DAUGHTER OF THE WOLF

VICTORIA WHITWORTH is a
historian and author of two
previous novels, *The Bone Thief*
and *The Traitors' Pit*, and of a
memoir, *Swimming With Seals*.
Having worked as a lecturer, tour
guide, artist's model and teacher,
she now lives in Orkney, where she
writes full time.

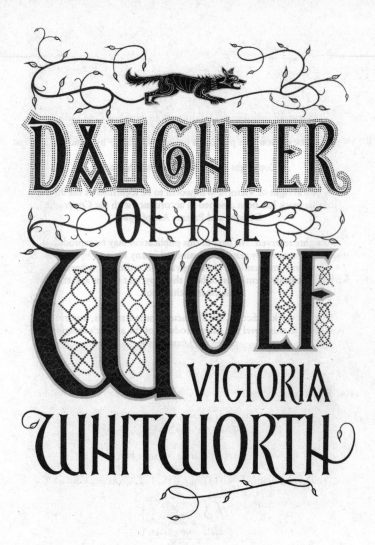

DAUGHTER OF THE WOLF

VICTORIA WHITWORTH

HEAD
of ZEUS

First published in the UK in 2016 by Head of Zeus Ltd

This paperback edition first published in the UK in 2017 by Head of Zeus Ltd

9 7 5 3 1 2 4 6 8

A CIP catalogue record for this book is available from the British Library

ISBN (PB) 9781784082147
ISBN (E) 9781781850909

Typeset by Adrian McLaughlin

Printed and bound by CPI Group (UK) Ltd, Croydon, CR0 4YY

Head of Zeus Ltd
Clerkenwell House
45–47 Clerkenwell Green
London EC1R 0HT

WWW.HEADOFZEUS.COM

For Stella, my bright star

PART ONE

THE CHRONICLE, YORK MINSTER SCRIPTORIUM

The first day of a new year. Time to look back and take stock. The chronicler was making himself a new quill, splaying the tip and slicing with the lethal blade of his pen-knife: brief, accurate strokes. He eyed the nib approvingly before dipping the sharp, shaped point into the little pot of gall-black ink, letting one or two drops fall back into the tiny midnight pool before drawing his first mark on the fresh sheet of vellum.

Up at a slant. Down again. Across. Straight up. Downward curve. Gathering speed a little as his hand accustomed itself to the new nib, to the consistency of this batch of ink, to the slightly rough surface of this calfskin.

AD DCCCLVIII In hoc anno…

His quill was the flight feather of a wild grey goose, tense and powerful in his hand even in this denuded and reworked state. Late March, and just that morning he had seen the first of the great mournful flocks turning north again, arrowing already across the Northumbrian skies to their unknown summer homes. Today was a day fit for new beginnings. The anniversary of that first separation of darkness from light; and of the day on which Eva's catastrophe had been reversed by the angel's *Ave* to Maria.

He sighed, looking down at the still almost empty page. *In this year...* How powerful it was, the desire to make some kind of mark, leave some kind of record, ink patterning vellum like footprints on sand. How long would it be before some little wave, harbinger of the rising tide, broke over this desk, this room, this great church, and washed the marks away?

He mused over the events of the last year, the news that had come in, brought by legates and royal envoys coming along the old roads; by merchants and sailors putting into the riverside wharves of York, whose cathedral sat like a spider at the heart of its worked net.

Time to dip his pen again. It hovered, while he hesitated over what might be worthy of record. Some events were easy enough. Tap a superfluous drop from the nib, little serif, strong downward stroke...

In this year died King Cinaed ap Alpin of the Picts; and also Athelwulf Ecgberhting of the West Saxons. Domnall ap Alpin and Athelbald Athelwulfing succeeded to the kingdoms.

Clumsy phrasing: he should have drafted it first rather than gone rushing in. The story of his life. Never mind, the meaning was clear enough.

Also in this year the pagans burned the minster at Tours.

He wiped the nib on a square of linen, and gazed at the white-plastered wall. There seemed so little that merited the effort of writing down. Who on earth would be interested in the small events that had marked out this last *annus domini* for him? *In this year a girl gave me a flower on the kalends of March. Her face and bosom were freckled, and her eyes were blue. She made me think of a songthrush egg.*

And what about the things that didn't happen? *In this year there was no famine, no murrain of cattle. The pagans were elsewhere.* Those were, surely, miracles in themselves.

He had never been to Tours, and now he would probably never get the chance.

Small events, unworthy of record. *In this year Ingeld was*

made priest against his better judgement and appointed to the abbacy of Donmouth.

He stroked the little tuft of remaining feathers that topped the quill against his close-shaven chin and smiled at the softness, lowering his eyelids the better to imagine the bird, high against the sun, heading north into a Hyperborean land of light. What did Northumbria look like to the geese? The estuary that gave the land its name, and the fan of rivers, the hills of chalk and limestone and grit stretching north and west until they ran out into the sea, the northern waters splitting the land, the territories of Dumbarton and the Picts. How far to the north had this supple quill carried its previous owner? His imagination lost itself in a dazzle of snow and sun.

Slowly he opened his eyes again, to the prosaic world of writing-slope and inkhorn, quill and knife and whitewashed wall. How marvellous it would be, to fly with the geese. To see the storms before they hit, to spot where armies were massing, the harbours in which the sea-wolves lurked, to swoop down and hear the treasonous speech men uttered in hall and bower when they thought themselves safe. To have all Northumbria in one's hand, its hills and waterways no more than the lines and curves that mapped his palm.

He smiled, and shook his head. That was a dream for the statesmen and the warriors, men like his brother. He would be happier with his eyes on the edge of the world, no care beyond the exquisite thrill of the moment, his wings riding the wind.

'End of the field and back?' Athulf was out of breath, cheeks pink and eyes bright under his rough-cut fringe. Elfrun thought he looked very like the unkempt ponies whose halters he was holding, hot in their shaggy winter coats and the late Easter sunshine.

She nodded. 'Dismount and vault three times, turn at the hawthorn tree, same again' – she gestured largely – 'finish here. And I'm riding Mara.' She glared at her cousin, challenging him for possession of their favourite, noting the beginnings of his frown, how that soft lower lip was already starting to pout.

'Come on!' Both the other boys who had accepted the challenge were already jostling their own mounts into position a few yards away. She knew one of them vaguely, had seen him before at other spring and harvest meetings, but his father's lands were in distant Elmet, several days from her own home of Donmouth. The other was a stranger, a tall, quiet-faced lad on a gleaming bay mare. They had come trotting up only moments earlier, just as the race was being planned.

Would Athulf throw a tantrum, with these strangers as witness? Elfrun braced herself even as she laid a possessive hand on Mara's halter.

Her cousin surprised her, however. 'As you like.' And he tugged Apple towards him.

But he was looking neither at her nor at the fat-rumped little pony whose bridle he was gripping. His gaze had gone flickering past her, and a look of calculation was crossing his round face.

'Come *on*,' the lad from Elmet shouted again, and all at once Elfrun decided that, whatever Athulf had seen, she didn't want to know. She tugged Mara round and scrambled on to her back, clapping her heels into the chestnut's flanks and screaming, 'Go!' A crazy headlong dash ensued, with hardly time to swing herself down, find her stride and bounce back on to Mara twice, never mind three times, before swinging round the hawthorn tree in its fresh green leaf. Her plaits were coming free, and though she had kilted her skirts they unknotted themselves, flying out and hampering her. No room in her head for anything but the exultation of the moment, not for her bashed ribs, not for the other riders, not for the clamour of rooks that rose raucous from the stand of elms at the bottom of the field; and certainly not for any of Athulf's funny faces. Elfrun came in a screaming second, mud-spattered and exhilarated. The tall lad on the bay had won.

But not by much, and he had noticed. 'Well ridden!'

She reined Mara in, narrowly avoiding riding into his horse's rump, grinning in return, flushed and too breathless to answer.

She might not have won outright, but she had beaten Athulf. Beating Athulf was harder than it used to be, and the pleasure that much greater. Sweeping a tangled skein of hair out of her eyes Elfrun slithered triumphant down from Mara's sweaty back.

Her grandmother stood in front of her.

Abarhild said nothing.

She didn't need to. Her face, framed in its neat white linen, was set even harder than usual, and her bony hands were clamped one over the other on the silver-gilt mount that capped her blackthorn stick. Elfrun eyed the distance between her grandmother and herself: she knew full well how fast and hard Abarhild could strike. And how she would be blamed for Athulf getting into trouble.

The silence lengthened and deepened. Elfrun could feel the hot blood mounting from somewhere near her heart until it had flooded her already flushed cheeks, her palms moistening where they clutched Mara's reins, her heart thudding and blocking her breath. One of the horses let out a long, stuttering fart, and Elfrun heard a stifled snigger behind her, but she didn't dare turn to see whether it came from Athulf or one of the stranger boys.

Abarhild lifted her staff, and Elfrun braced herself, but her grandmother was only gesturing, not lashing out – not yet. 'Athulf, take that animal. You' – she stabbed the staff at Elfrun – 'come with me.' She turned and began stumping her way up the field in the direction of the Donmouth tents, whose bright roof-poles and finials were visible above the hedge, never once turning to see whether her orders were being obeyed.

Elfrun thrust Mara's reins blindly at Athulf. 'You knew. You saw her coming.' Her breath stuck in her throat. 'You could have said.'

Her cousin just smirked. She turned, hot and wet-eyed with anger and humiliation, and hurried after Abarhild.

Her grandmother began speaking as soon as Elfrun fell into step, marking each word with a vicious stab at the turf. 'You – are – fifteen – years – old.' She stopped, and turned, the sunlight flickering on the gold crosses embroidered on the border of her veil. The Gallic accent that still buzzed around the edges of her grandmother's voice, even after fully fifty years in Northumbria, was stronger than ever when Abarhild was angry. 'Is this sin, or just stupidity?' Her eyes were watery, pink-rimmed and folded deep in her wrinkled face, but Elfrun knew she missed nothing. 'I thought you were going to show the world your bare arse.'

Elfrun clapped her hands defensively to her buttocks. 'You did not!'

But her grandmother was shaking her head. 'You have no idea, do you? Look at you' – another stab with the gnarled blackthorn – 'bringing disgrace... Strangers...' She clamped her mouth and breathed in through her nose. 'Nearly sixteen. *Pro Deo amur* – for the love of God, Elfrun, where is your dignity? In your good blue dress, too. And in the field next to the king's tents. This is absolutely the last time I want to have to say this to you.'

Abarhild glared at her granddaughter, looking for a sign that her words were getting through to her. Elfrun was a good girl at heart; Abarhild was convinced of that. Never been beaten enough, though, or given the responsibility she needed. Elfrun's father had always been too easy on his only surviving child, and since the girl's mother had died… *Spoiled*, she thought now, looking at the wild hair escaping from what had earlier been neat brown plaits, the spatters of mud across Elfrun's wide forehead, her cheeks' hectic flush – a flush begot, Abarhild suspected, by excitement rather than shame; and her mouth tightened again.

Elfrun bowed her head and bit her lip, doing her best to look remorseful, but there was a smile tugging at the corners of her mouth.

Biting back her anger, Abarhild turned and started walking up the slope again, her stick thumping into the grass and the keys chinking at her belt, and Elfrun hurried to catch up.

She knew fine well her grandmother would want to see compunction and penitence before any reconciliation or absolution could be offered; and she did feel a scruple of genuine shame. But more, much more, she was angry with Athulf for not giving her some warning. It would have been so easy – a wink, a jerk of the head… She dug her nails into her palms. She would get him, later.

Abarhild never talked about *Athulf's* dignity.

'What was that? Did you say something, girl?'

'Sorry, Grandmother.'

'What?'

Louder this time. 'Sorry!' And somewhere, deep down, against all desire, she had to admit that the world would agree. Abarhild was right; she was getting too old for these games. But admitting it, even to her private self, felt like a betrayal, a little death.

Abarhild huffed. 'I'll have more to say about this later on. Just now there's no time. Your father wants you.' A third, lesser sniff. 'Clean and well turned-out.'

'Where?'

And now Abarhild did swing her stick, but it thwacked only into the flesh of Elfrun's calf, not the bone of her ankle, and she knew from this that the worst of her grandmother's wrath was on the ebb. 'He's on his way to attend on Osberht. You're to wait with him, until you're called.'

'The king?' Elfrun's eyes went wide. 'What about?'

'You'll find out soon enough. Something particularly concerning you.'

'Is there something wrong with the wool? The lambskins?' Their home of Donmouth was famous for them, their number, their quality, and the way they were processed, both with and without the fleece. Both king and archbishop relied on them, and there was a constant demand from the fine leather-workers in York. The wool, raw, spun or woven, might be Donmouth's mainstay, but the lambskins were their fame. Under the tutelage first of her mother, and now of Abarhild, Elfrun had been learning not merely the spinning and weaving that every girl started mastering as soon as she was tall enough to hold a spindle, but all the complex economy of wool and parchment, milk and cheese.

Her mother used to joke that all Donmouth's glory balanced on the back of a sheep.

But why would the king ask for her, if all he wanted was to talk about lambskins?

She opened her mouth again but one look at her grandmother's face deterred her. By now they were almost back at Donmouth's little cluster of cheerfully striped canvas. Abarhild's lips were pursed and her brow drawn tight; and it hit Elfrun that her grandmother was as much in the dark as she was herself.

2

er scalp was smarting from the tugs of her grandmother's fine-toothed antler comb, her face and hands were glowing and abraded from the coarse linen towel, even her fingertips stung from the gouging Abarhild had been giving her nails. And dressing her down all the while, listing her seemingly endless faults of morals and manners while Elfrun squirmed under her grandmother's glare and the interested regard of the other members of their party.

Especially Saethryth's. The eldest daughter of the Donmouth steward, she had been roped in to dab the mud off the blue dress, and Elfrun still felt hot at the memory of the other girl's disingenuous cornflower gaze, directed alternately at the spatters of filth on the wool and at Elfrun herself, fidgeting in her linen shift under her grandmother's litany of shame. It wouldn't have been so bad if it had been any one of the other girls, but Saethryth's angelic fairness always had Elfrun feeling angular and grubby. And Saethryth's talent for well-aimed and malicious comments was second to none.

Elfrun had hardly had another moment to wonder why the king might want her.

Now, her grandmother chivvying her as she might a wayward ewe, they were walking as fast as Elfrun's stiff leather shoes would allow her on the dewy grass to the thronged open area outside the king's tents. To her great relief her father was there already, seated on the bench nearest the entrance to Osberht's tent. She could pick him out from any crowd in that blood-red cloak.

A gift from the king only a few days earlier, and far and away the gaudiest thing he owned, he was wearing it over the much more characteristic wolf-grey tunic which was the last thing her mother had ever woven, soft and light with all its worth in the fineness of the weave. His only glitter came from the silver tags weighting the woven bands that fastened the cloak at his shoulder.

But, plainly dressed though he might be, in his daughter's eyes Radmer of Donmouth shone brighter than any half-dozen of the more gaudily clad dish-thanes and riding-men who hovered wasp-like around the king's court, bullion glinting silver and gold at shoulder and wrist and throat, and on the sword-belts they insisted on wearing even if the swords themselves were packed away.

No weapons in the king's presence, not at spring and harvest meeting. Stakes were too high, old feuds always simmering too close to over-boiling. Northumbria might have been at its fragile peace since Elfrun was little more than a toddler, but she had heard the threats chewed over and spat out in the hall often enough. Internal dissent, brooding exiles, sea-wolves and the warlords of Mercia and Wales, Pictland and Dumbarton. The king's cousin, Alred, banned from coming south of the Tees since his rebellion seven years earlier. She knew fine well there were stories of disloyalty and over-leaping ambition attached to some of the faces she could see here, too. But she found it difficult to take any of the hard-edged talk seriously. With her father at the king's side, what could ever come to hurt them?

Radmer was gesturing to the bench beside him. No smile, but the lack of a frown was enough to fill Elfrun with relief. She knew only too well the drawn brows – worse than any spoken reproof – that would have greeted her if she had arrived in her former muddy and tangled state, and she felt a burst of still half-sulky gratitude to the old lady stomping along beside her.

Abarhild lowered herself on to the bench in silence, back straight and mouth still clamped.

'Mother.' Radmer bowed his head, still fair rather than grey in the spring sunlight, and she nodded.

Radmer looked beyond her, at Elfrun's demurely bowed head, the neat, pale parting in her rich brown hair. 'Daughter.' She came to stand in front of him, hands folded, gaze still lowered. 'The king has summoned me,' he said quietly. 'And he said you should come too. Something to our advantage.' Radmer set his hands on his knees. 'Well, I've been here for a while, and still waiting. There are legates come from Canterbury, and Archbishop Wulfhere is with them. But Osberht's steward said he'll see us next, whatever it is.' He reached out his hand and gave hers a brief pat. 'How have you been amusing yourself? Not frowsting in our tents, I hope, not on a day like this?' She lifted her steady brown gaze to his, and he smiled reassuringly.

Elfrun could feel the auger gaze of her grandmother boring into her. 'Watching – watching Athulf with the horses. Racing.' Not quite a lie, even if truth fell down through the crack between her words.

'Did he win?'

She wished suddenly, passionately, that her father had seen her ride. Radmer might have been – no, he *would* have been – angry, but no one had a better eye for horsemanship. And she was as good as Athulf, she knew she was. Better. The way the wretched boy had been sawing at Apple's mouth... 'He – I—'

'He did well,' her grandmother said. 'The other boys were older.' She shot Elfrun an inscrutable look. 'And he was riding Apple, not Mara.'

'Athulf.' Her father sounded thoughtful. 'Now your uncle Ingeld's home from York, it's time he took that lad in hand. Promising boy, but he's been left to run wild for far too long.'

'He should be trained for the Church.' Abarhild's tone was flat, uncompromising. Elfrun stared at her grandmother. Sulky, whining Athulf, a cleric?

And it seemed her father shared her incredulity. 'That puppy? Less fitted even than his father.'

11

Elfrun braced herself for the blast. But Abarhild had set her withered face hard, the lines between mouth and chin deep and oppressive. 'The boy is our responsibility. What's the alternative? Will you make him your heir?'

'Promise him the hall?' Radmer turned on his mother with a swiftness that startled Elfrun. 'Ingeld's brat? I'll be damned first.'

'Why not? Who else is going to take over Donmouth after you?'

'Don't bury me, Mother.' Radmer glanced from his mother to his daughter, and then turned his stare back to the king's tent. 'I'm not dead yet.'

'Radmer! Don't ignore me. You need to do something for Athulf.'

'Why?' Her father's voice was flat and hard as stone. 'Ingeld got him. Let Ingeld look after him.'

Abarhild levered herself to her feet and stalked away, her very shoulder blades eloquent of disapproval.

Radmer was drumming his fingers on his knee. 'As though I haven't done enough for Ingeld already.' He bared his teeth, white and strong in the silver-blond beard, but there was no smile in his eyes. 'Sit down, daughter, and learn the virtues of a king's good servant from watching me.'

'What are they?' The bench stood on uneven ground, and it lurched a little as she sat.

Radmer snorted. 'Obedience. Patience. Anticipating every need. And never asking questions.'

It sounded very like Abarhild's standard lecture on being a good granddaughter, and Elfrun wanted to say as much, to see if she could make her father smile. But Radmer was no longer paying any attention to her. His whole body had stiffened, like a wolf that scents the hunt on its heels. She followed his gaze across the thirty feet of open grass that served as an antechamber to the royal tent, but she could see nothing.

Just men.

But as she watched she realized a bustle of activity had been starting up across from them, like one of the little sand-devils that whirled on the beach at Donmouth on windy days; and then the clump of men parted left and right to let a solid figure, his bald head gleaming in the sun, emerge to walk across the grass towards the king's awning. Although he paced steadily his eyes went sweeping this way and that: Elfrun could see his gaze flickering over every face, and stopping, sudden and hard, when they sighted her father. But he never broke his stride. Elfrun only realized how massive he was when he stood next to the king's steward. This newcomer overtopped the tall steward by half a head, and was broad in proportion. With that lumpy, lowering brow he only needed the addition of a pair of polled horns, and he could easily be mistaken for an ox. On its hind legs. She put her hand to her mouth to stifle the giggle that threatened.

The steward listened, and nodded, and ducked into the tent.

And now Elfrun was beginning to realize that her father was not the only one to have been transfixed by the arrival of this stranger. The hangers-on were shifting, staring, regrouping. Men bending to mutter in each other's ears, listening with wary faces, drifting away from the quarter whence the stranger had come, to form new alignments. But that tight little clump of men from which he had emerged still clung together, all stout, weather-beaten, with something alien about them, though she would have been hard pressed to say quite what. The angle of a cap, the way in which leggings were bound, the nature of a pattern on a braid...

And then she realized as they moved and turned that they weren't all men, that the bundled figure of a woman stood among them, and a tall boy behind her, holding a horse.

Had he been alone, Elfrun might not have remembered the boy: she found boys of little interest in themselves. But she recognized his neat-boned bay mare immediately; the thrill of the race, and how even in the heart of the moment she had observed how mount and rider moved as one.

The boy had noticed her watching.

He was staring back, half raising his hand in acknowledgement. She stuck out her chin, forcing herself to hold his gaze. She could look, couldn't she? Even Abarhild couldn't object to her *looking*. What business did he have bringing a fine mare like that to the meeting if he wasn't prepared to let folk look? But the thought of Abarhild made her blush and shift her eyes elsewhere.

Now that Abarhild had left them, that round little woman in her swathes of brown twill was the only other female present. Were she and the boy kin, then, to each other and to the big bald man? The lad was tall enough, but russet-headed and slender, and looking every bit as out of place as she felt herself.

Her father was still set as though in stone. She noticed that the mutterers were glancing at him, and then back at the tent, an endless flicker of eyes. The big man, the ox-man, was still waiting, but even as she watched a couple of priests emerged, and then the new archbishop, the king's cousin. Wulfhere's narrow, vulpine face was pinched and annoyed.

And the big man was summoned in.

He was important, then. Important enough for the king to cut short a meeting with his grace of York and these foreign visitors.

And important enough, she realized with a little cold shock, for the king to break a promise to her own father. He had said Radmer would be next, and then this man had appeared out of nowhere and gone barging up to the steward as if he owned the place.

Abarhild would have berated her for worldly curiosity, but Elfrun dismissed all thoughts of her grandmother. She had to know what was going on.

'Father?' He ignored her. 'Father, who is that man?'

She put out her hand to tug his sleeve, but she was forestalled. One of the mutterers was making his way over to her father, cautious and stiff-legged as a cat approaching a mastiff. Elfrun recognized him, a distant cousin of her dead mother's.

'Radmer.'

Her father nodded. 'Edmund.'

Edmund was a liverish-looking man a few years older than Radmer, with weary, wary eyes and an ill-tended brown moustache. 'So. He's back.' He sat down on Radmer's other side.

'They. They're back.'

'Osberht must have known. Did *you* know?' Edmund waited, but Radmer said nothing. 'Well, it's been seven years. More.'

'He's done his time in exile. He's entitled to ask forgiveness.' Her father's voice was studiedly neutral.

'Men are saying they've been in the Danish marches all this while. Hedeby, and around the Baltic Sea. Making friends. That these' – he jerked his chin – 'are some of them.'

Radmer shook his head. 'They went to Frankia.'

'That's where they were supposed to have been. But men say otherwise.' Edmund raised his eyebrows. 'Do you believe it?'

'I believe nothing on hearsay.' Radmer let out a sigh. 'And ever since we exiled Tilmon it's been one goddamned rumour after another. That he's been in the Danemarch is only the latest. But the king he tried to force on us is dead, and Northumbria has changed a lot since he left us. New alliances. New faces.' Radmer paused, his face tightening. 'With Wulfhere in the archbishop's seat Osberht has never been stronger. Alred has been well bribed to stay in line, and he's in the north. So, let Tilmon come back – at least let him try. See if it does him any good.'

Edmund glanced at the king's tent. 'Osberht has a lot to forgive.'

'And he's not the only one.' Elfrun stared at her father, startled by the sudden harshness of his tone, but he seemed oblivious to her presence.

Not so Edmund. He caught her eye, smiled a little, then dropped a slow wink. Radmer frowned, a brief contraction across the brow, and he turned to look down at his daughter. 'Big talk for my little girl to listen to.'

Edmund snorted. 'That's not a little girl, Radmer. Not any longer. And more like her dear mother' – he signed himself with a sketchy cross – 'every time I see her.'

Radmer's face tightened. He turned and stared across the grassy forecourt once more. 'So Tilmon has brought his wife and son back with him. He must be very sure he'll be returned to Osberht's favour.'

'Either that or he's planning to send Switha in to fight his corner for him.' Edmund grinned on an outbreath. 'I'd rather take him on than her, any day.'

'True. She always was a foe to reckon with.'

They laughed, but their words made Elfrun squint all the more curiously across the grass at the bulkily clad woman. Switha. She looked quite ordinary, so small next to the men. As big a menace as her husband, the ox-man? And so the boy with the bay mare, he was their son. What was it like, having a father like that?

'If Tilmon has been in the Danemarch,' Edmund said slowly, 'and if he is still shoulder to shoulder with Alred, then Osberht will have to buy his loyalty back somehow. How will he lime that branch? Do you know? Are you privy to this?'

Radmer eyed him sideways. 'Think I'd tell you?'

'Everyone's wondering.'

'Let them.' Radmer stretched out his legs and clasped his hands behind his head. 'You want to look at me?' His voice was louder, more challenging. 'You want to speculate, boys? Come on then, and welcome. Be my guest.'

'Don't push it, Radmer.' Edmund sounded nervous.

'Don't push me, then.'

Elfrun's eyes flickered from one man to the other, wondering at the sudden thundery crackle in the air between them.

Edmund stood up and yawned, showing his back teeth. He caught her looking at him, and frowned. 'And what about this one, Radmer? What plans?'

'Elfrun's needed at Donmouth. She'll take over the hall from her grandmother. In the fullness of time.'

'Not marriage?' Edmund looked at her appraisingly. 'There's many a family would value a Donmouth alliance. Does the girl have a voice?'

'She wants to stay with me.' Her father put a hand on her shoulder. 'Don't you, Elfa?'

Elfrun squirmed at being the sudden focus of both men's attention. But she didn't have to answer. The king's steward had appeared at her father's side, beckoning urgently.

'No, Radmer. Not the girl. Just you.' He glanced at Elfrun. 'For the moment, anyway.'

Her father frowned. 'Stay here, Elfa. I don't like leaving you on your own.'

Elfrun looked round, but there was no sign of Abarhild.

Her father was still frowning. 'Keep an eye on her for me, Edmund?'

'As though she were my own.' Edmund's voice was hearty.

She watched the king's steward usher her father to the tent and lift the heavy embroidered door-curtain. The ox-man, this Tilmon, he hadn't come out yet. So the meeting was between the three of them.

3

Edmund had drifted away a few feet. Little as she warmed to him with his sad, straggly moustache and his heavy, lingering eyes, he was at least kin, however distant, and her father had appointed him as a bulwark between her and all the other watchers. She tried to straighten her back and fold her hands in a way Abarhild would have approved. 'Are you well, cousin Edmund?'

'So, you do speak.' He sighed. 'Well enough, cousin Elfrun. Well enough. Tell me, how are matters at Donmouth? Do you still have that fine smith?'

'Cuthred?' She knew full well they had good men at Donmouth, but it was gratifying to know that the world had noticed. 'Indeed we do, and his son has started working with him at the forge.'

Edmund shook his head. 'Your father's a lucky man. Smith, steward, shepherd – it's a tight ship at Donmouth. And Widia – your huntsman is envied by the king himself. I hope Radmer counts his blessings?'

She nodded.

'And, tell me, what has your father said about marrying again?'

'Nothing!' She was startled into a yelp.

'Nothing? Really? It's been a couple of years.'

Elfrun knew exactly how long it had been.

'Nothing to you, at least.' Edmund ran his tongue over the lower edge of his moustache. 'How about naming an heir?'

She shook her head, increasingly uncomfortable under this arrow-storm of questions.

'Well, well.' He looked at her for a moment, a calculating light in his eyes. 'But that holy priest your uncle has a son or two who could step in, am I right? Is that the way the dice are rolling?'

And all at once Elfrun hated him, the hint of malice in his voice and the way that his moustache drooped raggedly over his mouth so that she could barely see his lips move when he spoke. 'One son,' she said coldly. Athulf's parting smirk was still rankling.

'Just the one? Really?' Edmund cackled. 'And no chance for Ingeld to get more, I suppose, now that he has to leave York and head the Donmouth minster. Every step stalked by your father. That's made us laugh!' Suddenly he was looming down over her, close enough for her to see the red veins that threaded his eyes, the pores pocking the tip of his nose. 'You want my advice? Don't let Radmer' – he jerked his head towards the king's tent – 'keep you withering on the vine at home. He will, you know, just because it suits him. I know him.' He spat in the grass. 'He should marry you off. You're getting valuable.' And now he sat down next to her and leaned in even closer, his thigh hard against hers, and she could smell last night's beef and beer on his breath. 'Are you ready for a man? You're a skinny little thing, but one never can tell. And Donmouth could make any girl look attractive.' She pulled back as far as she dared without being rude, revolted by his proximity, and he laughed.

'My father asked you to keep an eye on me,' she said stiffly.

'So he did.' He looked her up and down in a way that made her skin crawl. 'And that's just what I'm doing. And you know what men call Radmer?'

'Call him? The King's Wolf.'

'The King's Wolf. Indeed. And do you know why?'

He was leaning in, and she shifted another inch towards the end of the bench, talking fast to keep him at bay, repeating words she had heard in the hall. 'Because Donmouth's the gate to Northumbria, and he guards it. Hold the river, and the estuary, and the kingdom is strong.'

'And that's not all he guards, is it, Osberht's pet wolf?' He seemed to think this was funny. 'Radmer's been growling and snapping at strangers on the king's behalf for twenty years. He's proud. He should be.' Edmund turned to look at the king's tent. 'But with Tilmon back he won't be growling. He'll be wanting to go for the throat.' He laughed. 'Exciting times.'

He was still much too close. Elfrun could feel the warmth and heaviness of him leaning against her, but she was right at the end of the bench now, the edge digging into her right buttock. Any further and she would fall off. All she wanted was to get up and walk away, but Abarhild would be shocked when she heard of such discourtesy to a kinsman.

And what if he followed her, shouted at her, made folk stare?

So she concentrated on her clasped hands, the pale half-moons on her thumbnails, not speaking, hardly even breathing. Edmund grunted enquiringly, but she kept her lips tight-pressed, and at last to her infinite relief she felt the bench tip as he hauled himself to his feet. When she dared to look up again she saw that he had rejoined one of the little clusters that hovered at the far side of the king's tent. Low muttering, sidelong glances – a few of them at her – emphatic gestures.

But it wasn't all about her. The Northumbrian riding-men and dish-thanes and hall-wards, with all their hangers-on, were clumping and forming larger groups. Tilmon's men were pulling closer together in response.

The boy with the bay mare had withdrawn himself a little, however, and was walking her up and down. Elfrun watched her neat lines, her forward-pricked ears and gleaming hooves, and the way the sunlight shone on her hide, so different from Mara and Apple. Her dainty head had something almost birdlike in its grace, as did her little pecking steps. That boy must spend hours clipping, and combing, and oiling. He turned his head and she looked away quickly in case he caught her staring yet again. It would be good to race that bay mare again, though Mara would never have a chance against her.

Dear, shaggy Mara and Apple – and a pang of conscience struck her. Could Athulf be trusted to look after the ponies properly, with all the distractions and temptations offered by the meeting? She cast a calculating look at the curtain screening the entrance to the king's tent. How much longer were they going to be? She could be quick: she could run.

Just to see that Apple and Mara were all right.

But what if they weren't? What if Athulf had just left them loose in the field? Still tacked up, even? She would have to catch them.

Elfrun half rose to her feet, then stopped, hovering somewhere short of standing.

Her father might come out of the tent, and she not back. What if the king had asked for her? And what if she got muddy again? If he didn't kill her, her grandmother most certainly would. So she slumped back on to the bench, still torn, trying to keep her face composed, her hands folded and her back straight. But the bench was hard, and getting harder all the time, her seat was aching, and her feet were cramped and hot and chafed, her heels blistering in the stiff leather shoes she almost never wore. She felt desperately self-conscious, sitting there alone, but it was still preferable to Edmund coming back. And all the while the sun was shining and every lark in Deira was pouring out its heart, singing its alleluias in the Easter sky, and from down towards the river Elfrun could hear splashing, and laughter. She had a suspicion she could hear Athulf's shrieks among the others.

Abarhild had been angry enough about her riding with the boys. What would she have said if she had caught Elfrun swimming?

Now she could hear other raised voices, not so far away.

Shouts, even. And coming from the king's tent.

Her hackles had risen without her realizing.

And she was not alone. Everyone had frozen, hands already halfway to absent sword-pommels. The woman in the brown twill and the boy were standing close together. The boy was

21

looking at the tent, but the woman was staring across the grass. Looking, Elfrun realized, at *her*. Perhaps she – Switha, that was the name – perhaps she too felt ill at ease in the midst of this throng of jumpy men.

But after that one outburst the voices inside the tent had fallen quiet again, as though belatedly aware of all those avid ears outwith its painted and embroidered canvas walls. Try as she might, she could hear nothing more.

Long, slow heartbeats, and the world began to breathe again.

The space under the tasselled awning darkened. Her father came blundering out into the daylight. She thought at first he was just sun-blind, but realized then he was snarling-angry, angry as she had never seen him. He came straight over to her.

'Get up.'

She scrambled to her feet. 'Why? What is it? Does the king want me now?'

But he had her hard by the bones of her elbow and was turning her away from the tent.

'Father? You're hurting me.'

Eyes. Everywhere, eyes.

Even she could see the eyes were noting his anger, his loss of self-command.

'Father? Is it something I've done?'

That got through to him. 'You, child? No, absolutely not.' He glanced behind them. 'I can't talk about it here. There are ears everywhere.' But he loosened his grip on her arm.

Ears as well as eyes. And tongues all too ready to twist what the eyes and ears had taken in. She longed for the familiar haven of Donmouth, where every face was known to her.

Radmer was looking over her, back towards the king's tent. 'Damn it.'

And the ox-man was there, out of nowhere, right in front of her, blocking the sun. 'This is the girl?' He reached towards her.

Radmer moved between them. 'You've had my answer, Tilmon.'

'Think again.' Tilmon looked back towards the tent.

'Don't insult me. A landless exile. A traitor. The king may be talking to you, but he still doubts your loyalty, and Alred's.' Elfrun could almost see her father's hackles rising, hear the low snarl. 'And he's right.'

Something touched her elbow, and she yelped.

It was the dumpy, twill-swathed woman. Close to, she reminded Elfrun irresistibly of a hedgehog, with her bright black eyes, pudgy face and sweet smile. Her veil was pinned slightly awry, allowing tight, dark curls, streaked with silver, to escape around her temples. 'Radmer.'

Elfrun's father nodded stiffly. 'Switha.'

Switha moved into the space between the men. 'We're on the same side now. At least look at my boy.' Her voice was warm and low, with a caressing note.

'Out of the question.' Radmer tried to turn away.

But, and to Elfrun's amazement, the woman laid an intimate hand on his sleeve, moving closer to him and dropping her voice still further. 'Whether Osberht trusts us or not, he needs us. He knows what's in the wind.' She turned, and her dark eyes scanned Elfrun, a long searching gaze, before she looked up into Radmer's face once more. 'How about letting bygones be bygones?' She sounded so reasonable. 'We were all good friends once.'

He shook himself free and stepped back, out of reach. 'Never.'

'Why, Radmer? You have to put her somewhere.' Tilmon made a sound that could have been laugh or growl, but Switha ignored him. She was still smiling. 'This could be so easy, Radmer. And you're making it so hard.'

4

The oars creaked with one last long pull. The oarsmen raised them dripping out of the water and drew them in over the topmost strake as the boat glided in among the reeds. Its mast was already unstepped, and the evening was a gloomy one, though the reeds were alive with little brown birds. It had been a wild day and a night, though one would hardly guess it now, and the whole crew was exhausted.

Finn crouched in the bows, his wickerwork pack balanced, ready to jump across to one of the little boggy tufts as soon as the boat-master raised his hand.

But instead Tuuri beckoned him over with a crooked finger. Finn set his pack down and stepped over thwarts and bundles and snoring off-shift crew to where the older man stood, by the keelson socket. Auli was crouched at his feet, whittling a new bone flute.

'We're earlier than we planned,' the boat-master said. 'A good couple of weeks. But we had to take that wind when it came.' His sun-battered face was giving nothing away.

Finn nodded. He remembered this stretch of the Lindsey marshes, and he wanted to strike inland while the light lasted, make for the great monastery at Bardney where they knew him from last summer. He knew he would get a hearty welcome and a place by the fire. The Hedeby market had furnished him with fine eastern incense, smelling of summer roses and wrapped in oiled parchment; and tiny clay phials of oil and water and soil that were said to come from Jerusalem, brought up along the rivers to the Baltic Sea. He also had his usual range of popular trinkets and random acquisitions. The good brothers of Bardney would be delighted. He would make for Bardney, and then this year his road would take him on a long loop, and ultimately north. Tuuri and he had talked it through. A counter-sunwise circuit that would end with him going up the old road to Barrow and the ferry, and along the Ouse to York, calling at the minsters and halls on the way, one hand outstretched in friendship, the other never far from the hilt of his belt-knife.

Finn bit back his impatience and waited. He knew Tuuri wouldn't be keeping him here merely to exchange platitudes about wind and weather. He followed the older man's gaze down the length of the boat, to where Myr and Holmi were lying, fast asleep, resting against Varri's broad, hairy back. The lads had been wrestling with rope and wind for much of the day, and he didn't grudge them their sleep, though it saddened him not to bid them farewell and good fortune. It would be a long season before he saw them again – and perhaps he never would. His world had no room in it for complacency.

'You know what we need.'

Finn nodded. He knew, exactly. How far upriver one might sail at low tide. Just what could be seen from a hall doorway. The number of armed men likely to be under a given roof on a given day. Whether the crosses and candlesticks were gold or silver gilt, silver or silvered bronze. His job was to see everything and forget nothing, to linger at high table and market stall when the transactions had been carried out and men's minds had moved on, the soft-spoken pedlar quite forgotten, except maybe by one or two of the girls into whose eyes he had smiled. He had done this job the navigable length of the Shannon and the Liffey, in the marshy hinterlands of Dorestad, along the Seine, and last year Tuuri had brought him and the others to the English coasts for the first time.

Of all the burdens he carried about him, this knowledge, this weightless, invisible merchandise, was by far the most valuable.

'You know this stretch.'

'I do.' Finn swallowed. His voice was scratchy, still sore from shouting against the wind.

'We're going north of the Humber.'

'The Tees, you said before.'

'Aye, the Tees, likely. For now at least. But there's a man wants to talk to us.' Tuuri's weathered face bent itself into a crafty, broken-toothed grin. 'Wants to pay us. Wants us to talk to our friends. Meeting on Humberside. Around the even-nights.'

'Where on Humberside?'

'Barton kirk. On the Lindsey shore. The big kirk. You remember it?'

'You want me there?'

'We'll want what you have to tell us.'

Finn nodded. 'I'll be there. At the even-night.' Five months away.

'Two days before and two after,' Tuuri said. 'Barton, remember?'

The boat bumped against a reed-thick islet. An arrow of north-bound geese flew high overhead. Finn hoisted his pack and settled it, and braced himself to jump.

5

Fredegar gazed down at his clasped hands, the interwoven fingers clenched so hard against each other that he could feel every bone under their thin covering of sallow skin. He pulled his hands apart and tightened them into fists, the knuckles showing white, the nails gouging his palms. The familiar heavy chill was in his stomach, like a slab of cold oat pudding, indigestible, although the air in the church was warm and close. *Pro Deo amur...*

But he had been fine all morning, head down at work in the vineyard, with his basket and shears and little hoe. No need to talk to anyone, or even to lift his gaze above the hard-pruned vines in their rows. Just as he had been fine yesterday morning, knee-deep in the mud and reeds of the fishpond, his robe kilted high and the spring sun hot on his shaven crown. Only when the little bronze voice of the bell started up again had the darkness and constriction begun once more to creep around the edges of his vision, to tighten about his lungs.

He took in a deep, ragged gulp of air and let it out again in his clear tenor, as true as that same abbey bell: *And our mouths shall show forth thy praise.*

But lifting his gaze, and standing up with the rest of the brothers, meant that he had to look across the choir, over to the row of Corbie's novices and oblates, and he couldn't bear it. The young, untouched faces, pink and scrubbed under their well-tended tonsures. *Innocentes*, was that the word he was scrabbling after? But *innocere* meant to cause no harm, and that wasn't right. Those boys could cause harm, right enough, in their thoughts and their words and their deeds, in what they had done and in what they had failed to do. *Ignorantes*, then? They had no idea of what might be coming, here at their inland haven. Even here.

O Lord, make haste to help us.

Better to die now, young and ignorant, than to live through what the future might hold.

'Father abbot wants to see you, Father.'

Fredegar nodded at the child and turned right along the shadowed, northern side of the church to the little stone *aula* where his new abbot held court.

'Failure to thrive.' Ratramnus steepled his fingers and looked at Fredegar over them, his grizzled eyebrows long and bristling as a stag beetle's horns. 'That's what I'd say if you were one of the lambs. And I'd advise putting you in a basket in the kitchen and feeding you from a bottle.' He sighed. 'But you're not a lamb. You're a monk and mass-priest of Noyon.'

'I was.'

'Noyon will be refounded.' Ratramnus's voice was dry. 'But until then we have to do something with you. And believe me, I mourn Bishop Immo and the others almost as much as you do.'

'Do you pray for them, Father?'

'Daily.'

Fredegar nodded. He respected Ratramnus, and he was grateful; since for some reason he was still walking God's earth then Corbie was as good a way station as any. But why was he, worthless as he was, here with every bodily comfort, when all his confraternity was dead?

'Not sleeping?'

Fredegar felt a wave of exhaustion roll over him at the question. He shook his head. 'I can't. When I close my eyes...'

But Ratramnus was raising one of those magnificent eyebrows. 'You do sleep, you know.' No confrontation in the abbot's voice, just the statement of fact.

Fredegar was startled into opening his mouth, almost into contradicting his superior, but Ratramnus was nodding at him, lifting a cautionary finger. 'The others have been in here to complain about the noises you make in the night.'

'Oh.' Had they? What, all of them? 'I'm sorry, Father.'

'They have a right to their sleep too, you know.' Ratramnus sighed again. 'What shall we do with you?'

'Just tell me what to do, Father, and I'll do it. Any job. The tannery. The pigs. I can sleep in the sty, if that would please the brothers better.'

'And let you fill your belly with husks? All honourable labour, to be sure.' Ratramnus sounded thoughtful. 'I had something in mind, and then word came to me yesterday.' He shifted sideways to lift his wax tablets from his writing desk. 'What did the man say, now?'

Fredegar waited.

'Ah, yes.' Ratramnus squinted at the thin leaves of wood, then looked at Fredegar through the overhang of his eyebrows. 'Now. I had been thinking I could use you in here. A petty enough task for a man of your abilities – I have seen your work, remember!' He waited for a response but Fredegar was silent. The abbot sighed, and went on. 'My treatise on the Holy Mass... someone to check my notes for me. You could sleep in the library. No one else sleeps up there but Gundulf, and he's deaf as stone.'

Ratramnus paused, weighing the tablets in his hand. He clearly had not finished, and Fredegar went on waiting.

'And then this.' The abbot gestured. 'Word from a cousin of mine. Distant cousin. She was a novice at Chelles, but then she got married, and then she got married again to an Englishman. One of the northern kingdoms. The messenger said she's in quest of a chaplain. Have they no priests left there?' He stopped and looked at Fredegar. 'Our library's warm, you know. And they'll speak English there. I don't suppose you speak English.'

'I've heard it spoken. Frankish is close enough.' No one would know him in Northumbria. No one would expect anything of him, or compare the man he had been with the creature he seemed to have become. 'Where is this place?'

'Somewhere in the middle wilderness of Britannia. The English bit.' Ratramnus squinted at his notes. 'How's your handwriting? I can't read mine. It would be such a help in my work, you know, Fredegar, to have someone with clear cursive.' He handed the little wooden rectangles over. 'What does that say?' A jabbing finger.

'Beginning with D?'

'*Donmouth*,' Ratramnus said. 'I remember now. There's been a minster there for a hundred years. More. But I don't suppose it's up to much. Too far from York.' He looked around. 'Not like here, you know, in the English kingdoms, not these days. No monks. Half the abbots are laymen and even bishops are as good as married.'

Fredegar nodded dutifully.

Ratramnus tutted. 'You don't have to go, Fredegar. There won't be a library. No scriptorium. Nor any other priests, for all I know. Maybe a boy to ring the bell for you. Maybe not even a boy.' He snorted. 'Maybe not even a bell.'

Fredegar closed his eyes. 'Father, with your permission, I'll go to Donmouth.' His tongue stumbled over the unfamiliar clot of consonants.

Ratramnus nodded. 'Ah, well. Pity.' He paused for a long moment. 'There's always a place for you here, if things don't turn out. As long as I'm abbot.'

'Yes, Father.' Fredegar bent to kiss the abbot's hand before turning to leave.

'We'll arrange your passage. By land and then from Dorestad, I think. I'll give you letters of introduction to Wulfhere of York, and the other bishops.' Ratramnus paused again and looked into the distance. 'Hexham, Lindisfarne – I think there's one more. And...'

Fredegar paused in the doorway out to the sunny courtyard. 'Yes, Father?'

'What happened at Noyon – *whatever* happened – it wasn't your fault.'

'Yes, Father.'

6

idsummer eve. The annual battle between Donmouth hall and Donmouth minster was well under way. Hours, now, since the lord and his brother the new abbot had stood on the mound and together thrown the keg hard into the crowd. They were not playing.

A shame, Hirel had thought, watching Radmer and Ingeld side by side. Little family resemblance, but they were both strapping men who would have been a credit to the fight. Not in those fine clothes, though! Hirel himself was stripped to the waist, in the thick of the scrum where he had been for most of the game, shoving with all his strength. Like most of the players he had had his hair and beard close-cropped for the fray, to deny the foe a handhold. He had no idea where the small wooden barrel for which they were all fighting might be, and just then he didn't care. Glory enough to be in the heart of this mindless mass of men, crammed together like bullocks, the air thick and damp from their sweaty bodies, without a care in the world except staying on his feet and using his bulk to keep the minster men at bay. As well, perhaps, that the abbot was not playing: with those broad shoulders of his he would be an opponent to reckon with. Hirel might care for the minster sheep as well as the hall flocks, but he knew fine well where his true allegiance lay.

Staying upright was getting harder all the time. The week before had been wet, so the grass was slippery and the ground soft and waterlogged beneath it. After the hours of fighting they had churned it to a buttery mush. Hirel thrust down with his feet and out with his arms at the same time, a great immovable wall of a man, trying to hold the scrum while some more nimble hall man could find the little keg and run like a hare. The battle was fought across the whole three miles between hall and minster but most years the real fight was here, at the stream by the stand of coppiced ash midway between minster and hall, where the keg was first thrown soaring into the forest of waving arms to disappear, often not to be seen again in daylight. Come the brief summer dark, someone would make a break for it. Already the sun was rolling along the tops of the hills to the north-west. Too many years they fought it out in the rain; this year the sun had shone from dawn to dusk, sparkling on river and estuary, gilding the hills and ripening the hay.

Nothing in the world existed except the battle, the moment, the hot press of grunting, swearing bodies. Hirel ducked his head and braced his shoulders again, trying to keep his stance strong. Many a man used the Keg as an excuse to settle old scores, but he had never had any truck with that. This was for sheer pleasure, the exhilaration of using all his strength, of being one of the many-headed, single-minded mob.

And he was at the heart of it.

So many years had passed since he had been anywhere else, Hirel could hardly remember being one of the striplings, the little lads who dodged round the edges, seeking to add their puny weight to the scrum before it overwhelmed them and they had to retire, purple-faced, wheezing and retching. He had heard that one such Keg, well before he himself had been born, had been the cause of Luda, the steward, breaking his leg, trampled underfoot by the oblivious throng.

Not the steward then, of course. Only a boy. Hard to imagine that sour pinched face with its suspicious expression ever belonging to a boy. Men said the lady Abarhild had patched him back together, but Luda had been too lame ever to walk straight again, never mind play in the Keg. The thought of Luda's bodily weakness gave Hirel a rush of illicit pleasure. He might be kept firmly under the man's thumb the rest of the year but on this one day of days he, the mere shepherd, was the better man.

He could see nothing but heads and shoulders; feel nothing but the treacherous ground below his feet and the great impersonal weight forcing in from all sides, that crushed ribs and stifled breath; smell nothing other than thick, rank sweat. But he could hear the crowd. Over-excited shrieks and exhortations from the women and children; bellows of advice and encouragement from the older men, many of whom had climbed into the trees the better to try and see down into the heart of the scrum, to guess where the keg might be, to shout strategy and tactics. Out of nowhere the sandy-haired deacon, Heahred, was facing Hirel, snarling and grunting, shoulder slamming into shoulder. Hirel shoved back even harder, looked Heahred in the eye, and laughed from sheer joy.

Then came one of those strange lulls that happened from time to time, by some unspoken accord. The pause rippled out from the centre, the men gasping for breath, wiping away the sweat, dropping their hands on to their knees and leaning forward, finding balance. And then the glances, the silent messages about force and direction. Hirel knew many of the eyes were on him, the biggest man in Donmouth. Something made him look out over the heads and shoulders of his foes and allies alike, to where the girls were clustered a little up the slope, clutching each other and pointing. Laughing. They were a mystery to him, these soft-faced creatures who took the fleece from his flock and transformed it into fine cloth by their secret processes. He'd been told he needed a wife. The dairy had not been well managed since the lady died. The girls were backlit with a rosy glow, and in his elated state Hirel truly could not have said whether the last rays of the sun gilded their edges so exquisitely, or whether they shone with their own inner light. The fair one, Luda's daughter. The one they all talked about. She was looking at him. She was looking right at him.

A roar from the scrum brought him back to his senses.

The sun had dipped now, and already the long, hazy light

was beginning to thicken. The scrum swayed and lurched, with a sudden break in the direction of the hall. Women and children scattered, screaming with excitement, as the mob lumbered towards them. Something thumped into Hirel's midriff. He looked down and saw the keg had been thrust into his hands. Without hesitating, he bent low, his arms clapped tight around it, and he barged ahead, ploughing his zigzag through the steaming crowd as though the burly men had been so many reeds. He knew he could outrun most of the heavy men from the minster, and none of the nimbler ones had the force to wrest the keg from him. Get it out of the scrum, carry it a furlong or two, and he could pass it on to one of the other hall men, one of the sprinters. He looked around for an ally. Widia, perhaps, the hall huntsman, wiry and nimble, and known for his merciless play. But once Hirel had broken free of the pack no one was at hand, so he just put his head down, and charged...

They brought him shoulder-high into the hall yard. They were shouting his name.

The feast was waiting, and they all piled in, thick with mud as they were, minster-men and hall-men all now the warmest of friends. It had been the best Keg ever. The stuff of song; the making of a man's reputation. The smell of roasting pork was thick in the air, and the biggest southern barrels had been tapped. For the first time in his life Hirel was at the glittering high table, with Radmer, lord of Donmouth, and his brother the abbot, the lady Abarhild and her granddaughter and the senior servants of hall and minster, and his keg, garlanded with ivy, stood on the linen-clad board before him. He watched the women moving about the hall with their heavy spouted pitchers, and they looked like angels from heaven.

It was the raw matter which would become legend. Twenty, thirty years hence, when he was an old man, they would point at him and tell boys whose fathers were striplings now of Hirel the hall shepherd and how he had won his keg.

He floated on a warm sea of approval, flavoured with sweet

wine and aromatic ale, his taste buds saturated with unfamiliar flavours and rare treats. The crisp greasy pork rind. Hare. Eggy bread made with some spice he had never tasted before.

The pitchers went round and the room grew louder and warmer, and the jokes and horseplay ever rowdier. Heahred the deacon was in the middle of the floor involved in some elaborate drinking game. The women had gone. Quite right, too.

No moon tonight. Hirel nodded sagely to himself, bleary-eyed. Very sensible. Who knew what dangers lurked in the summer-dim, on such a trowie night as this one? He pushed down hard on the board and lurched to his feet. He was the hero of the hour: he should be down on the floor in the thick of the games. He stepped down from the dais to a roar of approbation, and the sound of his name in men's mouths was sweet music to his ears.

And now he found he was regretting that the women had gone. He wanted them to admire him. He wanted the fair one to look at him again.

7

'Enough. You've had my answer.' Radmer stood up, his head narrowly missing the beams. 'You stay at the hall. We need you there for the time being.'

Abarhild hissed through her teeth. Now both her sons were thwarting her. Her sons, who never, *never* agreed with each other. The alpha and omega of all her child-bearing in her English marriage. The survivors.

Radmer, who from his first moment in her arms had contemplated her with that same stiff, judgemental stare he was using now. And Ingeld, unexpected Lammas lamb, born when she had thought she was past child-bearing. Ingeld, who gave her so much pain.

So much pain and so much joy. She had a sudden vision of him pinching her heart in a pair of tongs as though he were a blacksmith, heating it to an agonizing radiance and hammering it new, over and over again, a vision so clear she could almost feel the warmth of the imaginary forge fire on her face.

'Time? A luxury I don't have.' She glared at her elder son. 'I need to make my peace with God. I need a chaplain of my own.' A haven for herself at the minster, and a guide to help her to Heaven. Why were they frustrating her? Had they not noticed how short life could be?

Radmer shook his head. 'We rely on you here at the hall, Mother. You insisted on bringing him' – he jerked his chin at his brother – 'back to Donmouth, and I agreed against my better judgement.' He folded his arms and glared at her. 'We've had ten years of you refusing to appoint a priest to Donmouth minster while you were waiting for him to be old enough. And now you want two?'

She hissed with annoyance. 'Get yourself a new wife, if you need a lady for the hall. Or let Elfrun have my keys.'

'Elfrun is a child.'

'Nonsense. And you know it.' She turned to her younger son. 'And you! I thought you'd welcome some educated company here. So you wouldn't be so lonely. Having to traipse back and forth to York all the time to hobnob with the archbishop! Very wearisome for you.'

Ingeld looked at her for a long moment. 'Not wearisome at all, Mother. Wulfhere is my good friend.' To her annoyance a smile tugged at the corners of his mouth, creasing the skin around his warm, brown eyes. His face was gilded by the fire-gleam. 'But another priest at Donmouth just means someone else to disapprove of me. Why would I want that?' His eyes flicked sideways. 'As though Radmer weren't doing a fine job already.'

'Where is this priest going to come from, anyway?' Radmer took a couple of long strides and turned again, his energy cramped by the little space. Abarhild wished he would stop his pacing. He was reminding her of the caged lion she had seen long ago when she was a child, visiting the Emperor's court at Aachen: that same barely contained fury, the cold pale stare. 'Who's going to feed him? House him? Priests are expensive. There's plenty the minster needs before another priest. Its own smith, for one—'

But Abarhild had had quite enough. 'I will deal with all the necessaries.' She looked up at her eldest child. Did he have to tower over her like that? 'I have my morning gifts.' Through all the long, difficult years, she had clung to the woods and fields that had come to her the morning after each wedding. Her comfort and her strength, and they brought in more than enough revenue.

'What's it to you, Radmer, anyway, if there's a second priest at the minster?' Ingeld was still sporting that infuriating smile. 'My business, surely, not yours?'

'Your business?' Radmer wheeled once again, stabbing his finger at his brother. 'While you have been living in idleness in Wulfhere's household all these years, Heahred and I have been managing the minster for you, day in, day out. I know the minster land, and its income, and its renders, and you have not the faintest idea. And you don't give a plucked hen for the minster, as long as it fills your belly and covers your back in silk.'

'Radmer!' Abarhild felt the familiar tightness across her ribs. 'Ingeld is a priest of God now. *Pro amur Deo*, show him a little respect.'

'Priest of God,' Radmer said. '*Ingeld.*'

The pressure on her heart was harder than ever. She clamped her mouth and gripped her fingers around her stick, wishing she could strike him with it now as she would have once. Ingeld might be at fault, needling his brother, but surely to goodness Radmer could rise above the needling. One would hope a twelve-year gap would be enough to create a little distance between her boys.

But no, never. It had always been like this. Big and little piglet, squealing and shoving for the same teat. And such sharp teeth.

At times like this she was sick to death of them both.

'If we had a second priest at Donmouth minster,' she said softly to her youngest, 'he could take on all the pastoral work. You'd be free to spend more time in York.' She reached up to brush her fingertips against his wrist. 'If that's what you'd prefer.' Away from her. But happy. In Abarhild's version of their story she had only ever wanted him to be happy.

'Drinking the archbishop's wine,' Radmer said. 'Well, better that than drinking mine.'

Ingeld's mouth twitched again. 'Wulfhere certainly has better wine.'

Radmer turned on his heel for the last time and walked out of Abarhild's bower.

Grip the stick, hard. Never let them see how much it matters. The heat and pain were almost more than she could bear.

'You never give up, do you, Mother?' Ingeld squatted easily at her side and put his hand on her back, warm and bolstering. 'You'll try any twist and turn, if it gets you your way. As for the pastoral work, Heahred does most of that anyway.' He gave a little laugh, freighted with self-knowledge. 'I'm not at my best at a deathbed.'

'Ingeld, Ingeld.' She fought against the spell cast by his easy, beguiling voice, the warmth of his presence. He needed a firm hand, this one. 'It should be such a comfort, having you here again. And instead it's nothing but trouble.' He was hunkered down behind her, and she couldn't tell without turning if her words had any effect on him. She wasn't sure she wanted to see his face. 'Why can't you be a good priest? There is such good in you.'

'There are no good priests, Mother.' He gave her shoulder a little rub, a little shake. 'We are all just men. You know that. Weak, fallen men, subject to the changing moon.'

She twitched away from the pressure of his hand, holding on to the tatters of her anger. 'York still calls you.'

'Yes.'

'Women? Drinking? Dice?'

'Hunting,' he said agreeably. 'Horses.'

'And that's all you do with yourself.'

He shifted round so that he could look her in the eye. 'Would you have me lie to you? I've never done that yet, and I'm not starting now.' He shook his head. 'My friends are there. And York has books, as well, you know. Isidore, Pliny, Virgil, Ovid. Wulfhere and I talk about the stars. Time, and the tides, and how one might travel to Jerusalem. The monsters of the encircling Ocean. Where the barnacle geese hatch, and where the swallows go in the winter.' He put his arm around her shoulders. 'Don't fret about me.'

No one else ever touched her these days, not with such affection, now that she was so old and ugly and bad-tempered.

How she had missed him, cherished his visits, all the years he was in York. And, as always, his face and voice were working their enchantment. That painful heat was easing into gentle warmth, a soft drowsy weight. Abarhild felt she would sacrifice anything to keep him close to her. 'Where do the swallows go in the winter, then?' She leaned into him again, as though she were the child, and he the parent telling some soothing story.

'Well…' and she could hear the smile, the affection. 'In Isidore we read that they go across the sea, and Pliny says they make for sunny valleys high in the mountains…'

'But?'

'But I prefer the tale that they clump together in great balls – *conglobulant* – and spend the winter at the bottom of ponds. Like avian frogspawn.' He gave her shoulder a gentle squeeze. 'You shall have your chaplain, Mother, if only because Radmer disapproves. Do you have a man in mind?'

'I have already sent word,' she said. 'Weeks ago, to Corbie. My kinsman Ratramnus will find me someone.'

8

An arrow smacked into the tree trunk no more than a yard from Athulf's head.

He whipped round to stare at it quivering there, his body rigid with disbelief. The arrowhead had embedded itself in the slender birch's smooth bark. As the shaft stilled he noticed the fletching was swan-feather.

Everyone at Donmouth used grey goose.

But he was on the other side of the river from Donmouth now.

He turned his head slowly, gut tight, eyes flickering this way and that, gauging the little variations of light and shade, movement and calm, among the thick-leaved high-summer trees. The thongs of his sling slithered through his nerveless fingers.

Widia had told him not to cross the river. 'What if you meet wolf? Or worse. Boar. I don't know the Illingham woods. There could be anything.'

Athulf had bristled. What did he have to do, to earn Widia's respect? 'I can cope.'

Widia had shrugged. 'Don't blame me if you get hurt.'

'Nothing's going to hurt me.'

But his uncle's huntsman had just lifted one dark eyebrow, in a way that made Athulf's cheeks burn again, remembering. *What if you meet worse...?*

What was worse even than boar?

Men.

Three of them, at least. And one a fine archer, to send

his warning shot through the dense undergrowth with that precision.

Damn Widia. Why did he always have to be right?

'Name yourself.'

They still hadn't stepped out from behind the densely packed shoots of the overgrown hazel coppice, but he could tell the middle one had spoken. The leader, his bow in his hand, with a man on each side to guard his flank.

'Athulf.' The word scratched his throat. He swallowed and spoke louder, trying to deepen his voice. 'Athulf Ingelding.'

He could see them better now. Older than he was himself, but not by much.

'And what are you doing in my woods?'

His woods? Athulf raised his hands slowly. 'Hunting,' he said truthfully. 'No luck though.' He shrugged his cloak back so that they could see he didn't have so much as a leveret or a brace of ducklings about his body. The urge to cringe, to apologize, almost over-mastered him.

The youth in the middle stepped forward a couple of paces. He was tall, bony, with a glossy thatch of red-brown hair and cheekbones like clenched fists under the sun-gilded skin.

'From Donmouth?'

Athulf nodded.

'I didn't think the lord of Donmouth had a son.' A tone that Athulf interpreted as disbelief. 'I heard he only had a daughter.'

'Radmer's my uncle.' Athulf couldn't see much of the other two, in the shadows behind. One dark and thick-set, the other slightly built and fairer. Neither moving.

The bronze-haired stranger pushed past Athulf and began working the arrow out of the birch tree. Gentle little rocking movements that would ease the wicked little dart out intact. The other two came a little closer.

'You could have killed me with that.'

One of the others, the dark one, laughed, but the tall stranger's face remained impassive.

'If I'd wanted to kill you,' he said, 'I would have.' One last tug and the arrow was free. The tall young man turned, and caught Athulf's eye. 'I've seen you before,' he said, frowning.

Athulf couldn't remember. His scowl deepened.

'At the spring meeting, three months ago. Racing, on that scrubby little pony? With that girl. But I didn't know you were from Donmouth.'

There was a half-smile on the other boy's face, and Athulf read it as one of contempt. He flushed. Bad enough having had to ride Apple; worse being beaten by Elfrun; worst of all to have had this witness. He wanted to say something witty, biting, but his mind was a blank.

At last the tall boy shrugged. 'Pick up your sling.'

But Athulf didn't move. 'Who are you?' For the last ten years the king himself had held the rich estate across the river from Donmouth, and his reeve had cared little who might be pillaging his woods and marshes. 'What are you doing here?'

'I'm Thancrad. These are my father's lands now.'

'And who's he?'

'Tilmon. Tilmon of Illingham, as of last week. And Switha's my mother.'

Athulf stiffened. He had heard no word of this at Donmouth. If they had known, no one would have been talking about anything else.

They didn't know yet.

Tilmon of Illingham.

'Go on,' Thancrad said. He gestured. 'Pick up your sling.'

Blood flooded Athulf's cheeks. 'You can't tell me what to do.' He wasn't going to scrabble in the nettles for the son of a notorious traitor, no matter how high he and his might now stand in the king's favour. A strip of leather could always be pilfered from the tannery to make another sling. He stuck out his chin. 'Make me.'

No one moved or spoke for a long moment. Athulf forced himself to hold Thancrad's gaze, but he was very aware of the shorter figures to either side, especially the darker one with the grimace and the balled fists.

The dark one said, 'I know who he is.' His voice had a mocking edge. '*Ingelding*. His father's the abbot.'

Athulf tensed.

Thancrad shrugged. 'What does it matter who his father is?' He turned back to Athulf. 'Get your sling and go.' He jerked his head.

Athulf folded his arms. 'I told you. Make me.'

The dark lad stepped forward, bristling, but Thancrad gestured him away. 'Stop it, Addan.'

'We should teach him a lesson.'

'Why? He's done no harm.' Thancrad looked back at Athulf with a shrug. 'Please yourself. It's all the same to me.'

Athulf turned with all the arrogance he could muster, and started for the river, half expecting the thud of a dart between his shoulder blades. The blood had drained from his face, leaving him cold and shaky. When he was sure he was out of sight he paused and leaned against the hollow bole of an old willow, fighting the hot, sour bile that came flooding up from deep in his belly. It had been so close.

But he had stood his ground.

Against three of them. As his fear ebbed little rills of pleasure came rushing in to replace it, as lively as the currents that patterned the river water where it met the salt of the estuary. It belatedly occurred to him that that last exchange had been interesting. Thancrad hadn't wanted a confrontation, even three against one. It had been scowling Addan who had wanted to fight, and Thancrad had stopped him.

Had he been afraid?

But then there had been that little smile, still rankling... And he had shot that arrow, close enough that Athulf had felt the wind of its passing on his cheek.

Athulf jerked to attention. The ripples on the water told him that the tide was on the turn. If he was going to ford the river he would have to do it now, before the water from the estuary came flooding up into the narrow channel.

And he knew he had to get back with the big news. *Tilmon of Illingham*. It might be that no one at Donmouth, hall or minster, would thank him for it, but still they had to know.

9

'When I get married...' Saethryth glanced around to make sure she had an audience. She dropped her voice even further and the other girls leaned in towards her. The sun glittered on the loose curls of her hair, pale and shimmering as freshly retted flax. 'When I get married, it'll be to a proper man. You know what I mean? I've been looking around.' Her eyes were gleaming, lips moist. 'And I've got a few in mind. One in particular, although it's a shame to have to choose...' A stifled giggle erupted. Abarhild raised her head sharply.

Instant silence.

They were outside because the summer light rendered the interior of the weaving shed gloomy beyond all bearing. The stink from the urine-vats, with their ill-fitting lids, had been making the girls' noses run and their eyes water; and even Abarhild had conceded that some work could be done as well in the open air. 'Just make sure you tether the goats first.' So they were seated on the grass in a ragged circle, heads bent over their carding combs and the little looms for weaving braid. Abarhild squatted on a creepie-stool, one eye on her embroidery, the other on her deceptively meek-looking charges.

Elfrun sat at her grandmother's feet, outside the inward-facing circle of the other girls. She was stitching a new border on to the skirt of her blue dress. Athulf might have overtaken her, but she too had grown lately and her grandmother had scowled at her exposed, winter-pale shins and wrists. 'You've just grown up and down,' she had said, rubbing the nap of the blue with her knotty fingers. 'Not outwards. No need for a new dress, not yet. Plenty of life in this one. And I want to see some more modesty from you. *Deo amur*, Elfrun! Behave like your father's daughter for once.'

Saethryth was talking again, low and intense, and the closed circle of other girls was listening avidly, but Elfrun couldn't hear the hissed words, and she wasn't sure she wanted to. Saethryth really got under her skin, the way she breathed through her mouth, her pigeon-plump body, her air of knowing more than she should. Saethryth, who had been the first of all of them to start her monthly bleeding, and planned to be the first to marry. She was the daughter of Luda, the hall steward; the two girls were of an age, and if anyone at Donmouth should have been Elfrun's natural ally, it was she. Yet Saethryth had always irked her, like a sharp-edged pebble in her shoe.

Not *her* fault. She was ready to be friends. But Saethryth always deflected such overtures, with her sharp tongue and contemptuous glance.

A ripple of shocked, stifled giggles, and Saethryth looked up to meet Elfrun's eye, a challenge in her gaze.

'What?'

Saethryth shrugged, and smiled, but she didn't look away.

'Yes, what is it, girl?' Abarhild looked up from her needle. 'If you have something to say, share it with all of us.'

Saethryth ducked her head and looked demure. 'Sorry, lady.'

Abarhild snorted, and Elfrun just had to hope that her grandmother wasn't fooled. She jabbed her needle into the thick blue wool and it went right through and pierced the ball of her thumb. She snatched her hand away, stifling a yelp, and jammed her thumb in her mouth before any blood could get on her clothes, bending her head in the hope that the others wouldn't notice, staring furiously at a head of cow parsley that was just coming into flower. The pain was astonishing for such a tiny wound, and she bit hard on the end of her thumb, hoping to blank out the first shock with a more manageable one. A small ladybird was crawling across the flower-head, a red bead.

Abarhild was still glaring at Saethryth, rheumy eyes narrowed. The familiar smell of baking bread was coming from the cook-house, and from the hillside above the yard she could hear the bubbling, swooping call of a curlew.

Saethryth caved in at last. 'Sorry, lady. We were just talking about weddings.' That bold glance at Elfrun again. 'We were wondering who might want to marry Elfrun.'

'That is none of your business.' Abarhild looked at the girl, eyes like chips of flint in the shirred, pouchy skin of her face. After a moment Saethryth had to look away. Abarhild gestured with her stick, its silver-gilt mount flashing. 'Bring me your work.'

'Why?' There was a little ripple and shiver in the group of girls.

'I want to see if you can weave as well as you can gossip.'

Saethryth rose to her feet and advanced a few slow paces, holding the little loom in front of her as though it smelt bad.

'Closer.'

Another two paces, and Abarhild's stick darted out and up, knocking loom and braid away from Saethryth's shocked hands into the long grasses. 'I don't have to look at it. I know you, you lazy lummock. You girls, you're all the same. I'm sick to death of you. Pick it up, undo it and start again.' Elfrun lowered her face and tried hard not to smile.

Saethryth scowled, massaging the knuckles of her right hand. 'And what if I don't?'

'I shall beat you, you know that, you idle lump. And so will your father.'

Saethryth was biting her lip, drawing breath. She clearly had more to say, but she was interrupted by a furious shout from the hill.

'Out of the way, all of you – out of the way!' A fair-haired figure came pelting down through the trees to the little grassy field where the girls were sitting. They scrambled to their feet, staring. Behind him now they could hear the thud of hooves.

49

'A boar—' The man bent double, winded, his sides heaving. It was Dunstan, Radmer's sword-bearer.

'There's a boar coming?' Abarhild was hauling herself up from her stool, keys jingling at her waist. 'Down this way?'

'No – no – Widia.' He panted hard. 'The boar charged... Lady, he needs your help.'

'Widia's hurt?' Saethryth was pushing in, her face pale, the corners of her mouth tugging down.

'Yes.' Dunstan was nodding, his sides heaving. 'It gored him. Ribs. His face.'

The girls were scrabbling after their tools and cloth-work, scrambling over against the hedge, and the horses coming into sight now over the ridge, two of them, one led not ridden, with loping hounds and a couple of boys tearing down in their wake. Staring, Elfrun realized Athulf was one. Cudda, the smith's boy, was the other. Her uncle Ingeld was in the lead, on grey Storm, with a long, bulky, wrapped bundle thrown over his saddle-bow.

Not a bundle. Oh God. A man. She could see his arm hanging down, the hand bouncing like a dead thing. Widia.

10

'**M**other! You're needed!'

Blood, great quantities of blood, soaking Ingeld's hands and the front of his tunic, but much, much more drenching Widia's clothes. How many pints ran through a man's veins? Storm's white hide was streaked with red, and Elfrun was amazed that the mare could tolerate the smell.

And Abarhild was there, even before Ingeld and Dunstan had eased the huntsman down. 'Elfrun, here's the key to the heddern. Get me some linen. Clean, new. The rest of you, go away.'

'It came from nowhere.' Dunstan still sounded dazed. 'Out of a bramble thicket, it came straight for the abbot. Widia pushed us out of the way...'

'Elfrun, *linen*.'

She had been staring at her uncle, her mouth open, barely recognizing him. Blood had splattered across his cheekbones, streaked in his hair, stiffening it to spikes. She had never seen anyone look less like a priest.

'It tossed him,' Ingeld said. 'I drove it off.'

'*Elfrun*.'

She picked up her skirts and ran for the hall. The heddern at the back was kept locked, and she had never before been entrusted with the key. It was stiff, and she struggled for a moment before the lock clicked open. Spices, and the money chest, and her father's weapons and war-gear, and the lengths of linen neatly folded on a low shelf. Grabbing an armful she hurtled back to the infield. Someone had brought water. Saethryth was pushing forward, trying to see. 'Is he dead?'

'Get away out of it, you girls. There's nothing more you can do.'

A groan from the wounded man, and Abarhild bent over him again. Elfrun could see a great flap of gory skin hanging loose from the side of Widia's face, a bloody sheen of pale pink exposed. She realized it was the bone of his cheek, and she looked away, revolted. 'Come on.' She forced herself to take Saethryth's arm. 'You heard my grandmother!' But Saethryth elbowed her away.

'Help me get his tunic off,' Abarhild was saying. 'No, *cut* it, you fool. Not over his head! There's ribs broken.'

'He'll be scarred,' Saethryth said. 'If he lives.' Her voice was low, lacking its usual truculent edge, and Elfrun thought the other girl must be as shocked as she was herself. 'And not just his face.'

Radmer was striding towards them. Elfrun was glad to have the excuse to drop Saethryth's arm and run to him, seeking comfort. But he pushed right past her, his face set hard, making straight for his younger brother. Fighting hurt which she knew to be unreasonable, Elfrun turned and watched.

He and Ingeld were only inches apart, and for a moment she thought her father was going to hit his brother, his wrath was so palpable. Elfrun couldn't hear her father's words, but she didn't need to. His expression was enough.

'If Widia doesn't die he'll be crippled.' Saethryth still had that unwonted quietness to her.

'We don't know that.' But Elfrun wasn't really listening to the other girl, absorbed by her father's simmering gestures, that jabbing finger. Now Ingeld was turning his back and walking over to Storm. Radmer was following him, hauling his younger brother around by the shoulder, but Ingeld threw the hand off and swung himself up into the bloodstained saddle.

'My fault? How is it my fault?' He was tugging Storm's head round.

'Whom do you blame then?' Radmer had to raise his voice to reach his brother's ears. 'I've told you before, gamble all you like with your own worthless life but leave me and mine alone. As though I haven't enough to worry me, with this news of Illingham.'

Ingeld didn't reply. He dug his heels into the mare's flanks and Storm set off at a jolting trot. Athulf stared at Radmer for a moment, then tugged at Cudda's arm and the two boys hurtled off in Ingeld's wake.

'I'm going to ask your grandmother.' Saethryth sounded as though her teeth were tight-gritted. 'Where he's wounded. If he's going to die or not.'

Elfrun only had eyes for her father, who was still glaring after Ingeld. 'Don't be stupid! Can't you see she's busy?' Didn't Saethryth know better than to interrupt at such a time? 'Anyway, no one can tell yet. If he lives, he might heal fine well in my grandmother's care. They taught her so much, the nuns, when she was a girl in Frankia.' She tried to remember what Abarhild had said. 'But, yes, he might be crippled. Or he might live, and then the wounds stink and rot and he would die slowly from that.' She could hear her own voice rattling away, hardly aware of what she was saying, trying to remember Abarhild's teaching as a way of distracting herself from the horror of what had happened. 'That would be awful. But nobody knows what's going to happen.'

'But I need to know. I need to know *now*.' Saethryth's face had drawn in on itself like a thundercloud. She stared for a long furious moment at Widia's bloodstained figure, with Abarhild bending over him; and Elfrun thought she really was going to interrupt, and at the worst possible moment. But just as she reached a hand to the other girl's arm to warn her off, Saethryth turned round, hauling in her skirts and hurrying away in the opposite direction.

Elfrun stared after her. But a moment later she had forgotten all about Saethryth, because her father was at her side, tight-lipped and shaking his head. 'Three ribs broken, your grandmother says. That ragged filthy slash down the flank. The tusk must have gone in and sideways. And his face. There are teeth gone. It's a downright miracle that his skull's not smashed.' He smacked his fist into the palm of his other hand. 'I said priesting Ingeld would make no difference. I told everyone, and look. Your grandmother should keep a closer eye on him. Her moving to the minster – maybe it's not such a bad idea after all.'

Dunstan and another man had come back with a rough stretcher and were gently lifting Widia on to it. It looked horribly like a dead man's bier.

Elfrun hung on to her father's last words as a distraction 'She can't look after the minster as well as the hall. They're too far apart. There's too much to do. She's too old.'

And Radmer laughed. She couldn't understand why, but she felt such relief that she laughed too.

'Don't let her hear you say that.' He was already sober again. 'And even if she is getting old, your grandmother's a fine manager. But she's been singing that old song about wanting to take the vows they never let her when she was a girl. Find herself a chaplain. Fasting and prayer. Not yet, I've told her. We need her.' That edge of bitterness had returned to Radmer's voice. 'But it seems Ingeld needs her more.'

As long as Elfrun could remember Abarhild had spoken wistfully of retiring to a little bower at the minster, devoting herself and her wealth to alms and prayer and fasting. She had been about to do so when Elfrun's mother had first fallen ill, almost three years ago. Was it really going to happen?

She reached for her father's sleeve. 'I can do everything she does.' Honesty forced her to add, 'Well, nearly everything.' But he had already turned away from her, heading towards the hall, where they had taken Widia.

Why wouldn't he listen? If she could manage the hall as well as ever her mother had, then perhaps there would be no more talking of marriage, of sending her away. That encounter at the spring meeting with Tilmon and Switha still haunted her. *You have to put her somewhere...* Something about that woman made her hard to resist. She had emanated a sweet reason, an almost-physical reassurance. But Elfrun's father had held out against her and whatever she was asking. Elfrun didn't begin to understand the simmering hostility between Donmouth and the new holders of Illingham, but she knew she had been glad to see her father turn his back on them.

But they were not the only threat. She had a sudden, queasy memory of cousin Edmund's ragged moustache, of the way he had pressed his thigh against hers on that rickety bench, the rankness of his breath.

A jolt of anger shot through her. How could her father just walk away? What she hadn't yet mastered around the hall, she could learn. She knew Donmouth, its intake and outfields, the shielings in the hills, the fish traps and weirs, the steady rhythm of summer harvest and winter hedging, the secrets of brew-house and bake-house.

She might not have Abarhild's mastery of loom and leech-dom, but she was learning, and she could go on learning even with Abarhild a vowess at the minster. How much easier life would be without the constant fear of Abarhild's hard stick and harder speech. Just her and her father, working together.

But he was walking away from her, as though this were no more than a bitten lip, a grazed knee...

Elfrun felt a powerful desire to hit something. She folded her arms across her chest and glowered.

But the sun was still shining. And Abarhild would have forgotten all about her and her sewing in the worry about Widia. She could beg half a loaf from the bake-house and go out on Mara, and the day would be nearly gone before anyone thought again to look for her.

11

Ingeld slowed Storm to a walk. The shock was beginning
to ebb, but he was still living in that moment, the one just
before the world had erupted around them. They had been so
careful, hardly breathing, treading so lightly that the grass barely
rustled, ducking under branches, the dogs padding silently at their
sides. They had left the horses tethered at the edge of the wood.
And under the trees the world had been noonday-still, the birds
quiet, the green-dappled shadow a welcome rest from the blazing
day he had left down at the minster. He hardly noticed the hot
sun now. His hands on the reins were slick with sweat, his heart
still thudding.

Why hadn't the dogs scented it?

The boar must have been asleep: they had almost trodden on
its body. Like a black rock come to life, it had reared up squealing out of a patch of brambles and swung round straight at him
and Dunstan. A great shove from Widia had sent him flying, and
then Widia – always so neat-footed – had stumbled.

The violent images repeated themselves over and over again
in his mind's eye.

He was riding into the minster yard now, dismounting, the
earth smacking into the soles of his feet. Athulf was at his side,
trying to take the reins from his hands, and that fair child who
dogged Athulf like his shadow hovering a few paces behind. He
waved them away, more abruptly than he intended.

Storm was distressed; he could sense it now. She was his darling, this fine, dark-eyed forward-moving grey. He had bred her,

and broken her, and taken her with him when he first went to the archbishop's household in York, sixteen years earlier, when she had still been too young to ride. He looked down in disbelief at his bloodstained hands, his clothes, the drying streaks and spatters on her white hide. Heahred, the broad-shouldered, ginger-haired deacon, was at his elbow. Athulf was gabbling, Heahred nodding, his gaze flickering back and forth.

'Not your blood then, Ingeld.' A pause. 'Father. Father abbot.'

That must be Heahred's voice. Athulf didn't call him Father, never had, even now they had priested him.

'Radmer said it should have been me.' Ingeld could hear the sounds his mouth made, but he didn't quite know what he was saying, or what he might say next. He felt hugely weary, his knees sagging under the weight of his body.

Heahred was clucking, fussing, calling instructions about cold water, hot water, fresh linen. 'Put your head between your knees.'

'I have to look after Storm.' Ingeld held her bridle tight and leaned against the strong curve of her neck. Care for the horses first, always. He took a deep breath and felt the world steadying around him.

'Come on, Cudda!' Athulf, at his heels again, was shouting at the fair boy. 'We'll see to Storm for you.'

'I can't.' Cudda looked trapped. 'My father told me to be back at the forge by evening. He said he'll lam me else.'

'And I'm telling you to help me here.'

Where had the lad learned that imperious tone? Ingeld turned on the pair of them. 'You – Cudda? If your father wants you home, then you must go.' He could sense Athulf bristling. 'No arguments. Go.'

And Cudda went, at a pace that suggested his father's threats had a heavy hand behind them. Heahred was at his elbow with a bucket of water.

'Father abbot. Give me the reins. Wash your face. You'll frighten the children.'

Obedient for once, Ingeld knelt on the packed earth and

splashed his face. Now that it was wet, the blood smelt sharp again. He leaned further forward and dipped his whole head in the water, a shock of cold that brought him startled to his full senses. Keeping his head under as long as he could, he ran his fingers through his hair until he felt the spikes of dried blood begin to loosen and come away. He came up gasping.

The water in the bucket had darkened, but his hands were still spattered with leaking clots.

Athulf had taken Storm into her stall, and Ingeld could hear the boy's voice, soothing and clucking.

A good boy, really, this son he had almost forgotten he had. His child with a girl who had died so long ago, and yet he remembered her more often than he did this boy in front of him.

Ingeld took the towel that Heahred was offering, tousling and rubbing, smearing the linen's glassy surface with Widia's blood, diluted to a dog-rose hue but still staining everything it touched.

Damn Radmer.

It had *not* been his fault. Widia was the huntsman; the hall lands were his preserve. Widia had known there were boar about, he should have read the spoor better, the dung, the bruised undergrowth.

Between them Abarhild and Radmer had dragged him away from his home in the archbishop's household, back to provincial, dreary little Donmouth, his mother promising him everything she imagined he wanted, his brother berating him about his duty to God and his obligation to king and kin and land alike. Did they think him an ass, at once to be beaten with a stick and tempted with a handful of withered grass?

And he had saved Widia. How was he to blame? Dunstan, the sword-bearer, the man of blood, had just cowered under the brambles. But he, the man of God, had gone in screaming and jabbing with the boar-spear as the great brute had stood over the huntsman's body, rooting in his ribs with its tusks. He alone had driven it snorting and squealing away.

A moment of triumph. That increasingly rare sensation of being fully alive, every vein and nerve thrumming.

Damn Radmer, for spoiling his moment of glory.

'Bring me another bucket, Heahred.' He would have to change his clothes. But what little his mother didn't know about getting stains out of linen, whether candle-wax or tallow-fat or blood, wasn't worth the knowing. He peeled off his tunic and linen undershirt in one sticky mass, and left them in a crumpled heap. The blood had soaked right through to his skin.

The water in the new bucket was warm, and this time there was real pleasure in plunging his head under and keeping it there as long as he could before flinging it back with a spray of drops, his lungs gasping like bellows.

When he opened his eyes, a girl was standing in front of him, blurred and sparkling. He stared as his vision cleared. Cream, and the first ripening blush of strawberries, and her hair pale tendrils of spun silk that clung to her flushed skin. For a good moment he thought he was dreaming, still giddy from the lack of air. *Quale rosae fulgent inter sua lilia mixtae...* Had he said that aloud?

'What?' She was as short of breath as he was himself. 'What are you talking about? I need to know what happened to Widia.' Roses and lilies to look at, but thistles and nettles, alas, in her voice.

But however much he regretted the harshness of her tone the lack of deference was in itself refreshing. Ingeld found he had grown very tired, very quickly, of the people of Donmouth and their tiptoeing and whispering in the presence of their new lord abbot.

'Who are you?'

She gave him a scornful look. 'Don't you know? Saethryth.'

He shook his head.

'Luda's daughter.'

Luda's eldest? He smiled, masking his astonishment, his ineptness. 'Of course.' He looked at her harder, searching for some resemblance to his brother's hirpling, grizzled steward. Nothing.

'And I was planning on marrying Widia. Now look at him.'

'And that's my fault, I suppose.' Water was trickling down his ribs, raising his skin in little prickles. Heahred had come up with a fresh towel, and he reached for it gratefully.

'Your fault?' She sounded surprised. 'No. It's dangerous, the hunt. I know that. I'm not stupid. But I'm not marrying someone who's a cripple from the start.'

'No?'

'Not if I don't have to. So, what happened to him? You saw it. Tell me.'

'Yes, I saw it.' Ingeld closed his eyes. The eruption of the black, squealing mass. Flash of tusk. Widia falling. Grunting from the beast and screaming from the man. 'Face. Ribs. If he lives he'll likely be lame, and I don't think he'll be as pretty as he was. But he should be able to get about. If he lives.' Bitterness settled back down around him like a cloud. 'If.'

'And what about…?' Her lashes were lowered and her voice quiet but the gesture she made was unmistakable.

'I…' Why was he so reluctant to answer? 'I don't know.'

Heahred offered the towel, his features tight and expressionless and still somehow disapproving, and Ingeld took it, burying his wet face, mopping up the water that still dripped pink-tinged. Widia had taken the force of the charge meant for him, and Ingeld still could not quite believe it was not his own slashed face, smashed ribs, spilled blood. But, as the girl had intimated, it could have been so much worse.

Guts. Groin.

Trux aper insequitur totosque sub inguine dentes… but this *aper* had only sliced into Widia's ribcage with its *dentes*, not buried them between the man's thighs as that other boar had done to Ovid's poor Adonis. And for that both the huntsman and his cream-and-roses girl should be grateful.

When he looked up again she had gone.

12

Wynn waited until the clanging of the hammer had stopped before going up to the open side of the lean-to that sheltered the forge from the worst the weather could do and shouting her message.

'What?'

She guessed the hammer-blows were still ringing in her father's ears. 'Mother says, will you be here for the night?' She set the cloth wrapping the hard black bread and harder cheese down by one of the upright posts that framed the smithy entrance.

'Aye, we will that. We've a stack of sickles to see to. No harvest without the smith!' Cuthred's grin split his narrow, bearded face in half. He set his hammer down. 'And I've had that long-faced misery guts Luda in here twice in the last couple of days telling me the barley's ripe for the cutting, as though I've no eyes of my own.' He spat. 'And that's just the hall-work, never mind the minster. Don't go anywhere. I need you to set your hands to the bellows. I told Cudda to be here long before now but there's no sign of him yet.'

Wynn looked down to hide the smile that, try as she might, was tugging at the corners of her mouth. She loved everything to do with the forge, but when Cudda was there their father had little time for her. Cuthred jerked his head, and she set her hands to the wooden top-plates of the leather bags that were the life and breath of the forge.

'Apron.'

She glared at him. 'It's too hot.'

'I don't care.' And when she didn't move, he said, '*Sparks.*

61

Your mam will have plenty to say to me if I send you home with cinder holes in your dress again.' When she stuck her tongue out at him, he laughed.

'Let me take my dress off then.'

'No.' Her father raised his hammer, only half-playful. 'You're plain enough as it is, I don't want you scorched as well. Put that apron on.'

'You let Cudda work naked apart from the apron.'

'Cudda's a lad.' He raised the hammer again. 'I'll have no more of this, Wynn.'

She snorted with frustration, but she knew when to stop testing her father's patience and without further fight she unhooked the leather apron and pulled the strap over her head. Stiff, weighty enough to drag at the back of her neck, and it came down almost to her ankles.

'Good lass.'

She looked up briefly and grinned. Despite the upright stones between her and the fire-pit the heat struck her face as a solid thing. Up, down, up, down, her whole body straining to find the right rhythm, and slowly the bags filled with air and the charcoal in the forge began to glow once more, red, then orange. Cuthred picked up his hammer and tongs, and thrust the bent and twisted sickle deep into the radiant heart.

'Hey!'

The smith never looked up as his son came running in, but Wynn twisted round, somehow managing to keep the rhythm of the bellows steady.

'That's my job! Get out of it, chicken-bones!'

Her brother was breathing hard, his fair skin flushed and damp, tunic filthy, bare legs spattered with mud. But he showed no sign of remorse for his lateness. Gripping the tongs carefully, Cuthred moved the bar over to the squared stone that served as his smaller anvil, squatted and began to beat with swift, measured strokes.

Cudda said no more. Both he and Wynn knew that to

interrupt at this point was to bring down their father's wrath. As the fiery curve of metal began to dim, slowly regaining its true shape under the steady, clanging blows, their eyes met.

'Where have you been?' Her mouth shaped the words but made no sound. She frowned as she took in the dark spatter on the skirt of his tunic, and this time she did speak aloud. 'Is that *blood*?'

Cudda grimaced. He was about to say something, but glanced swiftly at their father and put his finger to his lips. The hot metal hissed as Cuthred thrust the sickle into the bucket of water that stood by the forge, and a sudden gust of steam billowed sideways through the smithy.

His children knew to wait until Cuthred had added the finished sickle to the pile. 'Right, lad. Take over at the bellows.' He reached over to grab another damaged blade, then paused, weighing it in his hands. 'You've been with Athulf again.' His voice admitted no doubt.

'And if I have?' Cudda's voice had a higher pitch than usual, and Wynn gave him another sideways look.

'I've told you before. Your place is here.'

'He told me to come—'

'Athulf's not your master!'

Cudda stared at his father. 'Athulf will be master here one day. He wants me as one of his men.'

Wynn held her breath, hoping for trouble. There had been a lot of this lately.

But, 'Athulf, master?' Cuthred turned and spat into the fire. 'You're dreaming. Stupid boy. Get to work.'

After a long moment, Cudda tugged his tunic off over his head and held out a hand for the apron. Wynn folded her arms across her chest. 'I was here first. I was helping—'

'Give.'

'Come on, Wynn,' Cuthred said. 'Don't you start making trouble. There's work needs doing.'

She could hear the danger in his voice, and knew she had no

choice. Huffing with annoyance, she bundled the bulky leather off and handed it over reluctantly.

'Off you go, chicken-bones,' Cudda said. 'Back to Mam and the other whinging babies.'

She shrugged elaborately, refusing to rise to his taunting, but her face was thundery and she dragged her feet on the way to the door.

'Still want a job, Wynn?' Her father jerked his head. 'There's more sickles need an edge putting on them, out the back. Get yourself a whetstone. And stay out from under our feet, you hear?'

Wynn retraced her steps, trying to keep the smile off her face as long as Cudda could see it, and grabbed a small whetstone from the great oak slab where her father kept his tools. Just as she was ducking out through the entry she noticed a rider coming through the trees on a chestnut pony. She tensed for a moment, but it was only Elfrun, from the hall. To Wynn's surprise the older girl reined in the pony and swung herself down to the ground.

'Is your father at the forge?'

Wynn stared at her. Could she not hear the sound of the bellows? There might be no hammer-clang, but the gasping lungs of the forge were loud enough. 'Yes.'

'I've a message for him.' Elfrun sounded as though her temper were none too sweet. 'I wasn't going to come this way, but Luda caught me as I was leaving the yards. And your father won't thank me for it.'

'What's the message then?' Wynn laughed shortly. 'No, don't tell me.' She pulled a pompous face and hunched up one shoulder, a nasal tone entering her voice. *Does that lazy fool of a smith not know the barley's ripe for cutting?* Her mimicry of the steward was cruel and accurate, and Elfrun had to half smile and nod in recognition. 'No need to take that message to my father,' Wynn said. 'He knows fine well, and he and Cudda are hard at it.' As though they heard her, the clanging of the hammer started up again.

'Cudda?'

'Acourse.'

'But—' Elfrun stopped, frowning, and Wynn eyed her curiously.

'What is it, lady? Is it anything to do with the blood on his tunic?' She felt a pulse of excitement. 'Has he been fighting again?'

Elfrun shook her head, to Wynn's disappointment. 'He and Athulf followed the hunt, and Widia was gored by a boar. It's Widia's blood.'

Wynn stared. This was even better. Bad enough in her father's eyes that Cudda was out climbing trees or fishing with Athulf, but hunting boar! She couldn't begin to tally the boundaries, spoken and unspoken, that he'd transgressed. This was power indeed! Would she do better to tell her father directly, or to keep Cudda wondering how much she knew?

But Elfrun seemed to misunderstand her wide-eyed silence. 'Don't fret – Cudda wasn't hurt. If he's got blood on his tunic, it's just because blood went everywhere. I thought he'd gone off again with Athulf.' She sighed. 'And Widia – well – it's bad, but my grandmother's looking after him.'

But Wynn had lost interest. The forge had little to do with the huntsman's preserve of kennels and mews, and Widia always looked after his own knives and spear-blades. 'If Cudda'd gone with Athulf again this evening our da would have killed him when he got back,' she said. 'He's always dodging off.' She scowled at Elfrun. 'You can tell your own da that it's me that keeps the forge going at least as much as Cudda. More. I do more than Cudda.'

Elfrun had turned to hoist herself on to the pony's back, but she stopped at that and looked hard at Wynn, holding the younger girl's gaze for a long moment. 'Yes, I'll tell him that,' she said. 'I will. He should know.'

13

Abarhild used her crescent knife first to mince the garlic fine and then to scrape it into the brass pot with the chopped leek, before pounding them together. 'Get me that little glass flask from my chest. No, the blue one. Bile.'

She took it from Elfrun's hand, pulled out the rag, shook the bottle and sniffed, her whole face pursed. 'I hope the damp's not got in. This was taught me for swollen eyes. Mother Gisela would have been shocked at the thought of putting it on a wound.' She frowned into the dark corner of the heddern where Widia lay restless and muttering.

Elfrun nodded. She too was disturbed by the sight of the taut, hot skin around the ragged gash across Widia's ribs. It was after her mother's death that Abarhild had started talking her through the salves and drenches, and what symptoms might prompt which response. Over the last couple of years she had helped with countless cuts and bruises, but this was by far the worst she had seen. At first he had seemed to be mending fine well, if slowly, but now the skin smelt wrong, and while his face didn't look too bad the wound on his side was oozing and hot.

'Make yourself useful.' Abarhild eyed her granddaughter. 'Go to Luda for me – take a pitcher and ask him to put a little wine in it.'

'Is it for Widia to drink?'

'No. It's for the salve. Get going, girl.'

Once outside the little storeroom and in the dim peace of the hall Elfrun drew a deep shuddering breath. The pitchers stood on a trestle table at one side and she grabbed the nearest by its gritty handle and went out of the hall, into a grey summer afternoon, where a light drizzle fell. Round the back to the storerooms and cook-house, her heels dragging despite her grandmother's injunction to hurry.

Luda was always best avoided.

But no one was at work in the cook-house, or in the little yard; no sign of life other than a few barn fowl scratching in the mud. Elfrun knew she should ask first, but Abarhild had said they should hurry. Surely Widia was more important? Shrugging to herself, she ducked under the thatch of the lean-to buttery, and turned the spigot herself. How much was a little, anyway? She watched the thin yellow liquid dribble through until perhaps a quarter of a pint stood in the pitcher, and then reached forward to close off the flow.

'Stealing wine again?'

Elfrun yelped and half turned, the wine sloshing. Luda stood close behind her, arms folded, a forbidding look on his pouchy, lined face. She hadn't heard a thing.

'I shall have to tell your father.' His nasal voice was serious, his face still disapproving, but somehow she could tell he was enjoying her discomfiture. She had always found it hard to look at him; his deep-set eyes were too close together, giving an unsettling intensity to his stare. The drizzle had beaded in his greasy grey curls.

'What do you mean, *again*? I haven't been stealing wine. It's for my grandmother!'

'Likely!' He clicked his tongue. 'Turn off that spigot.'

She hadn't even realized that the wine was still trickling out and dripping on to the packed earth of the floor, and her face was hot as she twisted the spigot round. 'Why do you always think the worst? My grandmother asked me to bring wine for a medicine she's making for Widia. There was no one around to ask, so I just took what she needs.' She stepped forward and pushed the jug at him. 'Look! There's hardly any in there.'

He peered in and snorted. 'Only because I caught you at it.'

'No!'

'We'll go to your grandmother and see what she says.' He gripped her by the upper arm and she tried to jerk away, relieved again that the pitcher held so little wine to spill.

'Yes, let's. Then you'll see I'm telling the truth.' She tried to barge past him, wanting to get round the clay-and-wattle walls of the cook-house and back into the big courtyard, but his hold on her arm was too tight. It was shameful being frog-marched like this, and she just hoped the courtyard was as empty at it had been earlier.

Jingling and a creak of leather, and they both turned, Luda's grip slackening. A dun horse she didn't recognize coming through the gate, but a rider who was vaguely familiar. One of the king's riding-men; she had seen him at the meeting. Luda dropped her arm and stepped forward, tugging his tunic down over his hips, trying to hide his limp.

In the flurry of greeting Elfrun ducked back into the hall, garnering a nod of approval from her grandmother.

'There's a man here,' she said. 'From Goodmanham, I think.' She was still flustered. 'Or wherever the court is? I think my father said they were at Goodmanham.'

'One of Osberht's men?'

Elfrun nodded. Abarhild's face pursed. 'Come to worry your father, no doubt.'

'He has a fine mount, but not as fine as Hafoc.' But – to be fair – few horses were as fine as Radmer's. 'Funny colour, though. Almost yellow.'

But Abarhild wasn't interested in horses. 'Bring that bowl over for me. The brass one. No, you silly girl, the one with the onion and garlic in.' She tipped in the wine, then covered the mixture with a coarsely woven piece of linen, weighted at the corners with little balls of clay. 'There, that just needs to sit.'

Elfrun glowered at the door. 'Luda thought I was stealing wine.' She rubbed her arm. 'He was angry, even when I explained. I thought he was going to hit me.'

Abarhild was silent for a long moment. Then she said, 'Luda is an old and trusted servant of your father's. It is possible that he still thinks of you as a child. More than possible, given how childishly you still behave sometimes.' She raised a reproving hand. 'Let me speak, please. But you are not a child any more, and we have to make sure that people understand that.' She drew in a deep breath, and Elfrun braced herself.

But Radmer was in the doorway of the heddern, blocking the light. 'Put up one of my good tunics and some linen in my saddlebags, Mother. The grey one will do. I'm away up to Driffield on the king's orders. He wants to talk something over with me.'

Not Goodmanham then, but still away to the north. Another of the king's many vills, a day's journey. Elfrun had never been to any of them, never been further than Barkston Ash for the spring and autumn meeting except for that one intoxicating trip to York last winter, to see Ingeld ordained priest with all the splendour the cathedral could afford.

Radmer was looking past her. 'How's he doing?'

'Badly.' Abarhild was tight-lipped.

Elfrun was suddenly consumed with horror at the thought that she would be spending the next few days trapped in the stuffy heddern watching Widia die by slow inches. 'Let me come with you?'

'You?' Radmer shook his head, frowning, turning away from her even while he was still speaking. 'No, no. You're needed here, Elfa. Where's Dunstan? I need my sword.'

'Get your father's tunic for him, child.' Abarhild turned to her son. 'No word waiting for me from York? No letter?'

'Were you expecting anything?' Radmer was hefting the leather bags down from their pegs. 'I told Athulf to saddle Hafoc for me. The brat is always hanging around here. Time he made himself useful, for a change.'

Abarhild bristled. 'Athulf has been looking after Storm. And he does a good job of it.' She hissed between her teeth. 'Give him something better to do, if you think he's wasting his time.'

Radmer turned his back, and Elfrun tried to look busy. Dunstan had come in and was sorting out sword and belt from the rack of war-gear. Elfrun turned to the great carved and painted chest where her father's clothes were stored. The lid was a heavy slab of oak, and it was an effort to lift it right up and over, and lean it against the wall. As she did so, the scents of costmary and mugwort came up to meet her, and she had a sudden blinding memory of her mother, picking the herbs, and hanging them to dry in their little linen bags, and showing her how to strew them in the layers of clothes. *Never forget the moths and their worms, Elfa, too small to see, almost, but they'll destroy all our work if we let them*. In her memory the chest was huge, so high she could hardly see into it, the raised lid a great slab disappearing into darkness: she must have been tiny.

The grey tunic was on the top, with its plain black and white bands at throat and cuff. Her mother had planned to embroider over them in silver, but in the end there had not been time.

Shoving the tunic under her arm, Elfrun banged down the lid more heavily than she had anticipated. Abarhild hissed her disapproval and whisked the tunic from her, following her son out into the big gloomy space of the hall. Dunstan was untangling a leather strap, fair brows contracted. He gave the sword-belt a shake, then scooped up sword and scabbard and turned to go after them.

'Elfrun.'

Hardly more than a whisper, half-formed: ... *frun*...

She could hardly bear to look at the scabbed red gash that seamed the left side of Widia's face from eyebrow to jawline. Abarhild had said to watch in case it too began to ooze and tighten. To bend close and sniff the bruised and swollen skin, hunting the whiff of rot. Her throat tight, she leaned in and did as she was told.

Widia reached up a hand.

'Stay still. Don't talk.' How it must hurt him to talk. 'Don't move your mouth.' The left half of her own face had begun to throb in sympathy.

He closed his eyes. She moved a little closer and hunkered down. 'Abarhild is making you some special medicine. Something she learned from the nuns at Chelles. It'll take a day or two, but you'll be well again.' Elfrun put all the conviction she could into her voice, but she knew she was talking to this tough, seasoned man as though he were a little child, and she winced at her own ineptitude.

Eyes still closed, he nodded, a tiny movement but it made him shiver. Then, lips not stirring, he whispered something she didn't catch.

'Sorry,' she said. 'Sorry, Widia. I didn't hear you.'

He opened his eyes then, dark and too bright at the same time, his pupils like black holes. He tried again, and this time she thought she did understand.

'*Saethryth?*' The last word she had expected to hear. 'You want me to tell her something? You want me to fetch her?' She jumped up, not waiting for an answer, relieved to have something practical to do.

The rain was hammering down now. She felt the mud spurt between her toes as she dashed across the yard and down the nettle-lined path that led to Luda's steading. To her relief she didn't have to go into the house. Saethryth was in the chicken run, her skirts kilted, one little sibling propped on her hip and another toddling after her with a basket.

'He what?'

'I don't know what he wants. But he said your name. And I think he's dying.'

Saethryth's face twisted in a scowl. Her hair looked darker in the rain. 'Why couldn't he just have died straight away? Why is it dragging out like this?'

'Look, are you coming?'

'How can I?' She shrugged, looking at the children. 'I've got to get the eggs and look after these brats. Mam would kill me if I just went off.'

'I'll take them.' Elfrun reached out her arms for the baby on the other girl's hip, but Saethryth turned away.

'No, I'm not coming,' she said over her shoulder. 'What good could I do? Are you sure it was my name he said, anyway?'

'I think so.' But no, she wasn't sure. 'Don't you care? He asked for you by name! I think he's dying. How can you not come?'

'Just go away. Before Mam comes out and wallops me. Or worse, Da.' Saethryth pulled a disgusted face.

Elfrun stared at her, but the other girl had already turned and was squatting to scrabble with her free hand under a thornbush for a stray egg, the little brother on her hip tugging at the damp curls of her hair and threatening to overbalance her.

14

The path wound down from the wolds, and the rising ground behind him cut off the westering sun. The track was steep-sided, and would no doubt run with water in the winter, but now it was late-summer dry with white dust and flint, though the leathery soles of his feet took the rough and smooth alike in their stride. Finn had had a good few weeks, following his instincts and the advice of chance-met folk on the road, meandering back and forth across these sparsely inhabited hills that marked the spine of Lindsey, dividing the coast from the flood-plains of the great river they called the Trent, the Trespasser. No one had set their dogs on him; no one had tried to rob him; though there was plenty of summer left yet for all that. His pack was lighter, and his little purse of silver heavier. His burden of knowledge was heavier too.

He wondered whether the monks and tenants of Louth would tell him the same story he had been hearing all summer, that the men of Mercian Lindsey lacked good leadership and had done for a generation. That the rising power of Wessex to the south took all the attention of Mercia's rulers away from this north-eastern province, which had never forgotten its own past, although it had been tugged back and forth between the Northumbrians and the Mercians for as long as men could remember. And that those rulers were themselves complacent, their rich heartlands far to the west. As far as Finn could tell this corner of Mercia was an overripe plum ready to fall from the branch, sweet and whole from a distance but come close and you could see the worm-holes, hear the buzzing of the wasps as they fought for the sticky prize.

And the Lindsey-men spoke with contempt of their great neighbour to the north. Ten years and more since Osberht had led an army south of the Humber! Finn had listened with interest to the criticism. 'We don't mind that he leaves us alone,' the Bardney guest-master had said. 'But it squashes ambition.' He topped up Finn's almost untouched cup of ale. 'And that does worry us. If he can't promote his old retainers and set up the young men, they'll be looking elsewhere. Nibbling at our edges.' He had laughed then, and shrugged. 'But strife between kin in Northumbria would also keep them too busy to bother us. As long as Alred – or whoever the contender might be – as long as he keeps off our turf we're happy.'

And he had looked happy, his jowly, freckled face half lit by the hearth-flicker.

Kin-strife. That was another phrase to file away. Every disaster brought its opportunities.

An evening blackbird called from a berry-freighted elder. Finn was hungry and thirsty, and he stopped to pull a few of the bittersweet little fruits from their dark-red stems and crush them with his teeth. Not too many though: they could do dire things to a man's insides. He would not, he guessed, make Louth before dark. And it would be dark soon: there was cloud coming in, and no moon, and it was now late enough in the summer that true night had returned.

Not much shelter up here on the high chalk, though, and the light would linger for a few miles yet. No folk, either. He could sleep fine well with no more than a bush as a windbreak, and despite the thickening cloud there was no hint of rain in the air, but, given the choice of that or a fire and a morsel to eat, he knew which he would pick. Finn stepped out, swinging his ashplant, in an easy lope that ate up the miles.

He had not gone more than a couple, though, when the sound of bleating floated in on the evening air. He stopped at once. Flocks meant a shepherd, and a shepherd meant dogs. His hand tightened around the smooth wood, an instant transition from walking stick to weapon.

They approached crouched and growling, rough, grey-furred animals not far removed from the wolves they had been bred to defend against. Two of them, or two that he could see in the dusk, flattened and with that insistent low lip-curled snarl that told him they meant business. Finn backed slowly, stick at the ready. There were no trees to climb. They were slinking closer, separating to right and to left, splitting his attention.

He breathed slowly, still stepping backwards, hands lifted appeasingly, the stick poised. Still that unnerving growl that had the hackles rising on the back of his own neck. Were they herding him, hunting him, or merely seeing him off?

A sudden, sharp whistle, and both dogs froze.

Finn did the same, keeping his breathing steady. They were still staring at him, and he knew that to turn and run would be an open invitation.

Another whistle, on a different note, and the dogs both turned with a last flash of white teeth and loped off into the thickening darkness.

Finn didn't shift, still concentrating on in-breath and out-breath, slowly lowering his weight from the balls of his feet back to his heels, letting his knees relax. The dogs could return at any moment. And where there were dogs, there were men.

'Who're you?'

He couldn't see who had spoken. The voice came from somewhere above and behind, on the bank that flanked the northern side of the road. He didn't move, still taking care to appear unthreatening. A high voice, a young voice. But the rash young could be far more dangerous than the wary old. 'A pedlar,' he said. He lowered his ashplant, angled his back to draw attention to his burden. 'See my pack?'

There was a grunt, and then a silence. Finn waited.

Then another voice, gruff. 'Buying, pedlar, or just selling?'

Relief coursed through Finn's veins. He shifted his weight on to one leg and flexed the other knee. 'I could be buying,' he admitted.

A crunch of flint and chalk as the young one jumped down from the bank. He looked half-sheep himself in his sleeveless coat of lambskins, the fleece on the outside. A jerk of the head. Finn followed.

The shepherds' shelter was half a mile off, a crescent of stacked turf roofed with bent withies, and a solid sheet of greasy felt against rain and wind. The fire had been banked with more turves, and the boy peeled these back and started feeding it with dry thorny twigs that crackled and sent sparks twisting up into the night sky. Dry oatcakes, and fingers of hard, sour cheese. Ewe's milk, warm from the teat and bitter with late-summer grass. The dogs skulked back and forth at the edge of vision, their eyes occasionally flashing an unearthly gleam as they reflected the fire.

They were silent men, and Finn let them be. If they had something further to offer him they would do it in their own time. Before he lay down he double-tied the fastenings of his pack and tucked his cloak around it as well as himself. The wicker was not only light to carry; it creaked and complained at the slightest pressure. He would know at once if anyone tried to open it while he slept. But he kept the hilt of his belt-knife in his hand, all the same.

No one tried.

He opened his eyes from his usual deep, dreamless sleep to a cold dawn. Fog, too thick a grey for the sun yet to have risen. The even-nights might be a month away but he could smell autumn in the air, the way the cold hit the back of his nostrils. He rolled himself on to one elbow to see his hosts the far side of the fire, their backs to him, talking too low for him to make out their words. He needed to relieve himself, so he got to his feet, making more noise than he needed to alert them to his wakeful presence.

When he turned back to the fire they were facing him, side by side. The older man nudged the young one. A boy, really. The boy looked down and muttered something. He had his hands behind his back.

The older man: 'He found it. When we were down at the steadings. He was hoeing his mam's little patch, and this came up.' It was more words than they had spoken all the past evening. He nudged the boy again. 'Go on.'

The boy held out his hand. It grasped a sizable thing of dull green bronze, still filthy with soil, like a giant spoon with a flat bowl: a disc with a series of welded loops for a handle. Finn took it carefully, turning it from side to side, hefting it. He had no idea what it might be, but the metal would be worth something, if only for scrap. He picked at the encrusted layers of dirt and corrosion. There was craftsmanship lurking there. His face kept its expression of mild, courteous interest, but behind the mask he was thinking fast. At Louth he could beg sour wine, flour, make a paste that would bring the shine back to the bronze. Give him an idea what sort of thing he held.

'What will I give you for it?'

The lad was silent, red-eared and shuffling.

'I've shared your bread. Never fear. I'll offer you a fair exchange.'

The big man laughed in his beard. 'A love charm, that's what he's after. A drink to make her lie down and welcome him in.'

Finn smiled, and spread his hands wide. 'Do I look like a cunning-woman? A leech?' He handed the bronze thing back to the boy and reached for his pack. 'What would she like, your girl? A ribbon? A bead?' He looked at the boy's unclouded face, his guileless blue eyes and smooth chin, and his heart twisted inside him. The big men, the hard men, they could shift for themselves. But the innocents, the children, their mothers, they troubled him. Reaching for his pack, he rummaged until his questing fingers found the little leather pouch they sought. Two blue and white glass beads tipped into his palm. 'Here. One for you and one for her. Wear them round your necks, on a good

77

thong. They'll protect your eyes, and guard against the Eye. And much else.' He held out his hand, a cool brown cup of palm and fingers cradling the little treasures. The boy scrabbled for them, pink and speechless, almost forgetting to hand Finn the bronze thing in his turn, until the big shepherd nudged him. They spat into their palms and clasped hands on the deal, and Finn hefted his pack once more.

15

'Osberht wanted to talk about Rome.' Radmer swung himself down from the high, gilt-tricked saddle. 'He should have asked your grandmother. She's been there. Or Ingeld. He claims to be a priest, after all.'

'Rome?' Elfrun felt blank as the newly woven linen stretched out and bleaching on the grass beyond the gates. Swallows and their new broods swooped and chittered about their heads.

'He needs someone to visit the Pope.'

'Someone to go to *Rome*?' Had her father said the Islands of the Blessed, or the Gates of Hell, she would have been no less incredulous. It had never occurred to Elfrun that Rome was still an actual place, one that folk might simply go to, as mundane as Barton or Illingham. Rome belonged to long ago – the setting for the improving stories Abarhild told her, of the virgin martyrs, those exotic holy girls like Agnes and Agatha and Lucy; of Abarhild's own pilgrimage to the threshold of the Apostles in her impossibly distant girlhood. And now her father was telling her Rome was real, part of the same solid earth she herself walked on. But there was the sea in between.

'Will they have to sail there?' She blushed as soon as she had spoken. Of course they would. There was no other way.

Radmer had his back to her, loosening Hafoc's girth. 'Is Widia still alive?'

Was her father trying to change the subject? Or perhaps he was just being kind, ignoring her stupid question. 'Yes! And mending, we think, though it's too soon to be certain.'

'Your grandmother is a miracle-worker.' He gave Hafoc's bridle a tug and Elfrun fell into step beside them as they walked towards the stable. She could see Luda making his awkward way towards them, and she wanted to keep her father to herself, learn as much as she could before the steward caught them up and blocked her out. She hunted for the proper words.

'The king is sending a mission to Rome then?'

'Me,' he said. 'He's sending me.'

He might as well have pushed her over a cliff. The yard around her, the familiar hall and heddern and women's house, were crystal in their clarity, and yet there was a boom and rush in her ears. Luda was gesturing angrily to Athulf to come over and take Hafoc's reins, and her father was turning to say something to Abarhild in the doorway of the hall, and the doves were cooing in the sun on the hall roof, and she was still falling. Something was wrong with her ears. She couldn't possibly have heard what she thought he had said.

Rome.

A confused babel of half-understood thoughts and images.

City of once-murderous emperors. Where they had crucified St Peter upside down. She had seen a carving of that on a stone in the great minster at York. Peter, the first Pope. Popes lived there now, in the city where the virgin martyrs had scorned their suitors and gone to their bloody doom.

A real place?

Something, he was saying something meaningless, about *honour* and *Peter's pence* and *before the autumn storms*.

Abarhild was taking over. Pointing with her stick, and speaking harshly to Luda, who was bobbing his head and rubbing his hands. They were going into the hall. Her father was saying something. *No, of course, I can't refuse.* But it made no sense.

She was still outside, with that rushing in her ears. Athulf was hauling Hafoc round and she fell mindlessly into step beside them.

'Going to Rome,' she heard Athulf say. 'How long will he be gone? What will that mean for us?'

Us? What was he on about, *us*? She twitched the reins away from him. Hafoc was her father's horse. She should look after him.

Unbuckling the girth, hauling the great saddle down and putting it away; twisting a wisp of hay to rub Hafoc's hot damp flanks, finding a handful of oats for him to nuzzle from her palm with his muscular, whiskery lips: all this was routine and a source of comfort. Athulf had turned his back on her and was shovelling dung, and she leaned against Hafoc's shoulder and ran her hand up his neck and under his mane. He blew through his lips and turned his head, and she thought she could see a shared concern in his liquid, long-lashed gaze.

Would Hafoc have to go to Rome, too? She couldn't imagine how her father would manage without him.

Hafoc was her father's horse. Luda her father's steward, Widia her father's huntsman, Cuthred her father's smith. And she was her father's daughter. Who were they, if Radmer went away?

16

I ngeld and Wulfhere had ridden out on the great road that led north out of York up into the heartland round the Pickering marshes, where the rich little minsters clustered thick as gems on a necklace, Stonegrave and Hovingham, Coxwold, Malton, Lastingham and Hackness, and all the way to Whitby. Not that they were going even as far as Crayke today, but the sun was shining, and why should the Archbishop of York and the abbot of Donmouth not ride out together, old friends as they were?

And here on the road, while they might be observed, no one could overhear their murmured conversation. York was several miles behind them already, and apart from the occasional herdsman they had seen few folk in the meadows, and on the road itself they had met only a single pedlar with his pack. Not many folk chose to build their home close to a road where armies marched. Life was dangerous enough without drawing down that kind of attention on one's head. Both abbot and archbishop were armed and in layman's tunic and leggings, and no one had done more than lift a cautious head to watch them pass. Still and all, their talk so far had been of matters that any man might listen to. Domnall ap Alpin, king of the Picts, had held a council of Church and State at Forteviot, and York's envoys had just returned with news of the great church his folk were building at Dunkeld to house the relics of St Columba. Word had come in on a merchant ship that back at the end of winter the Saracens had martyred the new archbishop of Cordoba.

'Eulogius. Poor man.' Wulfhere shook his head. 'I never met him, but by all reports he was a good and learned priest. Never even enthroned as archbishop, either.' He sighed. 'There have already been miracles, the man said.'

'Saracens and sea-wolves. Hispania is truly beset.'

'Are you making a song about it?'

Ingeld shook his head. 'I'd rather write an elegy for my brother.' He twisted round in his saddle. 'Radmer is going to Rome. *Radmer.*'

Wulfhere said nothing. They were riding knee to knee, Ingeld on a borrowed mare from the archiepiscopal stables as Storm was resting after the two-day journey from Donmouth. Their servants kept their horses a discreet dozen paces behind.

Ingeld wasn't going to let the matter drop. 'You must have been part of this. After everything we've said...' His tension was communicating itself to his horse, and she jibbed a little, swivelling her ears. Ingeld leaned forward and stroked her neck. 'Hush, beauty, hush there. It's not you, it's me.'

Wulfhere clicked his tongue and his horse stepped out a little more quickly. 'You've only just taken up your place at Donmouth minster. Why do you want to leave so soon?'

Ingeld urged his own mount to keep pace. 'Only just? It's been half a year already, and now the winter's coming.'

'You have your mother for company.'

'My mother, to whom I am a disappointment. My stiff-necked brother, who finds his only pleasure in thwarting mine. And my not-so-little niece. I thought her a fine fighting spirit but they're crushing her between them. Millstones.' Ingeld fell silent, intrigued by his own insight. 'She should fight back. I want to smack her sometimes.'

Wulfhere was not interested. 'Radmer is going to Rome on the king's orders, not mine.'

'But it's a mission to the Pope.' Ingeld was very ready to push thoughts of his family away. 'You must have been involved.'

'Peter's pence is a royal tithe, not an episcopal one.'

'But it gets sent every year, without a man of Radmer's stature going as escort.' Ingeld twisted round again. 'Why not me? We've always talked of going to Rome.'

'Aye, and Ravenna, and Constantinople.' Wulfhere raised an eyebrow, the closest his cautious face ever came to smiling. 'We'll make our pilgrimage one of these years, my friend. Jerusalem, too, if you like. But Osberht has it in mind that Athelwulf of Wessex went to Rome, with his youngest son, just a few years since, and returned with powerful new friendships, not just with the Pope but the kings and princes whose lands he passed through, coming and going.'

'And a thirteen-year-old princess as his bride, if memory serves.'

'Indeed.' Wulfhere's tone was dry.

'So why isn't Osberht going himself?'

'Now is not the time. You know that.'

And Ingeld did know. Radmer might think him a lightweight, but he paid attention. From a safe distance the violent machinations of court politics held all the illicit thrill of a cockfight.

'Tilmon.'

Wulfhere nodded. 'Tilmon and Alred have been seen together, close as they ever were. South of the Tees, where Alred is not supposed to be.'

Ingeld was quiet for a moment, working out all the implications. 'Osberht must be wetting himself.'

'He wants them at hand, where he can watch them. Tilmon and Switha, safely at Illingham.'

'And yet he sends the King's Wolf to Rome.'

'He shows the world the King's Wolf is still tame, still his to command. And that Northumbria's monarch has friends the length of Frankia and Lombardy, as well as at the Lateran.' Wulfhere looked thoughtfully at his friend. 'Osberht is angry with Radmer. Osberht thinks the way to hold Tilmon is a Donmouth–Illingham alliance, and Radmer is a stubborn fool who is still fighting over the wars of seven years ago. The world has changed, and Radmer hasn't noticed. So Osberht is using this opportunity to show Radmer who rules Northumbria. That a good dog obeys his master. *Sit up. Roll over. Die for the king.*'

'And you approve?'

'Why not?' Wulfhere shrugged. 'Osberht may be my cousin, but I don't think my fortunes rise and fall with his. Let him run his risks. So yes, why not?'

Ingeld ruminated, casting the odd sidelong glance at his friend's narrow face. He was probably right, that the fortunes of king and archbishop ran on their separate courses. Kings and their thanes were subject to the vagaries of fortune. The court shuffled endlessly between the king's many vills, from Driffield and Goodmanham in the south to Bamburgh and Edinburgh in the far north, faces continually changing as men fell into and out of favour. But the wealth and power of York's archbishopric were stable and eternal. Its radiant churches: St Peter, Holy Wisdom, St Martin, St Mary, St Gregory. The greatest library west of Milan. Always something new in York, something beautiful, to distract him from the ever-present threat of boredom. And worse than boredom, despair.

He glanced once more at the archbishop to find that Wulfhere was watching him, still with that eyebrow raised. 'You know what they say in Frankia?'

'What?'

'While the wolf's away the little foxes frolic.'

'Ha.'

They rode in silence for a little while. The sun was hot, but a breeze was freshening, and to the north, over the Hambleton hills, thunderheads were beginning to build.

'We should turn back.' Wulfhere reined in.

Ingeld baulked. 'Must we? Speaking of wolf, we could go into the hills. Look for tracks now, and come back later with the hounds.'

Wulfhere sighed. 'Haven't you noticed, little fox? We're not novices any more.'

'Really, my lord archbishop? How did that happen?' With an exaggerated shrug, Ingeld tugged his horse's head round to the south. The surface was good here and they trotted for a while.

Wulfhere was right. He had been too distracted by ridiculous, childish outrage at his older brother being given this exceptional treat. Radmer's absence could offer advantages. He would have to think about that.

The roofs and walls of York's great minster were just coming into view. 'Come on,' Ingeld called. They might not be novices any more, but he was damned if he was going to let his closest friend dwindle into middle age without a fight. 'I'll race you.'

17

As soon as the shout went up that the sail was sighted Radmer walked to the stable.

'Tell Elfrun to come after me.'

He swung himself on to Hafoc's blanketed back and headed for the hill that sloped away and up behind the yards. The late-summer grass was long, pink and bronze with seed heads, spangled with the last of the buttercups, all a green-gold haze, though the wind that rippled through the grass was the same nagging easterly that had set in over the last day or two. It had brought the ship at last, weeks after they had first started looking for it. Lambs, stocky now and hardly distinguishable from their mothers, bolted at his approach, tails bouncing in their wake. When he got to the row of barrows that marked the crest of the hill as seen from the shore he slowed and looked around.

He was forty-two years old, and for fully half those years he had held Donmouth. He had travelled the length of Northumbria over and over; he had been in fights with the Mercians and men of Lindsey whose north-easternmost lands marched so close to his own estates; the Picts north across the Forth; the men of Dumbarton on their rock on the Clyde; and as far as Wales. And he had the scars to prove it. But his easterly horizon had always been bounded by that restless blue-grey mass of water. It glittered on the edge of vision now as he tugged on Hafoc's halter, and turned the horse's head to gaze back down the way they had come, over the roofs of hall and heddern and bower, cook-house and weaving shed. A couple of his men were up on the hall roof, patching the shingles. He was glad to see Widia in the yard, holding Mara while Elfrun scrambled on to her back. Such a relief that his huntsman was back on his feet at last. There was not a soul in Donmouth whom he didn't value. This huddle of buildings, and the fields and pastures beyond, moor and salt marsh and fen, the hundred or so folk who laboured incessantly to make Donmouth what it was, under his guidance, bounded by sweet and salt and brackish water. This was the whole of his world.

But Donmouth was more than just his hall and its lands. There was the minster, itself a rich endowment.

Radmer shook his head. The minster wasn't visible from the hall: the spur of land that jutted where the stream flowed down blocked his view. Three miles away, but not nearly far enough, he was finding, with Ingeld as abbot. Radner knew his anger was bad for him, body and soul.

Things would have to change.

When he returned from Rome he would do what his mother had long advised: build himself a little oratory by the hall. He could see it so clearly. A house fit for God, painted and plastered without and within, and a gilt cross finial attached to the gable end, so that when he was in his dotage he could totter out of the south door of the hall and its sunlit promise would be the first thing on which his eyes would alight.

It would give him comfort, Abarhild had said. Balsam for his soul. He could start working for the forgiveness and reconciliation he so sorely needed.

Hafoc shifted and tried to walk forward, and Radmer gripped harder with his thighs.

His dotage. There would be time enough then to repent all the deeds of violence, the hard counsel, to make amends with God. For his family, for Donmouth, for Northumbria. Never yet for himself – at least, that had never been his intention. Surely God would understand.

But he wasn't in his dotage, not quite yet. Radmer had a

sudden urge to knee Hafoc into a headlong gallop, to go whooping and shrieking down to the shore and set sail, leaving all the worries in his wake. Instead he breathed deeply, allowing himself a little smile, and settled his red cloak more securely over his shoulders, its silver tags chinking gently against each other.

The last weeks had been full of such endless planning – for the voyage, but much more for Donmouth and how it would manage in his absence. The hay-harvest was long gathered and stored; the barley was in; the apples were ripening; but he could already feel the long winter coming up hard on the harvest's heels. Rationing and maintenance, killing the pigs and the bull-calves, the endless threshing, the predictable... and the unpredictable.

And that was just Donmouth.

Elfrun came trotting over the grass on Mara, breathless and pink-cheeked. As she reined her pony in Radmer raised a hand in greeting, batting away the anxieties that buzzed around him like summer blowflies. Beyond her, across river and estuary, the headland that marked the corner of the Illingham lands slept in the shifting sun and shade. He wasn't used to indecision, but he had been trapped into going to Rome, and he didn't know whom to trust.

Trust his instinct then. It had always served him well.

Osberht valued his loyalty. Osberht owed him his life. He and the king had been side by side for twenty years.

Osberht would never send him to Rome if there were anything to fear from Illingham. But for all that he couldn't rest easy, not with Tilmon and Switha so close.

'You wanted me, Father?'

He nodded. He had been planning to talk to her ever since getting back from Driffield, and now he was running out of time. Abarhild was right: his little girl was leaving childhood – had left it, indeed, somehow without his noticing. She was as old now as her mother had been when he had married her, God forgive him.

And even now the words were almost impossible to find.

How did he put his fears for her into words? It was tantamount to an admission of failure as father, lord, guardian.

'Father?'

They were right, the gossips; they had all been right: he should have seen her safely stowed by now. Either with the good nuns north at Hovingham, as Abarhild had always wanted, or married to some steady man. He was letting her down.

He had been afraid of this parting, that there would be tears, tantrums. But she met his gaze directly, brown eyes wide and clear.

He nodded a greeting. 'We'll be back in the spring. As soon as the mountain passes are clear.'

'Abarhild says the mountains are dangerous when the snow melts. She says you mustn't take any risks you don't have to.'

This wasn't the conversation he wanted to have. He sighed. 'Your grandmother is lady of the hall while I am gone.' He raised a hand to forestall her. 'I've told Luda. And I want you to listen to them. Follow their orders in everything.'

He had told Abarhild and Luda his decision only the previous day.

Abarhild had been furious, of course. 'You are doing this to thwart me, aren't you? Elfrun is more than old enough.' He had tried to speak, and she had jumped down his throat. 'Of course she is childish, Radmer, and she will be as long as you treat her like a child.' But he had folded his arms and set his teeth and let her bitter words flow over him until finally she fell silent.

And then disagreement from the corner he had least foreseen. 'With all due respect, I agree with the lady Abarhild.' A sideways glance from Luda and a judicious sucking of his teeth. 'I find it's the same with my own eldest daughter. These girls need responsibilities to steady them. Marriage, babies. Something to break them to the saddle.'

Even to himself, Radmer couldn't fully explain his own reluctance. He knew only that the thought of Elfrun taking up that load of duty, without him being there to watch and guide her, broke his heart.

And if he were away then she would have to be lord as well as lady, with all the burden of judgement and punishment, record and render, to add to the overseeing of brewing and baking and loom.

No. It was too much. Far too much, and too soon. He knew Elfrun thought she could carry out her mother's tasks, and she was probably right. Next summer, when he returned, and they could let Abarhild retire. But not the lord's duties as well.

Abarhild had tried to stare him down, but he could meet her fury with his own cold, adamantine anger. Luda, however, had rubbed his hands together, ducking his head and smiling in the obsequious way that set Radmer's teeth on edge, and that was much harder to fight. He valued his steward, both for his skills in managing the day-to-day drudgery of the estate, and for his supervision of the tanning of skins for leather and their tawing for parchment. He had also felt a powerful obligation to the man ever since the nightmare of that midsummer day over twenty-five years ago when Luda had been trampled in the playing of the Keg.

One can, however, trust and respect a man without liking him.

They had knuckled under, as he had known they would, but it left a bitter taste in his mouth.

Elfrun was frowning, her face flushed and clearly wanting to respond, so he went on talking himself, fast, to forestall her. He didn't know how he would get the words out otherwise. 'Elfa, I'm concerned' – he couldn't bring himself to say *frightened* – 'about Illingham. They're trouble. Avoid them.' She was frowning now. 'Tilmon, you remember? The big man, at the meeting.'

'The ox-man.'

He nodded. 'Good description. Stubborn. Powerful. In it for the long haul.' He was talking to himself as much as her. 'And perhaps I'm wrong. Osberht may be doing the canny thing, keeping him close. But I've fought alongside that man as well as facing him over the shield wall, and, friend or foe, I don't trust him.' His heart beat faster, remembering. 'Them.'

'I understand. But I'm hardly likely to see much of them, except at the meeting.' She paused. 'Will Grandmother have to speak at the meeting?' She had looped her reins, and Mara had her head down, tearing at the tall grass.

'What? I doubt it.' He was still fighting the old battles, and he took a deep breath, trying to steady himself. But down in the distance a rider on a white horse was coming along the track that led from the minster to the harbour, and Radmer's agitation only increased. How much of that unexpected desire to be gone had been inspired by a longing to be free from his gadfly little brother? Heahred was following on a mule, and Radmer had no doubt that the bundle on the deacon's saddle-bow would be Ingeld's ridiculously ornate yellow silk chasuble. Fit for the bishop Abarhild still, incredibly, dreamed of him becoming.

Radmer turned back to Elfrun. 'Get Ingeld to speak for the hall at the meeting, if needed. He seems to have plenty of time on his hands.'

'Father...' She hesitated, then said in a rush, 'Leave me your cloak?'

'What?' He frowned at her. Where had that request come from? The red cloak was the harvest of the loom of the king's wife and her women, dyed in the wool with costly carmine from the far south; the tags were worth a little fortune for their craftsmanship, never mind the weight of the silver. He might think it a flashy object, better suited to a young warrior on the make than a grizzled old war-wolf like himself, but the gift had been an honour and he was proud to wear it.

'They say it's hot in Rome.' She lifted her chin, her eyes bright. 'You won't need it. I want something' – she wrapped her arms around herself – 'just something... Oh, never mind.'

Such a childish request, he thought, like a toddler clinging to a rag that smelt of mother's milk. And there was a long autumn-into-winter road by land and sea and a high mountain range between him and his destination. And he was the king's envoy: it was crucial that he keep fitting state. But, and without

92

quite knowing why, he slid the tags out through the loops and shrugged off the weight of wool. 'Here, then.' He nudged Hafoc closer and draped it awkwardly over her shoulders. It swamped her, and he had to look away briefly to hide a smile. His little girl. 'Something to remind the world that you are Elfrun, Radmer's daughter. Elfrun of Donmouth.'

18

In the estuary the broad-beamed coastal trader was dropping anchor. Shallow though its draught might be, the ever-shifting sandbanks between Donmouth and Illingham posed a constant hazard, and a wise captain stood well out in the bay. Even from here Radmer could see the bustle in the yard, hear the faint shouts as Luda ordered the bundles brought down to the shore. So much baggage, to make certain that the king's envoy maintained a proper state on the long road. There was Dunstan's unmistakable butter-coloured head, his arm pointing up the hill. Radmer had been spotted. It was time to go back down. He leaned forward and patted Hafoc's neck. Widia had charge of the horses. Hafoc would be fine.

Everything would be fine.

He had done all he could. His house was in order.

And, under all the hammer-blows of worry, that sense of excitement was still there, like one of the fresh rills that came down from the summer pastures. Time to go. The wind smelt of salt and rotting seaweed, a scent that he had always known, but today it hit his nostrils as though for the first time.

A little four-oared boat was putting out from the Donmouth shore, and Radmer thought yet again that it was high time they built themselves a jetty, save all the slog over the wet sand.

When he got back, perhaps.

He was needed down there, to oversee the loading. To make sure that the fine red leather purses with their gilt fasteners, heavy with tribute for Pope Nicholas, were stowed as safe and dry as they might be. The letters for the Archbishop of Rheims. His safe-conduct, the introductions, the list of monasteries that would provide shelter on the long trawl through Frankia and into those fabled mountains...

He sighed and urged Hafoc forward, Elfrun falling in behind him. But halfway down the slope he paused. From here he could see the Illingham shore more clearly, and a little gaggle of men gathering just above the high-tide line. And no reason why not. But they weren't mending their nets, or caulking their boats: they weren't doing anything. Just standing around, watching; and even from here he could make out Tilmon's looming bulk among them, bald head gleaming, and that russet-haired lad of his at his side. No great surprise, to be sure. The sight of a vessel was always fascinating, whether threat or promise. But that group of interested observers chilled him, finally quenching the last sparks of excitement.

Tilmon, and his son. Radmer's face tightened, and he glanced across at Elfrun.

Would he have loved his daughter so much if his sons had lived?

They trotted into the little group by the shore and reined in, looking out to sea. The men in the Donmouth boat were shipping their oars and catching the line thrown down to them. The coaster was a vessel well known to them, putting into their harbour twice a year, and the folk of Donmouth had known for weeks that this would be how their lord would leave them. Even at this distance the burly shoulders and grey curls of the ship's master, jumping squarely into the four-oarer, were familiar. Not so the tentative, hooded figure who followed him, though.

'Where have you been?' Abarhild was waspish. 'There's rain coming in on that wind. To keep me standing around like this! And what is she doing in your cloak?'

The boat had turned and was making for the shore with long, strong strokes, speeded a little by the easterly breeze. The men of Donmouth knew their sea fine well.

The thin man's hood had fallen back as he scrambled down

into the Donmouth boat, and Radmer could see now he was dark, and tonsured. An envoy from the archbishop, to accompany him on the journey? Slowly the folk of Donmouth were gathering to bid their lord farewell. Luda, with Saethryth and the throng of little ones. Hirel the big shepherd stood a few paces away, his dark, jowly face reminding Radmer of a faithful, mournful hound. Cuthred the smith with his wife, and another string of children, Cudda standing a little aloof. Widia, still haggard, the line of the scar across his face purple and angry, and Radmer knew from the way he held himself that the newly knit bone and flesh along his flank were hurting him too. If he wasn't careful, Abarhild had said, he would set like that, tight and hunched on the one side. And a wound like that could turn a man bitter. Not many managed as well as Luda, with his game leg.

The boat slid into the shallows and canted as its keel met the sand. The master was helping the tonsured stranger over the side, into ankle-deep water. The stranger had a box clutched in his arms, of golden oak, finely made but undecorated, and a heavy bag of double-woven linen slung over his shoulder and skewing his balance. The box was the burden that was fussing him, though. More gifts for the Pope, perhaps.

The stranger turned, and made straight for Radmer. He stiffened, pulling his shoulders back, readying a greeting. But no, that dark, hollow gaze was to the right, just a little, and it was in front of Abarhild that the stranger knelt, awkward, the box clutched in his arms like a heavy, hard-edged baby. He had sallow skin, so green-tinged that Radmer thought he must have had a choppy crossing. A high-bridged nose between eyes grey as glass. The tonsure was neatly cut, but the dome of his skull was stubbled. He bowed his head. '*Domina*.'

And Abarhild came alive. A babble of the Gallic she hardly ever spoke, fluting and sibilant, as she bent to cup the man's elbows and draw him to his feet, to gesture with an abrupt motion of her head to Luda to take the box. A clumsy, passionate exchange, and Abarhild knelt stiffly in turn to receive the man's blessing. At some point Gallic transmuted into Latin, but Radmer could not have put his finger on the moment.

He slid down from Hafoc's blanketed back. 'What's this?'

'We brought your new priest for you.' The ship's master grinned briefly, teeth white in the leathery face. 'He shipped with us at Dorestad – lucky for him, as there weren't many vessels plying the lanes. Rumours of sea-wolves too thick for most men's taste.'

Radmer closed his eyes. He had been prepared to give in to his mother's request for a chaplain, in his own good time. Having one thrust upon him was infuriating. But he could feel the wind on his cheek, and see the little choppy waves on the sandbank. The wind was shifting its airt; the tide was turning. He wanted to be gone.

He turned his back on his mother and this new cuckoo in his nest, and on Ingeld, who had indeed donned the yellow silk, along with that particularly infuriating smirk of his. Radmer knew his brother would be off to York again as soon as the sail was out of sight. Heahred was kindling incense in his thurible, cursing the easterly wind. Radmer had no grudge against Heahred: the deacon had kept the minster going during the long hiatus without a resident priest, after their uncle's death. He was a good man, and a solid one – a kinsman; and Radmer thought now that they should have left Ingeld to amuse himself in York, drinking the archbishop's wine and reading his books, and made Heahred abbot of Donmouth in his stead, for all Abarhild's scowls.

Another matter for his return.

But the last thing he wanted just now was some travesty of a blessing from Ingeld, some pretence of sorrow. Easier just to pretend that his brother wasn't there. 'Get my gear and men aboard.' He nodded at Dunstan. 'You can oversee that, can't you, with the master?'

Abarhild was tugging at the red cloak. 'What are you doing

in that, Elfrun? Give it back at once. Your father'll need it twice over crossing the Mont Jouve pass.'

They both ignored her. Radmer knew he should kneel for his mother's blessing, but he was too frustrated with her. He pulled Elfrun into his arms for a last rough embrace, then thrust her away and turned back to the ship's master, without looking at her. 'Come on. We'll miss the tide.'

PART TWO

THE CHRONICLE, YORK MINSTER SCRIPTORIUM

The chronicler looked down at the words he had last written, on that still-unfolded creamy-silky sheet of vellum. It was good to be back. No one had touched the desk in the weeks he had been away. All the way down the page, and where the other pages would be once the quire was folded and the pages cut, he had lightly pricked the guide-lines for continuing the list of noteworthy events, enough for years to come. Enough for the rest of his life, surely, even if that life proved long and full of years, and witnessed great happenings. Straight and evenly spaced, the ghostly lines marched down the white surface, trapping the future behind their bars before it had even happened.

The inkhorn was dry, just a rusty stain – there would be more in the store. But instead of going at once to fetch it he hitched himself on to his stool, gazing at the blank area of the quire until it blurred under his gaze, and thought about the nature of time and space. Here they were, living somewhere towards the end of the Sixth and Last Age in a world grown old and tired with sin, and in these islands on the farthest edge of the Ocean, as far from the hub of Jerusalem as one could well be. He thought of the feast they were celebrating that day; of the Empress Helena doggedly ordering her men to dig until the true cross emerged from the mud and filth of Calvary. Nation by nation, God was gathering in his harvest, corn-cockle, darnel and tares as well as the good wheat. He looked down at his fine linen, his red leather shoes, the gold ring on his hand. *If God so clothes the grass of the field, which is alive today and tomorrow thrown into the furnace...* He had no doubt at all that, gilded lily as he was, a just God would assign the furnace as his destination.

He shoved the stool back and went to fetch more ink.

In this year, also, Amlaibh and Imhair made an alliance with Cerball against Mael Sechnaill, and Meath suffered greatly because of it. His pen stumbled over the alien names of Irish king and sea-wolf alike, heard the previous evening at the arch-bishop's table from a vagrant priest of Kells. *Athelbald of Wessex married his father's young widow, and the bishops of the West Saxons were much troubled thereby.*

The alliances between kings and warlords, the anxieties of powerful bishops: these were great events, but were they the events that men would say mattered, looking back a year, a hundred, a thousand years from now, if the world should still be limping on? He paused, his pen hovering over the vellum. *In this year, King Osberht of the Northumbrians brought Tilmon back into his favour, and granted him Illingham. In this year also, the same king sent Radmer of Donmouth to Rome. Men wondered at both these things.*

And the smaller things, and the things that didn't happen. The arrows that missed their target, the seeds that fell on stony ground. Once he and the archbishop had dreamed of writing a sequel to Bede's great history of the Northumbrians. 'Bede stopped writing a hundred years ago, and more,' Wulfhere had said. 'Think how much has happened since.' But Bede's work was dauntingly perfect. How could they cobble something together, and hitch it on behind?

They had never gone beyond dreaming.

And now, ten and more years later, the chronicler found

Bede's great book even more troubling. That old monk of Jarrow had been so sure of the working out of God's plan in history. But he himself saw no such pattern. Rather, disjointed purposes. Messages that came too late or went astray. Accidents of ill-health or childbirth and death that put men and women where they were by chance, pure chance. Who could tell if a man were a saint or a black-dyed sinner? God, surely only God. Men could not make these judgements about each other, stumbling as they were in the dark.

The only heart-secrets he knew for certain were his own.

No, better he penned this petty chronicle. A little job, fit for a butterfly mind. Brief sentences, elliptical phrases, with no moral commentary attached or deeper meaning intended. How little human actions mattered. A just God would damn them all, every last one, with no hope of appeal. A merciful God would put out a hand to catch a faltering sparrow.

In this year the swallows came back to their wonted places on the ides of April. The cuckoo called in the woods. The sun shone.

19

The morning after her father sailed away, Elfrun woke with a strange hollowness under her breastbone. Her dreams had been restless ones of hunting for something she had lost, behind wall-hangings, down the cracks between the floorboards, and the sense of absence lingered, unsettling her. The sheltering sky had gone, and in its place was the void.

It wasn't as though he had never been away before. Even though his campaigning days belonged to her early childhood, he accompanied the king often enough; and travelled the roads of southern Northumbria on Osberht's behalf, one of the king's senior *prefecti*, the royal eyes and ears, assessing renders and seeing that they were paid, hearing complaints and channelling them back to the king. He could be gone for long weeks, and still Donmouth went trundling on.

Why should this be any different? Perhaps because there could be no word, of him or from him, with him gone across the sea. He would be on board even now, probably awake. Cold, without his red cloak, listening to the slap of the waves and the creak of the strakes, watching the edges of the world take shape as grey seeped into the sky.

She had always minded him being gone, even when it was only for a couple of weeks, even before her mother had died.

Elfrun lay very still. For the last couple of years she had slept in the women's house, which served Donmouth also as its weaving shed. Few of the housesteads had a loom at home, and the older girls worked here. It was easier if they also slept here, they and some of the older women who had nowhere else to go. Half a dozen sleeping bodies huddled around the hearth. It must still be very early. She could feel the autumn chill seeping through the thatch and the daub.

Was it because he had gone over the sea? Elfrun could never think of the sea, the deep sea, without a twitch of the skin. The dunes were home territory, and the ebb, and she didn't mind the shallows. She was well used to foraging the shore in hungry times for crabs and cockles, samphire and sea-kale. But the deep water was another matter. Even the men who fished didn't go out further than they needed, and still they came home with stories of vast whales, strange mists and calms, of uncanny cries and groans that echoed through the strakes of their vessels. The songs of the drowned.

Her scalp crawled and a shudder went through her, as though a rat had gone scrabbling across her blanket. This would never do. She rolled over and got to her feet, treading a careful path between the sleepers. The world was colourless, dawn too far away for even the cocks to have noticed yet. Chilly, with a little mist. A visit to the need-house, an apple and a handful of cob-nuts, and she would find something useful to do, to drive off the last rags and shreds of dream.

She had left the wool she was carding together with her combs in a basket in her grandmother's little bower. Abarhild slept badly at night though she napped readily enough in the afternoons, and Elfrun thought her grandmother might welcome her company.

But when she nudged open the door of the bower and peered cautiously into the gloom she found that Abarhild wasn't there. The two women who attended her were snoring on their pallets by the banked hearth, but the fine wooden bed that Abarhild had brought across the sea from her first marriage was flat and empty. Puzzled, Elfrun ducked back out under the low thatch and looked around. The first cock crowed from a nearby dung-hill, and another answered from further away. Surely she couldn't have gone far? Elfrun walked around the bower, checked the need-house and the cook-house, and stood outside the hall, feeling foolish.

The world was beginning to stir. She could smell hearth-smoke, hear the call and response of sleepy voices.

And then realization dawned. Her grandmother must have slept at the minster. They had all stood watching the patched red-and-white sail dip and bob and vanish at last over the grey horizon, and then Abarhild and her new priest had headed for the minster. Abarhild had commandeered the mule and told Heahred to bring the new priest's bag.

Elfrun had been too wrapped up in her father's departure to take much interest, but she had overheard Heahred asking, 'Did you know about this?'

Ingeld had shrugged. 'She told me she had written to the abbot of Corbie.'

'And you didn't think to let me know? Or Radmer? For God's sake, Ingeld!'

'What would that have achieved?' Ingeld was still looking seaward, to where the sail had finally vanished behind Long Nab. 'It might have led to nothing. Never trouble trouble...'

... *till trouble troubles you.* Was this new priest trouble? Her father had been angry. Heahred had looked angry, too, although usually he was so bluff and easy-going. Ingeld seemed to push everyone to the limits of their patience. And yet it seemed everyone loved him. Or almost everyone, she amended, thinking of her father.

How did he get away with it?

It was mid-morning before the creak and rumble of the ox-cart announced that Abarhild had returned. Elfrun tucked her heddle between the warp threads and came out into sparkling September sunshine to find her grandmother snapping orders. Her big carved bed had been unpegged and carried out of the bower, and now it was being loaded piece by piece over the tail of the cart. One of her women was standing guard over Abarhild's dowry chest and a neatly folded stack of wall-cloths.

Elfrun stared. 'What's going on?'

'There you are at last.' Abarhild didn't even look round. 'I am moving down to the minster.' A small, tight smile creased her withered face.

'But where will you live? And what about the hall? Father said you weren't to! Who's going to look after the hall?'

Her grandmother waved a dismissive hand. 'As for where I will live, Heahred and Fredegar are seeing to all that.'

'Fredegar?' The name was alien. 'The new priest?'

Her grandmother nodded, then reached out and tapped Elfrun's shin smartly with her stick, not punishingly, merely indicating the way she was to go. 'Into the hall. We need to talk to you.'

We?

She had never seen the hall looking so forlorn, so dark and dull. Radmer had taken so much of their splendour with him. There were men there, but her first thoughts were about absence, not presence.

'Sit down, Elfrun.' Abarhild pointed with her stick.

'What, in the chair?' She was taken aback: too many memories of being told not to sit in it, not to climb on it. The thick cushion with its latticework of red and yellow embroidery had gone to Rome, but even in her father's absence the great elm-wood chair with its lathe-turned finials embodied him and his authority.

But, 'No, no, you silly girl. Down here, on the footstool.' Abarhild hobbled forward, and one of the men in the shadows loomed forward to offer his arm in support, but her grandmother brushed him aside. Now that her eyes were adjusting to the hall's dim light Elfrun could see it was Hirel, the shepherd. Hard to miss. No one else was that big, not in Donmouth.

He was a good shepherd, but Elfrun had never been comfortable around him. He was so massive, he moved and spoke at such a ponderous pace, and his nails were always black-rimmed, his hands stained rust-red. Still, she knew fine well the stains were only raddle and sheep-grease, for all they looked like dried blood. He had a name for being famous with the sheep, and his worth had only increased after that sensational run with the keg, back at midsummer.

Hiding her uncertainty, she came forward and lowered herself on to the stool. And now she could see that Luda was there too, and the knot in her belly tightened. Her father had told her, more than once, that Luda had all the virtues of a good steward. 'He's sharp with my wealth. Never wastes anything. Honest as the recording angel.' And perhaps his suspicious glares were part of that honesty. But there were too many memories of him telling her off for the things she had done and those she had failed to do, and the skin of the nape of her neck and her shoulder blades twitched and shivered in his presence as though a horse-fly's feet were crawling there.

'You want to be lady of Donmouth.' Her grandmother's tone was dry.

It was completely unexpected. 'Yes, but...'

'Here are the keys.' Abarhild's gnarled fingers were slipping the brass loop from her girdle. 'Go on, girl.' They jingled faintly. 'Take them.'

'But Father said—'

'I am tired, Elfrun. I am sick to death of arguing about this. If you need me I will be at the minster.'

Elfrun couldn't think of anything else to say. She stared at the ring of keys – money box, spice chest, heddern.

'Take them.' Abarhild shook the ring. 'Your father has no idea. When I was your age I had had my own household for three years and I'd already buried two babies.' Her grandmother shot a sideways glance at the men. '*Amur Deo*, Elfrun. Grow up. This is not the place to argue.'

Elfrun felt as though she'd been punched in the gut. But she couldn't challenge Abarhild, not with the shepherd and the steward looking on. And did she even want to? Her thoughts were rattling like dried peas shaken in a jar. Her father had planned otherwise. But her father had gone away.

For the first time she began to realize what that absence meant. How angry would he be, when he got back? But again, this was her chance.

She reached out, watching her hand extend, still unbelieving, and took the loop from her grandmother. The keys rang against each other as she unknotted her own girdle and tied them in place.

Luda moved in, one hand rubbing the other. 'We need a word from you, the shepherd and I.' He paused. 'Lady.'

Luda, speaking respectfully to her? It was still hard to breathe, but a thrill shivered through her. She needed to keep pace. 'Is there some dispute?' She tried to find the right words. Over what might these two men clash? 'Is it to do with lambing? The lamb-leather, the parchment?' Was it her imagination, or did Hirel jump?

But Luda moved in, smoothing hand over hand as though he were rubbing bacon-fat into cracked skin. 'No, no, nothing to do with the sheep. A family matter, that's all. A formality.'

Elfrun felt so small, her knees on a level with her chin, staring up at the men. Her father's cloak hung on its peg, only feet away, and wrapping that round her might give her some of his authority, but she could scarcely ask them to pass it to her now. She must look such a child, in her patched blue dress, with her feet and head bare. If only she had a claim to the veil that married women and widows wore, that would make her look older, give her some ballast...

'His daughter,' Hirel said, loud and sudden. 'I want her.'

'Saethryth?' This was so unanticipated, and so much less serious than Elfrun had been picturing, that she was hard pressed to stop herself laughing out loud.

'It's past time that girl was married,' Abarhild said sharply. 'She's a flighty creature, even more than most. Marriage will burden her, slow her down, like it did the rest of us.'

Luda darted a sharp look at Abarhild, one that smoothed away to a tight-lipped smile when he became aware of Elfrun's curious gaze. 'She's a good girl, lady, as you well know. A great help to her mother. A credit to her, as well. Handy.'

If Elfrun had been listening she might have taken issue with some of that, but she hardly heard a word. If Saethryth were to marry Hirel she would go and live up at the sheepwick, miles away, on the edge of the hill pasture.

No more Saethryth in the women's house, with her endless whispering, that speculative giggle, the conversations which were hushed as soon as the other girls became aware that Elfrun was present. With Saethryth gone, she could start again. Hard enough being Radmer's daughter without the extra burden of Saethryth's malice.

But if she were to do this, she had to do it properly. There was more involved than just granting permission; she had seen her father go through this a dozen times over the last few years. There were rules for this kind of thing, and to Elfrun's relief she could remember them. 'And the maiden, is she willing?'

Luda was nodding. 'We wouldn't be here otherwise.'

Hirel said, 'I wanted to ask her at midsummer, but she had gone. Now was my next good chance.'

Elfrun nodded. The sheep were back from the hills now, now all the fields were cut, feeding on the barley stubble and the aftermath of the hay, and enriching the soil with their dung. The shepherd would have more excuse to come down to the yards.

The temptation just to take Luda's gilded words at their surface value, to say yes, to wave a hand and make it happen, was palpable: she could feel the yearning in the palms of her hands, in her midriff, her shortness of breath. How delightful, how *convenient*, the thought of sending Saethryth away. With a mere nod of her head she could confound all the other girl's power over her.

But how she would hate it if this were her own future, being decided behind closed walls.

And she was acting for her father. Anything she did, was in his name.

She had to get this right.

'Go and fetch the maiden,' she said, hiding her diffidence with the formal words, a haughty voice and a chin held high.

Luda glanced at Hirel, shrugged, then turned and limped to the door.

The moments stretched out. A trapped fly was buzzing loud up in the rafters. Elfrun was longing to question her grandmother but Hirel's big silent presence inhibited her. He had taken off his greasy felt cap and he was twisting it round and round in his massive hands, breathing hard.

If she thought for a moment that Saethryth was reluctant, she could stop this wedding with a word.

And she would, too.

But when Saethryth came in the other girl was loud, fast-talking and full of flashing smiles. Hirel was clearly besotted, following her with doting eyes, and many of those smiles were sent in his direction, although Elfrun noticed that whenever Saethryth had cause to look instead at her father her eyes narrowed and her lips tightened, and she kept well away from him.

'Come with me,' she said, scrambling up from the low stool which had left her feeling at such a disadvantage. 'Just Saethryth. Outside.'

Saethryth hovered in the doorway, although the big yard was deserted.

'Come *on*.' Elfrun was frustrated. 'I'm on your side. Tell me, where they can't hear. Do you really want to marry the shepherd?'

Saethryth flung her head up and stared at Elfrun defiantly. 'I can't pretend I had the idea. Hirel asked Da, and Da told me he wanted it.'

'But what about you? You don't have to if you don't want to. I'm not going to make you.'

Saethryth was pink-cheeked now. 'I've got to marry someone, and I want to do it soon.'

It was Elfrun's turn to stare. 'Are you... Is there a baby coming?'

'What's it to you?' Saethryth's eyes narrowed and she gave Elfrun much the same look as she had been giving her father. 'Why don't you want me to marry the shepherd? Are you saying I'm not good enough for him?'

'What? Where did you get that idea?'

Saethryth tossed her head, pale braids swinging. 'I know what you think of me. The way you look at me. You're loving this.'

The shot was too close to home. 'You're imagining things. Why would I—?' Elfrun gave up. 'Oh, never mind. Marry him tomorrow, for all I care.'

20

Tuuri wrapped the rope twice around the tree stump and tied it fast. 'You're in charge.' Auli nodded. She had already set a couple of men to gathering firewood. Myr and Holmi were baling. Varri gave a wet, pink yawn, showing all his surviving teeth.

Tuuri set off up the track, kicking his way through a yellow drift of birch leaves. It wound along a ridge of high ground, heading for the terrace where the kirk was nestled. Never straightforward, these meetings. He was true to the day, to the very hour, that he had promised, but that was no guarantee that his paymasters would have done the same. And he could not blame them. Apart from wind and tide, there were so many things that could go wrong.

Men planning treachery were always vulnerable.

Northumbrians here on the Humber's southern shore, in the land of Lindsey, could never be certain of their welcome. The men with whom he had his appointment might have run into any sort of trouble.

As he climbed the path a silvery-grey ash bole unfurled itself and stood up. He squinted, and made out Finn's face.

'Good man.'

Finn nodded.

'Have you been here long?'

Finn shrugged. 'Two-three days. I came from Lincoln.'

'Business?'

'Good. I have silver for you. I buried it. And some new stock.'

They fell into step together, Finn keeping pace with the bigger man. No more words were exchanged until the ditch and bank around the church came into view.

Tuuri said, 'Did you make yourself known to them yet?'

Finn shook his head. As they approached the causeway he fell back a pace or two, his already reserved face taking on a more servile, closed expression. Tuuri threw back his shoulders.

But there proved no need for swagger. Horses were already tethered outside the kirk, and the hall doors, north and south, stood open. They were welcome. White doves preened in the autumn sun.

The usual courtesies, new ale and mead, the words the same in the tongues spoken either side of the North Sea. Then the abbot of Barton left them, well pleased with his gift of silvered-copper cups chased with vines and strange beasts, and they got down to business.

Finn watched, taking everything in as was his second nature.

'Here's Northumbria.' Tuuri was holding out his left hand, fingers splayed, back of the hand towards his audience. 'This' – he pointed with his other hand to the big gap between thumb and index finger – 'this is the Humber. Here's the Tees' – the gap between index and middle fingers – 'here's the Tyne' – middle and fourth fingers – 'and here's the Forth.'

The big man's face had plumped and creased with amusement. 'So your little finger is Fife, and here in Barton we're sitting on your thumb.' He had no neck, just rolls of fat. Where did a man get fat like that?

Laughter, louder and longer than the quip merited.

'So, tell us where and when.' Tuuri was nodding, waiting for their merriment to run its course. 'We can bring you three ships.'

'Sixty men?' The quiet, mouse-haired man spoke this time.

Tuuri nodded again.

'And they'll be good men? Fighting men?'

Tuuri began to answer, but the big man overrode him. 'You wouldn't ask if you'd seen them! Manning those boats, it bonds men together like nothing else. They're kin, anyway. Lads from good families, know how to use a sword. But the boat's the key. Clinch this now, and I'll take word to—' He stopped, and winked, and nodded.

'Ships,' Tuuri said mildly. 'Not boats. How much will you pay?'

'Forgive me. Ships.'

The mouse-haired man said, 'Excuse us.' He indicated the door.

The courtyard was enclosed from the wind, and Finn could feel himself relaxing and opening up under the kindly rays. He closed his eyes and lost himself in a red haze, listening to the crooning of the doves on the roof and the chittering of the sparrows, but opened them again when Tuuri said, 'Do you know who they are?'

'The big man, I've seen him before. At Hedeby, I think.'

'Hah. No missing him, even with eyes like mine! Tilmon. He's been in the Danemarch for seven years. The other one is Alred. He wants to be king north of the Humber.'

'What's wrong with the king they have now?'

Tuuri shrugged and spat. 'Nothing.' He grinned. 'Everything.'

'Only three keels?'

Another broken-toothed grin. 'Got to keep some stock in reserve.'

'Not much of an army. Three keels. Not for winning a kingdom.'

Tuuri sucked his teeth. 'They'll be starting small. Harrying. Causing little bits of trouble, up and down the coast. Choosing choice spots, spots that will hurt. Trying to get his man to come out and fight. That's how these things start.'

There was a servant at the doorway gesturing them back in.

The big man said, 'My lord and I accept your terms.'

They settled down to talk through the detail, suddenly cosy. Finn watched and listened.

21

Abarhild waited a long moment, then reached out with her stick and prodded Elfrun sharply in the ribs.

'Ow! I was listening!'

Only partly a lie. The day had been a long one even though they were in October now and the light was shortening; long and all the harder for having been spent in Luda's company, going through the tallies, reckoning the paltry stores of grain against the mouths that would need feeding, human and animal alike. And the job not done yet. Only a few weeks since Radmer had left, but it felt like a lifetime.

Her grandmother seemed to have been ensconced forever in her tight-built little bower, pentice to the minster's common hall, where Heahred and the boys, and now Fredegar, resided. The foreign priest had become a familiar, though still a chilly, figure presiding over offices and masses alike. They had hardly seen Ingeld. He had been in York for weeks, even missing the riotous day and night of Hirel and Saethryth's wedding.

Within days of her father's departure Elfrun had begun to realize that she didn't know the Donmouth economy half as well as she had thought. The weights and measures and forecasts Luda had been putting before her set her head hurting.

Abarhild had begun again. 'But Agnes said, "I am already promised to the Lord of the Universe. He is more splendid than the sun and the stars, and He has said He will never leave me..."'

Elfrun had always enjoyed her grandmother's stories of the virgin martyrs, whose feasts had marked out her winters as long as she could remember. Lucy on the shortest day; Agnes and her lambs in late January; Agatha, whose miraculous veil could quell a flaming mountain, just half a month later. And with her father gone to Rome the tales had taken on a new reality. But this evening she found it hard to pay attention, when the stories were so familiar and she had so much else fretting at her.

She pulled the fleece from her combs and looked at it critically before rolling it and putting it in the basket.

'Don't frown like that.' Another sharp little prod. 'The wind might change.'

Elfrun winced.

'You should sleep here.'

Elfrun shook her head. The little bower was small, the straw pallet thin, and her grandmother snored mightily. 'No. I'll go back to the women's house.' Even though she suspected the other women and the girls would be whispering about her, like everyone else, wondering if she would make the right choices to pull them through the coming winter that lurked on the edge of everyone's mind like the wolf that slinks round the sheepfold in the dusk. The harvest had been poorer than they needed. Feed was lacking for the cattle as well as for the men. She sighed. 'I've got to make an early start tomorrow. I need to talk to Luda again.'

Abarhild rapped her stick on one of the stones that edged the hearth. 'I don't like you walking all that way in the dark on your own.'

'But I do it all the time. I've always done it.'

'You're not a child any more.'

Elfrun managed not to roll her eyes. 'What, you think the sea-wolves are going to take me?' She meant it as a joke, but her grandmother wasn't amused.

'I want you to stay here.'

'The moon should be up by now.' She got to her feet, ignoring Abarhild's hiss. 'It's a fine night, Grandmother. Don't worry about me.'

Indeed, the hunter's moon was just rising, round and white as church-bread, his face veiled by scudding hanks of cloud. A cold muddy league lay between her grandmother's little bower by the minster and her own bed in the women's house at the hall. The damp autumn wind was coming straight from the north, over the sea, and it went through wool and linen as though she were naked. Her toes were already going numb, and before she was halfway home Elfrun was wrapping the folds of her father's cloak tightly around her and more than half wishing she had agreed to spend the night by her grandmother's hearth after all.

Moonlight gleamed in fitful ripples on the wind-stirred estuary as she rounded the spur of the hill, and her nostrils caught a welcome whiff of distant hearth-smoke. She quickened her step. In the women's house there would be a banked and glowing hearth, and plenty of warm bodies, and because she was her father's daughter she would have her usual place close by the fire and no one would have dared steal her pallet. She put her head down against the clammy breeze and hurried into the great thicket of coppiced ash that spilled down the slope, straddling the path and flanking the stream.

A horse snorted, somewhere close.

Elfrun stopped dead in her tracks, head thrown back, ears pricked.

Another, softer, snort.

She could see the horses now that she knew where to look, four or five or them in the shifting moonlight, their outlines disguised by the tall thin tree trunks. No riders? But there were dark bulky shapes on their backs, shapes that made no sense... What trowie business was this? Why on earth had she dismissed her grandmother's fears so frivolously?

She leaned back into the shadows, not daring to breathe.

'Who's there?' A hiss from an unseen speaker, somewhere below her. 'Elfrun? It's me, Athulf.'

The breath went out of her in a long shudder. 'Are those our horses? Is that *Hafoc*?' She moved down the slope towards

118

his voice and nearly tripped over him. He was just getting to his feet. There were two other lads with him, their crouched forms barely visible. She couldn't make out faces, but Cudda was bound to be one of them. 'How dare you ride Hafoc?' She was starting to be angry, now that the fear was ebbing out of her. She stumbled over a dead branch and put out a hand to the flank of one of the horses. 'They're wet!' Realization dawned. 'I can guess where you've been! Across the river to Illingham. You idiot, Athulf. You know better than that! You'd never dare do this if my father were here.' She lifted her hands to strike at him, but he grasped her wrists and held her at arms' length.

'Never mind that.' His voice was impatient. 'Look what we've got. Feel this.' She resisted, but he ignored her, pulling her towards him and guiding her hand to one of those big dark lumps burdening the horse. Her hand met the rough weave of burlap. He pushed her hand down into it. Something familiar ground and shifted under the pressure of her fingers.

'Barley?' She had never heard of anyone stealing barley. Cattle were another matter, though surely Athulf wouldn't dare...

His voice was fierce with satisfaction. 'Ten sacks.'

'Did you meet anybody?' The ox-man, she thought. That boy with the beautiful bay mare.

But he shook his head. 'We were in and out quick. Stole our moment. With this tide, the river's easily forded. Cudda's been back and forth, spying for days.' He clapped one of the seated lads on the shoulder and Cudda looked up, his fine-boned face and fair curls suddenly silvered by moonlight. 'He told us the lord's gone away, and we struck.'

Cudda shuffled his feet in the dead leaves and muttered something, but Elfrun could sense his pleasure at Athulf singling him out.

'But they'll miss it. They'll come looking...'

'Let them.' His voice was larded with scorn. 'We're ready. And they may not even miss it. Their granaries are full, compared to ours. Even their rats are fat.' He dropped his voice a notch and took her shoulder to turn her away from the horses. 'What do you think, Elfrun? Did we do well?'

Ten sacks wouldn't fill the shortfall that she and Luda had been agonizing over. But they would go some way. 'You did well, I suppose,' she said grudgingly. But she was still angry, beyond all reason, and she hunted around for a cause. 'I don't know what you're thinking of, keeping the horses standing around wet in this wind.'

'We'd only just—'

'Don't *we'd only just* me!' Her voice was really sharp now and she twisted away from him. 'What's the one piece of holy writ your father seems to know? *A righteous man regards the life of his beast?* Get them into the stable, and rub them down. And don't you ever dare to take Hafoc out again.'

'You can't tell me what to do!' She had hurt him, she could tell by the edge in his voice. It had always been easy to goad him to tears.

Well, let him snivel, and if he was driven to do it in front of his friends then so much the better. While she had been fretting indoors over Luda's scratchings in the wax, he had been in the woods, plotting action with the other boys. Why should he have all the fun? 'Of course I can. I'm the lord of Donmouth, not you.' Pushing past her cousin, she tugged Hafoc's halter, and the big horse fell in obediently behind her.

22

Thancrad stood in the great dim space, taking in the wash of rich background colours and small points of glimmering light. He had no memory of ever having been in this church before, although they had told him he had been baptized here. There were painted faces on the wall, their eyes large and lustrous, gazing right through him. In the woods and fields of Illingham, on the hunt, riding Blis, wrestling or at single-stick with Addan and Dene, he was in his element. But in here he was like a fish on the ebbing strand, or a kitten in a bucket of water, floundering.

His baptism had been long ago, when he was a baby, when they were last in the king's favour. He had been ten when his father was exiled, but the years before the exile had been unsettled, harrying, campaigning, always on the move. And then seven years on the fringes of Frankia and the Danemarch, living on promises and threats and charity.

No one trusts a traitor, no matter how useful they might find him.

And a traitor's son is tainted by association.

Thancrad took a step forward. There was an unfamiliar scent, half-sweet, half-acrid, and a little grey haze in the air. The rise and fall of holy song from somewhere ahead of him.

The guards on the great gate had told him the man he wanted would be here somewhere, but Thancrad was nervous of interrupting.

There had been no churches like this in the Danemarch.

His parents were lodged with a Frisian contact in the merchants' quarter. Muttered conversations and sidelong glances. He couldn't stand it. They had paid no attention when he had slipped away.

The song was coming to an end: even he could recognize an *amen*. Figures in long robes coming from behind the screen of carved stone. He caught at a sleeve. 'Excuse me...'

A lad younger than himself. When he heard the question he grinned. 'Try the library. That door, and across the courtyard. Right opposite.'

Stone buildings, limewashed, patched and thatched. Hearth-smoke and dusk. A door stood ajar, and he pushed it a little further open on silent iron hinges. The room was full of presses and chests. Two men seated on stools, a book open in front of them on a slanted stand, their backs to the door. Half a dozen honey-scented candles. One man, taller, broader, was reading aloud to the other, in Latin. Thancrad had no idea what the words might mean, but the rhythm and the music of the language was intoxicating.

After a long moment, hoping they would realize he was there, he lifted a hand and rapped on the doorjamb.

They turned as one, almost guiltily. 'Yes?' It was the slighter, plainer one, his narrow face annoyed.

Thancrad ducked his head respectfully. 'Father Ingeld?'

The other man smiled. 'Leave me to tidy away, Wulfhere. It was getting too dark to read, anyway.'

Thancrad stood back as the narrow-faced man came towards the door saying over his shoulder, 'We can read some more tomorrow.'

'I should start back for Donmouth tomorrow.' The other man beckoned Thancrad in. 'What can I do for you?'

Thancrad looked at the book open on the desk. It was huge, the vellum impossibly smooth, like the surface of a bowl of cream, the little scratchmarks like insects that had fallen in and drowned. He had never been so close to a book before. 'Is this a bible?'

'This?' The priest laughed. 'No, this is the *Historia Naturalis* of Pliny. The best guide to all the wonders of God's creation. I was reading to my lord archbishop about the manticore, which has three rows of teeth and sings like a pan-pipe blended with a trumpet.'

Thancrad nodded, disconcerted. Now he had found the man he didn't know what to say to him.

The priest waited, one eyebrow raised. 'Do I know you?'

Thancrad shook his head. 'No, Father. I am Thancrad of Illingham.' He waited, and watched the expressions flicker across the man's handsome, mobile face. He was expecting the shutters to go up, but the hazel eyes met his frankly.

'And?' The priest's eyes went beyond him, to the door. 'Do you want to make your confession? There are more experienced confessors than me at this church, you know.'

Thancrad had no more than a hazy idea of what the man meant, but he shook his head firmly. 'I want your advice.'

'You would do better—'

'Not a priest's advice.' He was gaining confidence. 'Yours. Ingeld of Donmouth.'

After a long moment Ingeld nodded. 'Go on.'

'Radmer is away. Who makes the decisions in his absence?'

'His daughter. Her grandmother has retired to live with me at the minster.' The priest's mouth twitched as though he found something funny.

Thancrad nodded. 'My parents...' This was harder than he had anticipated. 'My parents want me to marry her. But Radmer has said no.'

And now the shutters did come down. Thancrad watched the priest retreat to somewhere deep inside himself to think about his words and their implications.

Then: 'And you want me to say yes?'

'Is it in your power?'

Ingeld thought for a moment. 'Probably. The king wants an alliance between Illingham and Donmouth; I did know that.

But that marriage was in the wind... no.' He looked hard at Thancrad. 'Do you want it?'

'I – I've never met the girl.' Thancrad squared his shoulders. 'But does that really matter?'

'She's a good girl.' Ingeld sounded as though his thoughts were elsewhere. 'Radmer has said no? In no uncertain terms? And contradicting the king's will?'

Thancrad nodded. The candles were drowning in their own wax, guttering, melting together and dying, and he could hardly see the priest's face, just their tiny flames reflected in his eyes. From the courtyard outside an evening blackbird burst into song.

He said, 'My parents have told me to make her marry me. But I don't know where to start.'

Ingeld laughed. 'Two things, young man. Always query your parents' wishes. And never ask a priest about women. Good priests know nothing, and bad priests know far too much.'

Thancrad could feel himself reddening, half-embarrassed, half-angry. Coming to find this man was perhaps the hardest thing he had ever done, and now he was regretting ever having entered under the shadow of the great gate of the minster precinct.

'Sorry. I can't help you.' Ingeld stood up, and the conversation was clearly over. Thancrad nodded, and muttered something, and found his way back into the yard.

Behind him, Ingeld stared at the door, unseeing. Thancrad's words had set his head spinning. What a chance to thwart Radmer, in all seeming-innocence and with the best of excuses. *The king wanted it...* Ingeld chewed his lower lip and stared unseeing at the floorboards. If Elfrun went to Illingham, she would need a bride-gift, but the estate would be left intact. This marriage might – just – free the way for Athulf, if he could coax the dice to fall right. His good boy, for whom he had never done anything. Donmouth hall, falling to him on Radmer's death, if the king approved. And this lad – Thancrad – seemed decent enough, though surely one should be wary of any child raised by Switha and Tilmon.

He had been on the verge of saying, *Yes, let's have a wedding*.

And then Elfrun's face had come to mind, her clear brown gaze, her little frown. So eager to please, so hard-working, so desperate to show she was lady of Donmouth and lord as well.

He had been unable to betray her, despite the powerful temptation. He closed his eyes, his gut tight and his fists clenched, and he prayed that he would never have to explain himself to Athulf. After a moment he opened his eyes again, and trimmed the wicks of the candles. In the last few moments of light remaining to him, he turned back to Pliny. *The manticore has the face of a man, and a man's eyes. It dwells in India, and it loves the taste of human flesh...*

23

Saethryth was kneeling on the ground with her skirts hoicked up and the little churn clamped between her thighs. She had been thrusting the dash-staff up and down for what felt like forever, but the butter showed no sign of coming. Pulling the end of the staff out once more, she peered at the bole of wood from which the cream still stubbornly dripped, and heaved a sigh. Why wouldn't the butter come? This late in the year, there wouldn't be much more milk.

Marrying Hirel had been the stupidest thing she had ever done. Looking back over the last few weeks, she didn't know what had possessed her. Yes, she had been furious over Widia's injury; and yes, she had been worried that there was a baby coming. Widia's baby, from that one time when she had given in. Two months skipped, and then she had bled, but by that time it was too late. She had already stood up in the hall and been handfasted to Hirel, the yards of gauzy white linen that symbolised the marriage draped over her head and shoulders, with Elfrun looking on with that steady brown gaze which had always made Saethryth feel about as small and dirty as a wood-louse or some other scuttling thing which came out when you moved a stone.

Three months now since the boar had gored him, and Widia was back on his feet, and hardly even limping any more. Not as pretty as he used to be – well, that was true enough, but there was more to a man than his looks. He'd not come within spitting distance of her, though.

Damn this trowie churn. She could hear her mother's voice, loud and clear: *With a face like that you could churn till Doomsday and the butter not come.* She had so looked forward to marriage and getting out from under her father's heavy hand. How could she have known what it would be like up here, all on her own out in the sheepwick without a single gossip to pass the time of day with? Even the two beardless lads who helped Hirel were away up in the pastures, looking for strayed sheep. They could be away for days.

This was the rest of her life, stuck up in the hills forever, bar sheep-shearing and haysel. She wasn't sure whether life was worse when Hirel was at home, or when she was left entirely alone. At least when she was alone he wasn't pawing at her, or throwing her those wistful looks which looked so ridiculous on his jowly, black-browed face.

She had known what a mistake she had made on their wedding night, watching him staggering and spewing and passing out. And her gradually realizing that no one else was going to clean up the mess. And that there was nowhere else to lie down but beside him.

Hirel was hoping hard to get her pregnant. *You'll be settled when you've weans of your own.* But there had been no sign yet, and for that she was thankful.

The day was surprisingly pleasant for October, the turning leaves of birch and rowan glowing against a deep blue sky; it should have been a good day for making butter, but the work was hard and weary, and her heart wasn't in it. She had discarded her housewife's veil – no one could see her, after all – and pinned her thick flaxen braid high on top of her head, and now the sun was warm on the back of her aching neck.

Weans of her own. Hard enough to learn to be his wife over the last few weeks, never mind mother to his children. As if she hadn't slaved all her life looking after little brothers and sisters! The last thing she wanted was to start again on that endless round. But if she went home, she would have to do just that. What choice was there?

And she couldn't go crawling back to the hall and beg to be let out of her marriage already. She just couldn't. The other women would snigger, and Elfrun look down that snotty little nose of hers. The staff thumped viciously back and forth in the wayward churn. Perhaps some more cream would hurry things along. She tipped a ladleful into the churn from the earthenware pot at her side, and poured a little down her own throat for good measure. It distracted her from the stink of the barrels where the lambskins were tawing.

Better get on.

Hirel had left his old hound with her while he took the young bitch down to the hall with him. Macsen was restless, prowling up and down and growling, but she ignored him. Wolves posed no threat, not at this time of day. Macsen just couldn't bear being too old to work, with his greying muzzle and stiff legs. Hirel said he had always been the best of the dogs, and it broke his heart to see him like this. He petted the dog, tickled him under the chin and stroked his ears, ran a scratching hand down his spine.

He knew how to handle the dog all right. So what made him so clumsy with her?

She shoved the staff up and down a few more times and at last felt the beginning of the heavy dragging response that meant some transformation was happening inside the churn. About time. The last time she had been down to her father's steading Luda had told her several times exactly how much butter and cheese the sheepwick would owe the hall, and that she was now responsible for all of it. She might be a married woman now, but she seemed more firmly under her father's hand than ever. At least he wasn't slapping her around any more. She sang furiously beneath her breath, '*Churn, butter, churn! Come, butter, come...*'

Macsen had frozen. He was staring past her, and lifting his upper lip to show what was left of his teeth as he growled on a single, unnerving note.

Saethryth half twisted round. A dark shape shimmered on

the edge of vision, in front of the sun. She squinted and it came a little clearer: a figure approaching on horseback just outside the wattle hurdles, hooves noiseless on the new grass. She tried to get up, but she had been squatting in the one position for too long, and her legs were stiff and awkward, threatening to fold beneath her as though she were a newborn lamb.

'I didn't mean to frighten you.' He was slithering down from his saddle and looping his horse's reins over one of the posts of the lambing pen.

She blinked into the dazzle, half-giddy from heat and effort, and from standing up too quickly. The lord abbot, walking towards her. She had been aware of him since his return from York, of course she had, and more so since she had gathered all her courage in her hands to run to the minster and ask what had happened to Widia, on that dreadful day. But apart from that one time, stripped to the waist and stained with blood and water, she had never quite been able to take him seriously: a shimmer of silk and golden thread, a blur of sweet smoke, a babble of eloquent gibberish. Now here he was clad as an ordinary man, though still with glitter at throat and cuff; and no ordinary man would ever have such a smooth chin or such clean hands, or ride such a sleek white mare. She ducked her head awkwardly, and looked up again to find that he was smiling at her, and coming closer still. She felt her cheeks reddening. His thick dark-brown hair was scattered with silver, but his eyes were dark and bright at the same time, and his teeth were white.

'Are you looking for my man? Hirel's not – he's not here, my lord. He's down at the hall, gone to meet my father...'

'So I'd heard,' he said. He was still smiling, though his gaze went flickering past her, to the little house beyond. 'You have cream on your face, did you know?' He reached out and stroked his thumb over her chin, and then very deliberately he touched his thumb to his mouth.

Saethryth felt an even hotter wave swamp her cheeks. She took a step backwards and stumbled against the churn. It toppled and fell, slowly – oh, so slowly... She could see the buttermilk lapping the wooden rim, ready for tipping out and sinking into the dusty soil... but at the last moment he grabbed the churn and righted it, setting it firmly down on a flat patch of ground.

'Looks like you need someone to keep an eye on you.'

Saethryth stuck her chin out. 'I would never have stumbled if it hadn't been for you.'

'Is that right?' He was looking at her avidly, like a hungry man staring at bread, and she knew her cheeks were still scarlet. If he touched her again, she didn't know what she might do.

But he didn't. Instead he smiled, a slow, lazy curve of the mouth that had her insides turning somersaults. 'I hope I haven't spoiled the butter. Bring some down to the minster when it's done? Tell them it's special, for me.'

And he had gone, just like that. Turned and swung himself back into the saddle and ridden away, leaving her flushed and restless and confused. She stared down the track for a long time, until the angle of the shadows reminded her that time was passing, and the butter wouldn't churn itself. Butter, he wanted, did he?

She would give him butter.

24

'Close the door. Was there anyone in the yard?'

Hirel stepped in, and shoved the door of the hall shut behind him against the hazy autumn sunlight. The day seemed strangely warm and airless for so late in the season. He shook his head. Luda was squatting on a three-legged stool by the cold hearth.

'Don't you have the lambskins?' The steward's voice was sharp. He stared at the shepherd's empty hands, his unburdened back.

'The ones that you asked me to hide for you?' Hirel wanted to be sure. He was afraid of this little man, now his father-in-law. 'This year's?'

'Not so loud!' Luda tutted. 'Of course this year's. What else would I mean?'

'No,' Hirel said slowly. 'Not with me.'

'Where are they then? I gave you plenty of salt and alum. I wanted them sorted out, ready for market.'

Hirel grunted. 'Aye. Skinned and salted each one the same day we killed it.' He paused, thinking back. 'I had Saethryth scraping the fat off, but there were so many, you hadn't given me enough salt.' He shook his head. 'Nor enough alum, neither. And a fair few were too maggoty to save by the time your lass got to them. The rest are still tawing.'

'My lass? Your lass now.' Luda grinned without humour, showing his long top teeth. 'Learning a bit more about her, are you? No matter.' He picked up his wax tablets. 'We'll set them all down as lost in the bad weather or taken by wolves, anyway.'

Hirel nodded. 'A lot was lost, you know.' He frowned earnestly. 'Really lost, I mean. The flock was scattered at lambing – too often the crows got there before I could. Not like you're putting down there.' He stabbed his raddle-stained index finger at the neat set of tablets. 'Much worse than last year.'

'You told me.' Luda shook his head. 'That's how it goes. Good years, bad years—'

'You don't have to tell me that.' Hirel was twisting his matted felt cap in his hands. Thunder growled in the near distance, and the air in the hall was unseasonally close. Hirel could feel sweat beading his forehead and prickling in his beard. 'Think she'll notice? The lady?'

'Elfrun? Never – not unless you let something slip.' Luda squinted at his son-in-law. 'So mind you keep quiet. She believes everything I tell her. Now the old besom's down at the minster we're much safer, believe me. That was a piece of luck.' He tapped his tablets. 'Where are the skins now?'

'Still up at the sheepwick. I told you.'

'And when will you bring them to me?'

Hirel's scowl deepened. 'I want my penny first.'

Luda snorted. 'I can't pay you till after I've taken them to York and talked to the scribes and the leather-workers. But my cousin should give us a good price.' He paused, looking at Hirel's lowering expression. 'Don't you trust me?' He leaned back on his stool and folded his arms.

Trust him? Hirel wasn't that much of a fool. He had been shepherd's boy then shepherd at Donmouth all his life, brought up to it by his father, and he knew the wiles of hall servants, even those that were now his kin. But he chewed his lip and twisted his cap and said none of this. 'What when Radmer comes back? What if he finds out?'

'He won't. But better safe than sorry.' Luda tapped his finger against the side of his nose. 'So mum's the word, eh? Even to Saethryth. You know what women are like.'

Hirel frowned. 'I want my penny now.'

But Luda was already pushing past him on his way to the door. 'While you're about it, pray for a kind winter.' The steward limped out without looking back.

As if Hirel needed telling. Every man, wife and wean in Donmouth was praying for a kind winter. It had not been the worst of years, but very far from being the best. It was wrong, the lord being away. It was as though the weather knew they were weak. So yes, they were all praying, just as the minster men told them to do. Ducking under the thatch and out into the yard, he kicked viciously and accurately at a stump of rotten wood by the path, and it splintered in a shower of tindery fragments.

The next pedlar who came through lugging his fardel on his back, the next merchant's boat to put in, Hirel had planned to buy as many pretty things as a silver southern penny could get him. Ribbons. Beads. Such trash as women liked.

Pretty things for that pretty wife he had somehow landed, who dragged around the sheepfold with a face like the thunder which was threatening. Hirel gnawed his chapped lower lip. He had been away from home for too long already. Four miles to plod, with the westering sun and the sweat in his eyes, back to the little sheepwick on the edge of the high summer pastures where he cared for a few sheep of his own and a great many of those belonging to the lord of Donmouth hall and the abbot of Donmouth minster.

25

'Will you take off your dress? And your shift as well.'

Saethryth just stared at him.

'What? Is it so much to ask?' He smiled. 'Cat got your tongue?'

But when he looked at her like that she lost the ability to think, never mind speak.

'I want to hold you,' Ingeld said. 'I want your skin next to mine.'

Hot blood charged through her veins. She had thought she knew so much, and yet here she was flustered to incapacity by this simple request. His little private bower was dim, but she felt as though the noonday glare was flooding through both the room and her body.

She mumbled something, more thoughts than words. Then she lifted her head and spoke clearly. 'Hirel never asks me to take my shift off.'

'If Hirel valued you properly you wouldn't be here, would you?'

There was only one possible answer to that.

In the end it hadn't been the butter that had furnished the means of her coming to him. That butter had been for the hall, and there would have been questions asked if the weights were short. After nearly two weeks of seeking excuses, she had come down with the cheese instead. Two big rush baskets of hard cheeses wrapped in the coarse leaves of butterbur and pinned with thorns, that had banged against her legs, their plaited handles chafing her fingers, for the darkening three miles between sheepwick and minster. At least the path was downhill all the way. And then the minster cook had tried to take them from her and shoo her away, but she had stood her ground. 'I want to see the father abbot. I have an important message for the father abbot.' And in the end, grumbling and shrugging, they had let her knock at his door.

And he had said nothing. She had come in and closed the door behind her, and when he saw her his face had lit up, and he had risen from his stool and taken her in his arms, holding the whole length of her close against him, a broad, solid wall against which she could rest. She had buried her face in his shoulder and breathed in the smell of him until the wool began to fret the skin of her cheek, and then she had lifted her face and let him kiss her as though he were trying to drain her to the dregs, leaving her gasping and unsteady.

Being slobbered over by Hirel was sickening; his thick, flabby mouth made her flesh creep. There was something cold about the way he touched her, that didn't realize she too was a living, responsive creature.

But every kiss from Ingeld had seemed a different question. *Is this what you like? This? And now?*

And now this.

He had taken a step backwards, wiping his mouth with the back of his hand and breathing hard before sitting down, and now he was on the edge of the bed, looking up at her, elbows on his knees and hands loosely clasped. 'Well?'

Saethryth narrowed her eyes. For all his passion Ingeld had an air of amusement, like an adult waiting for a little child to catch up, and this made her furiously angry. She didn't want him quiet and smiling, she wanted him hungry and desperate. 'Don't laugh at me.'

'It's a sad world if we can't laugh at things that make us happy. Has Hirel never seen you naked, then?'

'I've not been naked since they washed me for my wedding,' she said. 'I mean, I've changed my shift. But only to put the clean one on.' She snorted. 'I don't think Hirel knows my shift comes right off me. And I don't think I want him to, either.'

He couldn't have missed the note of bitterness, but he was too wise to comment on it. 'So will you?'

'Stand around and catch my death while you stare at me? Not likely.'

'Come and sit down then.' He patted the embroidered cover.

But she stayed standing where she was, knowing that she could turn and run if she wanted to, looking down at him. All was new, and exciting. Her lips were tingling, grazed from his stubble.

'Give me your hands,' she commanded. Obediently – and that, too, was exciting – he held them out to her, palms upwards, and she took them in her own and looked at them carefully, letting him curl his fingers round hers. Clean, dry and warm, with well-trimmed oval nails, no dirt in them, no ragged edges, though the hands were hard-palmed and sun-browned. Strong fingers, and the thought of him touching her made her breathe a little harder. She turned his hands over, looking at the scatter of dark hairs on his wrists, tracing her thumbs along the courses of his veins. His right hand was weighed down with the massive gold ring of his office. Saethryth had never touched gold before.

He shivered suddenly.

'What?'

'Nothing.' He closed his eyes. 'A goose walked on my grave, isn't that what they say? I want you. I want you very much. I want to see your breasts. I've been dreaming about them for months. Your mouth.' He opened his eyes and looked straight up into hers. His eyes were brown and green in equal measure. Their hands were still clasped. 'You. Can you blame me?'

She wriggled a little at the intensity of his gaze. 'Why are you looking at me like that?'

'I'm looking for judgement. *Weighed in the balance and found wanting...* But all I can see is acceptance. And roses, and lilies.'

She smiled at that, feeling little leaves and tendrils of power begin to unfurl and grow inside her. She stroked his palms with her fingertips, wanting to make him shiver again, thinking about his words. 'You owe me, you know.'

He creased his brow.

'I was going to marry Widia.'

'You blame me.' He dropped his hands.

'It was your fault,' she said boldly. Too boldly, because she saw him flinch, and she quickly changed the subject. 'The other day, other week I mean, the day when you came up to the sheepwick—'

He nodded.

'You wanted me then. Why didn't you – you didn't do anything about it. You could have. Nobody else was there. You could have done anything you wanted.'

'I know.' He raised an eyebrow then, a little rueful, self-mocking.

'So? Why didn't you?'

'But where would the challenge be in that?'

She frowned at him. 'I don't understand.' He was making her feel stupid again, and he must have seen that all was not well, because he took her hand once more and cupped it in his, tracing the lines and whorls of her palm with his index finger and making her feel as though she were one of the blown glass vessels they used at high table in the hall, that if he exerted one more ounce of pressure she would shiver into fragments.

'What I *wanted* was for you to come here. For you to want me.'

26

Abbot Ratramnus had been almost right. Donmouth had no library, never mind a scriptorium. The only books in the place were a tattered missal, full of rites Fredegar only half recognized, and the abbot's collection of pagan Roman poetry, in a commonplace book the man had compiled for himself. In what world were Ovid's *Art of Love* or *Book of Changes* suitable fare for a man in holy orders, the putative shepherd of this little flock? All the spiritual wealth of York at his disposal, and he frittered his time and his soul in this way, reading of erotic love and the discredited gods of Rome.

The man could read, and he read of profanities. He could sing, and now, joining his voice to Heahred's and Fredegar's own in the *De profundis*, his light tenor sounded as merry as though he were singing love songs at a sheep-shearing.

An abbot whose idea of duty ran to singing mass only when he was in the mood to wear that ostentatious yellow chasuble, and hunting on Sundays.

It would have been easier to bear if Ingeld had been stupid, or ignorant, or ugly. As things stood it was a damnable waste of talent and resources. And charm. Imagine that smile harnessed to a will to do good in the world! Fredegar had no illusions about his own forbidding aspect. He might compel people towards God through fear of Hell; Ingeld, had he been so minded, would have had them come rejoicing through the door of his little church as though he were St Peter welcoming them in through the gates of Heaven.

But in one important respect Ratramnus had been wrong

about Donmouth. The minster had a bell, made of true brazed metal, and two boys who took pride in ringing it. And every time that clear note rang out Fredegar felt the old clench in the guts, tremor in the hands, prickle of sweat in the palms.

Out of the depths I have cried to Thee, O Lord...

The sun had set behind great banks of wind-torn cloud, and neither the thick autumn twilight coming through the church's door nor the guttering rushlights on the altar shed much light on the page. But Fredegar hardly noticed. While he loved the sensation of the smooth pages under his fingers, soothing as a mother's touch, he had no actual need for the book.

He stroked it now, his racing heart slowing a little. Would he ever hear a bell again with equanimity? That bright beacon, which should be the sound of salvation. The ringing of the bell at Noyon, which had let the sea-wolves know that the whole community was processing to the church for Easter, that gate and guard-house were untended.

It was a cold evening, but he was sweating.

Vespers ended with the abbot's usual rapid gabbling of the prayers and Fredegar fell into step behind Ingeld, the deacon and the boys following. Elfrun and Abarhild had been standing quietly in the darkness of the western end. They both crossed themselves and bowed their heads as the little procession trooped past, and Fredegar amended his previous verdict.

Not entirely godforsaken.

Perhaps hope would return yet. Perhaps he had fled far enough, and he would find himself and his God again at the end of the road.

Barely were they out in the churchyard and the chilly autumn dusk before Ingeld was shrugging off his choir-robe and bundling it into Fredegar's arms. 'Put this away for me? Good man.' He slapped the other priest on the shoulder and walked over to where his grey mare stood, ready-saddled and -bridled, young Athulf with his hand on her reins. Ingeld waved a dismissive hand without turning round and swung himself up into the saddle. He clicked his tongue and turned his horse's head west and up the slope, and the gathering darkness rapidly swallowed them up, Storm's whiteness glimmering in the dusk.

That iniquitous man was warm and alive and enjoying the good things of God's earth, when so many better men were in their graves.

'Do you know where he's going?' Fredegar found Abarhild at his side.

He looked down at her over the crumpled bundle of white wool and began smoothing the cloth. Even to the man's mother, he would not criticize his abbot. Vows of obedience were right and proper and he would keep them as best he could. She had spoken in the Gallic of her childhood, and he answered her in the same language. 'I'd better put this away, *domina*.' How his patroness, this wizened creature compounded of fine parchment and holy water, had given birth to that big, ruddy, vital, blaspheming man, he could not begin to imagine.

He came out of the hall again to find that Abarhild had retired but Elfrun was still waiting for him, alone. 'Father Fredegar?'

He nodded, but he could guess from her diffident expression that he still had a forbidding air about him. He took a deep breath and tried to unbend. 'Elfrun. *Domina*.' He switched to the Frankish which was so like her own language. '*Frouwa*.' Then English, 'Lady.' Did she have something she wanted to confess, out of season? There was a burdened look about her which he associated with the Noyon novices and their fevered guilty dreams.

But, 'I have a favour to ask you.' She was twisting her hands together, but as he watched she stilled them consciously, clasping one hand firmly with the other.

He nodded again, and waited.

'Will you teach me how to read? Latin, I mean? Grammar.'

He thought about it. 'Wouldn't your uncle be a more suitable tutor?'

'I asked him. But he said he doesn't have the time.' She must have been able to read his expression, because she said quickly, 'I know. He has time for a lot of things. But not, it seems, for this.'

'I can teach you, of course. I have no Priscian, or Donatus, but we can use the psalter.'

'And...'

'And?'

'Renders,' she said. 'Tithes. Taxes. The kind of thing Luda has written down on his tablets. Can you teach me how to read those, as well?'

27

Elfrun lifted her head abruptly. A cry, like a strange bird, or a plaintive cat, just on the edge of hearing. But it went on and on, the same note.

Puzzled, she went to the door and looked out. Early morning had brought silent autumn mist, and she could see little beyond the nearest buildings. Beaded moisture hung in the thatch and the cold damp air made her flinch after the warm fug of the women's house. Her bare soles curled away from the cold ground.

The sound went on, a thin droning. Somehow it spoke of pain more eloquently than any scream could have done.

She looked this way and that, frowning, trying to trace the sound to its source. One of her women was near her time, but this wasn't the familiar bellows and blasphemies of labour. This sounded more animal than human.

A scuffle in the courtyard and a girl tugging at her sleeve. 'Lady? Please come! Please help!'

The smith's girl. Wynn.

'What is it? What's happened?'

More frantic tugging. 'Just come!'

There was no gainsaying that intense brown gaze, and the girl's thin fingers clutching at her cuff had an astonishing strength in them.

'Is someone hurt? At the smithy?'

The girl nodded, eyes bigger than ever. 'Burned.' She opened her mouth to say something more, then clamped it shut. Her face was pale.

'My grandmother, she'll know what to do. Go to her.'

'But you—'

'Yes, yes, of course. But I'll need more help.'

The girl nodded and scudded away.

Elfrun picked up her skirts and ran in the other direction, heedless of the mud and the sticks and small gravel. A clear half-mile down to the forge and she had never covered the ground so fast. Her heart pounding, she rounded the lean-to to find the smith in the doorway.

'He fell, lady.'

She peered into the gloom.

A sprawled figure was lying on the beaten-earth floor. Someone had turned him over, rolled him out of the fire-pit.

The smith was blocking Elfrun's view. The moan went on, rising and falling a little, like the east wind in the cracks between the wall-boards.

'Let me see him.' Elfrun took a step forward. 'Is it Cudda? It is, isn't it? I need to go to him.'

The smith was standing legs apart and arms folded. 'There's nothing you can do, maid. Go away. Get your gammer.' He closed his eyes briefly. 'Though I doubt me there'd be much she could do, either.'

Elfrun couldn't let him get away with this. 'I've already sent for help from the minster, but I need to see him myself.' She had always been cowed by the smith, not just his ropy strength and his gruffness but his easy mastery of the mysteries of fire and iron. Every wise lord knew his power over land and men alike lay in the palm of his smith. But none of that would bar her from her plain duty. 'Let me in.'

They stared each other in the eye. At last, to her huge relief, Cuthred dropped his gaze. 'Maybe you're not the little maid you were. I see that.' He glanced behind him at his son. 'Do what you can.'

Burning gorge rose in her throat as she ducked under the overhang. The smell...

Half his face was ruined. His arm... Oh, God. She could do nothing with this.

He must have stumbled sideways into the fire-pit, and lain there until the flesh had started cooking. Nothing else would explain the depth of those burns. Why hadn't he scrabbled himself out?

She whirled to his father, dark against the slanting October light. 'What happened? How did he fall? Why didn't he get himself up again?'

Silence.

The bones of her skull were shivering under the strain.

At last the smith said, 'He's drunk.' His voice was a growl. 'Dead drunk. And I was outside. Wynn found him.' Rising to anger: 'Don't you look at me like that, maid. Don't you even think it. Why would I push my son in the fire? He's the hope of my forge.'

She stared at him. 'I wasn't thinking that! I was wondering if...' But she looked at the smith, and her words faltered.

'What?'

She had been wondering if this was Illingham's retribution. Every night since the raid on the Illingham granaries a few weeks back she had been waiting, startled out of sleep by every nightbird's shriek, waiting for the smell of smoke, the screams, the thunder of hooves and the clash of steel. Was this the beginning?

But she couldn't put her fears into words. 'Where's his mother?'

'At her sister's, with the new baby. She doesn't know yet.' He let out a long ragged breath. 'I was just out the back, I told Wynn to go in and stir him up a bit. She and I, we'd been away for a week getting a new load of ironstone. He came in at dawn, singing. I was outside – I shouted at him to get the fire hotter. Thinking back' – he closed his eyes – 'I shouldn't have sent Wynn. I should have come in myself. I could sense he wasn't right, but if I'd known how drunk...'

Drunk. Was it possible? Cudda was much the same age as Athulf, and she still thought of him as one of the children. But he wasn't a child any more.

None of them were.

Elfrun steeled herself to crouch at the boy's side. She had no idea how long she stared at him. Hard to tell blackened and curled skin from the charcoal embedded deep in the burns. Disturbing smells of singed hair and roast fat. His skin had been seared away... When she came to herself again, she was longing for her grandmother to arrive, endlessly calculating how far Wynn had to run, how long it would take to harness the oxen, how slowly they would lumber along the rutted track... Her mouth trembled and she pressed her fingers against it, fighting back the tears.

'I had the right of it, didn't I? You can't help him.'

Half his face was untouched. But the other side... How could he keep up that steady drone of agony, with his lips blistered and eaten by fire?

Elfrun was used to pulling thorns out of the children's feet, salving eyes; under her grandmother's guidance she had even splinted a broken arm. And she had helped with Widia. But this...

This was different. Far, far worse even than Widia's hurts.

Tentative, she extended a hand to touch the unburned shoulder, wanting to offer the boy some comfort.

Neither she nor his father was prepared for the scream that seemed to erupt not from his lungs but from every pore of his body. Elfrun scrambled backwards to find the smith close behind her.

'Rutting Mother of Christ, that's all we needed. That'll bring folk running.'

Did he want folk to keep away? Elfrun stared at him, blinking hard, trying not to cry.

Abarhild would know what to do.

Abarhild wasn't here.

She pressed her fingers against her forehead. What had Abarhild told her? 'Raw onions,' she said under her breath. 'Eggs. St John, holy apostle...' Thank heaven it was only October, and the hens were still laying. 'To lay on the burns.'

But she would need to clean him first, to extract those

blackened lumps from where they had burned themselves into his flesh. She stared, and swallowed, and began to steel herself to touch him again, as ready as she could be for another world-shattering scream. And then she drew her hand back. She would harm as much as she healed. She didn't know where to start.

'Don't you go fainting on me, lady,' Cuthred said. 'I've enough on my mind. I told you you can't help. Nothing anyone can do.' The man's voice had a savage pleasure in it, as though he were glad to be proved right.

'We have to wait,' she said.

So they waited, for what felt a lifetime. There was nothing else to say. Cudda's breaths were a steady drone of pain.

Footsteps, and the doorway darkened at last.

'The child said I was needed?' Fredegar sounded breathless, urgent, a world away from his habitual dry, level tone.

Elfrun gestured wordlessly.

The priest took a few paces into the forge and his dark, narrow face contracted further. '*Jesu Maria.*' He crossed himself on a long out-breath. 'A blessing I brought my oils, *domina.*'

'You came so quickly, Father.'

'I rode Father abbot's mare.'

'You rode *Storm*?' Even in the middle of her shock Elfrun was taken aback.

'Your grandmother's coming in the ox-cart.'

'There's nothing you can do, mass-priest.' The smith's voice was gruff.

Without so much as acknowledging his words, Fredegar pushed past them and knelt at the boy's side.

'It hurts if you touch him,' Elfrun said hesitantly.

'I'm sure it does.' The priest sat back on his heels and stared down at the boy. The moaning had slowly dwindled in the aftermath of that scream. Now all they could hear was painful, harsh breathing, blended with the occasional whimper. Fredegar had a satchel with him, and he opened it to take out the long white band of his stole. He draped around his shoulders, his lips moving. Next he took out a small wooden box. The smith and Elfrun watched in tense silence. He put the box down on one side, and the satchel on the other.

'Can I help, Father?' Elfrun felt she had to ask.

Fredegar ignored her. His whole face had shut down, lips tight and thin, brows drawn down over the dark, liquid eyes. He was looking intently at every inch of Cudda's burns, moving in closer. She watched the flicker of his gaze taking in each detail, and his face not so much as twitching. His hands were hovering above the boy's skin, fingers splayed, assessing but never making contact.

'I need a knife,' he said at last, without looking up. 'I forgot my own, in my hurry. At least a finger-length blade, narrow and sharp as you can find. Have you such a knife?'

'I do. But it's not as sharp as it might be.'

'Put on a new edge then.'

The smith turned away to the massive wooden slab where sickles and knives of all kinds lay waiting his attention.

Elfrun wanted to ask a dozen questions of both men but she didn't dare open her mouth. Apart from Cudda's ragged wheezing the only sound was the steady hiss of the whetstone.

Fredegar shuffled his way down the length of the boy's body. Below the knees, Cudda was unburned. Elfrun had a sudden, blinding vision of how it had happened, the muzzy-headed boy stoking the fire, stirring the glowing bed of charcoal, turning, tripping, falling, sprawling head-first, bashing his head perhaps on one of the upright stones that shielded the fire from the wind, too numbed by the drink to heave himself up again...

Drunk.

If he had been drinking, he would have been doing it in company.

Silently she withdrew and made her way to the forge's opening, where the smith circled the blade on the stone.

'He'd been out with Athulf again, hadn't he?'

'That's it. Him and his little friends.' Hiss, hiss, hiss. 'What did my lad want with them? He's got his place, his life, here with me at the forge.' Hiss, hiss, hiss. 'He's got nothing to prove, not like some. If I told him once, I told him a hundred times.'

Elfrun thought of the treasure-house represented by the hall's buttery. Fragrant ale. Thick sweet mead. Southern wine from over the sea. It didn't matter which of the lord's barrels they'd been tapping. Any strong drink would go fast to the head of an empty-bellied lad raised on small beer.

And how a boy whose life was mapped out from the first breath might respond to the promise of adventure.

Fredegar had opened his box and taken out two little phials. Elfrun turned back to watch the priest's elegant, economical movements.

'You're giving him the last rites,' she said suddenly.

'The rites for the sick and those for the dying have much in common.' His voice was flat.

'So you think we can save him, Father?'

He ignored her and went back to the prayers, his rapid Latin barely audible.

'Father?'

Elfrun tried to keep her breathing steady. The burns were bad, yes, but they could heal. He would lose the sight of his eye, and the sinews of his right hand looked to be burned away, but Cudda had a chance of living. She could light a candle. Three candles. Beeswax ones. St John for burns, St Agatha, St Lucy... Lucy was good for eyes.

'I've got you the knife, Father.' Cuthred was back, and seemingly chastened into greater courtesy. 'What would you be needing it for?'

Elfrun too was puzzled by the knife. This wasn't some pus-bloated wound, or a boil that needed lancing. She tried to think through the care the boy would need, and her brow cleared. Of course. They would have to cut his clothes free. No balm could possibly be applied to that mess of ravaged skin while charred cloth and burned wood were still embedded deep in the flesh.

Voices were audible outside the forge, and the rumbling creak of a cart. A spring tide of relief flooding through her, Elfrun ducked outside and went round the building to where the surface was hard enough for the wheels. 'Grandmother!' At last. The driver was already helping the old lady over the side-planks and on to the wet grass, handling her as though she weighed no more than a hank of wool. The girl, Wynn, was scrambling down in her wake, still corpse-pale. Storm, Ingeld's precious grey mare, was hobbled and cropping the grass beyond.

'Burned, Wynn said.'

Elfrun nodded.

'Bad? Don't say anything. I can see it in your face.'

'Your basket, lady.' Wynn was at her side, her face taut.

'Carry it for me, girl. I'm stiff as a board this morning.'

Another appalling scream tore through the misty air. They all froze for a long moment. Elfrun caught the old lady's eye, and turned to hurry back round to the forge. 'My grandmother's here—'

The two men had their heads bent over the boy. The smith was sitting cross-legged. He had lifted his son's head in his brawny hands. That must have been why Cudda had screamed again. Fredegar was kneeling. The glow from the fire-pit lit them from below. Elfrun could only see the unburned side of Cudda's face. He looked so young, with his fair curls and smooth chin. As she watched, incapable of movement, Fredegar lifted the knife, its newly honed blade sparking in the light. He paused, his head on one side, for a long deliberate moment, looking down at the unspoiled skin of the boy's exposed throat, the extended tendons, the Adam's apple, the hollows at the base of his throat and above his collarbones. Then, almost casually, he lowered his hand and slid the knife home.

28

Elfrun had gone blundering out past her grandmother, not waiting to answer the old lady's anxious questions, just gesturing wordlessly behind her, her face too stiff and shocked for tears.

But tears were coming now. She had been walking blindly down from the smithy to the river's edge and then turning east, along the shore where the water ebbed and flowed salt and sweet in turn. She only realized how far she had come when she stumbled on the edge of the stream that came down from the summer pastures and marked the boundary between hall and minster. She wanted to be alone, and here was as good a place as any, down through the trees and along the shore to where the treacherous reed-beds gave way to dunes, and the narrow confines of the river to the wide horizons of estuary and sea. The stream ran out on to the sand in wide braided rills, spilling and soaking away before it ever reached salt water.

Elfrun found it hard admitting even to herself that her strongest feeling was relief. That early mist had cleared, but the morning was a chilly one despite the fitful sunshine, with the wind coming straight in off the sea, and she wrapped her father's cloak more firmly round her as she slithered down through the dry sandy hillocks towards the beach. The tide was on the ebb, exposing a great half-moon of fine wet sand, its smooth gleaming surface interrupted by the broad streaky banks of old cockle shells that testified to the riches waiting to be harvested. Oysters here as well, and razor clams. This hungry autumn, they were all reliant on ebb-meat, but it took a lot of search and struggle to make a meal's worth. A few children were usually to be seen picking their way over the sand-flats with baskets on the ebb of the tide, but the hour was early and low water some time away, and Elfrun was thankful to see that the place was still deserted.

She found a sheltered hollow and sat down, looking out to the endless sea, swallowing hard. She wasn't sure what had frightened her most, Cudda's fearful burns and that unbearable drone of pain, or the calm, lethal way in which Fredegar had responded. Something about his patient assessment of the boy's agony, and then the way he had struck, reminded her of the windhovers, the way they trod the air, winged bodies a blur but head quite motionless, waiting for their moment to kill.

Kill.

She hunched forward, the air driven out of her as though by a sharp blow to the guts. How was it a mass-priest's part to kill? She had thought Fredegar a true priest, not like her uncle the abbot with his hunting dogs and his feasting.

But Fredegar had stopped Cudda's pain. She had wanted to stop it, but she had been able to do nothing. Even her grandmother wouldn't have been able to spare the boy months of hurt, perhaps a lifetime of it. And a certain lifetime of humiliation. No future at the forge for a one-eyed man who could use only his left hand. No more running with Athulf and his band. A lifetime of charity. Pity, if he were lucky; otherwise contempt. A burden, a deadweight, existing on the margins of other men's tolerance.

So why was it so bad, this thing that Fredegar had done?

What kind of man could kill with that dispassionate detachment, as though he were snapping the neck of a hare the hounds had mangled but left alive?

She wrapped her arms around herself, fighting feverish nausea. Poor Cudda. Poor, poor Cudda. And Cuthred, and the family. They had lost a couple of newborns in recent years, too. Cuthred would have to take a stranger in to train up under the forge's roof. That was something else a good lord would oversee.

A good lord. Athulf saw himself as the leader of men. Always having to prove himself, pushing at the edges, mocking her authority. No good lord would have left a drunken child to stumble into danger like that.

But Cudda wasn't a child, and she remembered her insight of a little while ago. Not one of them was a child any more.

She should have seen this coming, or something like it, some disaster. She should have stopped Athulf. With her father away and Abarhild withdrawn to the minster, who was the lord of Donmouth, if not she? Not Athulf, with his pathetic attempt at cobbling together a war-band out of churls' sons, beardless boys with blunt belt-knives.

Why was he claiming to be a leader of men, when he couldn't look after them? When he laid all Donmouth open to a retaliatory raid from Illingham? When he never did any real work, boring work? Those hours and hours spent tallying sacks of barley and weighing wool with Luda: that was lordship, if you like. Not pretending to be a warrior.

She was lord, not him.

Elfrun closed her eyes and breathed in deep, trying to break the iron band that had somehow cooped her ribcage. If she were lord, then she should lead. Her place was at the forge, comforting Cuthred and his family, not skulking on the beach. She rose shakily to her feet. The wind had dried her tears but her face felt stiff and she scrubbed at her eyes with her knuckles.

When she lowered her hands, she saw a figure walking towards her, some way away, a slight fair-haired shape against the pale gleam of the sand and sky behind him.

Cudda, come back, hallowed in a shiver of silver light, raised up like a drowned sailor from the deep haunts of the sea.

She froze, as suddenly cold as though she too had fallen into deep water.

But the picture melted and remade itself, and she saw that though this man was young, and finely built, he was still older and taller than Cudda would ever have the chance to be, and he was a stranger.

Breath shuddered through her.

But where could he have come from? The trail of footsteps he left on the wet sand was already dissolving back into nothingness.

Elfrun drew herself up tall, put her shoulders back, lifted her chin, and waited. When he was around twenty paces from her she raised a commanding hand. To her inordinate relief, he stopped at once. 'Who are you?' Her voice was higher than usual, but she didn't think it shook. 'What are you doing on my land, unannounced?'

He bowed, and stood again, his right hand on his heart. 'I'm a pedlar, lady. A chapman.'

'Why didn't you blow your horn?' She would have said she knew all the wandering pedlars, those weathered men, bent and sturdy as wind-twisted thorns, who followed the coast road, coming through three, four, five times a year. The same faces at the same festivals, over and over. She knew at once she had never seen this fine-boned face before.

'I didn't know there were folk so close.' He dipped his head again, but there had been nothing humble about his upright stance, his open gaze. When he raised his face he was smiling. 'I'm new in these parts. Come across from the Lindsey shore.' He nodded his head southwards.

'Where's your pack, then?'

He jerked a thumb. 'Hidden in the long grass. My back needed a rest.' He put his head on one side. 'Shall I show it to you? Prove myself?'

'Go on.' Elfrun's hackles were still up. Why hadn't he come to the hall by the road as such wanderers usually did, instead of lurking along the shoreline? She was wary, running through her choices. She could clamber back up over the dunes, and summon one of the men to deal with him; but no one would want to be bothered about some chapman and his pack, not on a day like this one.

Or she could simply walk away while he was out of sight. But she couldn't allow wanderers to go unchallenged on her father's inlands, even if the man had been below the high-tide mark when she had first seen him.

She was lord of Donmouth, after all.

And she was clawing for any excuse not to go back to the forge, at least not until Cudda's body had been safely shrouded, and the blood had soaked away into the hard-packed soil of the forge floor.

Long-legged birds, redshanks and plovers, were picking their way over the gleaming sands, and sea-mews screaming above her head. The sky was hazing over, turning tarnished silver. If the stranger didn't come back soon, she would just walk away. Where had he come from, anyway? She could make out no sign of a boat either seaward or along the shore, although the estuary had so many little creeks and bays, and the fen extended so far inland in places, that a half-hundred ships might hide there if they had their masts down and put in with muffled oars on a moon-dark night.

But here he was again, skidding down the dune beside her. And she wondered now how she could ever have mistaken him for Cudda's after-walker, except that he too was fair and fine-boned. But this young man's hair was ashy-fair, not flaxen, and it fell straight; and now that he was close again she could see he wasn't so young as all that, years older than she had thought, somewhere in his early twenties though his beard was so slight; and that wind and weather had found the time to engrave delicate lines in the corners of his grey eyes. His cheekbones were wide and high, keeping the impress of his smile even after it had faded from his mouth.

But the smile was back now, illuminating his face from within, and Elfrun found a sudden sharp breathlessness afflicting her, a weakness of the knees which was a new sensation, together with a fierce longing to learn more about this stranger.

Of course she did. He was a welcome distraction – and she ignored the racing of her heart. A new face, someone who would talk to her of frivolities, anything to blot out the memory of Cudda's peeled and blistering skin, the ravaged eye-socket, the bone.

She wanted him to tell her something new, something she had never heard before. She needed different pictures in her head.

He was shrugging the densely woven wicker pack from his shoulders.

'I'm not buying,' she said, and regretted the words as soon as she had blurted them out. If she wasn't buying, why would he linger?

That radiant smile again. 'But these are my credentials, lady. So you know not to set your hounds on me. And if not you' – he shrugged easily – 'maybe someone else might be interested?' His eyes flickered past her, inland.

'Not today. No one would be interested today. There's – there's been a death. An accident.' She was trying to place him. His light voice had an accent which struck her as strange, but not as strange as that of the West Saxon hostages who had companioned the king last time he had come to hunt their woods and eat their stores. She fought the desire to press her cool hands to her hot cheeks. She was lord of Donmouth, was she? She could hear Abarhild, loud and clear. *Time you behaved like it.* 'What's your name, and who are your people?'

'Tell me yours and I'll tell you mine.' He looked up from his straps and buckles, his face expectant. 'And I'm sorry for your troubles.' He frowned at her. 'I thought it was the wind, but now I can see you've been crying, haven't you?'

Taken aback by his directness, Elfrun dashed furiously at her eyes with the back of her hand. She hadn't meant to pass the time of day with this stranger, never mind let him know what was bothering her. 'My name is Elfrun. My father is the lord of Donmouth.'

'And this is Donmouth?'

'Of course!'

'I thought perhaps these might be your husband's lands.'

'I'm – I'm not married.'

He raised his hands. 'I didn't mean to pry. Sorry, Elfrun.' *Alvrun*, he made it sound. 'And Donmouth is a fine estate, no doubt? A splendid hall and a high seat? A church, rich in silver and gold?'

She nodded, too proud to put him right, thinking ruefully of the hall-treasures her father had taken with him, of the shabby little church still earthen-floored and wooden-walled and likely to stay that way, for all Fredegar's disapproval. They would never build new, not with Ingeld as abbot, not while her father was gone. 'And you? Your name?'

'Finn. That's what men call me.'

She nodded again.

'Do you want to see?' He was opening the lid of his pack. 'I have some pretty things.'

'I told you, I'm not buying.'

'And maybe I'm not selling. But I'm proud of my wares. Come on, lady. Show courtesy to a poor wanderer.' He laughed. 'Now I've made you blush for your shabby welcome.'

She knew he spoke the truth, both about her treatment of him and her treacherous blood mounting in her cheeks. She could feel her face growing still warmer, despite the nipping, insistent wind. Nonetheless she moved closer, intrigued despite herself by the bundles and packets visible in the basket, eager for any distraction to wipe away even for a few moments the haunting presence of Cudda's burned face.

'Now...' Finn the pedlar said. 'Shall I show you some white furs? Silk ribbons from the court of the eastern Emperor? A little amber – some glass beads, nothing fine enough for you.'

Was he laughing at her? She was feeling grubby and shabby enough already, and she flinched at the mere sight of the silk ribbons. He offered a coil of them, but she thrust her hands behind her back, painfully aware of the charcoal smears and the way her rough skin and work-worn nails would snag on the gossamer stuff. The high silver haze was lifting and the day beginning to brighten, if not to warm. She shook her head at him.

'No? Are you sure?' He trailed a handful alluringly over his forearm. The ribbons slithered and shimmered enticingly, but she was more aware of the light dusting of golden hairs on the smooth brown skin of his arm, and the play of the muscle beneath.

'No!' More sharply than she had meant.

'Have you ever smelt kanella?'

Frowning, she shook her head.

'Cinnamon, you might call it?'

Again, bafflement.

He unscrewed the lid of a little wooden cylinder and she peered in. Scraps and curls of brown bark. She lifted her face to his, puzzled.

'Pinch a little. Crush it. Rub it between your fingertips. Take a deep breath, through your nose.'

Sweet and yet acrid, the scent hit the back of her nose: heady and utterly foreign. She closed her eyes and breathed deep, as he had told her. From somewhere came bubbling up the familiar words of the wedding psalm, *murra et gutta et cassia* – and she must have spoken aloud, because Finn said, 'What was that?'

'*The sweet scent of the spices, myrrh, aloes, and cassia, covers your royal robes,*' she said in English. She opened her eyes, still savouring the extraordinary smell, hardly seeing him. '*You delight in the music of harps in palaces decorated with ivory...*' Her breath caught tight somewhere between her breastbone and her throat.

'Beautiful,' Finn the pedlar said. 'Don't stop.'

Elfrun could feel her face hotter than ever, and shook her head again. She should not be here alone with this unknown man; she should not be enjoying herself, not on the day that had also seen Cudda's death. She had no idea why she was behaving like this. But she might be dead herself tomorrow.

Heaven knew the psalmist had enough to say about that. *Like sheep they are laid in the grave, and death shall feed on them.*

'Beautiful,' he said again. 'Like you.'

She shook her head.

'Not beautiful, you think? Then I have just the remedy, lady.' He looked into her face and frowned. 'Don't make that mardy face.'

'What face?'

'I can read you fine well. You were thinking I might insult you with some ointment.' But the thing he was unwrapping from a roll of sheepskin was no flask or jar. Something flat and metallic, highly polished, a disc a little larger than her hand, with a handle of welded loops. He passed it over and she took it with both hands, bemused again. Too many new things. She bent over and peered hard. Red enamel set into the greenish-goldish handle, and the flat surface of the disc finely incised with swirls and spirals of great beauty, some fields smooth, others minutely cross-hatched. Dents and scratches enough to show that it was an ancient thing, but not so many that they marred the design.

'Turn it over.' He was refastening the buckles on his pack, not looking at her.

She did so, wondering. On the other side, the disc gleamed as though newly cast. Again barring a few scratches, the surface was perfectly smooth, shining as though the bronze were still molten.

'Look into it.'

'I am looking at it.'

'Not at. Into.' He lifted his hand. 'Like this.'

She raised hers, mimicking his gesture, and gazed clearly at her own face for the first time in her life. She was startled beyond words. Where had the chill October gone? In the polished metal, a face was painted in the light of a warm summer evening, a rich golden glow. And that face, staring forthright and wide-eyed back at her... It reminded her of the Madonna picture in St Peter's Minster in York, the one men said had come from the holy city of Constantinople, further even than Rome...

Only gradually did she realize she was looking at no icon but her own true self. The reflection was softened round the edges, but she could see her face clearly enough. Wide brown eyes, and strong brows, the shadowed hollows of eye-socket and cheek-bone, strands of her chestnut hair escaping and softening her face, and a big smudge of charcoal across her broad forehead. She lifted her free hand with an exclamation and rubbed it away.

'See?' Finn the pedlar was close at her shoulder, but the mirror was too small to reflect both of them. 'Now tell me you're not beautiful.' His voice was warm and teasing.

'Do I really have so many freckles?' She peered at the dusting that overlay the bridge of her nose and spilled across her cheek-bones. No one had reminded Elfrun about the freckles since her mother's death. Suddenly she felt a deep self-consciousness. 'This is silly. Beyond silly.' Sickened by her own vanity, she pushed the mirror back at him. 'While we're blethering on, poor Cudda's lying dead back there.'

His face had grown sober again. 'I am sorry.' He reached out and took her hand confidently in his. She stared at him in dis-belief as he pressed the handle of the mirror into her palm and folded her fingers about it. She shook her head violently, but he kept his hand firm-clasped round hers. 'I'll come by your hall again, maybe, on a luckier day. Your father and mother might like to see what I carry. You have a church, you said?' She nod-ded, unable to speak, to correct him about her parents. 'I'll bring the things priests like, one of these days. Oil. Incense. I can get the vessels, too, given enough warning. Books, even.' She nodded once more, still dumb, as he took his hand away. 'Keep the mirror by you for a while. Think it over – though if you ask me, Alvrun, the man who made it had your face in his mind.' He looked at the distant, restless horizon and frowned slightly. After a moment he said, 'This day week. I'll look for you here. Sunset.'

'But—'

'No buts. If you're not here I won't bear a grudge. We'll meet again.'

He was smiling again, a smile that started with his eyes, and despite herself she could feel her face answering in kind, and though he had taken his hands away their warmth still lingered. 'I—' *could never afford it*, she was going to say, but he had already swung the pack up on to his shoulders and was loping away along the shoreline, waving a hand in farewell but never looking back. It felt as though he were taking something of hers with him, something beyond price.

29

The two motionless figures knelt side by side on the cold earthen floor of the dark church. Not so much as a single rushlight guttered on the altar.

'I could have saved him,' Abarhild said again. Her knees were agony. 'I am disappointed in you.'

'*Domina*.' Fredegar's voice gave nothing away.

'Our people are not your cattle to put down at will.'

Outside, a patch of freshly turned soil lay a few yards from the minster's south door. Ingeld had been startled at the request to admit the boy to the family lych-yard, and minded to refuse, but Fredegar had taken him to one side. Abarhild hadn't been able to hear his muttered words but she had approved the priest's dark frown, and his fierce, stabbing gestures from the boy's swaddled corpse where it lay on its hurdle to the minster and back again. Her last-born child needed firm handling. Men – and women – deferred to him far too much. How would he ever grow into the good man she knew he could be?

'You think Cudda would have been grateful for your cobbling him back together?' Fredegar gazed up at the dim altar.

'More grateful than he would be for you cutting his throat.' She peered up at the priest's hawklike profile, backlit from the little window high in the north wall.

'You are wrong, there.' He spoke to the stone cross carved in the wall above the altar. 'His father knew it, and so do you, *domina*, in your heart. I'd seen that boy around the place, running with your grandson. He lived in his body, as the beasts do.

Lose his health and he would have nothing left. If he had been able to speak, he would have begged for the knife.'

'You play at being God.'

'He is mercy as well as justice. I did what I hope to be God's will. Father abbot knows it, too, for what that's worth. And so does your granddaughter.'

The old lady rose to her feet with an audible creak. The silent slave-woman who had been waiting in the porch stepped forward and offered Abarhild an arm just as she staggered.

The priest said, 'If anyone is to blame here it is that whelp Athulf.' Grey-faced Athulf, who had watched the ceremonial from a sulky distance, never dismounting from his cobby little chestnut. As soon as the first spade-load of earth had slid over the shrouded body and the women had stopped their keening, he had tugged his reins around and forced his horse up the slope behind the church.

'How is it Athulf's fault?' Abarhild turned to look at him, still at his devotions. 'How? Cudda should have known better than to go near the forge fire in that state.'

Fredegar shook his head, but didn't answer.

Abarhild hobbled away from the altar, dipping her fingers in the holy-water stoup by the door and crossing herself as she came out into the lengthening daylight. She was convinced she was right, and she also knew that she was alone in that belief. Elfrun had confessed as much.

'He would have died in agony, Grandmother. It would have taken days... and if he had lived, what sort of life...?'

Such specious arguments.

Agony.

And what was so wrong with that?

God sent men agony to make them into something worth welcoming into Heaven. That boy would have been purified by pain as the prophet Isaiah had been cleansed by the seraph who brought a burning coal to cleanse his mouth of blasphemy. How fitting that the fire of the forge had been God's tool. Cudda should have been left to live or die, and, if he had lived, to have learned to accept his lot. Used it to grow his soul in wisdom and acceptance of what God had willed for him.

She expected little of Ingeld, and in her secret heart she admitted as much. But Fredegar had been trained in a house that knew proper discipline: she hadn't thought him capable of such weakness. She tightened her grip on her woman's arm. Pain was good for men's souls.

It had to be, else why would there be so much of it in the world?

She thought of Elfrun's white, horrified face, watching the blood spurting from Cudda's neck, soaking into the packed earth of the smithy floor while the boy had gurgled and choked his life away. She had always thought the best thing for that girl would be to take her out of this world of sorrow and put her away somewhere safe. Such a shame she had never made Radmer see sense about sending the child to that house of nuns, north at Hovingham. Elfrun would have made a fine abbess in the fullness of time, spared the pain that was the allotted fate of women.

Burying your children.

At the grave-edge Wynn stood with her parents, with the baby nestled in the crook of its mother's arm and a couple of smaller children clinging to her skirts, though most of the rest of the mourners had long since peeled away, back to tending their hearths and their hedges. Cuthred and his wife looked as though they were exchanging angry words. Wynn was glancing from one to the other, quick bird-like movements, her arms wrapped around her skinny body. As Abarhild watched, the girl turned her back on her mother and took her father's arm. The gesture had something final and defiant about it. The woman watched her husband and daughter go with a look of disbelief before dropping her head and burying her face in the swaddling cloth of her infant. Her shoulders were shaking. Abarhild wondered whether she should go to her, offer such feeble comfort as she was capable of, but another woman was there before her, and the two walked slowly away.

Abarhild felt a sudden weary desire for her narrow pallet. Could not the world just have done, and let her go? God had made it, but men had marred it: a bitter, horrible place, and she wished that she and those she loved were safely out of it.

But in Radmer's absence she could scarcely send the child to a nunnery. And these Northumbrian houses. Lax and ill disciplined, with little tradition of learning. Not that the men's houses were much better. Abarhild thought wistfully of her own old home. Was there anyone still at Chelles who would remember her? *Hilde*, they had called her. The fresh-faced novice of some sixty years ago, that girl who had been taken away so suddenly. The white-washed building where the novices had slept, always clean and sweet and comfortable, and the sun always shining, always warm. She had always been warm in those days.

Abarhild shook her head and muttered below her breath, and her woman eyed her sideways.

Luda was waiting for her outside the door of her little pentice attached to the minster's common hall, wax tablets clutched in his hand. He started speaking while she was still several yards away.

'I need a decision about the hall cattle, lady. We haven't the inkeep for half the ones I wanted to over-winter. The barley that should go to them we'll be needing for ourselves, and we can't leave the beasts to starve.'

Abarhild scowled at this vision of a hungry winter. 'Why are you asking me? Speak to Elfrun. She wants to be lady of the hall? Let her decide.'

Luda gave his lopsided shrug. 'She told me she didn't understand. I thought it better to come to you.'

'Kill them, then, while they're still fat enough to be worth the salting. Why do you even need to ask?'

He was opening his mouth to reply, but a ringing ululation from the hillside above the church cut across his words. All three turned to see Athulf on horseback, skidding down the slope, past the minster and the fresh earth of Cudda's grave with never a pause, his reins in one hand and his other arm gesticulating violently to the north. He was shouting something but they could make neither head nor tail of his wild words.

'What is it now?' Abarhild had had enough for one day, even of her beloved grandson.

He brought his mount to a wheeling halt only feet from them. 'In the estuary! Get your men!' His voice emerged as a painful rasp after that ringing shout.

Abarhild felt a pulse of anxiety. 'What is it, boy?'

But Athulf was ignoring her, addressing his gasping words to the steward. 'Dozens of them! The good sort, the black ones. Heading past the river-mouth! Quick – get everyone! I'm down to the boats!'

He clapped his heels to his horse's flanks and was away.

'Please, my lady?' Her woman, hissing. 'Please – my arm. I'll be bruised tomorrow.'

Abarhild unclenched her fingers but didn't relinquish her grip. 'What's happening?'

30

Further along the estuary, to Athulf's fury, the Illingham boats were already putting out. But the men of Donmouth were only moments behind.

Widia was at Athulf's side. 'Neap tide,' he said tersely. 'This is as high as it will get. And we're only just past slack water. We can do this. Off your horse, lad.'

'We'll have to share, with them.' Athulf's tone was bitter. Widia turned a frowning face up to the boy. 'Yes, I know there'll be more than enough,' Athulf went on. 'But they never offered to help us... And I saw them first.'

Widia knew fine well where those ten sacks of grain had come from, but he also knew when to hold his peace. Sometimes one should just accept blessings, and not ask too closely. 'Into the boat, lad.' He half turned and shouted to the men running the boat down to the water. 'Got your billhooks? Gaffs?'

They had been meaning to put out far into the bay and harry the herd from behind. But there was no need. The whales were coming landward by themselves.

Athulf's belly was growling with desire at the sight of those short, sharp fins and blunt heads. They were the small black whales called Wade's cattle, and they made fine eating.

And, best of all, they were swimming round the headland. If they carried on that course they would be grounding on the sandbanks downstream from where the river fed into the estuary.

Athulf let out an exhilarated shriek, higher-pitched than he would have liked, and slithered down from Mara's back.

Pausing only to loop the reins round his saddle-bow, he plunged forward, tugging his knife from its sheath. 'To me!' With his left hand, he grabbed a gaff from the pile Hirel had just set down and waded forward into the ebbing tide. He had only seen a whale-drive once, and then he had been too young to be allowed to do more than help the women gut and strip and pack. But he knew he could do this. 'To me! Over here!' He had to lead. He had to do this, and then he would be forgiven for Cudda's drunken stumble.

Not the dozens he had proclaimed in that first, over-excited moment on the hillside when he had spotted the sleek black backs arcing through the water. But at least twenty, propelling their way towards him with great up-and-down thrusts of their curved tails.

Athulf was thinking fast.

Widia had said this was as high as the water would get, and that it was on the turn. Athulf could already see the change in the current, out where river water met sea. His first impulse had been the right one. He waved his arms at the men in the boats, pulling hard on their oars to counter the gathering tide that wanted to take them out to sea. 'Over here!' he screamed, and again, 'To me!' Get at least some of the whales on the shoreward side of the sandbank, and their job was done.

There were half a dozen boats now, Donmouth and Illingham side by side. Four men at the oars, and one in the bow of each, lobbing stones, beating the water with spare oars and bellowing.

The water was boiling, dark green and streaked with foam. Impossible to tell just yet where the sandbank lay, and how far under the ebbing surf. Athulf became aware of others in the water, hungry men with drawn knives to his left and right. Fredegar was only feet away, soaked to the waist. Widia stood on his other flank, holding one of the great flanged spears they used for boar. Athulf waded in deeper. The water was heart-stoppingly cold.

More boats, a crescent of shrieking, bawling men, drawing the trap ever closer. The sea was an explosion of fins and flukes and the round black heads. Athulf swallowed in almost painful anticipation of the sweet blubber melting on his tongue.

And a whale loomed right in front of him.

Sweet Mother of Christ, it was so big. Like a black pig out of a nightmare, barrelling straight at him with great thrusts of its tail. Its mouth was open, showing two rows of neat, pointed teeth framing a pink mouth. He raised his knife. Coming so fast! How was a man supposed to deal with a beast like this? Widia had the right of it, you needed a great, flanged boar-spear, not a mere knife.

He was still staring at the monstrous thing, wondering at its size and force, the speed of its approach, when it hit him in the chest with a thump that shook creation, and he went under.

His eyes and nose and mouth were full of water. The whale was somewhere above him; he could feel the water pushing this way and that as it thrashed past. The force pulled the gaff from his hand and tumbled him round till his head spun, and he lost all sense of where up was, and where down. He wasn't sure whether he was being bumped against silt and sand or the belly of the whale.

His only thought was for the knife. He would need it to kill his whale; he mustn't lose it. And, oh God, he mustn't fall on it. His free hand flailed wildly, finding the slick surface of the whale's skin above him, but no purchase was to be had. His whale was literally slipping through his fingers.

Where was the air? Why couldn't he see anything? He opened his mouth to breathe, to shout, and swallowed half the sea.

Someone had him by the scruff of the neck.

Athulf came choking and spluttering back into the world, his sinuses burning from the through-rush of salt water. The sea had turned a startling red. His whale. Where was his whale?

'Come on.' His saviour had him by the shoulder still and gave him a slight shove. 'You don't want to be the last to make your kill.' They were chest-deep in the scarlet water, and the whale was right there, between them and the shore. Athulf pushed the sopping hair out of his stinging eyes, still gasping for breath that wouldn't come.

No one else had claimed it. He felt a surge of power. No one would dare claim prey to which he had once raised his hand.

Where was the place to strike? The whale might be grounding, but it was still thrashing around, more than three times his length and vastly bulky, the tail whacking the water with unbelievable force, sending the spray yards into the air and soaking him again. He forced his way through the foam to its head and stared at the tiny eye and beaky nose, panic rising inside him.

Beyond the bulk of his whale, through his stinging eyes, he caught glimpses of Widia and Fredegar, expertly dispatching another leviathan. And beyond them, on the shore, others were already dragging their kills on to the beach where the women were waiting with gutting-knives. Elfrun was in charge, her skirts kilted, standing in the foam, shouting and gesturing, but he couldn't hear what she was saying.

The whale writhed its great body, sending a wash of water that nearly knocked Athulf down again. He was chilled to the marrow and he knew he wasn't thinking clearly. The air was filled with whimpers and cries, the voices of the animals being slaughtered all around him.

'I've never done this before,' he said aloud.

'Me neither.' An urgent voice at his shoulder. 'But I can see what the others are doing.' A hand with a gaff reached past him and hooked the whale in the blow-hole. 'Quick. You've got the knife. Just there. A foot or so down the spine.'

Athulf shoved the hair out of his eyes again with the back of his left hand, and brought his knife down hard, slicing into the gleaming black skin till only the hilt was standing proud. A great red spray of blood leaped out and soaked him once more, startlingly hot after the numbing cold of the sea, and he stifled a gasp. The blood stung his already sore eyes and was warm and sweet in his mouth.

The whale gave one final, immense shudder and was still.

'Here, I'll finish it off.'

Still blinded, Athulf relinquished the knife.

When he opened his eyes, he was shocked to recognize Thancrad of Illingham, his strong, bony face streaked red, standing across the great bulk of their kill.

'That was well done,' Thancrad said. 'Now we need a rope.'

Athulf turned, eyes blood-bleary and still stinging, and peered up the beach. 'Elfrun!' He could do no more than repeat Thancrad's words. 'We need a rope.' Their whale was one of the biggest, he realized, coming nearly up to his hip. One of the big bulls of the herd.

Their whale?

His whale.

He had spotted the whales first. The rest of the meat would be divided up and shared out according to household, but he had the right to a whole carcass.

Now that the water had stopped foaming it was redder than ever. The boats were putting into shore.

'That girl.' Athulf followed Thancrad's gaze. Elfrun was making her way towards them, skirts kilted high above her knees, coils of rope in her arms. She was soaked, breathless and bloodstained. 'Who is she?'

'My cousin.'

'That's Elfrun? But she's the girl who was racing with us. At the meeting.'

'Yes, that's right.' Athulf wasn't sure he liked Thancrad's expression, and he certainly didn't like being reminded about that race. What was so interesting about stupid bossy Elfrun, anyway? He turned back to the corpse of the whale, rocking gently in the ebbing water. 'Where do we tie a rope, anyway?'

'Round its flukes.' Elfrun waded up to them, gasping with the effort. 'Here.' She thrust the heavy coils into Athulf's arms and pulled one end free. 'Get this done. I want to get out of the water.'

'Elfrun, this is my whale.' She had her back to him, already turning for the shore. 'This is my one, isn't it? I saw them first.'

She stopped, shivering in the thigh-deep sea. 'I think so.'

'Our boats were out before yours.' Thancrad's voice was mild.

'I saw them first,' Athulf repeated.

'No, I think we did.'

'And anyway they came to our shore, not yours.' Athulf squared his shoulders and clenched his fists. He could feel the wind drying the blood stiff and clotted on his face. The air above them was noisy with wheeling crows and the great black-backed gulls, waiting their moment to descend and feast.

The two young men stared at each other, eyes narrow in bloodstained masks. Elfrun looked from one to the other, her sudden nervousness written on her face. Behind his steady gaze, Athulf was totting up men and calculating support, and he was pretty sure Thancrad would be doing the same.

And perhaps they came to the same conclusion, because in the end Thancrad just shrugged and offered Athulf the knife, hilt first. 'I expect you're right. It was your kill, certainly.' He glanced sideways at Elfrun, with a little smile. 'Does he always get his own way?'

'Don't worry. We'll see you get your share,' she said. Her skin was blotchy with a chill that Athulf had stopped feeling.

Thancrad's smile deepened and warmed, the skin tautening over his cheekbones. 'I'm sure you will, lady.' But she didn't smile back.

On the strand, the messy business of gutting and flensing had begun. Sharp knives were slicing great square flaps of skin, easy as opening up trapdoors, and the glistening grey ropes of intestines were spilling out. The children were shoving each other, balancing on slippery carcasses, fending off carrion birds with sticks and stones, pestering adults for strips of the pinkish, nut-sweet blubber. Athulf's mouth was watering.

He and Thancrad bent their shoulders to the rope. The air was thick with the hot, heavy smell of blood and guts. They swung the great beast round while the water was still deep enough to help them, and then began the arduous task of hauling it in.

Eager hands came to add their strength, and to slap him and Thancrad on the shoulder; their startling white teeth grinning in gory faces, his friends and kinsmen indistinguishable from the men from the Illingham shore.

'This is my whale,' Athulf said. He glanced at his new comrade. Thancrad raised his eyebrows. Thancrad was bigger. Older. His father was a king's thane. Hiding his rapid calculations behind an exultant grin, Athulf grabbed Thancrad's hand and held it up. 'We killed it.'

31

'Your father wants you.'

'What for?' Athulf was grooming Storm with a hard-twisted hank of straw. Ingeld had let her have a good muddy roll when he had got back, and her white coat was spattered, legs black with dirt up to the hock. The lad was the far side of her, rubbing firmly at her flank with circular movements, and Fredegar couldn't see his face.

The priest could imagine it though, the little scowl, the lower lip jutting, the defensive hunch of the shoulders. He sighed. 'That is not an appropriate answer. When someone to whom you owe respect summons you, you come, without question.' This boy had not been beaten nearly enough.

'I'm filthy.' Athulf's tone was hopeful.

'So wash your hands.'

Athulf stood up straight and came out from behind his father's mare. 'I stink. My tunic's stained. She's been rolling in her own sharn.'

And even in this light Fredegar could see that the tunic was also still tainted with blood and filth from the whale-drive several days earlier. He sighed. 'Surely you have more than one tunic? Your father's son?'

Athulf nodded reluctantly.

'Then get cleaned up. He said he'd be waiting with your grandmother.' The priest turned on his heel.

Athulf wiped his hands front and back on his tunic before pulling it over his head and changing it for the slightly fresher one that hung on a nail. His grandmother's women did his washing, but he never noticed when things were dirty or remembered to take them a bundle. Giving Storm a last affectionate pat he made his way out of the stable and round the common hall to his grandmother's well-built lean-to annexe, the new oak and reed-thatch still pale-gold, head down against the driving wind and rain.

He had not seen his grandmother to speak to since Cudda's body had gone into the ground. Despite the cloud of anger and self-righteousness Athulf had wrapped around him he had been painfully aware of her simmering disapproval. But he had also noticed that those tight-lipped frowns were not directed at himself alone; and he had experienced a savage thrill of pleasure at her anger with her foreign priest. Athulf had had about enough of Fredegar pulling his shoulders back and pinching his nostrils as though he stank of something much worse than horse-sharn.

What gave that foreigner the right? He was no better than any of them. Worse. He had killed Cudda, in cold blood. Athulf had not seen his friend's body unshrouded, and his imagination glossed easily over the injuries. How bad could they have been? Elfrun had refused to tell him more than the bare minimum, but those burns would have healed, surely? What man was ever thought less of, just for a few scars?

Making his way across the yard, he scuffed his heels and glared indiscriminately at anyone who happened to be in his line of sight, but cheered a little when he saw Heahred ducking out of the church and nodding a greeting. Deacon though he was, he had always treated Athulf with friendly courtesy. And in marked contrast to Fredegar, Heahred was his father's man, blood, bone and marrow.

In the months since his father had come home for good Athulf had been learning that there were plenty of men who admired Ingeld: his horsemanship, his conviviality, his skill in the hunt. It meant something, at spring and harvest meeting, to be known as the son of the abbot of Donmouth.

Even if Ingeld seemed to forget, most of the time, that he existed.

Athulf choked back the bitter lump that threatened to rise in his throat. Why was he wanted, now? His desire for his father's approval was like a hot, painful wave washing through him.

He hesitated at his grandmother's door, unsure of his welcome despite the summons, but Abarhild's plump-faced servant beckoned him in impatiently. 'You took your time.'

'I had to clean myself up.'

The woman looked him up and down and scowled before stepping back. 'You call that cleaned up?'

What business was it of hers?

And where was his father?

His grandmother was warmly wrapped in lambswool and close to the fire, her hands planted on her stick. For all her frailty she was sitting erect and her face was stern.

'You are out of control,' she said.

Athulf felt the blood hot in his cheeks, but he hoped that his grandmother, with her rheumy eyes, would never notice in this dim, hearth-lit space. He stood up straighter. 'I spotted the whales. I killed the bull whale.'

'I am not talking about the whales. Raiding Illingham. You and the other little foxes, playing at being wolves.'

He winced at the contempt in her voice, and tried to counter it. 'Well, what am I supposed to do?'

'What you are told.' She gestured at her women. 'Leave us be.'

Athulf waited until the door had closed behind them, then took an impetuous step closer to the fire. 'Told, Grandmother? But I'm never told anything that matters. And I always do exactly what they tell me – I look after Storm, I—'

'You're not a child any longer.' Abarhild beckoned him closer, and he squatted a few feet from her, pretending not to see her nose wrinkle as his clothes warmed and steamed in the heat from the little fire. She looked at him hard, and suddenly he was far from sure that anything about him would escape her disconcerting gaze. She went on staring, and he could feel her eyes dwelling on every aspect of his face, until his skin burned again and he looked away.

He heard her sigh. 'So like your father.'

'What's that supposed to mean?'

'Don't be stupid,' she said irritably. 'That can't be news to you. What's done is done.' She gestured him down, and he hunkered once again, but wary this time, balancing his weight on the balls of his feet, ready to pounce or flee. 'The question now is what we do with you. Fredegar and I have been talking—'

'That foreigner!'

Abarhild hissed with disapproval. 'No more foreign than I am myself.'

'It's not the same! What gives him the right—'

'Oh, shut up, boy.' Abarhild batted his protest away as though it were some impertinent insect. 'Fredegar thinks you are unsuited for the Church.'

Athulf stared.

But his grandmother ignored his startled look. 'He is wrong, however. All you are is young. Ill disciplined and poorly educated, yes. But' – she paused and glared at him – 'young. We can correct all that.'

Athulf just gaped at her, until she poked his foot with her stick. 'Close your mouth, boy. You look like a fresh-landed sturgeon.'

She had the right of it. Athulf felt as though he had swum unseeing into a wicker weir, and now he couldn't find the way out.

'No.' He was on his feet, with no awareness of how he had got there.

'No?'

He didn't hear the warning in her voice. 'I'm going to be a warrior. I need a sword. I'm going to join the king's war-band.'

Abarhild was shaking her head. 'Not the wisest choice, boy. Nor the safest.' She tapped her stick on the floor. 'Sit down again.' She waited. 'Sit *down*.'

He could feel his will beginning to bend when the door eased open behind him and Ingeld came in, closing it on the daylight, the fire glinting in the raindrops that beaded his hair. Athulf turned to his father, hand extended, mouth open, eyes pleading. Ingeld had never wanted to be a priest. He would understand.

But Abarhild hadn't finished, and Ingeld held up a warning hand.

'That matter with Cudda.' She was pursing her lips, choosing her words. 'Bad. Your fault?'

He clamped his mouth shut against the cry of protest that threatened.

She was relentless. 'How else would he be drunk? That drunk? You'd been at the buttery.'

He scuffed his toe against the floorboards. 'Yes, Grandmother.'

'Warriors carousing in the hall, eh? Your little war-band?'

He shrugged, his eyes roving to every point in the snug little room but their faces.

'What are you hoping? That Radmer will make you his heir?'

There was a snort from Ingeld, and Abarhild grunted confirmation. 'Quite. That will never happen, boy. He's said as much. We only want the best for you.'

'But I want...' He couldn't get the words out past the lump in his throat.

'Speak up!'

He stepped back, out of reach of her staff. 'I want to take my sword to the king.'

'Your sword?' It was his father who had spoken. 'Where have you got a sword from?'

'I don't – I haven't.' Athulf could hear what he thought was an undercurrent of amusement in his father's voice, and it made him sick and desperate. 'Not yet.'

'You've no claim to a sword, you stupid boy.' Athulf could tell his grandmother was reaching the end of her patience, but anger made him reckless.

'I would, if I killed a man who had a sword and took it.'

'Enough of this nonsense.' Abarhild levered herself to her feet. 'We have decided everything. Ingeld, you will write to Wulfhere about finding the boy a place at the minster. It's not too late, even for learning to read. I have known older oblates, and stupider ones.'

Ingeld shrugged his acquiescence. 'Yes, Mother.'

Athulf turned on his father, his mouth contorted with the effort of fighting tears. 'You never wanted to be a priest!'

Ingeld stared at his son. 'How would you know what I wanted at your age? What boy gets to choose?'

'I have chosen! I'm good. Thancrad said so.'

His words fell into silence. Ingeld was staring at him.

'Tilmon's son?' His grandmother's voice was sharp.

He nodded, sticking his chin out. After the whale-drive he and Thancrad had agreed to meet: once to go into the marshes with the fowling-nets, once to practise single-stick. Just Thancrad and him – not those other lads, Addan and Dene. They might be Thancrad's cousins, but they were cousins he hardly knew after his seven years of exile across the sea.

Thancrad had his sword already.

Thancrad had praised his strength in the single-stick combat, his dexterity, his endurance.

'Did you know about this?' Abarhild was looking at Ingeld.

Ingeld just shrugged. 'What does it matter how he spends his time at the moment?' His voice was tight. 'You've got it all mapped out for him.'

'I don't want to go to York.' Athulf's voice was scarcely more than a mutter, but Abarhild heard him.

'Very well. Starve.' Abarhild coughed, a ragged little grumble in her chest that went on and on. When she recovered her mood seemed to have softened. 'You don't like the idea of being a churchman, Athulf. I can see that.' She reached out her free hand and patted his arm, ignoring his flinch. 'No one could say you were cast in that mould. But not many men are. Not many priests.' She dropped her hand and shifted to look at Ingeld.

'There's plenty to keep a boy like you busy in York, from all I hear.'

Athulf also turned to his father, frantic as a netted waterbird. 'Can't I stay here? I've been working hard for you! Storm has never been so well looked after—'

His father's face closed like a stone.

Abarhild leaned her weight on her stick, the corners of her mouth tugging downwards. 'Think about it, you stupid boy. Who will hold Donmouth minster after your father? Radmer would give it to Heahred tomorrow if he thought he could get away with it, just to spite Ingeld. If there's no one here, the arch-bishop will give it to some other friend of his, come the day. Hmm? Thought of that?' She stopped and breathed hard. 'Is that what you want? Forty hides of fine land, given to some stranger? What will you live on then?'

Athulf realized to his horror that the tears which had been threatening for some time were leaking, hot and painful, from the corners of his eyes. He sniffed, and swallowed hard. 'If I join the war-band the king will reward me.'

Ingeld shook his head. 'He won't, you know. There are too many others ahead of you. Ten years of peace!' He gave his habitual wry smile, and Athulf read it as mockery. 'Fine and well for the farmers, but the fighters are hungry and restless. The king has long run out of rewards.'

Abarhild thumped the tip of her stick on the floor. 'Enough of this. You wear me out, boy. You may be an accident, but you're still my grandson. You can't be your father's stable-hand forever.'

'I want—'

'You want!' Her voice had taken on a cruel edge of mimicry. 'You want to be a warrior. You and a hundred other idiot boys. Think Osberht has room for an untrained child like you?' She raised her voice. 'Come back here!'

Athulf was tugging the door open. But for all his inability to keep back the furious tears, he could not disobey that imperious note. He would not come back to her fireside, but he did stop and half turn round, his hand still on the latch. Abarhild's women were hovering outside, agog.

'I will write to the archbishop myself.' She looked very tired suddenly, and one of her women stepped through the doorway, pushing past Athulf, and helped her back to her stool. When she was seated again, she looked up at him, still poised on the threshold between anger and flight. 'You foolish little boy. When a man gives you a horse you don't stop to check its teeth. Thank him, and get in the saddle.'

Athulf could feel the women's eyes, inside the room and out, curious, judging. This couldn't be happening. 'Father?' He had never called Ingeld by that name before, and to his fury his voice gave its tell-tale swoop and break as he did so.

But despite the anguish in his son's voice Ingeld was spreading his hands and shaking his head. 'I'm sorry.' He seemed about to say something more, but in the end he just shrugged, and smiled.

32

Elfrun looked over her shoulder at the grey clouds to the west, and back to the deserted beach. She didn't think the sun had yet set, but, with that louring sky and the veils of rain that had draped themselves over the hills, who could tell?

A week of autumn storms, and she had spent most of it on the foreshore half a mile from here. Her hands were chapped and sore with salt and water, and a weary ache tugged across her shoulder blades, but the job was done, the whale-meat salted away in its barrels, the skeletons left on the beach above the high-water line to be picked clean by birds before being transformed into everything from weaving battens to writing tools. Another good source of profit in the York market.

Her father would be pleased.

Wrapping the thick red folds of the cloak around her, she padded down to the waterline, trying to keep her bare soles from skidding on the thickly plaited coils of weed that strewed the sand. Much more weed and many more shells than usual, the seabed churned by the force of wind and water, but the wind had died right back now and all was still, though the scent of rot was thick on the chilly air. Sea and wind were quiet for once, and the loudest sound was the trickle of the stream where it ran down from the hill and soaked into the sand.

She had a plaited-rush basket on her arm and a rake in her hand, and if anyone challenged her she planned to say that she was looking for cockles and razor clams. Rain was drifting in a slow grey smirr down on to the beach, and the daylight was failing fast.

At the bottom of the basket lay the mirror, ready to be returned to its owner. She set down rake and basket and pulled the mirror out from its hiding place.

Beautiful. The word had made itself a nest somewhere under her ribs, warm and curled like a fox cub in its den of dry leaves. All through that blood-soaked, back-breaking week she had been aware of it, and had found herself pausing in her work, the corners of her mouth tugging upwards, an answer to the memory of Finn's smile that came not so much as an image but as a rich, sleepy sensation that made her think of honey and drowsy, laden bees. The scent of meadowsweet, already half-forgotten on this dreary feast of All Hallows.

Beautiful. She peered at her frowning face, and shrugged, and turned the mirror over to look at the patterned side. Now this was beauty, if he wanted beauty. Her eyes danced along the lines, tracing those coils and whorls inscribed by some long-dead master who must have known what was in God's mind when He first drew up the plans for this shifting world, that never-ending pattern which reminded her of eddies in the river where it ran shallow, or the sky when fragile clouds were stirred by the winds of the upper air, harbingers of storm.

Fredegar had said that tomorrow they would celebrate another mass for the souls of all the faithful dead, both those whom they often commemorated and those whose names no one remembered any more. This was a new thing, this mass for All Souls, that they had started doing in the churches of Frankia. One of the many important matters of which the Northumbrian churches were ignorant, he had said, his nostrils pinched as though against a bad smell.

Forgotten souls. Those souls felt tangible in the twilight, by the ebbing sea, as though the gauzy pall of drifting rain were the veil between this world and the next. Perhaps that was what was meant by the patterns on the mirror, that everything was always changing, that everything you loved slipped away on the tide, the solid world proving itself liquid, vaporous, gone...

The mirror was cold in her hands, and she had a sudden horror of looking into it again, of what she might see.

Finn wasn't coming. Of course he wasn't.

The beach was almost dark, and she was a fool. The sun must have set long ago. The chill had seeped even into that little secret haven under her breastbone.

Shoving the mirror back into the basket, Elfrun walked out on to the flat grey sand and started raking furiously. The cockles were densely packed just under the surface, and she set her rake aside and squatted to burrow beneath and scoop up the thick, ridged shells with both hands before dumping them into the basket. Sand and shell further abraded the raw skin of her fingers but the pain came as a welcome distraction.

After some moments of furious activity Elfrun found herself calmer as well as warmer, and the sides of the rush basket were bulging. But half her haul was made up of wet sand, and she decided to go down to the edge of the ebb and wash the shells before lugging them back to the women's house. Her belly was growling, and she thought wistfully about prying open a few of the cockles there and then, but it would be hard work with just her little knife, and she knew fine well they would be full of tooth-cracking grit. Far better to take them back and rinse them properly, and steam them. Too late in the year for wild garlic, though there might be some dried leaves left in the store. Saethryth had brought some butter down from the sheepwick just the day before, warning that it would likely be the last of the season's. Butter, and a little salt. Her mouth watered.

She was soaked now, kneeling in the shallows with her skirt hoicked up, drenched from rain above and salt water below, the red cloak a heavy, dragging burden, matted and weary. She was glad he hadn't come. No one would think her beautiful this evening.

Finn. No other name. No people. Some unreliable vagrant of the roads. What did she care what he had said, anyway?

Hot tears pricked her eyes, and she had to sit back on her heels and wait for the iron grip around her ribs to ease. An errant wave ran up and over her feet, further drenching her hem, but she barely noticed. She could hardly be wetter, anyway.

Had she in fact come down to the sands too late? She had left the women's house as soon as she could decently get away, but perhaps the sun, invisible behind the lowering clouds, had set earlier than she had thought. Finn could have come and seen the beach empty, and left again, perhaps only moments before she herself had come hurrying down through the dunes.

She closed her eyes. Another wave ran over her toes.

'Lady?'

Elfrun scrambled to her feet, grabbing for rake and basket.

'Lady, the tide's coming in. I wouldn't have spoken, but...' The smith's girl. Wynn. Twisting her hands together and sounding embarrassed. 'I saw you from the top of the dunes, and you weren't moving, and the tide's coming in fast, your cloak was in the water, so I thought I'd just see...'

Elfrun could feel the blood rising and heating in her own face. 'I was washing cockles. Do you want to take some to your mother?'

They had begun to walk up the beach but Wynn stopped there, just before the dunes. 'I'll take them to my father, lady.'

'Is your mother still at her sister's, then?'

Wynn nodded.

'All right. Hold out your skirt.' As she shovelled handfuls of damp shells into the fold of cloth, Elfrun said, 'Your brother will be much missed at the forge. Has your father said anything about how he's going to manage without Cudda?'

Wynn contemplated the question, her pointed little face suddenly taut, eyes narrowed. 'Too soon to say, lady. It's only been a week. You leave us be for a bit.' Her gaze suddenly shifted. 'Lady...' she said on a panicky in-breath.

Elfrun half turned. And there he was, loping along the edge of the ebb-line, from the south.

'It's… Don't worry. I know him.' She set down the basket and rake, and raised a hand as he approached.

'Lady.' He bowed his head, grave and formal. 'I have kept you waiting, and I ask your pardon.'

She nodded, trying hard to mask her pleasure. How, in a week, had she forgotten his easy, light-footed grace, and the way that the curve of his eyebrow and cheekbone conspired to make his expression so warm and open even when, as now, he was not smiling?

She wanted him to smile.

More than that. Oh God, please, let him smile at *her*. She had been so cold and clenched, and now there was warmth in her veins, a bubble and a fizz and a lightness as though the dreich November had turned into May.

Gradually the world widened out again, and she became aware that Wynn was staring. She picked up her basket again and foraged beneath the layers of wet, sandy shells for the soggy little bundle of sacking. 'Here.'

Finn nodded and took the bundle from her, and she felt a pang. He shrugged off his pack and set it down on the drier sand of the dune-edge, before turning back and unwrapping her careful little parcel.

'I've taken good care of it.' How defensive she sounded.

'I've no fear of that, lady.' He was running his fingertip along the sensuous curve of the red-enamelled pattern, his face remote and thoughtful. Elfrun became aware of Wynn edging closer, her fists still bunching the cloth of her skirt to make a bag for the dragging weight of cockles, but all her attention on the mirror.

Finn glanced at the girl. 'You want to see?'

She nodded, speechless.

'Sit down.'

She subsided gracelessly, legs folding under her, her wet lap still heavy with shells, and Finn hunkered down and offered her the handle. Wynn used both her hands to hold the mirror, confident and enquiring; and Elfrun, watching her turn it this way and that, was startled by how much she minded seeing another woman handling it, even such an awkward, childish creature as this. The girl squinted at the polished bronze; and Elfrun was intrigued despite herself to observe that Wynn appeared more interested in the narrow edges than either the broad, engraved and enamelled surface or the burnished one.

She squatted, the better to look over the other girl's shoulder. 'What are you looking at, Wynn?'

'Cast handle.' The girl appeared to be talking to herself. 'But the flat bit is a sheet, beaten. How do you beat it so flat? See how they've fitted the one into the other?' Elfrun hadn't registered how the T-shape of the handle was more than simply beautiful, that it allowed the fragile front and back plates of bronze to be supported and braced. 'And three rivets… but the back was engraved before they ever riveted it…' Her voice faded away, and she had bent so low over the mirror that both it and her face were hidden by her lank brown hair.

Finn caught Elfrun's eye, and they stood up, leaving Wynn for a moment to her musing.

'Who is she?' His voice was low.

'The smith's girl.'

Finn nodded. 'That makes sense.'

Elfrun swallowed. 'It was her brother who died, last time – last week – when you—'

'Ah.' He nodded again. 'Hard times for Donmouth.' He glanced towards the dunes. 'Too dark now for visiting, but is tomorrow a better day, lady? Will I find a welcome under your mother and father's roof?'

Tomorrow? She had simply taken it for granted that he would be coming back to the hall with her now. Without realizing, she had clasped her hands tightly, one over the other, and she did her best now to relax them, to breathe, to speak with the ease and command which Abarhild had been trying so hard to teach her. 'My mother is dead. And my father is from home.'

Where had this man come from, that he didn't know that? 'I am lord in his absence.'

'You? The lord? I see.' He was silent for a moment. 'Then, like me, you know about shouldering a burden.' And at last she saw that radiant smile, and she could feel her own face lighting up in response. 'Has he gone far, your father?'

'Rome, on a special mission for the king.'

'And you are proud of him.'

She nodded, pressing her lips together hard and breathing deep through her nostrils. After a moment she said, 'It's strange with him gone. It's not just him – he's taken a few of his men, his sword-bearer – and so many of the hangings, and the cups, and the cushions... He needs to look good on the journey, and in Rome, to show the world that the legate of Northumbria's king is a man to be reckoned with. But Donmouth feels very' – she groped after the words – 'small and grey and – and *fragile* without him.' She stopped abruptly. She had never meant to say so much, and such vague, stupid things too.

But he was nodding, not laughing, and his face was interested. She found her breath catching in her chest.

'How much?' At the sound of Wynn's voice they both turned. Elfrun thought the girl had been asking the price of the mirror, and she bristled. But Wynn hadn't been talking to them. She was still looking hard at the mirror, and her voice sounded angry. 'How much tin?' She tilted it this way and that, peering at the surface, scowling hard.

'How would you make such a thing?' Finn went to crouch beside her again.

'Me?' Incredulity. 'I couldn't make this. I couldn't coax the metals to make this colour. The warmth of it!' She sounded more furious than ever. 'And look at it. Just *look*.' She thrust it up towards Elfrun, who peered obediently at the engraving. 'It's perfect. That pattern. *Perfect*. I could try for a month and not make lines like that. Not a single line.'

'I've seen a gospel book,' Elfrun said slowly. 'In St Peter's

Minster, in York. My uncle showed me. It had patterns like that.'

'A *book*.' Wynn's tone was rich with contempt. 'They say on vellum you can make a picture of anything, and if it goes wrong you can scrape it out and do it again. But this' – she gave the mirror an angry little shake – 'there's no room for a slip here. It won't forgive. This is a perfect thing. Take it away.' She shoved it, handle first, at Elfrun, who took it tenderly. 'It hurts me to look at it.'

Elfrun looked helplessly down at the little bronze object. She had thought it beautiful, but she had none of the sense of craftly achievement which was causing Wynn such anguish.

'You're a maker,' Finn said.

'I want to be.' The girl had gone sullen, her voice flat. 'But I'm not.'

'You can learn, though, can't you? If you truly love it, you can learn.'

A shrug, and a contemptuous glance.

Elfrun's temper flared at the girl's bad manners. 'Wynn! Show some courtesy to our guest.'

'Sorry, lady,' and she turned to Finn. 'Sorry I was rude.' The girl's voice was pure misery, and Elfrun was bitten by remorse.

'I'm sorry, too. I spoke more harshly than I meant,' she said. 'Go home now, Wynn. Take the cockles to your father.'

Wynn rose awkwardly to her feet, clutching the damp and sandy folds of her skirt around the sea-fruit. She ducked her head at Elfrun – 'Lady' – then nodded to Finn – 'Thank you' – before she turned and dashed away, sprinting up the slope of the dune despite her burden, as though she were some long-legged shore-bird.

'So,' Finn said.

They were alone, and Elfrun didn't know what to say. She looked down at the mirror, and then held it to out to him. 'I can't afford it. I should have said before—'

'You don't know the price.'

'It doesn't matter.' She was dreadfully embarrassed. 'You heard what Wynn said. It's a perfect thing. It's fit for the king's wife. You should take it to York, or Driffield, or bring it to the market at the next spring meeting.' She could hear herself babbling, and despised herself.

'I could do.' He folded his arms, ignoring the proffered mirror. 'But I don't know where I'll be, come the spring.'

'Not round here?' The words were startled out of her.

He smiled. 'Folk like me are like the swallows, Alvrun. Here for a season, but who knows where the winter might take us?'

'Will you really not come up to the hall now?' He shook his head, and she felt it like a blow. 'Then you must take this with you.' She held the mirror out to him again. 'I have to go. I need to take this lot home' – she gestured at the basket with her free hand – 'they'll be wondering where I've got to.'

'And where have you got to, Alvrun?' He was ignoring the outstretched hand, looking out at the dull grey water, his hair beaded with wet.

'What?'

'You're kind,' he said, 'which is more than beautiful.' He was hugging himself with his arms, not looking at her, and she turned to follow his gaze, towards the hungry, choppy waves. 'You said sorry to that child, and you didn't have to. She was rude, and you are her lord. You were well within your rights to rebuke her.'

'I – She – she's not having an easy time.'

'That was plain, for those who know where to look.' He sighed thickly. 'Keep the mirror for me. Keep it for the winter.'

'But what about tomorrow?' She could hear the anxious keen in her voice and tried to temper it. 'You'll come up to the hall for food and fire?'

'If I can.'

She wanted to cry out, to ask what might stop him, but she felt she had trespassed on his patience enough. 'And if not, you'll be back for it? In the spring?' Oh God, she was like one of Widia's hound-puppies, begging for scraps.

'I'll try.' He was nodding. 'Go home. Get dry. Eat your cockles.' He smiled, at last. 'Warm, with butter.'

She nodded, clinging to the smile and trying to muster one of her own in exchange. She knew she had already been dismissed, but she felt a terrible reluctance to leave him. Just one more smile, one more kind word?

'Go on,' he said.

'But—'

'Go.'

So she went, awkward, balancing the rake on one shoulder and lugging the cockle basket with its sacking-wrapped treasure tucked in safe on top, her wet skirts dragging at her thighs. Every few steps she turned and peered back through the thickening mist and dusk, but he wasn't looking at her, he was gazing out to sea, and he didn't turn or call her back. Before long the high curve of the dunes and the green-grey prickly grasses blocked him from her sight.

33

'Who's this, then?'

Athulf pulled his elbows in and stiffened his spine, but one man couldn't hide himself in a group of four, and the others had stepped away from him anyway. They had come in out of the freezing rain after a long and fruitless day trying to net duck in the marshes with the aid of a couple of dogs, and now they were jostling their way to the hearth, the others flinging down their sodden cloaks, talking big and shouting for a cup of ale.

He had been to Illingham a couple of times over the last few weeks, but had never yet been invited into the hall, and now he was trying not to stare. It was longer and higher than Donmouth's, with beams whose carving was fresh-painted; and where Donmouth was sparse and poor with the lack of Radmer's trappings, Illingham was a blaze of colour, with embroidered hangings on the walls and a finely worked cloth draped centrally over the high table. Smoke, and sweet hay crushed underfoot, and something good cooking.

'Go on, Thancrad. Where are your manners? Who's your new friend?'

A woman no taller than he was himself, round and soft, with black eyes in a doughy face, and a sweet smile. She was offering him a pottery cup, and he took it gratefully, realizing as he did so that the others had not yet been served.

'Be well, guest.'

He scrabbled after the proper reply. 'I drink your health,

lady.' He raised the cup and sipped. Mead, with a different blend of herbs from the little vats of Donmouth. Sweeter, and very much to his taste.

'See, Thancrad?' The little woman had turned. 'Some young men have lovely manners.'

'Athulf is my name, lady.' This must be Thancrad's mother. Switha of Illingham. He badly wanted her to think well of him.

'Let's get you out of your wet cloak.' She snapped her fingers and he relinquished the sodden square of wool into friendly hands. 'We'll hang it by the fire. Now, where are you from, Athulf? Who are your parents?'

'He's from Donmouth.' It was Addan or Dene speaking, from somewhere behind him. 'The abbot's son.'

His stomach tightened painfully, waiting for the cutting remark, the cold shoulder.

But her face lit up. 'Ingeld?' She made it sound as though this was the best news she'd heard all winter. She clasped his elbows and stared intently into his face. 'You're Ingeld's son? Of course you are! Look at you! How could I ever have missed that? The spirit and image of him. And you're wet through. Come and have a seat. There are some oatcakes, fresh from the stone.'

Confused and flattered, he let her lead him, chattering sweetly all the while, bring a creepie-stool forward with her own hands, refill the cup of mead. He hid his face, leaning forward and fiddling with the wet bindings round his calves, feeling as though all the world was mocking his hot cheeks.

The others were joining him, taking up all the space round the fire. One of the women was bringing more wood, feeding it carefully into the blaze. Thancrad's mother was at his elbow with hard cheese, more oatcakes, some relish of onion chopped with herbs. He was starving, and he ate and drank everything she offered. He was always hungry, and usually it felt as though there was not enough food in the world to satisfy him, but at last he shook his head, and she motioned away the woman with the basket of flatbreads.

'Now,' and she was sitting next to him. He looked down at the hand she had placed on his arm. A little, pale paw, broad with stubby fingers and tidy nails, Silver-gilt shimmered on one finger. 'Tell me about your dear father.'

'My father?' A wave of bitterness and exhaustion rolled over him. But she had called Ingeld *dear*. She wouldn't want to know his true thoughts.

'Is he settling into being the abbot of Donmouth?' She laughed, and her tone was warm and affectionate. 'It's so hard to imagine. Pious, virtuous... I remember how we all sighed over him, before I had to go away, when he was still only in minor orders. Of course, I was long married, and already a mother, but even so...' She shook her head. 'But he would never have looked at me, even then. I was never pretty enough to catch *his* eye.'

Athulf couldn't work out if she was praising his father or criticizing him. Whichever, it made him uncomfortable, and he wondered how old she was. It was so hard to tell with women; once they were veiled they all looked the same. As old as his father, by the sound of it, and his father had turned thirty last year. That was why they had made him be a priest. You couldn't be a priest until you were thirty. His cup was somehow full again. The others were talking over the day's adventures, the flocks of duck that had stubbornly dodged the net, the valour of one dog and the stupidity of the other, the hilarious moment when Addan had stumbled and tripped backwards into the bog.

'Ingeld's not pious,' he said. Despite everything Athulf felt the need to defend his father. 'He says mass, of course, but apart from that...'

Dene had hauled himself to his feet, re-enacting the story of Addan's fall. Misjudging his step, he collapsed heavily into Athulf's lap. Athulf's cup went flying from his hand, and to his horror he saw it land and break in two on the edge of the hearth.

He cowered, waiting for the reprimand. But it was Dene on whom Thancrad's mother turned her censure. 'Get off, you great oaf. That's no way to treat a guest. Let me get you a fresh cup, Athulf.'

So this was what it felt like, when you were the man who mattered most in a company. Warm, glowing, cosseted. Athulf thought he could easily get used to this. He looked across the fire to find Thancrad was watching them, his face solemn, hands loosely clasped between his knees. Thancrad could be such a bore, reining in him and the others. So serious, stern even, he reminded Athulf sometimes of Radmer at his humourless worst.

But he was being given no time to dwell on Thancrad's shortcomings. Switha was at his elbow again. 'Try some of this. It's a different brew. There's more meadowsweet in it.'

He sipped. Cloying and sticky and so sweet it set his teeth on edge. He drained it at a draught.

'I'm so glad that you and Thancrad have become such good friends. That was wonderful, you spotting the whales. That'll help us all through the winter. Tell me about it.'

'Yes,' he said. He wanted to say something interesting, so she would go on thinking him wonderful. 'I saw them first.' But his tongue was thick in his mouth, and he couldn't find the words.

It didn't seem to matter. She went on talking, asking more questions about the whale-drive, drawing him on to tell stories about his life, about Donmouth hall and minster. Shy at first, the words started coming willy-nilly. What it was like with Radmer gone. Cudda's death, and he felt the tears he had not yet shed prickle the corners of his eyes. How Abarhild and Ingeld between them had thwarted his hopes.

'But of course you must have a sword! Are there no swords left at Donmouth?' She pulled back and stared at him, those warm, dark eyes round with astonishment. 'Look at you! It's not just who you are – who your grandfather was – but such a promising young man…' Her eyes were flickering this way and that, assessing his shoulders, his thighs, her gaze as palpable as a spider darting over his skin. He sat up taller. She tutted. 'Why on earth would they think to make you a priest? You could have

Donmouth as a lay abbacy, if they put their minds to it. Surely Osberht would see the advantages to that? Whatever is Ingeld thinking of?'

'It's my grandmother.' He cradled his empty cup and tried to remember everything Abarhild had said. 'She says if I don't become a priest I won't get anything.'

'Abarhild.' There was contempt in her voice. 'That meddling old besom. She always did think she knew best.'

For all the fog and muzz of the mead, Athulf felt as though he had climbed a steep slope to emerge on a sunlit plateau with views to the far horizon. He had been trapped in confusion and anger for days. But it didn't have to be like that. *Meddling old besom.* The phrase was delightful. Everything was delightful. Switha was holding up a jug, those sparkling black eyes quizzical.

'There are swords at Donmouth,' he said slowly. 'But they're locked away.'

'And who has the key?'

Athulf opened his mouth to say that Elfrun and Abarhild had the keys to the hall heddern, but a sudden lurch of nausea prevented him. Switha had turned away to replace the jug and, looking across the hearth, he found Thancrad still watching him, the firelight flickering on his cheekbones. Thancrad's eyes narrowed, and he got to his feet. 'Come on.'

Athulf clenched his throat against another queasy surge, and he was only too relieved to let Thancrad steer him outside, into the chilly yard. He barely had time to register that the rain had stopped before he staggered and spewed heroically against the side of the hall. Retch after retch, until his throat and eyes were burning.

Thancrad was laughing softly under his breath. 'I was watching you putting it away. I knew there'd be trouble.' Laughing, but he sounded bitter rather than amused.

Athulf was cold and sweating, but now that the mead was out of his belly he was more master of himself. His first instinct was to swing his fist against Thancrad's face, but he reined that in, swallowing down the bile. When he could speak he said, 'Your mother is very kind.'

'My mother?' Thancrad was outlined against the open door of the hall, and Athulf couldn't see his expression. 'Yes, she's very good at drawing people to her. I can see why you'd like her.'

People? He wasn't *people*. Athulf needed very badly to think that Switha's smiles, her questions, that assessing, admiring gaze, had all been special, all been for *him*.

34

'Come to bed, wife.'

Saethryth was sitting between him and the hearth, a dark shape with a faint golden outline. She had said she was going to finish her carding, but he had been watching her ever since lying down himself, and she had not moved, combs and fleece left untouched in the basket at her side. Her back was to him, and she sat with her arms around her knees, gazing into the little fire. If she wasn't working, she should come to bed. She still had her dress on over her linen and a shawl around her shoulders, as though she had no idea that he was waiting for her.

If he reached out his arm his fingertips would graze her back, and yet he felt as though there was a yawning gap between them, one that he could not bridge.

Hirel propped himself up on one elbow. 'Wife?'

She neither moved nor answered, and this annoyed him. The night was cold, and he wanted her body next to his, to warm him as much as for his pleasure and the kindling of the child he wanted so badly. And she was sitting so as to block the little heat from reaching him. 'Bank the hearth and come to bed.'

She responded with a shrug of her shoulders that could have been designed to anger him, but he was determined not to let her goad him to fury, not this time. Tucked in the pouch around his neck was the silver penny that Luda had finally handed over, and Hirel came to an uncharacteristically sudden decision. Putting a smile on his wife's face was not something that could wait until the first merchant ship or wandering pedlar came by in the spring when the sea-roads reopened. Give her the penny, and she could pass the winter with the pleasure of planning and choosing for herself.

'Do as you're told...' He paused. '... and I've a gift for you, wife.'

That shrug again.

'Wife?'

She muttered something.

'What?'

'Stop calling me that!'

Hirel felt an increasingly familiar surge of fury rising up from some pit of fire deep inside him, and he forced himself to keep breathing, to swallow it back. Shouting at her had got him nowhere. 'Be firm with her,' Luda had told him, 'that lass needs a strong hand. Belt her if need be.' But if he yelled at her, she just screamed back at him; and the one time he had taken her father's advice and given her a smack she had brooded and huffed, and refused to let him near her for days on end. That had been a few weeks back, when he had first brought the flocks down to graze the home fields, and the blow had come because he had been so hurt and angry at her chilly welcome.

'Saethryth? Look.'

He was fumbling with the tight thongs of the pouch, all his attention engrossed in unpicking the hard little knots. But, when he looked for her again, the silver penny pinched between his clumsy, stained fingertips, she was gone. The door was settling back on its leather hinges.

Hirel swore. His first thought was to go after her, and then he felt aggrieved again. He was bone-weary, and the heap of blankets, topped with a couple of sheepskins, was only just warming up. This wasn't what he had bargained for when he and Luda had gone to Elfrun to tell her that the marriage was in the wind and Saethryth was willing.

Willing.

He swore again, and shoved the blankets to one side.

Outside the house the night was even colder, the heavens clear and a filling moon tangled in the top branches of the elder thicket. There would be ice on the puddles come the morning. Somewhere off to the west a vixen barked. Hirel turned east and south, he wasn't sure why, towards the sheep-track that led ultimately down to the minster pastures. He trod softly, bare feet careful on the slick grass, but if she wanted to avoid him it would be easy enough, he knew. He was a big dark shape lumbering and crunching though the silver night.

Was he even going in the right direction? He stopped, and peered back up the slope. The moon was bright enough to cast a long shape, and he could see nothing moving, nor could he make out any huddled shadow that might be Saethryth holding her breath, waiting until he had gone.

What was wrong with the woman?

He was a good catch, a steady worker, a free man. He was young and healthy. There were sheep of his own running among those of hall and minster. He might not have the standing of her father, but he had thought her glad enough to get away from under her parents' roof. You didn't have to stand and gossip like the old women to know that Luda had a heavy hand. You only had to be near the steward's house with a pair of ears on you. His wife fought back, though. That would be where Saethryth had learned her shrill curses.

Married all these weeks, and he'd only smacked her once. She should be counting her blessings.

Hirel carried on down the hill, for lack of a better option. She could have gone down the other track, the one that led to the hall. Back to her parents' house, as well, though. Or turned uphill, and followed the winding path that climbed at last to reach the summer pasture. But she would find no shelter up there, not in December.

He wanted to call her name, but the midwinter night was too huge and silent. He felt as though his voice would be swallowed up by the moonlit emptiness. What if he tried to shout and no sound came from his lungs?

'Wife?' His voice was tentative enough. But she'd asked him not to call her that, though he loved its soft syllable. 'Saethryth?' The land rose before falling away again, and from here he could see the moonlight on the still waters of the sea, a silver streak on the horizon. The cold in the back of his nostrils told him again that ice was coming.

How far did Saethryth expect him to follow her? Hirel had thought he would have found her by now, waiting for him, chilled and penitent, wanting him to plead with her just once more to come home. He thought with a sudden savage pleasure of the satisfaction it would give him to put a ring in her nose and a rope through it, force her to do his will that way, as though she were one of the beasts.

The beasts were so much easier.

And he had had enough. He was cold, and his bed was waiting for him. From here the path went down into the stands of timber, and she could be hiding anywhere. She could play her stupid little games on her own. Hirel turned abruptly, and as he did so he stumbled. The silver penny, which he had forgotten he was clutching between his cold fingers, flew into the sagging tangles of winter grass.

Hirel stared after it in disbelief. There would be no finding it, not in this light which made everything shine silver. But that didn't stop him from falling to his knees and rummaging through the dead grass after the little hammered disc of metal. Fruitless, and he knew it, and after a few moments he stopped and sat back on his heels.

Above, the silver circle of the moon mocked him.

Hirel wept.

35

Fredegar was alone in the church, broom in hand. He had been sweeping every corner of the muck and wind-blown detritus that constantly found its way in, despite his constant sharp words to the other clerics, especially the two boys. They never kept the door closed, and the birds had been constantly swooping in and out, soiling the altar.

The door was open now, but that was only because without the light that came through it he could not see to clean this hovel that passed for God's house in Donmouth. The last of the old season's filthy rushes had already been heaped and were outside the door, ready to be carted to the midden. A fitting job for Lucymas, the darkest day of the year. Lucy, whose very name meant *light*. The returning sun would shine on a clean church, whether the abbot liked it or not.

Like it? Ingeld wouldn't even notice.

His jaw was tense and his hands had tightened around the broom handle as though it were a weapon. Fredegar was finding it hard to breathe. He knew his anger with Ingeld was what kept him going, a source of dark energy on which he could draw when the shadows started closing in again. But he also knew that it was a sin, and a danger. Spend too long wandering down that path, and he might never find his way back.

He began sweeping again, focusing on long, even movements of the broom as though each one were the strophe of a prayer, and slowly the hard heat around his heart began to ease. The dirt floor would never be really clean, and the thatch of the church roof had been full of mice since the first frost. The sparrows congregated up there as well: he could hear their cheeping now, and he wished the folk of Donmouth spent half as much time singing in their church as those little grey-brown birds did. Fredegar stopped sweeping, a smile almost forming on his face at the thought of the busy feathered flock in the roof at their ceaseless devotions, despite all the work they gave him.

His face grew sombre again.

Only the previous day, after supper in the minster hall, he had suggested to Ingeld that come the good weather they might replace the thatch. 'Look at it, Father abbot. Sagging, so thick with moss, almost black in places! And it lets the water in.'

Ingeld hadn't even turned to face him. 'Order the reeds cut, then.'

'I had thought perhaps oak shingles...' Donmouth great hall, Radmer's hall – that had shingles. No birds there that he had ever seen, and few signs of mice. The hall also had beautifully carved barge-boards and elaborate finials.

'If you pay for them.' Ingeld had pushed past him and out into the yard.

He pay for them? He had nothing of any value but his books: his psalter, his gospels, and his battered penitential... Did the abbot mean he should sell those to pay for timber? He was sure he could find a buyer for them, in York, but why should he? He didn't need them – the words they contained were inscribed on his heart – but he loved them. Cold, sick fury sat in his belly as he stood in the doorway and watched Ingeld stroll away.

Fredegar began sweeping again, short vicious jerks of the twigs against the packed dirt. Bare earth. Bare earth and thatch for God's own house. Ingeld's own snug little hall might be thatched, too, but at least it had floorboards... Again, he forced himself to be calm. No merit in gouging little ruts in the consecrated floor.

After he had finished sweeping he would have to put his mind to the altar furnishings. The cloths were of fine quality, but old, dotted with ancient stains of wax and smoke, threadbare in places, their embroideries unravelling. In the dark of the church one hardly noticed their maculate state, but he had had them out into the light and he found it painful to look at them. He would talk to his *domina* Abarhild.

Wooden candlesticks.

A chalice of horn. Base horn, for the *Sanguis Christi*.

Only the processional cross had any beauty or richness in its making, and that had been the minster's chief treasure since long before Ingeld had been born. Heahred had told him it had been a battle standard in its day, carried against the Mercians a hundred years ago and more. Certainly the prayer inscribed along its arms, *Rise up, Lord, and scatter thy foes*, was as fit for a fight as a mass.

Three months, he had been putting up with all this. Quite long enough.

As the strokes of his broom brought him gradually closer to the door Fredegar became aware of an unexpected shadow, long in the solstice light that shone from low in the south. Certainly, someone was waiting outside. Someone restless and fidgety, to judge from the shadow's twitching. Had one of his flock summoned up the courage to consult him? Fredegar rested the besom against the wall and walked towards the door. His bare feet were almost silent, but as he came to the threshold the shadow darted away, and when he ducked under the thatch and squinted into the cold December sunlight he found the churchyard deserted. He peered to right and left. The frost was still thick on the grass, and he could see where feet had left their marks, but that shy visitor must have run with the speed of the wind.

Fredegar let out a long sigh. If someone among his folk had a troubled conscience he could only hope that whoever it was, man or woman, would find the courage to come back. He turned towards the church door again to finish his chores, and as he did so his eye fell on a small, ragged object just outside the doorway.

A scrap of brown sacking, carefully tucked around its contents.

He picked it up gingerly, not knowing what it might contain, but the edges of the cloth unfurled to reveal a little cross, carved of bone, on a leather thong. A simple enough object, but made with some skill, highly polished and symmetrical. As he turned it in his hands, his brow furrowing, he realized that it had exactly the same proportions as the minster's great treasure, the gilt-bronze processional cross, the same flared arms and pattern of little bosses. Someone had been observing minutely, and working with great patience, to make a gift that he might cherish.

But who? Which of Donmouth's residents would take time out of their winter evenings to make a thoughtful offering to their foreign priest? The cross swung back and forth on its leather thong, teasing him.

A gift from an unknown hand was a disturbing thing. He did not know, by accepting it, to what obscure compact he might be setting his own hand. If such a gift had been left for Ingeld he would have been in no doubt that it was some light love token, from one of those shuffling, giggling girls who swarmed at the hall. But there was nothing, surely, in his own aspect or behaviour to prompt such inappropriate devotion. They shied away from him, rather. He was sure the story of Cudda's death had lost nothing in the telling.

Still, Ingeld's folly cast a long shadow.

Lucymas, and the shortest day, and this was the first time in all the long weeks Fredegar had been at Donmouth that anyone other than Elfrun and Abarhild had lifted a hand to make him feel welcome. At last, shrugging and still thoughtful, he slid the little knots together and eased the thong over his head to settle around his neck, the cross tucked out of sight under his robe. From whatever source, it was welcome.

But he paused again in the doorway before going back into the church, feeling the shape of the cross under the coarse wool of his robe. Were his first instincts wrong? Could Abarhild have left it, or asked someone to leave it for him? Possible, of course, always possible, but his instincts told him otherwise.

If his *domina* wished to make him a gift, there would be no subterfuge. Elfrun, then? He had wondered about her, her clear singing voice and the regularity with which she obeyed her grandmother's request for her to attend the offices several times in the week, despite the long walk and the many responsibilities which visibly burdened her. He would look up sometimes to find her disconcerting brown gaze fixed on him, as though she could see every mote of dust and cobweb that cluttered the darker corners of his soul. He knew Abarhild had been considering a convent for the girl, and he thought it would be a wise choice. She felt too deeply, that one.

But no. The little bone cross surely did not come from her. Like Abarhild, if Elfrun wished to present him with a gift she would do it openly.

Someone else cared enough to make him that small donation. As he went back into the church and began readying the altar Fredegar had tears in his eyes.

36

Elfrun traced her fingertip around the whorls and curves incised into the bronze. Finn had not come back. All that long day of All Saints, and the next, and a few days after that, she had been hoping every moment that he might yet come through the gate and into her yard.

But that had been weeks and weeks ago; and now, with Yule and Candlemas behind them, try as she might, she could barely recall the details of Finn's face, and that troubled her. Nonetheless, looking at the mirror was a certain way of summoning once again that unfamiliar sensation of heat and light which his presence had given her. Sunlight glinting on the golden hairs of his arm as he drew the silk ribbons over his skin. The warmth of his hand pressing her fingers around the mirror handle. She could close her eyes and breathe in, letting the memories course along her veins, until she felt like a flower unfurling its grateful petals and opening itself to the generous sun.

Somehow she had managed to keep the mirror a secret all winter. Without having to ask she knew that Wynn had told no one. Taking it out and examining its patterns had become her great pleasure, all the more intense for being rare and guilty. She might spend a little time looking at her own softened and gilded features, searching for whatever the pedlar had called 'beautiful', but her reflection never held her for long.

No, the real attraction the mirror offered was its other side, those harmonious curves, one endlessly flowing into the next without seam or break, no beginning and no ending, and all perfect proportion and grace. The more she contemplated the pattern, the more certain she was that it encoded some secret, one that she could unlock if only given time enough and calm.

But, oh, God, how she wanted Finn to come back. She talked to him constantly in her head, telling him things that she could mention to no one else. How weary she was, how busy and how bored. Luda's frustrating evasions, the way he told her in so many words not to make such a fuss about nothing; that he had everything in hand. Fredegar was teaching her how to read, and how to tally, but it was a slower and more painful business than she had ever imagined. And Luda's records were kept according to some arcane formula he seemed to have drawn up himself, and she didn't understand.

When she said as much, however, the steward had shrugged, and told her that Radmer never bothered checking the details. 'Your father lets me do my work.' That unnerving stare from eyes set too close together for comfort. 'You should do the same, lady.'

Everything would be fine, surely, once Radmer returned?

Elfrun spent far too much time looking out, down the wintry, windswept river and estuary, to the open sea, and if she was honest with herself she admitted she was no longer sure whether she was looking for her father, or Finn. But the last few weeks had been proving dark and wet and muddy beyond belief, and Elfrun knew that she was a fool to imagine any ship would put into their harbour, or for that matter any wanderer of the roads would be seen at Donmouth, before Eastertide.

She sighed. There would be a long Lent first.

A clatter and a scuffle, and Elfrun hastily wrapped the mirror in a length of ragged linen and tucked it at the bottom of her box. Shoving the box away she scrambled to her feet, hot and confused. 'Am I needed?'

Saethryth was in the doorway, gesturing. 'Are you blind or something?' Elfrun had never even noticed the goat that had wandered in and was now nosing enquiringly at the nearly finished length of tabby on the loom. They shooed it out together, and Elfrun closed the latch firmly behind her. Had Saethryth seen the mirror? Surely not – she had been crouched with her back to the door; and if the other girl had caught a glimpse she would surely have asked what it was.

There was nothing wrong in what she had been doing; surely there was nothing wrong. But for all that, she didn't want to share her secret with anyone else. And especially not Saethryth. What was she doing down here anyway?

Coming out of the women's house and peering at the leaden sky Elfrun found the morning further advanced than she had thought. Fredegar had promised her a Latin lesson after terce, and she would need to make all decent haste. But first she needed to go back to the heddern to fetch the neatly folded lengths of linen she had promised her grandmother. New cloths to embroider for the altar, Abarhild had said. And Fredegar was quite right, her grandmother had added, their little church was a disgrace.

It was the closest she had ever heard her grandmother come to criticizing Ingeld.

The three miles to the minster were claggy underfoot, and Elfrun was hot-faced and breathless when at last she raised her free hand to knock on her grandmother's door, which was standing ajar. At that precise moment, a voice spoke, harsh with anger and only just the other side of the wood.

'You should have had me gelded then, as well as tonsured. I've always said Radmer would have been the better priest.'

She jumped backwards and stared at the door.

Her grandmother's reply was inaudible.

'You did it to me, and now you're doing it to Athulf. And Elfrun too, from what I hear.' Elfrun had been about to retreat, but the sound of her own name trapped her like a bird in lime. 'Just because they wouldn't let you stay at Chelles—'

'Athulf would make an excellent priest, given time and training.' That was loud enough.

'Excellent?'

'Good enough.'

'Just like me, then.' A creak of the floorboards.

'He knows I have his interests at heart.'

'Really? Are you sure of that, Mother?'

There was a long silence, and then a muttered, incoherent response from Abarhild. When Ingeld answered he sounded weary.

'Then you should have let me marry. You and your ambitions.'

This time her grandmother's voice was perfectly clear. 'As if wedding would have stopped you. You've broken every other promise you've ever made.'

'I only gather fallen apples, Mother.' He paused, and when he spoke again his voice had softened. 'Besides, this one's different.'

'*Fallen apples?* She's still a bride.'

'She's no innocent.' Still that smile in his voice.

There was a pause, then Abarhild, snappish: 'That's not what I meant. I know that girl, remember. You're not giving that marriage a chance.'

'You don't understand. This one's different. Not since Athulf's mother—'

'I don't want to lose you.' Abarhild voice cracked with emotion. 'In this world or the next.'

There was silence.

Elfrun could feel her cheeks heating still further. A sudden horror of being caught eavesdropping had her backing away from the threshold, still clutching the now crumpled linen. She turned to find Fredegar contemplating her from the door of the church, his psalter in his hand.

'Next,' the priest said quietly, 'my lord abbot will protest how sorry he is, and she will say she's ashamed to have given birth to him and make him promise to stop, and he will tell her he's her good boy.' Fredegar's fastidious tones told Elfrun more than she wanted to know.

'This happens often.'

'Let us say I've heard it before.' The priest jerked his head. 'Come on. Don't worry about him.'

Elfrun flinched at the cold distaste in Fredegar's voice. 'He'll have to behave better when my father comes home.' Ingeld's words were still ringing in her ears. *This one's different...* Who could the woman be, to have put such a soft edge on her uncle's wry, mocking voice? But she couldn't imagine asking such a question of the sallow, austere man walking at her side.

'Your father coming home. Would that change the way the abbot behaves?'

She looked at him in surprise. 'Of course. Everyone always does what my father tells them to.'

Fredegar was silent. They went into the church, and Fredegar lit a candle. She joined him in a brief prayer to St Agatha, on this her feast day, and Elfrun settled herself on the bench that ran along the north wall of the church, looking up at Fredegar expectantly, more than ready for the distraction of Latin verbs. But instead of sitting down beside her and opening the book as usual he stood looking down at her, a frown pulling his dark brows together and making him look more aquiline than ever.

'What is it, Father? Is it too dark to read? Should we light more candles?' He was silent for a moment; then to her surprise he reached under the collar of his robe and tugged a leather thong over his head. A little bone cross dangled before her eyes. 'What's that?'

'You didn't make it?'

'No.'

'You haven't seen it before? Are you sure?'

She was indignant. 'Why are you asking? Where did it come from?'

Fredegar jerked his chin towards the door. 'Come on.'

'But it's too cold outside!' Elfrun was confused. 'The wind's right off the sea this morning.'

'The wind here is always off the damned sea.' Fredegar was already standing in the open door. 'I shouldn't go on teaching you, not until we know whether your father would approve.'

'But—'

'And I shouldn't be alone with you. Your uncle's reputation taints all Donmouth minster.'

'Reputation. You mean...?' Elfrun frowned at him. 'People would never believe that of you!'

He tilted an eyebrow. 'Of course they would. And you as well. They're probably gossiping already. Don't be childish. You're not a child.'

Elfrun pulled herself up tall. 'Of course I'm not a child.'

'Your grandmother has been talking of making you a nun. She has the right of it. Why didn't your father send you to some convent, for safety, before he left?'

'Because my father wants me to run the hall. This is where I belong.' She shook her head. 'What do you mean, making me a nun?'

'Would that be so bad? Leaving you here, in charge of this' – he gestured broadly in the direction of the hall – 'it's lunacy. What if the sea-wolves attacked?'

'The sea-wolves haven't attacked our shores for a decade,' she said furiously. 'And besides—'

'Not yours perhaps.'

'Our king is too strong—'

'You have no idea what you're talking about.' The flat certainty in his voice startled her into silence. 'Do you think they've gone away? Ask the men of Kent. Ask the traders of Dorestad. Ask the brethren of Redon, or Saint-Florent.' He paused, and then added, 'Or my own old home of Noyon.'

She felt numb with sudden fear, lips cold and belly tight. 'What – what happened at Noyon?'

Fredegar closed his eyes. She waited, but in the end, eyes still closed, he just shook his head.

'It might help you,' she said hesitantly, 'to unlock...' She was afraid of blundering in, but she couldn't imagine that it was good for him to bar and bolt himself away like that. But she was equally afraid of what he might have to say, if he did decide to tell her about the scenes which she was convinced were play-ing themselves out behind his eyelids. 'Father?'

Slowly he opened his eyes. 'I am sorry, child. I didn't mean to frighten you. But as to why you are still in the house of your father – well, it puzzles me. And until he returns, no more Latin lessons.' He was already at the door. She tried to hide her anger, bred from disappointment. He was Abarhild's servant to com-mand, not hers.

'But what about the counting, and the record-keeping?'

'No.'

'What if I ask my grandmother to chaperone me?'

But he shook his head.

37

Luda tugged the cloak more tightly around his head and shoulders. He knew he was a distinctive enough figure, with his thick grey curls and his limp, but he had hopes, on this dreich evening, of passing unremarked by curious eyes. There was a whole quarter, in the lee of York's great minster, of craftsmen and artists who served the archbishop, and also the king and the great men of the court. One of them was his cousin, Beonna, a fine leather-worker who could make a beautifully patterned cover for a little gospel-book as easily as shape a gauntlet for a falconer.

Luda had been the lynchpin in cutting a deal for Donmouth that meant Beonna had first claim on the best of their lamb-skins. A good deal for Radmer; a good one for Beonna; and happy clients who could rely on the quality of raw material and craftsmanship alike. And a very good deal for Luda. For the last several lambing seasons Beonna had been accepting some of the finest of both tanned and tawed skins from Donmouth's flock above the board, and just a few below, with the silver from the latter finding its way into Luda's pouch. A little, thin-voiced, singing-jingling trickle of possibility, getting faintly but steadily sweeter, year on year on year.

But things were different now. Better. The shepherd was bound to him by kinship ties. Radmer had gone away. And the old witch had gone into retirement at the minster, leaving that arrogant snip of a girl in charge. Elfrun, who thought she knew everything that was needed to run hall and estate. Luda snorted. That little trickle could be enticed to run more freely now.

To get to the craftsmen's quarter the path took his feet past the office of the archbishop's own officious steward and, though there was no good reason for anyone to object to him visiting his cousin, Luda pulled his cloak even tighter.

Radmer trusted him, without question. They had been boys together.

Radmer was a fool.

Big, stupid Radmer, who saw enemies everywhere outside his own bounds, and never stopped to think that the people who hated him most might be right under his nose. Radmer, who took his health and his wealth and power for granted.

Luda knew he would never take his silver for granted. Sometimes he lifted his little bag of coins down from the rafters while his household was snoring, and took it out into the chicken run at night to let the little discs flow through his fingers; and nothing in all his forty-odd years had ever given him so much pleasure. He didn't even know exactly what he was going to do with the money. It represented wonderful possibilities, the idea of freedom, a sweet embodiment of his own superiority, his greater cunning.

Freedom. Whatever that meant.

No, he knew. Getting away from being Radmer's enforcer, from the menial round of stewardship. And more: away from the sharp-tongued, grey-faced woman he was married to, and the endless procession of babies. Seventeen years of babies, puking and screaming, and half of them dying, and nothing to look forward to when they did come through but sulky, ungrateful creatures that glowered at him to his face and slacked in their work when they thought he wasn't looking.

Luda knew he had a name for being a heavy father, and he despised the people who criticized him for it. Give them a daughter like Saethryth, and see how they responded.

One possibility would be to go south, to one of the rich monasteries of Lindsey, to Bardney or Louth or Caistor, hand over his purse and retire, much as that old besom Abarhild had done at Donmouth. Nothing to do but sit in the sun or by the fire, depending on the season, rest his ever-painful leg, shuffle through a few services, let someone bring him a bowl of broth morning, noon and night.

The vision had its charms.

But not yet, and certainly not while Radmer was still away.

He had twenty-five silver pennies. Once it would have seemed wealth beyond all dreaming. Now he knew he would not be content until he had fifty.

He ducked down the narrow alleyway that led to his cousin's house and workshop, in the muddy triangle of land between the rivers. Bad for flooding, but good for business, with the ships putting into the low, shelving river foreshore that made a fine trading station. And closely managed by the archbishop's steward, but not closely enough, not for men who knew a thing or two.

Beonna didn't even look up as Luda stooped under the lintel of the workshop that fronted his lodging.

'Did you bring them?' His lack of teeth slurred his words. The little room was gloomy, smelling of old leather and damp thatch.

'Yes.' Luda unhooked the satchel and brought out the sheaf of skins.

At that Beonna did turn round, his forehead corrugating. 'These your best?'

'Some of them.' He grinned.

'I thought you weren't coming.' Beonna indicated the rush-lights. 'Too dark to work. I've been hanging on, waiting for you.' He sniffed. 'Wouldn't have been the first time.'

Been waiting, had he? Then let him wait. Beonna thought he was an important man because king and archbishop sent their servants to him. Let him learn how dependent he was on getting the finest lamb-leather, at a price that meant he could undercut those ever-hungry rivals. A place in the archbishop's quarter always attracted envy. Luda riffled the sheaf of lambskins knowingly. 'Want to check their quality?'

Beonna just grunted and held out a thick-veined hand. He took his time, running his fingers over hairside and skinside, looking for holes, wrinkles, flexing each sheet and tilting it this way and that in the dim, guttering light.

Let him look. Luda knew these half-dozen skins were flawless. He had done the same himself, and in full daylight.

Beonna sniffed again but he said nothing, and Luda felt a little thrill of satisfaction. His cousin had been longing to find some flaw that would mean he could beat down the price, and he had found nothing.

'Is this all? I had a dozen from you last year. Of the special ones.' Beonna winked, and Luda grinned back at him.

'Another twenty of this quality. Around forty almost as good.'

That surprised him. 'Sixty? Below the board, you mean? So many?'

Luda shrugged. 'A bad year for the lambs, according to my records. A good year for you and me.'

'And Radmer gone to Rome.' Beonna sucked his gums and nodded.

'As you say.' Their eyes met in full understanding.

'What about the girl?'

'As simple as her father. She doesn't understand the half I tell her.'

'And the shepherd married your daughter, I hear.' Beonna's face took on a knowing expression. 'Keeps him too busy for the flock, does she? I've heard other things, as well.' He dropped a wink.

Luda sat up straighter. 'What have you heard?'

Beonna raised a hand. 'Steady! I don't reckon much to idle chatter, you know me too well for that.'

The man did little else, when he wasn't at his bench. But Luda knew he would do better to swallow the lie. 'You've heard something.'

Another of those crude, lingering winks. 'We know your shiny new abbot fine well in York, remember.' The next wink was augmented by a toothless smirk. 'He comes by here often enough. He buys my work. A man of taste. Gloves. Shoes. We all like to hear that he's happy.'

Luda was thinking fast, feeling for what the man was saying in the gaps between his words. He waved a hand, pretending that none of what Beonna was saying was new to him, or interesting. 'Let's get back to the lambskins.' He reached out a hand. 'Seen enough?'

Beonna shrugged. 'I'll take what you can give me.'

'Price?'

'Same as last year. I can give you bronze now, or silver later.' Beonna riffled through the skins again.

'The same?'

'No. You can have more if you take bronze.'

Luda narrowed his eyes. The handy little bronze coins from the York mint were useful where the rule of Northumbria's king held good, but he knew fine well they were sneered at south of the Humber. 'Silver. I'll be back in two weeks with the rest.'

'I hope you've a safe place for all that silver.' Beonna shook his head. 'What are you going to do with it?'

But two could play at that old game of never giving a straight answer. Luda just shrugged and turned away.

38

After a winter of the stuff Abarhild was so sick of eating whale.

Not so much the flavour, though that had palled long ago in the dark, hungry days of midwinter. The chewing. Hard enough for those with their full complement of teeth, she thought angrily. One of her women had stewed the air-dried leathery strips all day to make something she could mince and manage, but Abarhild tilted the bowl and supped out the broth alone, leaving the indigestible nuggets for someone else. Sunday had come at last, and she surely deserved something better after the six long hungry days of the Lenten week. Fredegar had suggested she fast before mass, but that was one reform she couldn't hold with.

The world was coming out of winter, with the equinox in sight, and Easter itself less than two weeks the other side of it. Celandines were flowering on the sunny side of the sheltered ditches, and every bush was full of busy nest-building. But for some reason the spring warmth wasn't reaching her bones, and Abarhild pulled her stool closer to the hearth.

'Careful, my lady!' Her woman was at her side, steadying her. 'We don't want you falling in the fire!'

They were both silent for a moment.

'It's nearly time for mass,' her woman went on at last, offering Abarhild her stick. And indeed, the minster bell was loud and close. 'You'll enjoy that.'

'I'm not going.' She took the stick and planted it in front of her, both hands gripping hard.

'Forgive me, my lady?'

'I said I'm not going.' Abarhild looked discontentedly at the concerned face, pink and foolish, looming over her. 'It's too cold in that hovel of a church.' She pulled her woollen wrap more securely around her. 'Who's singing mass, anyway?'

'Father abbot, my lady. Your son Ingeld. Let me help you up.'

'I know who the abbot is, you gabbling fool.' Abarhild shifted away from the source of her annoyance. 'And I'm not going. You go. Tell him I'm not well.'

'But I can't leave you if you're not well!'

'Then tell him I'm too tired. Tell him anything you like. Just get out.' She raised her stick.

Her woman backed away, and bolted.

Abarhild stared at her hands where they clutched the smooth blackthorn. Her hands were famously white and smooth, long-fingered and skilful, with oval nails which her women rubbed with sweet oil until they shone. She was proud of them, she deployed them artfully when she spoke in the hall, lifting her arm in a practised gesture so that the embroidered linen fell back, exposing the pale skin; and her gold rings and gleaming nails scattered the firelight. At the harp. At the loom. Reaching out to move a gaming-piece triumphantly across the board. Those were her hands. Who had stolen them, and replaced them with these useless lumps of gnarled wood, hideous with their veins, their massive knuckles and withered skin? Once she had thought there could be no worse fate than being taken from her cloister. But this was worse. What sorcerer had done this to her hands?

She began to struggle to her feet. The stool shifted behind her, but she managed somehow to keep her balance. Her hands – no, not her hands, those travesties that belonged to some old woman, not her, never her – groped for her stick. When had she started to use a stick? Something was terribly wrong.

Someone was behind her, supporting her. Strong arms. Gentle. 'Grandmother? Are you all right?'

'Yes,' she said.

That boy. Ingeld. No, Ingeld was her son. Her darling son. Her last-born. It couldn't be Ingeld. Why would he call her grandmother? That other boy... a dear, good boy, angel-faced, They said he was wild. But it was right and proper that boys should have a spark about them. She had always liked the wild ones. Not girls. Girls shouldn't be wild, for their own good.

Her wild boy. What was his name?

'Grandmother, there's a boat in the bay! We think it's my uncle come home!'

And at that some of the fog cleared.

'Radmer,' she said. 'Oh, dear God. At last.'

The boy – Athulf, that was it – was helping her out into the sunlight. Her eyes watered with the brightness of it.

'They're just harnessing the oxen, Grandmother.'

'You don't want him to come home, all you little foxes,' she said, loud and clear. 'You've been having a splendid time while the wolf's away.'

Silence, but for the *tee-ick tee-ick* of an alarmed lapwing, somewhere down by the shore.

The boat was a pot-bellied coaster, ugly but serviceable. It stood out in the estuary while one of the Donmouth four-oared fishing boats was rowed over with Luda aboard. They watched the steward standing unsteadily in the rocking bow of the little vessel and shouting up at its captain, but they could hear nothing of the words. Elfrun observed the little glinting rills of the waves coming over the mudflats, and thought back to the day her father had left. Was it truly only half a year? What a child she had been. Her only thought then had been to please him, and do as she was told. She looked sideways at Athulf. He still looked like a child, beardless and soft-chinned for all the greater breadth and height, but he had changed too.

Luda was shouting at his oarsmen now, and the boat's prow was turning. No one new had scrambled over the strakes and down into the little shell. Elfrun scanned the ship again, looking for her father's familiar bulk, for a second boat putting out, but as far as she could see there was nothing.

A cold hand gripped her heart. Was this ship bringing the bad news she had been telling herself and everyone else was never going to come?

'Father abbot, there's a gift for you aboard, the man says, from friends to the north.'

'For me?' Ingeld's voice was urbane as ever but Elfrun could not miss the relief on his face. 'From whom?'

Luda jerked his head. 'They're coming. It's a Frisian trader, been up to Tayside over the winter and heading homeward now.'

And indeed even as he spoke the little broad-beamed yole belonging to the trader was pulling for the shore, five men aboard, four rowing and one standing. Or was it six? A smaller figure, much smaller, also standing.

As the boat drew closer they could all see there were the backs of several shaggy animals on board, stowed between the middle thwarts. Very small horses? The tide was low, and even such a shallow-keeled little craft couldn't come right into shore. It grounded itself some twenty yards out, and rocked sideways, and the men aboard started jumping over the strakes and into the thigh-deep water.

The new arrivals were being lifted over the topmost strake and carried to the shallows.

'They're dogs,' Elfrun said in disbelief.

Athulf's eyes were shining.

Enormous, leggy dogs, with shaggy coats variously in pewter-grey, creamy-red and ashy-black, and pointed, intelligent heads. Three of them. And a little child to lead them.

The red-cheeked captain was bowing to Ingeld. 'From his grace the lord abbot of Meigle, my lord. I have a letter' – the captain pulled it from the neck of his tunic – 'but I can tell you, my lord, that these are pearls among hounds. From the bloodlines bred by the ancient kings of Fife, celebrated in song and story, and as valiant in the hunt as they are on the field of battle.'

'I know a good hound when I see one.' Ingeld held out his hand.

'I've no doubt of that!' The captain grinned and passed the letter over. 'Only obeying my instructions, my lord.'

Ingeld looked up, his dark eyes gleaming. 'Their names are Gethyn, Bleddyn and Braith.'

Elfrun looked at the hounds. Indeed, they looked like creatures out of legend, standing up to the chest of the silent, brown-haired boy who held them on their red plaited leashes. Their collars were also of red leather, with gleaming bronze buckles. One yawned, and she had to keep herself from flinching at the sight of the great teeth and lolling pink tongue. 'And the boy?'

'There's nothing here about the boy.'

The captain stepped forward again. 'The boy goes with them.' He grinned and spread his hands. 'He doesn't speak. But the abbot's dog-master told us that he was raised in the kennels himself and has tended these three since they were pups. He's a good boy.'

'You mean, he doesn't speak, or he can't speak?'

A shrug. 'Whistles, lady. Gurgles. But the dogs always know what he means.'

She stared at the boy. Small, with glossy nut-brown hair and eyes, surely no more than seven or eight years of age. He gave no sign of knowing that he was the subject of their talk. Deaf as well as dumb? Or did he only comprehend the language of the Picts? She would have to try him with Hirel or one of the others who spoke British, and see if anyone could make himself understood.

Elfrun took a deep breath. 'You must come up to the hall.' She waved an arm to show she meant crew as well captain. 'Uncle, you may house these creatures in our kennels for the time being. You must all come – we must feed you and reward you for the service done to our house.'

Ingeld had stepped forward too, but he was greeting the hounds not the men, letting the great shiny black snouts sniff and lick his palms and nuzzle between his fingers. Athulf had joined him, and for the first time Elfrun could see how alike her uncle and her cousin were, now that Athulf was growing, at last. The dog-boy was still standing in the fringes of the sea as his charges thrust themselves forward to make friends with their new master. His large hazel eyes looked downward, at his chapped hands clutching the plaited leather, at the chilly little waves that came breaking around his heels.

39

'What are you doing in here?'

Athulf ignored her.

The heddern, at the back of the hall, had been dark even before Elfrun had come to the doorway, but she knew what she had seen.

'You shouldn't even be in here. Put that down.'

He had his back to her, not so much as acknowledging her presence.

She felt a screeching fury threatening to hatch inside her and choked it back. 'Put it down,' she said again. 'How did you get in here?' There were only two keys. Abarhild had the spare for safekeeping. All their wealth was in here, of wool and linen and treated lambskins, of stored garments and precious spices, of the war-gear and hall-gear that her father had left behind. No one was allowed in here without her say-so.

It was the war-gear that was troubling her now.

'How do you think I got in?' Athulf had lifted the sword and was squinting down its length. 'You're blocking my light.'

'That's my father's sword.'

'My father's father's. *Our* grandfather's. And his father's before him.' Athulf sounded as though his teeth were clenched hard.

Elfrun bit her lip. 'That still doesn't give you the right—'

'And look at it!' He still had his back to her. 'I can't believe stupid scar-face Widia keeps his precious hunting knives in a barrel of oiled sand, while this gets left to rot in its scabbard. *Look* at it!'

He swung round, his hand high, holding the sword with the point down. 'There are nicks in the blade not whetted, and *rust*...'

True enough. Even in the murky light of the heddern Elfrun could see the dull, rough-brown patches, like a malevolent mould that had crept across the old steel. The hilt and guard still glowed, though, their gold-wire ornaments standing proud and untarnished against the dulled silver.

'It's not Widia's job, looking after the swords,' she said. 'My father took Dunstan with him, remember—'

'I know that!'

'Put it back.' Elfrun took a deep breath. 'I'll tell Widia to see to it, if that would make you happy.'

'No.'

'What?'

'Widia's only a huntsman. He's no swordsmith.' His arrogance was blinding. 'I'm taking it. I'm going to get sand and some goose fat to deal with the rust, and then I'll take it to Cuthred. If I'm going to carry a sword I want it properly maintained.'

'You can't have that sword!'

'Why not? No one else is using it. It's not your father's best. I wouldn't have touched that one, even if he had left it behind.'

'But you can't just take this one, either. He'll be so angry—'

'I'm nearly sixteen!' It came out at a shout, and long force of habit had them both looking guiltily at the door. In a lower voice, Athulf went on, 'If your father were here, he would have invested me with my sword by now. Long ago. Thancrad had his sword when he was fourteen—'

'So that's what this is about.' Elfrun sat down heavily on a barrel, her back against the wall. 'Thancrad of Illingham. I should have known.'

'They said if I have my own sword I can join their wolf pack. Him and his cousins. He said I was good.' Athulf extended his arm, lifting the sword first this way and then that. The blade was a heavy one, and for all her anger Elfrun was impressed by his steady grip and smooth, graceful turns. 'I am good.' He turned his wrist and brought it down suddenly, whistling through the air, and she flinched and faltered despite herself.

'Athulf!'

'See? As good as he is, any day. I need a shield, too.' He turned his head and scanned the shelves and racks.

'Athulf, this is madness. Put that sword back. My father will be back soon. You can ask him then.'

He turned and looked at her, and Elfrun did her best to hold his gaze. Hard to see anything but the little cousin, the pest with the floppy, mouse-brown fringe, dimpled and desperate for attention, always toddling after her on his sturdy legs. He was walking towards her now, the light from the doorway falling on his face. His eyes were a hard, pale blue.

'You really don't understand, do you?'

He lifted the blade to the horizontal in one even gesture that made it seem a living extension of his arm, while still moving towards her. She forced herself to stay still and keep his gaze as he came closer and closer, stopping at last with the point resting lightly on her left breast. 'My bossy big cousin,' he said. 'Always telling me what to do. Always judging me. Like Grandmother. Telling me I should become a priest.' The scorn in his voice was palpable, *priest* spat out like an obscenity.

'Is that really how you see me?' Elfrun stared down at the tip of the rusted and pitted blade. His words were hurting her much more than the metal. It was hard to breathe. 'Be a warrior then, if it means so much to you. Find another sword. Maybe there's one lying around at Illingham. Join Thancrad's wolf pack' – she forced her eyes up to meet Athulf's – 'if he's fool enough to have you. With any luck you'll both be killed. But you're not having my father's.'

'I am, you know.' He prodded at her with the blade, and she could feel the point testing the soft flesh beneath its coverings of wool and linen, meeting the resistance of muscle and rib. 'And, yes, perhaps we will be killed. Would you weep for me, Elfrun? Or would you mourn for Thancrad, instead?'

'I hardly know him!'

'He knows you.' Athulf gave her another little jab with the sword-point, hard enough to hurt properly this time; and now she was really angry, too much to respond easily. 'He likes you.' A jeering note had entered his voice.

She turned her head away.

'Look at me!' Reluctantly, she did. Athulf was smiling in a way she found unsettling. 'Don't you want to know what he says about you?'

'No, I do not! Stop this stupid game. And I don't believe for a moment Abarhild gave you her key. You stole it, didn't you?'

She jerked her head sideways and put up an arm to push the sword away, expecting resistance, a fight even, but to her surprise he stepped back and lowered the blade. When he turned away from her to the rack of pegs she thought that he would replace the sword where he had found it. But instead he unhooked the scabbard and sword-belt that went with his chosen weapon, and, with one last rueful glance along the length of the blade, he pushed it home. 'These need refurbishing as well.' He gave the harnessing a shake. 'The leather's all dry and cracking. But that I can do myself.'

And he walked out, right past her, without another word.

Elfrun was shivering with anger. She breathed in hard though her nose, forcing herself to unclench her fists, and leaned her back against the smooth-planed boards of the wall. She found herself sinking into a squat and wondered for a furious moment if she was going to faint.

At least there had been no witnesses.

She put her hands to her face. Thancrad and his wolf pack. Athulf had been nuisance enough when he and Cudda had run wild across the Donmouth hills and fields. Why was Thancrad encouraging him to lift his gaze higher?

Nothing but trouble from Illingham.

40

'I want to leave him.'

Luda gave no sign of having heard. He was watching two of the hall-men high up on the sloping roof, weeding and pulling the thick growth of winter moss out of the thatch of the women's house.

'Da?' Saethryth stepped closer. 'I've had enough.' He didn't turn. She moved a step or two nearer still. 'Da?'

He looked round at last, squinting at his daughter as though he'd never seen her before. 'What are you doing down here? We're milking three times a day down here – you can't tell me there's not enough to keep you busy up at the sheep-wick.'

'I'm doing my share!'

'For the first time in your life, if that's true. Now go on back up there. I don't need you hanging around, wasting everybody's time and getting in the way.'

She scowled at him. 'Didn't you hear what I said? I've had enough of the sheepwick. And him. The shepherd.'

Luda folded his arms and glowered at her. 'You've made your bed. And sort out that sour face or you'll spoil the cream before you've had a chance to churn it.'

She glanced up at the men working on the roof, sensing their curiosity, and lowered her voice. 'I can't stand him. I can't stand him touching me.'

'Ah, well, daughter. That's marriage for you. Did no one ever tell you that?' Luda nodded sagely. 'And where is it you would go, exactly, if you left him?'

Saethryth was surprised by her father's milder tone. She looked at the muddy ground and shifted her weight from one foot to the other. After a moment she said, 'Come home?'

'Really?' His smile broadened, showing his large yellow teeth. 'Your mam would be pleased, especially now you've learned what hard work is like. She's short-handed enough.'

Saethryth chewed her lip, still scowling.

Luda leaned in and lowered his voice. 'You think I don't know what you're really up to? That I don't know all about you and the holy father abbot?'

Her eyes widened but she recovered quickly. 'What's to know?'

'Your mucky little games? All Donmouth knows, and probably all Illingham as well.' His voice was tight with contempt. 'The archbishop on his high seat in the cathedral, I expect. Everybody with eyes to see or ears to hear.'

'Hirel doesn't know.'

'He will, soon enough.' Luda hawked and spat. 'And look out when he does. I've told him you need a firmer hand.'

'He won't find out.'

'Why not? When everyone else knows!'

She pulled her shoulders back and raised her chin. 'And if they do? I'm entitled—'

Her father grabbed her just below the elbow, hard enough that she felt the paired bones grind together. 'You are entitled to nothing, you stupid little bitch. If you come back under my roof these bed-tricks of yours will stop. But you're not coming back. And that's an end to it.'

'I can't stay with him!' She jerked away, tears of frustration in her eyes, rubbing the soft flesh of her arm. 'I could just leave him.'

'Leave him?' Luda feigned surprise. 'Ah. Hirel, you mean? And go where, if you're not coming here?'

'Ingeld would look after me.'

'*Ingeld would look after me,*' he mimicked, high-pitched and nasal. 'How can you be my daughter? Where's your sense? For half a year, maybe, until he gets sick of you and your whining and finds some other stupid girl ready to scratch his itch.' The corners of his mouth tugged down with disgust.

'It's not like that with us.'

He father shot her a glance that made her redden with anger. He held up his hand. 'Wait.' He limped over to the base of the ladder and barked a few instructions, waiting for the men to come down and move the base of the ladder-pole a few yards to the right, before they clambered up again.

Then he came back. 'Not like that, eh? How old are you?' She opened her mouth, but he ignored her. 'God knows, you look enough like a woman, and I thought you were old enough to know better, but maybe not. I'm of an age with Radmer. I've a decade on Ingeld. I grew up with them. Do you really think I've never seen this happen before?'

Saethryth wanted to stop her ears, or – better – shut her father's mouth. 'He says I'm different.'

'Aye, well, maybe that's true.' He paused, then spat out his next words. 'Even more stupid than most. Readier to lie down and open your legs when he gives you that smile.' His face darkened. 'Are you having a baby yet?'

Saethryth folded her arms and hunched her shoulders. 'Not that I know of.'

'Well, see that you get one going. It doesn't matter who the father is, but a wean or two will soon put a stop to this messing about.' He laughed shortly. 'Then you'll find out what hard work really means.'

'It's not fair.'

'That's been your song all your life. God doesn't deal fairly with us, so why should we deal fairly with each other?' He turned to pick up the full basket of damp moss and rotten reeds, and thrust it into her arms. 'Go and empty that into the ditch, and then get back to work.' His close-set eyes were hard and narrowed. 'Shift on, lass. What you want doesn't matter. I need you married to Hirel, and I need you working harder at the dairy. Cheese doesn't make itself, you know.'

Saethryth stared at him, then glanced down at the filthy basket she was holding. Her face twisted. She shoved it back at her father, hard enough to make him stagger. He managed to regain his balance but not to hold on to the basket, which thumped down and toppled on to its side, spilling its load. She wiped her hands on her skirts. 'You can't have it both ways. If I'm a married woman, then I'm not yours to order about any more. One master's enough. Go find someone else to bully. Try Mam.' Saethryth snorted, her cheeks pink with excitement, aware of fascinated eyes. 'Good luck.' She turned on her heel and walked away.

41

'They pay their geld to Burgred of Mercia,' Athulf called across. 'They're fair game, never fear.' He and Thancrad were riding abreast, the latter on that truly fine horse of his, not large but nimble and responsive. Nine years old, Thancrad had said, and he'd been training her since she was a filly. Behind them Athulf could hear the hoof-beats of the ponies ridden by Dene and dark-bearded Addan, Thancrad's slightly younger cousins – and shadows, Athulf thought contemptuously. Followers.

Addan and Dene were riding serviceable skewbald nags, not like Thancrad's soft-eyed, proud-necked bay. To an impartial eye, Athulf's own mount, the elderly chestnut with a bristling blond mane out of his uncle's stable, might look little better than theirs but he and Elfrun had both learned to ride on Mara; the mare could read his half-formed thoughts and wishes before he could himself, and he would hear nothing against her. They were rid-ing at a steady trot through the thin belt of scrubby woodland around twenty miles south-west of Donmouth, on the edge of the marches dividing Northumbria from Mercia, hills on the sunset side, bog and reed-bed on the other, stretching to the sea.

He knew quite well that Addan and Dene were not pleased at him leading this raid. But they didn't know the paths through the trackless watery lands that spread so far around the estuary. Without him they would flounder into the fen and be swallowed up. And if they didn't show him more respect he might just let them go right ahead.

Athulf's pilfered sword banged against his thigh, giving him a deep sense of satisfaction. He had replaced the key on its hook before Abarhild and her women had emerged from the minster church. So easy, as though he had been meant to have the sword. He clapped his heels to Mara's flanks and pushed her into a faster trot, eager to keep ahead of Thancrad and the others, though the going was rough and the light fading. They were cresting a low ridge, coming through a gap in the trees, and the ground fell away before them, down into the broad lush stream-threaded plain of the Trent valley. He reined his horse in just before the thick-crowded trees petered away into lighter cover of hazel and rowan. 'I was last here a week ago.' He pointed to where a lazy coil of smoke unravelled in the early spring air. 'Their hall's there.' His arm swept westward. 'They've been out-wintering some of their cattle on the high ground, with only a couple of little lads to watch them.'

'Seems rash,' Thancrad said.

'They've stopped thinking that danger might come from the north.' Athulf grinned, a wolfish look that transformed his soft, round features.

'What are we waiting for?' Addan urged his pony forward.

Thancrad's hand shot out and grabbed his cousin's rein. 'Dark, you fool. Listen to Athulf. And don't let yourself be sky-lined.' He jerked his head backwards, indicating that they should return the way they had come. Once they were back under the cover of the trees they all slid down from their mounts and hobbled them to let them graze, then sat or squatted deep in shadow.

Athulf looked thoughtfully at the other three. Thancrad was the oldest; Thancrad's father was one of the king's thanes; Thancrad was the unacknowledged leader of their little group. But this was his raid, and he intended to lead it. He was prepared to let Thancrad show some initiative. If either scowling Addan or taciturn Dene tried it on, though, he would discover his mistake. They had never yet warmed to Athulf or admitted him as one of their tribe.

He had unbuckled his sword, and now he was sitting cross-legged with it lying across his lap. Reaching down into his pouch, Athulf pulled out a little lump of suet wrapped in a scrap of muslin. He began working the grease with his fingers and rubbing it into the dry, peeling leather of his scabbard. The light was fading fast, and his fingers were stiff and cold.

He glanced up suddenly to find all three of the Illingham lads were looking at him.

'What?'

Addan was grinning. 'They say you shouldn't judge a sword by its sheath, but I don't know.' He shook his head. 'Where did you find that one? Your mother's midden?'

'Don't be too hard on him.' Dene glanced warily at Thancrad for approval before going on. 'Poor little Athulf didn't even have a sword last time we saw him. He doesn't have a mother, either.'

Addan laughed. 'Is there really a sword in there? Or are you just posturing with an empty old scabbard your uncle had thrown away?' He rose to his feet and started walking towards Athulf. 'Let's see your blade.'

Athulf looked at Thancrad, but he had risen silently and was seeing to his horse, his back turned to the others. Athulf was absolutely certain that Thancrad was listening, but he gave no sign. Addan was standing over him now. Athulf clenched his fist on the warm lump of suet, feeling it softening and moulding to the shape of his fingers and palm.

'What's the matter?' Addan looked ostentatiously around him. 'Not got your little churl-bred friends with you? What kind of warrior are you? Oh, I forgot. Your mother was a slave, wasn't she? No wonder you're tongue-tied when you're out with your betters.'

'Be careful,' Athulf said softly.

'As careful as you and your little friends when you were sneaking around pinching our barley last autumn? What?' Athulf heard Addan snicker. 'Did you think we didn't know about that? You should have asked. We'd have taken pity on poor, hungry Donmouth if you'd begged us hard enough. Maybe you should beg now.' He glanced round, assessing the mood of the others. 'On your knees, slave boy.'

Athulf sprang to his feet, grappling with his hilt. Thancrad had turned round, and he and Dene were both watching. Addan had his hands on his hips, his head cocked to one side. Athulf couldn't see too clearly, but he was sure the other was smiling.

Athulf pulled his sword from its sheath. There had been no time yet to take it to the smithy for regrinding. But he had brought it back to brightness with sand, and used Widia's whetstone to polish away some of the smaller gouges in the blade-edge; now was not the moment to agonize over all that he had left undone. He tossed the belt and scabbard to one side. 'Come on then. I'll show you how hungry men of Donmouth can be.'

Addan glanced over his shoulder, and Athulf realized, first, that the other lad was unarmed and, next, that he was frightened. Exhilarated, he took a step forward, lunging with the sword, and Addan flinched. 'Thancrad? Dene?'

But they stayed where they were.

'Where's your own sword, Addan?' Athulf took another step forward. 'You should know better than to step away from it. Didn't your bones tell you battle was coming? What kind of warrior are you?' He gave his blade a little shake, knowing that if he didn't take care the wooden hilt, smooth from the grip of men long dead, might slip from his greasy fingers. 'My sword doesn't look so useless now, does it?'

Without realizing it, Addan had backed himself against the broad trunk of an ash tree. Slowly he raised his hands to shoulder-height.

Athulf lifted the sword to tap the point of the blade against Addan's chest. He almost smiled, remembering his encounter with Elfrun in his uncle's treasure-chamber. 'You're not half the man my cousin Elfrun is, for all your beard.'

'Enough.' Thancrad straightened up, and only then did Athulf realize he had been keeping a restraining hand on Dene's shoulder. 'No need to prove yourself against an unarmed man, Athulf. We get the point. All of us.' A smile tugged at the corner of his mouth. 'And, Addan, you're a fool.' He made an exasperated, flicking gesture. 'I say we ride out at midnight. In the meantime, tend to your horses and get some sleep. Athulf, do you want to keep the first watch?'

Suggestions, not orders.

Athulf decided he could acquiesce without losing face. And he wouldn't have slept, anyway, not in that company. He kept his sword loose in its scabbard, close to him under his cloak, and stared into the half-dark, waiting for Addan to come back and get his revenge. High thin cloud covered the sky, and somewhere behind it a waning and westering moon, against which the bare trees formed a dark lattice. The night was full of rustles and creaks. The occasional harsh bark of a fox came up to his ears, and the horses shifted their hooves and snorted and tore at the meagre grass, but as far as he could tell the other three slept soundly until the stars told him the middle of the night had come at last.

It was exhilarating riding down to the pastures, the hooves of their horses muffled with rags. Picking out four likely cattle, then charging in and heading them off for all their frantic bellowing, driving them up and away while the sleeping children who should have been watching them were still scrambling to their feet in panic terror. It was also a thrill to be on guard at the rear while they escorted their shaggy, bewildered prizes – all, he suspected, in calf – back along their trackless route as the sky slowly lightened. He had felt a deep sense of triumph when they came riding through Donmouth at dusk and his own darkbrown, long-horned prize was singled out and driven into the yard, while the women and children came tumbling out of doors to stare and point and wonder.

But nothing of all this – *nothing* – could compare with the pleasure he had experienced when Addan had taken that first step backwards, the corners of his mouth tugging down in terror and his shaking hands rising to shoulder-height, half fending, half appeasing. Athulf found himself smiling in reminiscence. Pressing his lips together, he glanced at the others where they were hauling their horses round to herd the three remaining cattle across to Illingham.

Thancrad caught his eye, and raised a hand.

Thoughtful, Athulf returned the salute. Thancrad thought he was master; that he could lead by making men love him. But fear might prove a more useful weapon than love.

PART THREE

THE CHRONICLE, YORK MINSTER SCRIPTORIUM

'We thought you'd given up on that project.' The librarian peered short-sightedly at the stack of vellum. 'It got put here somewhere in the waste pile, to be scraped back, but I don't think anyone's done it yet.'

'I can see it, sticking out.' The chronicler would not have cared, especially, even if that carefully prepared quire had been lost. But it lay near the top of the sloppily stacked pile, sitting askew, folded as though prematurely readied for binding and cutting. And since it had crossed his mind, and he had taken the trouble to come into the quiet scriptorium and ask, and it now lay under his hand, he might as well do some work.

'You can't really expect us to keep your desk for you,' the librarian scolded. 'Not when you're only here every couple of months.'

'I don't expect it.'

The old man softened. 'You're missed, you know.'

The chronicler laughed, and the librarian looked indignant. As well he might. The old man had taught the chronicler to write, and to ready vellum. Had chased him round the tannery threatening to throw him into a reeking pit and be tanned himself if he didn't mend his wicked ways. A lifetime ago, and through it all, always, a steady undercurrent of affection.

'What will you set down?'

The chronicler shrugged. 'The death of kings. Battles. A great synod. A new pope.' He spread out his hands. 'Always new and always the same. Does it matter?'

The librarian said, 'I'll see this doesn't happen again. Just leave it here, and I'll make sure it's kept for you.'

The door swung slowly shut. Was it really a year since he had first conceived the idea of writing a chronicle? It seemed too grandiose an idea now: he wondered how he had ever had the audacity. Who was he, to give events significance by scratching them down with his little pen?

In this year, a woman's breasts were like mounded cream tipped with strawberries, and they moved me more than pen can express. In this year, I have trespassed on other men's woods and fields, and hunted their private runs. In this year, I have lost my soul, and found it.

The chronicler looked down at the marks his pen had made and shook his head. These were secrets to whisper to a girl in the warm dark of midnight, or pour out in the confidential space between the penitent's mouth and the confessor's ear. There was no room for this kind of detail in the written record. A matter for the recording angel, to be sure, but not for other men's eyes. He watched the ink slowly turn matte and dry on the page. In a moment, he thought, he would pick up the knife and painstakingly scrape at the surface of the vellum, shaving away his words until the least, faintest, ineradicable trace remained. And then he would write again, write what had really happened.

42

Elfrun felt odd in her new shoes, her gait off balance and unfamiliar. They fastened with thongs that pulled tight round her ankles rather than the usual horn button, and she wasn't sure they had been a good choice, but last year's pair were worn right through. No matter how tight she tied the thongs, the shoes were still too loose round the heel, and her toes had to grip the insole with every step. Her feet had yet to mould the stiff leather into a comfortable form, and the slick spring grass made an untrustworthy surface. It was perhaps the thing she disliked most, at spring and harvest meeting, that her grandmother insisted on her looking her most respectable in the presence of all their neighbours.

Respectable, to be sure, but shuffling and gawky and afraid to stride out for fear of falling over.

In order to be set up in time to greet king and archbishop the Donmouth party had left home as soon as the eastern sky had begun to lighten. Now it was mid-afternoon, their tents and shelters were pitched, and everyone was exhausted. They had the same place every year, on good, flat, well-drained ground close to the great hollow ash that marked the meeting site but it was still as well to get there early in case any of their neighbours tried to take advantage.

Someone was always ready to take advantage.

Radmer had the best of the Donmouth tents with him to Rome, but Elfrun had set two of her women to embroidering a new awning over the winter and it made a brave show now, the blue and yellow dancing in the spring winds along with the sunlit daffodils that dotted the field's edge. It brightened her mood, and Heaven knew she needed something to cheer her, after the wrangling that had already marred her morning. Athulf had tried first to wheedle and then to bully her into letting him bring Hafoc.

'Come on, Elfrun! How can it hurt? Last autumn you said maybe in the spring! Riding Hafoc, I'll make us look good in the races—'

'No. And I never promised anything. You're making it up.' But had she? Maybe, and she had forgotten as he was claiming, but she didn't believe it. It would be just like Athulf to make up some story then keep badgering until she came to believe it herself. Still, she wanted to be concessionary. 'You can have Mara.'

And then as soon as Mara was tethered, rubbed down and fed he had streaked off, looking for friends with whom to plan the races and the wrestling and that insane match they fought with pig-bladders and wooden staves. Leaving her to oversee everything.

Last spring she would have been with him, for some of it anyway, dodging Abarhild, exhilarated by new woods and streams to explore, and new company. She thought back to that crazy, wonderful race on the ponies. She had beaten Athulf, but that had been the last time she had had the chance to ride like that. What a difference a year could make.

Even as these thoughts ran, yet again, through her mind, she saw her uncle duck out of his equally colourful tent to stand and stretch in the sunlight. Donmouth hall and minster always tented together, although most of the minster-men from the various big and little church communities had their habitual pitches a half-mile or so to the south, near the archbishop's estate at Sherburn. And for all the burden of tradition Elfrun could wish the tents of Donmouth minster further away. She looked away now, but too late. Ingeld had seen her and came smiling over.

'Little niece. How are you doing on this blessing of a morning?'

'Father abbot.' She couldn't find a smile with which to answer his. She was angry with Athulf, and some of that was rubbing off on his father. And she was still unsettled by Fredegar's refusal to go on teaching her Latin. Remembering that overheard conversation made her hot and uncomfortable.

He raised an eyebrow. 'What a mardy face you're wearing. Have I done something to offend you?'

He had, but she couldn't possibly tell him. She blurted out the first thing that came to mind. 'Why do you pitch your tent with us, and not with the other minster-men?'

'What? Whatever put that into your head? We've always done it like that.'

'And look at you!' She could hear the pitch of her voice rising to shrillness. 'No one would know you were a priest! No tonsure—'

'I know.' He ran a rueful hand over the thick dark-brown hair that crowned his scalp. 'I'm planning to get it cut before the archbishop's party arrives.'

'And your *clothes* – and Storm is finer than anything in my father's stable, and—'

He put out a hand and grasped her wrist to forestall her. 'Why, I do believe you were about to fly at me. Who would have thought it? The little brown bird has found her beak and talons at last.' He leaned back and assessed her at arm's length. 'I thought you were a sparrow, but you're a falcon! And I rejoice to see it.'

She twisted herself free, furious. 'Don't laugh at me. I'm lord of Donmouth. I have to guard our honour.'

'I'm not laughing. I'm impressed.' But she could hear the rich golden-brown note in his voice, like sunlight in ale, and knew he was, at least in part, lying; that for all her fury she was managing to do little more than amuse him. 'And as for my clothes – Elfrun, do you really expect me to dress like a beggar? What honour would that do to Donmouth? Or perhaps you think I should travel the mud and dust of the roads vested for mass?' He sighed.

'I've all the silk and gold thread I need packed away in my chest, and no doubt the worthy Heahred is getting the creases out even as we speak. So, stop fretting.' He patted her arm. 'The sun is shining at last. It's been a long, filthy winter. Come on, little niece, count your blessings, then head out and make the most of them.'

She pulled herself up tall, wrapping her father's cloak around her, and glared at him, and this time he did laugh.

'Sorry! Forgive me, Elfrun, but no one who wasn't watching just now would ever believe you could look so much like your grandmother.' He lowered his voice, and she had to lean in to listen. 'She tries to change me, and so does your dear father, and now you. Look at you! You used to be such a lively child.' He shook his head, keeping eye contact, keeping the smile. 'Why on earth do you think you should succeed where they have failed over and over again?'

She was beginning to understand Abarhild and Radmer's frustration. 'But doesn't it worry you?'

'Doesn't what worry me?'

'That everyone's talking about you? That they say you're a bad priest?'

'Do they? Then the very best of good luck to them.' His face broke into another of his irrepressible smiles. 'Little niece, if the king, or his grace the archbishop, were to threaten to deprive me of Donmouth minster and its revenues I might think again. But that's hardly likely. A king tried that trick on us a hundred years since, and the Pope himself stepped in and put matters right. And besides…'

'What?'

He looked to right and left and beckoned her closer. Frowning, she took another step towards him.

'What is it?'

He put a warning finger to his lips. 'Can you keep a secret?'

'Of course I can.'

His face was still stern but his eyes were laughing. 'The archbishop's a worse sinner than I am myself.'

She recoiled as though he had slapped her. 'You disgust me.' Elfrun turned on her heel. Her intent was to march away, but he caught her by the shoulder and hauled her round, thumb and fingers digging in hard enough around her collarbone to make her catch her breath. This time he wasn't smiling.

'Elfrun, I've been very patient with you. I have fought battles for you about which you know nothing.'

She stared at him, startled by the force of his grip, speechless.

'But I will not tolerate this. Not from you, not from my mother, not from that damned meddling Frank she's imported who has the cheek to suggest he should be my confessor. My soul and the sorry, spotted state of it is between me' – he gave her a shake – 'and my God. Do you hear me?'

She was too stunned to reply.

'Do you?'

She nodded mutely, and Ingeld let go at last. She rubbed her shoulder, and at once he looked concerned. 'Did I hurt you?'

She shook her head, fighting tears.

'I'm glad.' But still he wasn't smiling. 'Remember what I say, Elfrun. My conscience is my business.'

She managed another nod, still too shocked to trust her voice.

'I'll see you at vespers, no doubt.' That mocking edge was back in his voice at last, and suddenly she couldn't bear it any more. She turned, eyes filling, and walked rapidly downhill and away from the Donmouth tents, wading through the tangles where the new spring grass was coming up fast through the withered and rotted remains of last year's weeds. She didn't really care where she was going, and had blundered a couple of hundred yards in a randomly chosen direction, close to another pitch of tents, when a voice shouted a warning. Without realizing the cry was addressed to her she took another furious step in her new shoes and went sprawling headlong over a hidden guy-rope.

The ground met her with more force than she would have thought possible, and her cheekbone and temple had struck something hard. She lay half-stunned and winded for a long moment before managing to ease herself up on to one elbow and assess the damage. Her ankle was agony, and she had flung out a hand as she fell and scraped it on something hidden in the grass. She tried to catch her breath but it wouldn't come easily. She pressed her hand against the bone of her right eye-socket and then looked at her fingers curiously. They had come away red, and warm, and wet.

'Stay where you are. Don't try to move. You half-witted fool!' A long moment and then she realized the voice was no longer addressing her. 'I told you not to put the pegs in the long grass before we'd had a chance to cut it back.'

Another figure joined the first. Her head was clearing a little, and she could see that one was thick-set, with a craftsman's leather apron. He had a mallet and more pegs in his hands.

'I know you,' she said to the tall one who had spoken first. 'But you were covered in blood.'

'You're the one covered in blood.'

It was true. Now she could feel the warm liquid trickling down her right cheekbone.

He was still talking. 'Can you stand? Or do you want me to carry you?' He held out a hand and pulled her to her feet. Her ankle crumpled beneath her.

'Sorry. I need to lean on you,' she said between gritted teeth.

'I'm going to take you to my mother.'

A dozen paces, no more, with her clutching like ivy around an oak, and a pudgy, sweet-faced woman, unveiled in the decent privacy of the tent and her black curls falling about her face, was drawing the tent door-curtain closed. A familiar woman, but from where? Now she was calling for bowls of warm water, untangling Elfrun from the folds of her cloak.

Stuffy, dim, airless. A straw pallet.

'I'm going to be sick.'

And a bucket was there at her side. She reached for it gratefully, ignoring the murmur of voices behind her.

'You're shaking.' The doughy-faced woman, kneeling beside

her and holding her hair away from the bucket. 'And no surprise. From what Thancrad tells me that was a nasty tumble, and a great big lump of rock in the grass. Thancrad says he told Hadd not to put the ropes up without cutting the grass back first, but that lazy good-for-nothing never lifts a finger unless you stand over him with a switch.' She was dabbing at Elfrun's temple with a warm damp cloth. 'Just a tiny little three-cornered tear, right on the eyebrow. Bruising fast, but that will sort itself out in a few days. You're young. The good God willing it'll heal right up and no one will know.' Elfrun opened her mouth, but the torrent of words swept on. 'Let me have a look at your ankle. Thancrad said you couldn't put any weight on it, but with a little bit of luck and the angels and saints on our side it'll only be sprained.' The woman was assessing her, head to toe. 'There's hardly any weight to you as it is.'

Switha, that was it. Thancrad's mother. Thancrad, covered with blood at the whale-drive, that was the image that had been nagging at her. She was in the Illingham tent.

Trouble. Avoid them.

But Radmer hadn't seen this coming. Why couldn't she have been more careful? Elfrun could feel the wretched shoe being eased off and warm, powerful hands flexing her foot. A throb of pain shot up her shin to the knee, but she bit her lip.

The door-curtain was pushed aside, and she winced away from the sudden glare.

'Yes, I know who she is. Radmer's daughter.' A man who blocked the whole of the sunlight. An ox of a man. 'I want a better look at her.'

Elfrun propped herself up on her elbows, feeling foolish, her head still swimming.

'Time and enough for that. Will you two get out of here and stop crowding the poor thing?' Thancrad's mother moved between her and the light. 'Go and get that mallet off Hadd and do the job yourselves, before I find myself tending any more of his victims.'

Elfrun tried once more to sit up. 'I'm sorry, I—'

But the black-eyed woman was using a softer voice now, turning back to her, and the tent had gone dark and quiet. 'Don't you listen to a word. I just wanted them out of here. Try bending your foot again.' A dark bristle sprouted in the corner of her mouth, and Elfrun wondered why the woman didn't tweeze it out.

'I'll go as soon as—'

'You're not going anywhere until I give you leave. Put your head back. If you were up as early as we were then you'll be worn out even without this silly falling-over.' She was frowning now, and her tongue darted out to make contact with the bristle and in again, fast and furtive as some half-glimpsed barn rodent. 'Look at you. Aren't you sweet? I've always wanted a daughter. No more children after Thancrad though; I had him too young, they say. I was only twelve. It spoiled me...'

Another cushion was being tucked in behind her head. Elfrun lay back and despite all the pain in her head and ankle, the vile taste in her mouth and the lingering nausea she felt a sense of deep calm. It occurred to her, in a distant, dreamy kind of way, that no one had looked after her like this for – how long – not since her father had left? Longer. Much longer. Not since her mother had fallen ill.

Why was Illingham tenting there? That bit of ground had been the prerogative of Howden, time out of mind...

Someone was wrapping her cloak around her, tucking in the edges. Elfrun gave a profound sigh, shivered violently and fell into a doze.

Somewhere in the drowsy dimness there were low urgent voices, but no one spoke her name, so she paid them no heed. Darkness took her.

When Elfrun came slowly back to wakefulness, the light through the tent walls had changed. Much of the day must have passed. There was a gentle hand on her shoulder. Switha. Kind Switha.

'Your uncle's here. Can you walk?'

43

Elfrun watched Tilmon of Illingham with all the greater fascination now that she had been a guest in his tent. Hard to see him as Thancrad's father, though they were both so tall. Where Thancrad was angular his father was a solid wall of shoulder and paunch, and if Tilmon's slab of a face had ever been adorned with those striking cheekbones they had long since been swallowed by the surrounding flesh.

Her eyes flickered sideways to where Thancrad was standing, stiffly upright, arms folded, mouth hard. Had he decided at some point that this was the appropriate public stance in which to present himself? He looked uncomfortable, even disapproving, but she was coming to suspect that that was the habitual set of his strong-boned face. Certainly there was nothing she could see for him to disapprove of in the little ritual that was being enacted between Tilmon and the king. The lord of Illingham was kneeling on the dais, bowing his head to rest his brow on the king's knee, offering the king his great red-knuckled hands and being sworn in as the lay abbot of Howden.

Which explained why they were tenting in Howden's stead.

This should have been old news to her. It would have been unimaginable to her father that a grant of this magnitude should be given without his knowledge, without his advice, his endorsement. Especially to a man with Tilmon's past.

Well, whatever that past, he was embedded in royal favour now. The king was smiling, rising from his stool to pull Tilmon lumbering to his feet, embracing him and kissing him on both cheeks, slapping the man on the shoulder and turning him to face the assembled thanes and abbots. Sun glinted off silver cloak tags and bullion-embroidered cuffs as the chief men of southern Northumbria roared their approbation.

A mellow murmur in her ear. 'Watch the king.'

Ingeld. She had had to forgive him for yesterday, he had treated her with such affection after her fall, fending off Athulf and his malicious comments: her clumsiness; how ugly she was with her bruised face; how she had only done it to catch Thancrad's attention. Ingeld had batted Athulf away, and examined her twisted foot and her cut face with real concern; and she had loved him for it.

Ingeld wasn't looking at her now though. His gaze was focused on the dais, where Osberht was now stepping back to allow the archbishop forward, and Tilmon to kneel again and take his second oath. And Ingeld was right. The king's face had slipped out of that enforced joviality as soon as he thought men's eyes were off him. He was concentrating on Tilmon and the archbishop as a cat might watch at a rat's hole, his fair-skinned, neat-featured face quiet behind his greying beard, his eyes never leaving them.

There were few other women present. Elfrun had already had to endure probing enquiries from Eadburh of Aberford. Only a few years older than Elfrun and widowed when her husband had broken his neck hunting in the first year of her marriage, their son still unborn, Eadburh had been holding her land in her little son's name for so long, and with such fire-forged determination, that Elfrun wondered whether, when the lad came of age in four or five years, he would find himself strong enough to prise his heritage from his mother's grip. In all their encounters the older woman had spoken to Elfrun as though she were a child – and a particularly simple and ignorant child too.

If the world was ever to treat her as an adult, she would have to behave like one. She could hear Abarhild's voice in her mind, scratchy but loud and clear for all that.

Men's eyes were coming away from Illingham now. While this new grant to Tilmon would be the subject of discussion and debate around the hearths for months to come, Illingham had had its moment.

Now it was Donmouth's turn.

She turned to Ingeld, expectantly. He was smiling at her, his left eyebrow lifted. 'What?'

'Hall first, then minster.' Surely he didn't need her to tell him what to do?

'Yes. I know.' He was still smiling. 'Let's hear you.'

She stared at him, hoping against hope that she had misunderstood his meaning. He jerked his head. 'Come on.'

'I can't! I don't know what to say, and it's not proper—'

'It's perfectly *proper*. Look at Eadburh.'

'Her!'

'You are lord of Donmouth. You were happy enough to behave like it when you gave me that lecture yesterday, Elfrun. So do your duty now.'

'You're punishing me.'

'I'm helping you. Supporting you in your lordship. Get moving, or people will think we've got something to hide.' He had his hand on her shoulder blade and he was steering her through the throng, bowing and smiling. 'Look, all friendly faces. Familiar faces.'

Yes. Thancrad of Illingham, eyes shadowed, mouth a straight line. Eadburh of Aberford, smiling in cosy, cloying, feigned sisterhood. Athulf gurning away at her through a gap in the crowd. Abarhild next to him, gimlet eyes in a frame of neat, gold-tricked white veils. Elfrun was never quite sure how she hobbled her way up on to the dais. What had happened since last September, anyway? What on earth was she going to say?

The whales.

Tilmon had said nothing about the whales, although the men of both estates had joined together to send the king his share. She could tell that story and by mentioning how the men of Illingham had been made welcome on their side of the estuary she could appear generous, a good neighbour and a good subject.

She stepped forward at the king's beckoning. The boards creaked under her unsteady feet. He was smiling at her, eyes creased in skin sun-weathered even after the long months of winter. Her mind went on scrabbling after Donmouth's news.

Things bade fair for a good lambing.

The dogs – but they were Ingeld's news not hers.

Cudda, falling into the fire. No need to mention Fredegar's role in that disaster. And perhaps to say that they needed a lad to work the forge? Perhaps someone here would have a likely lad he could both command and spare. Or would that be an admission of weakness? No, best say nothing that her father would later regret.

And, as ever, remembering the day of Cudda's death made her thoughts flash to Finn. How would she describe him? A pedlar who had come, so mysteriously, from the sea. Come, and gone, and it was as though a hand had tightened around her heart.

Should she mention him? Her very reluctance suggested not – how important could he be? He might even be here, one among the merchants and hucksters who swarmed around the hem of the great meeting. Just because she hadn't seen him...

Ingeld prodded her sharply in the arm.

The king was looking at her. His eyes were kind. 'Radmer's daughter.'

'My lord.'

She knelt and pressed her brow to the fine twill covering his knee, and she felt his hands press down, brief and gentle, on her head before bringing her back to standing.

Just start, and pray that the words would come.

'My lord king.' Deep breath. Head up – and never mind the black eye. Heart pounding. 'My lord archbishop.' Louder. 'Men of Northumbria. Donmouth is in excellent heart. Last October we had a fine sea-harvest—'

Shouting at the edge of the crowd, and a sudden hiss and

babble of talk. They weren't listening to her. They were turning away from her. What was going on? Hadn't they realized she had begun talking? Was her voice too low?

A rider on a black horse was pushing his way through the men on foot, heading for the dais, shouting for the king. He had the look of a mariner, or a foreigner, eyebrows startlingly fair against his red-brown skin.

'My lord.'

'What news?' Osberht had risen and come forward to join Elfrun at the front of the dais. It was a long moment before Elfrun recognized the newcomer. Gaunt as well as tanned, but the mop of butter-coloured hair was the same, and the way he sat a horse.

Dunstan, her father's sword-bearer. She staggered as though buffeted by a gale, and, recovering, looked immediately beyond him, for Radmer's familiar outline.

But Dunstan seemed to be alone.

Somehow, they were all in the king's tent. It was hot in there, a little private space created by embroidered hangings and dividers, the awning lowered, painted canvas underfoot. Everyone was making a fuss, finding a creepie-stool for her despite her protests. Why were they wasting time? Ingeld was there, and Athulf, and her grandmother, also seated. Heahred. And Tilmon. Why was Tilmon there?

'What news?' the king asked again.

'My lord, we delivered all your letters. We – we reached Rome.' He stopped. 'We gave the money to the Holy Father. He received us well. We...'

'What?'

'Radmer wanted to get home. We took a boat from Massalia, a merchantman, that was taking the sea-road past Iberia, and Ireland. There was a storm. A terrible storm.'

Elfrun heard a voice saying, 'Dunstan, where is my father?'

He was crouching in front of her, taking her hands but she couldn't feel the pressure of his fingers. 'Elfrun, I'm sorry. I'm so sorry.' Another unbearable pause. 'I saw him go over the side.'

44

'This is damnable.'

'You knew the risks.'

'I'm sorry for the girl.'

'Soft, my lord,' Wulfhere said. 'There's no room in this life for softness.'

'My conscience...'

'We have been indulging your conscience for over a fortnight.' Wulfhere tapped the table. 'Her grandmother wants to send her to a convent.'

'It's one solution.'

They had been walking up and down in Wulfhere's great hall, where the great stone walls and columns the Romans had left behind supported a towering superstructure of carved beam and gilded shingle. Osberht's attendant men-at-arms were standing near the door, passing the time of day with Wulfhere's retainers. Hard to tell king's men from archbishop's, all in their bright cloaks, their gleaming gilt-tricked helmets tucked under their arms. Places for the young men, rewarding the young men. So much of Osberht's power depended on them, on harnessing their desire, their ruthlessness, their glorious physical energy, to serve his needs.

How many of them were wondering what he was going to do with Donmouth?

Osberht looked at his cousin, keeping his face a careful mask. Wulfhere's authority came from God and St Peter, not from the swords and spears he could command. The lands of the

256

archbishopric extended more widely than those of the king, and he had authority outside Northumbria of which a king could only dream. Osberht's mouth tightened briefly. How long would Wulfhere's glory last without the men with swords to do God's will for him? *I bring not peace but a sword...*

He could feel power sifting away from him, like flour through a riddle.

Wulfhere picked up Abarhild's letter and looked it over again. 'Send her to Hovingham, she says.' He tossed the letter back on to the oak slab. 'I see no merit in it.'

'It would free up Donmouth, and see the girl safe.'

'Is that what you want?'

'Radmer was my old friend.' Shield wall and council table and feast in the hall. Twenty years. More. Osberht picked up the letter and looked at the little scratch marks, like the foot-prints of a bird in mud. He felt an obscure and – he knew – unjustified resentment. Why had Radmer been so careless? If he had to drown, could the man not have left his affairs in better order? 'He cherished that daughter of his. I wish he had said yes to Tilmon. I feel an obligation...' He tailed away, looking at Wulfhere's narrow face, his teeth showing in the vulpine smile that always made Osberht nervous. 'What?'

'Stop thinking about the girl. However did you manage to stay in power before you started coming to me for advice?'

Osberht wasn't sure if his young cousin really wanted an answer to that question. He stared at the embroidered hanging behind the high table. King Edwin, seated in council, debating the coming of the Faith to the Angles of the north. Paulinus, Wulfhere's predecessor, at his side. An old retainer, gesturing at a bird in flight. He couldn't read the words that surrounded the wool-and-silk figures, but he knew the song.

...We come from winter; and winter takes us again.
Brief as the birds are we; and our bones lie long in the grave...

He gave himself a shake. 'What are you saying?'

'I'm asking you what you really want. You've been playing

tag with Tilmon all winter, as though you were children again. Illingham, and now Howden. You know he won't be happy. He's been seen with Alred. Alred may have stayed north of the Tees but he's been keeping funny company. Tilmon's been in the Danemarch. You can count to four, can't you?'

Osberht grunted. He could put two and two together better than most. How else had he kept power? He didn't need Wulfhere to tell him that. 'I want Tilmon on my side. Should I give him Donmouth? Is that what you're hinting at?'

'You won't get his support that road. The man's a blackmailer by nature. Give him Donmouth!' Wulfhere spat into the straw. 'Try to buy him with land, and he'll think you weak and ask for more. You know he's a traitor. Once and always.'

Osberht scowled. 'I have no proof. I cannot exile him again without proof. He has too many friends.'

'He has friends because he and Alred are promising them rewards. Opportunities. You should be doing the same.'

'Give someone else Donmouth? I've been thinking about that. There are solid men who need land.' He gestured at Abarhild's letter, then swung round to look at the promising young men of his bodyguard. Would they still look out for him if they were being offered rewards elsewhere? Or would they be watching his back in another sense, waiting for the moment to strike? They might be doing that already. 'That's why sending her to Hovingham seems a good idea. If I give the girl with the land it would need to go to a younger man. Unmarried.'

Wulfhere smiled again. 'We've known men put away their old wives for plums less ripe than Donmouth. But that's not what I meant. You want Tilmon and his worms to come out of the woodwork?'

Osberht nodded warily.

'Then do nothing.'

'*Nothing?*'

It was Wulfhere's turn to nod. 'Leave the girl where she is.'

Osberht stared. 'As lord of Donmouth?'

'How do the shepherds lure the wolf pack so the huntsmen can take them down? Stake out a lamb, and wait.'

Osberht turned the idea over, testing its soundness. 'I don't like it.'

'No one's asking you to like it.'

And that was fair enough. God knew he had done enough things for which he had no appetite in his time. His dislike made them no less necessary. A thought struck him. 'Will you tell Ingeld? Can you trust him?'

Wulfhere smiled. 'Ingeld is my dear friend.' His eyes met the king's. 'Of course not.'

45

T he great boar came snuffling through the brushwood. It stood a yard or more high at its dark, bristly shoulder, and its tusks were a good five inches long. Widia had been stalking it all morning, but the beast had been following a meandering path and it must have circled back on itself while it had been out of sight in the burgeoning undergrowth. The wind came from the boar now, a rank, musky scent, unmistakable. It was a big old beast, it would make challenging eating, but Widia wasn't planning on eating it. He had a suspicion that this was the same animal that had gored him a year ago. He bore no grudge, but he needed to know its habits, as he did those of every stag and every dog fox, guarding the wild wealth of Donmouth against Radmer's return.

Radmer, who would not be returning.

Widia had been doing a lot of thinking in the weeks since Elfrun and Ingeld had returned from the spring meeting with the dreadful news. He knew he could trust the dog-boy with the mews as well as the kennels, and he was wondering whether he should just leave, and not return. His loyalty had been to his lord: with no lord he was a free man.

Radmer had promised land, and a wife.

Well, the wife was lost to him, married to that lumbering fool, although despite everything he still found the sight of her cut him to the bone. Elfrun might yet grant him land, but what use was that, now? No prospects, a scarred face and body and a lord lost on the whale-road. What was there to keep him here?

His face twisted further. Everyone knew that the abbot had developed a new and unexpected interest in the wellbeing of his flocks, their fleeces and especially their milk. He didn't blame Radmer for being drowned, exactly, any more than he blamed the boar for goring him. But the bitterness and anger which were becoming habitual needed a focus of some kind.

He gave himself a shake.

Such thoughts were dangerous in the forest, and it was while he had been brooding earlier that the boar had gone in a loop and come round behind him. A beginner's mistake, and possibly a fatal one. As though his ribs and cheekbone weren't reminder enough.

The boar lumbered along, its bristly head low, casting this way and that along the slope, grinding its tusks as it went. Widia noticed a slight foam at its jaws and tensed still further. Although it was early in the season it could mean breeding sows were around. Every few paces the boar stopped and rooted in the mulch. A sudden flash of red, and Widia spotted the bright-eyed robin, following in the boar's footsteps, head on first one side then the other, hoping that the animal's vigorous snouting of the soil would turn up some overlooked seeds or worms.

Widia gritted his teeth. He felt a strong kinship with the robin, dependent on unwanted scraps that the great men of this earth never even noticed they let fall. The robin had seen him and stared, brazen and unafraid. Why was this one little bird so confident, when most would flee the approach either of men or the massive, blundering boar? The beast was ambling off now, downhill, heading towards the stream, and Widia guessed it would be making for its favourite wallow. He was getting to know its perambulations of the woodland bounds intimately.

At least Athulf had stopped pestering him so relentlessly to be taken out on the trail of boar. Since the news had come of Radmer's death he had hardly seen the boy. That in itself was new, when for most of the last two years Athulf had spent what free time he had in making a nuisance of himself hanging around the mews and the stables.

Widia spent as little time as possible listening to the endless round of gossip that inevitably characterized the free hours of the folk of Donmouth. Too much petty-minded filth. Too much that he didn't want to hear. But that Athulf was running with the lads from Illingham, he couldn't help but know. He didn't care what they got up to or where they went, as long as they stayed out of his woods and drives.

The boar was out of earshot now. Widia straightened up, tension ebbing from his body. When he had been no more than ten, long before he ever took service at Donmouth, he had been handling dogs on a boar hunt when the quarry had exploded out of the bushes and made straight for the master huntsman. One quick flash of those razor-sharp tusks, and the man's thigh had fountained blood. He had died right there among the trees, bled out like any slaughtered pig. Long before his own violent encounter, Widia had had profound respect for these monsters of the dark woods, more than for stag or even for wolf. The boar were the only creatures that frightened him.

Thinking of wolves reminded him that weeks ago he had promised Luda to go round the high fences and the pens, looking for scat and spoor, and keeping an eye out for any unmended winter damage. He wouldn't have to go near the sheepwick, just walk the boundaries, hunting for any sign of coming trouble. Now was as good a time as any. Turning to make his way across the slope and out of the trees, he stopped dead as he heard a lightly whistled cadence of notes.

That was no bird.

'Huntsman.' It was an acknowledgement, no more. Ingeld raised a hand as he came past, picking his graceful way through the briars and the fallen branches. Ingeld, who had held a requiem mass for Radmer and the other men lost at sea, but showed no other signs of grief.

Widia tensed again, his face giving nothing away. He nodded, refusing to call this man lord, or father. 'Where's your mare?'

'Storm?' Ingeld paused mid-step. 'In her stable with a capped hock. I thought she should rest it. I expect Athulf's looking after her. What business is it of yours?'

'Have you been riding her too hard?'

Ingeld had a smile hovering round his mouth. 'Tend to your hawks and your hounds, huntsman. I know what I'm doing.'

'That's not what I hear.'

Ingeld paused for a moment. 'Are we still talking about Storm? Or have we moved on?'

'You know what I'm talking about.'

Ingeld still had that smile. 'She's lovely, isn't she?'

They stared each other out. Widia bit his lower lip. The urge to violence was almost too strong for him, and his hand twitched towards the hilt at his waist.

'Come on then.' Ingeld spread out his hands. 'What's stopping you? I'm not armed. Do as your conscience lets you.'

Widia jerked his hand from the smooth ash of the knife-hilt as though it had bitten him. 'Don't tempt me.'

'You're very ready with your temper for a man who has no claim.' Ingeld was still smiling, but his eyes had narrowed. 'I saved your life last year: you might do well to remember that. If you've said all you have to say, I'll be on my road.' He turned back to the pathless route downhill back to the minster. As he watched the dark-blue shape dwindle rapidly among the trees, Widia heard him pick up the whistled tune again.

One throw. Just one…

For all the mass of scar tissue down his ribs, he could still aim a knife with force and precision. He took a savage pleasure in imagining the sharp blade flying end over end, embedding itself neatly between the abbot's shoulder blades, Ingeld gasping, his arms flying wide, staggering, slumping to his knees and falling face down.

The image in his mind's eye was so vivid that it was almost more shocking to see Ingeld still picking his way down the slope.

Yes, Ingeld had driven off the boar. There was a debt there he could do without.

Debt?

He had shoved Ingeld out of the boar's path first. And now Ingeld had taken his girl.

Donmouth owed him, not the other way round. Donmouth owed him a lot, and Ingeld most of all.

Widia watched until the solid, confident figure was out of sight. He had never yet attacked any man from behind and without warning, but he could wish he had fewer scruples.

Perhaps next time the boar would do his work for him.

46

A tiny woven basket, containing a folded butterbur leaf. Someone less sharp-eyed than Fredegar could easily have passed it by or trampled it unnoticing. The priest looked left and right in the early light but as ever when the gifts arrived the churchyard appeared deserted.

This was the fifth. First, there had been that little bone cross. Then, on a bitter morning, just before Lent, a benison of two early eggs in a nest of fleece, small and speckled but delicious after the months of dearth. Then a few weeks later a hare, its neck broken, and the noose still dangling, early on a Sunday morning. A gift from someone who knew that the Lenten fast was lifted on the Lord's Day? Most recently a wreath of spring flowers, long-stemmed daisies tight-woven, buttercups and blue-bells threaded through, already fading by the time he found it. Other than the hare, everything had been beautifully presented, and today's little offering was no exception. Fredegar unpinned the thorn that held the leaf together to find a couple of dozen wild strawberries gleaming beneath. To seek out so many per-fectly ripe fruits this early in the season must have taken time and trouble, and once again Fredegar found himself profoundly moved. He lifted the basket to his nose and inhaled the essence of summer.

Someone wanted to give him pleasure. It was not a thought to which he was accustomed, and it made him uncomfortable.

Half a year this had been going on, and he had come no closer to finding out his benefactor, although he had been scanning the

Donmouth faces at high days and holy days. Was there some unmarried girl nursing an unlikely and illicit passion for her sallow priest? Did one of those stolid churl's faces conceal a guilty secret that would be revealed some day in confession, these gifts left in the hope of a lighter penance?

But although plenty of folk blushed or scowled or averted their eyes under his scrutiny he was no wiser. He fingered the bone cross where it lay on his breastbone between linen and wool, and wondered where to put the basket. It had been skilfully plaited and coiled out of straw, and though he knew never to underestimate the marvellous delicacy of which men's hands were capable, he rather thought that small fingers had made this, and female ones. A few white petals had been scattered over the garnet fruits.

Again he wondered about Elfrun, and again he shook his head. She had a generous spirit and an impulsive one, but her gifts were public ones from her and Abarhild, like the new altar linen, and made to the clerics as a group, or to the church. This furtive practice was surely alien to a girl like her, although of late she had had a haunted look about her which disturbed him. Had an oblate or a young cleric in his care had that look he would have pressed the lad to make his confession and clear his conscience, but he was not Elfrun's novice-master and he felt deeply inhibited about raising the question of her soul's wellbeing with her. Some six weeks ago she had made her Easter confession to him, instead of to her uncle, but it had been perfunctory – should he have challenged her then?

Neither age, nor sex, nor rank should prevent a confessor from doing his plain duty, scrutinizing a penitent's soul as a *medicus* would a flask of urine. And usually Fredegar was scrupulous in his duty. He was sealed to silence, and he held the grubby secrets of the souls of Donmouth in his heart, as though in a locked and iron-bound chest. But he had been unable to put Elfrun to the test, although something heavy was lying on her, the depth of those once-clear brown eyes shadowed and sad.

Something more, he thought, even than the burden of her father's death. The shadow had fallen on her before that dreadful news.

He shook his head, walking back into the church. Without meaning to, he took a strawberry from the basket and put it in his mouth. A moment of grainy nothingness, and then as his tongue crushed the fruit against his palate a burst of pure flavour, like sunshine and sweet music, that tasted every whit as good as it had smelt. The strawberry was the plant of the Holy Virgin, in flower and in fruit at the same time, and he had heard it said that these little fruits would be the food of the blessed in Heaven.

But, God forgive him, he was supposed to be fasting before mass. With renewed resolve, he folded the leaf over and pinned it back into place. Fresh linen gleamed on the altar. The year's first harvest of rushes and sweet flag was strewn on the floor. The little church looked as fine as he could make it. He set the little basket down at the base of the altar. A gift to him, or to God?

47

'**Y**ou're not doing so badly, child.'

Elfrun wasn't sure to what her grandmother was referring. The fine-woven diamond-patterned twill which her gnarled hands were tugging this way and that, or the management of the hall? Or just that Elfrun was still somehow moving through her life, despite the awful numbness that deadened her to the world, the sense that she was walking on eggshells, this monstrous clawed grief that gripped her, bear-like, and took away her ability to breathe?

She nodded, and said nothing.

Abarhild had been making one of her unannounced visits to the hall-women's house and the weaving sheds, examining both the work still on the looms and the finer bolts of cloth and braided bands that had been their winter's labour. Not a woman present had escaped having her work dissected, and some of the younger ones had been left in tears. Abarhild appeared highly satisfied with this result now, and she patted Elfrun's arm with her free hand. 'We'll make weavers of them yet.' She sniffed. 'Lazy, slapdash creatures, girls. You have to be hard on them so that they learn to be hard on themselves.'

'Yes, Grandmother.'

'They think because I'm old they can get away with poor work.' She sniffed again, and yawned. 'You're not as bad as some.' She patted her granddaughter on the shoulder. 'I never thought you would manage so well. But we have to think about the future.'

If the news of Radmer's death had frozen Elfrun it appeared

perversely enough to have brought Abarhild back to life. She was spending a lot more of her time at the hall, and somewhere through the fog Elfrun knew that she was grateful to her grandmother. The last few blurred, stumbling weeks would have been impossible without her.

'Take me to the hall, girl. I'm worn out. I need a seat by the fire and a cup of wine.'

'Yes, Grandmother.' Elfrun pushed her cloak back and waved an arm at a scurrying child. 'Go and tell Luda he's wanted in the hall.'

'Yes, lady.'

A snort, and the faint sound of hooves, and Elfrun half turned to see Athulf trotting into her yard, on Mara. She still minded the old sword that hung permanently now at his belt. For that matter, she minded that he had got in the habit of saddling Mara and taking her out without asking. She herself had no heart for riding, however, and she hoped she was not such a dog in the manger that she would deny the same pleasure to him. Besides, Mara needed the exercise.

But she would not let him have Radmer's best sword. Dunstan had brought it safely home, and she had seen Athulf eyeing it. That sword and its scabbard weren't in the heddern any more: they were tucked under the thick-plaited rush of her pallet.

Not a chance she would let Athulf have that sword, though she didn't quite understand why it mattered so much to her.

Athulf was not alone. The spring sunshine glinted in the russet hair of the tall young man riding in behind her cousin, and with a slight tensing of her gut Elfrun recognized Thancrad of Illingham. One thing to know that Athulf spent his waking hours riding and hunting with him; quite another to have Thancrad trotting into her father's yard on that beautiful bay mare of his, with his shoulders back and his head high, looking about him as though he owned the place.

Elfrun knew Athulf would gladly have ignored her, but he could hardly show that same discourtesy to his grandmother. Both young men were slithering down from their saddles to make their bow just as Luda came bustling up, an officious squint on his long face.

If she ordered wine now as her grandmother had commanded, she would have to offer some to Thancrad. It would be too pointed a snub otherwise. But she hated the way he was standing so easily, resting his weight on one foot, holding his horse's reins and looking around him with that cool, narrow-eyed stare, assessing the hall and the stables and the hounds the dumb dog-boy was leading out of the kennels.

Luda was waiting, his eyebrows raised.

It was no good. Abarhild was tired; she was old; she needed warmth and wine and a comfortable cushion. Elfrun was going to have to swallow her pride. But she hadn't been able to forget the jeer on Athulf's face a couple of months back, the way he had menaced her with his blade. *Don't you want to know what he says about you?*

No. She didn't. She had a positive horror of finding out. Just having Thancrad here made her jumpy. Even absent, Radmer had been a bulwark against bad things happening. And Illingham was the nearest likely source of bad things. *They're trouble*, Radmer had said. *Avoid them.* Almost the last words he had ever said to her.

Luda was still hovering.

'Young man!' A long moment before Elfrun realized her grandmother was addressing Luda. Abarhild put all her weight on Elfrun's arm and thrust her stick at the steward. 'Wine in the hall.' She turned back to Elfrun and said loudly, 'Keeping us waiting. My father would have had him flogged.'

'He's a free man, Grandmother.'

Abarhild grunted with amusement. 'As if that would have made any difference.' She waved her stick again, at Athulf this time. 'Let me see that sword.'

Athulf came forward unwillingly, and Abarhild peered at belt, hilt and scabbard. 'My father's sword. I thought so.'

'Yes, Grandmother.' Surprise was making Athulf's voice

swoop unnervingly. Elfrun had to repress a sob of laughter, and he noticed. His face tightened and flushed, and he was clearly bracing himself for a row.

'My father's sword, on a boy destined for the priesthood?' But unbelievably Abarhild was smiling her hard-faced smile, nodding and tapping the ferrule of her stick on the ground. 'And his father's before him. It hangs well on you. I was beginning to think you'd never grow.' She nodded at Athulf. 'Wear it for the time being. And we'll have to think again about your future now.' She half turned to include Elfrun. 'Everything's different now.'

Athulf was shifting uncomfortably, and Thancrad stepped forward, deflecting attention, and bowing. 'I am Thancrad of Illingham, lady.'

'I know who you are.' Abarhild cleared her throat, almost growling. 'I knew your father when he was a wisp of a lad not half your size.'

The thought of Tilmon, massive as a side of beef, ever having been *a wisp of a lad* was almost enough to set Elfrun off again. She could feel laughter coming up inside her chest like the punch of a fist. What was wrong with her?

'And how is your mother settling in at Illingham?'

'If my mother had known I would be seeing you I am sure she would have sent greetings.' He bowed. 'She is well enough, but she complains about the damp.'

'Really? After where she's been?' Abarhild snorted. 'Come on, inside.'

Elfrun sat on a stool at Abarhild's feet, her head lowered and her hands clasped around her untouched glass, the thick brown plaits hanging down the sides of her face and hiding her hot cheeks. She wished they would go away.

Abarhild was interrogating Athulf endlessly, about the sword, and his riding and where he had been, tutting and hissing occasionally, but mostly nodding in approval. Thancrad tried to join in, but she ignored him, and after a little while he shifted round to hunker down by Elfrun's side.

'How are you?'

She turned to look at him. 'Really?'

'Of course, really.'

'Then, *really*, I wish I was dead too.' That threw him, as she had intended, and he was silent for a long moment.

Then, 'And is that all?'

'All?' Her voice was too loud and she lowered it. 'Listen to my grandmother. You know why she's asking Athulf all these questions? Because she thinks maybe he can take over Donmouth now. She doesn't have to try to force him to be a priest.'

Thancrad frowned. 'But Donmouth is yours. The king said as much. Everyone knows that.'

'Till someone steals it from me.' She was perilously close to tears, and she had to stop, breathe, swallow.

'Drink your wine.'

She nodded, and sipped, but it stuck in her throat.

Thancrad huffed a sigh. 'You want your father back, but sometimes I wish mine would just disappear.' He glanced at her, looking for a response, but she felt no curiosity. He and Tilmon were her father's enemies. Why should she care about them, and any quarrel they might have? Thancrad went on, 'He's got so much, but he always wants more.' Again that glance, that pause, as if he were waiting for her to answer. Why did he think she was interested?

Eventually she shrugged, staring into her wine, and he gave up, moving back to Athulf, and the conversation turned to cattle.

Only slowly did she realize that Abarhild was falling asleep. The stick was slipping sideways from the old woman's hand, and Thancrad leaned forward and fielded it easily, propping it against the stool.

'She lives at the minster, doesn't she? She should go home.'

Elfrun scrambled to her feet, relieved beyond measure. 'I'll tell Luda to see the oxen are harnessed.' She spotted her chance to escape. 'I'm going back to the minster too. So, goodbye.'

'No need.' He was standing too. 'Put your grandmother up

on your pommel, Athulf. I will be honoured if you ride with me, Elfrun.'

'But the oxen—'

'It's nearly dark,' he said. 'It'll be much quicker on horseback, and more comfortable. Why go jolting over a rutted track when you can ride in style?' She could tell from his voice that he was smiling now, though the hall was too dark to see his face clearly, with the hearth behind him. 'Athulf tells me you like horses. You'll love Blis.'

Something odd in the way he said the name. 'Bliss? The bay outside? The one you were riding when...' She tailed off. It was more than a year since that crazy race, and Thancrad had never given any sign that he had recognized Elfrun of Donmouth as that wild-haired, screaming girl who had so nearly beaten him. Where had that girl gone? She seemed like a stranger now.

'Blis,' he corrected, the vowel oddly long. *Blees*. 'I've had her from a foal. She's nine now. She's perfect.' He jerked his head and turned, leaving what felt like no choice but to follow. Elfrun looked longingly at her grandmother, but Athulf was already helping Abarhild to her feet and out into the courtyard, still lit with the afterglow of the sunset.

And Blis was certainly extremely beautiful: a neat head, her brow marked with a white flash, lustrous dark eyes and eyelashes, a nose soft as moleskin and a fragile grace which, Thancrad told her, was wholly misleading. 'Strong as an ox. And a great heart, haven't you, girl?' And, watching him run his hand up under her mane and caress the soft fur beneath and around her ears and the way the pretty mare rubbed her head against his shoulder with such obvious pleasure, Elfrun almost found herself warming to him.

Thancrad had been riding bareback. He gathered his reins into his left hand and grabbed a handful of mane, and almost faster than Elfrun's eye could follow he leaned his weight on his left leg and swung his right foot up over Blis's back, hooking and hauling, his knees gripping her hard and his whole body following. He grinned at her from his vantage point. 'It's handy being tall.' Her eyes followed his to watch Athulf's ungainly scramble, and she smiled unwillingly. Luda was helping Abarhild up to sit in front of her grandson.

Elfrun thought of riding three miles with Thancrad's arms tight round her and his breath hot on the back of her neck, and she felt queasy and a little giddy. 'I'll go up behind you.'

'As you will.'

And she didn't want Luda to help her, either. She called with relief to Widia, who seemed to be in urgent conversation with the dog-boy. Had they found a common means of understanding one another? He patted the lad on the shoulder and came over to make a step of his hands and throw her up, with her skirt rucked up to her knees.

She had ridden behind her father a hundred times. Why should this be so different? She gripped loosely with her bare calves, feeling the calm, gentle lurch of Blis's pace, leaning away from Thancrad and putting her hands on the mare's warm back rather than around his waist. But then Blis moved into a trot, and she had to hold on to him, trying to clutch the soft brown of Thancrad's tunic rather than his midriff, uncomfortably aware of his rangy strength beneath the cloth. She had known he was strong from the easy way he had handled her after her ridiculous tumble at the spring meeting, helping her to his parents' tent. As Blis picked up her pace Elfrun had to hold his waist harder with her left hand while she rubbed at her eye-socket with her right, feeling the shape of the bone beneath. Finn's mirror had told her that the bruising had long gone, but even all these weeks later a tenderness lingered.

Blis had a lovely, forward-going pace, much smoother than Elfrun was used to. She couldn't help saying as much.

'You like her?' She could hear the smile in his voice.

'I love her,' she said frankly, and bit her lip.

'She's my truest friend.' He dropped his voice, and sitting behind him as she was she had to lean forward to hear. 'My parents and I, we were always moving from one court to another. Here and there in Frankia, the Danemarch. It's strange, being the son of an exile. You have no kin, no foster-father, godparents.' He shrugged. 'Athulf is always complaining about being left out, but from where I sit...' He let out a long breath. 'And now it's strange having land, being the son of somebody embedded... My father has fitted right back in. But me...' He half twisted so he could look at her. 'Sorry. Very dull. I just wanted you to see why Blis matters to me.'

Not dull. Certainly not dull, though the thought of him unlocking his heart's secret for her made her profoundly uncomfortable. She made some non-committal noise, and they rode on in silence, with the colour slowly leaching from the sky.

Athulf and Abarhild had been left well behind. Elfrun tried to keep her breath steady. He was her good neighbour, doing her a kindness, nothing more. The familiar path wound up and down and to and fro, avoiding the patches of bog to one side and salt marsh to the other. The stream was high with the rain of the previous day, and Blis splashed through the rills that ran down among the trees before the path made for the higher ground over the big spur and down at last into the sheltered, spring-rich combe where the minster sat on its little plateau. Blue smoke curled gently up into the dusk, smelling comforting and homely. Abarhild's women would have some broth or some porridge waiting, and at the thought her stomach grumbled loudly.

Thancrad laughed. 'Ready for your dinner?'

Oh, Lord in Heaven, did he expect to be invited? But as they jolted into the yard she saw Fredegar ducking out from under the thatch of the clergy house, and she slithered and bumped down even before Blis was quite at a standstill, hurrying to him in relief. The priest was frowning at her, but his brow cleared when she said loudly, 'Athulf is bringing Grandmother, and Thancrad kindly carried me,' and then in a hurried mutter, 'Please, get rid of him, Father.'

Fredegar nodded, his face still stern, and he put his hand on

275

her shoulder. 'Thank you, young man, for bringing our daughter home.' His voice was loud and firm, his tone both courteous and dismissive. 'Go into your grandmother's house, child, and see that all is ready for her.'

Elfrun went, feeling both graceless and grateful. Thancrad had been kind, that was all. Very kind. She paused in the doorway and looked over her shoulder to see him lifting a hand in salute, but she pretended she hadn't noticed and hurried inside. The pot on the hearth smelt as savoury as she had hoped, and it was good to be out of the chill.

Fredegar came in a few moments later, ushering Abarhild and settling her down on her stool. Her woman came clucking forward with a soft shawl, and the old woman grumbled and muttered to herself. Fredegar stood in the shadows and watched. When he was certain Abarhild was comfortable he jerked his head. 'Come.'

'But I'm hungry!'

'Bring a piece of bread then.'

The first stars were appearing, though the western sky was still streaked faint green and orange above the hills. Not frosty, but not far from it.

The young men had gone.

Elfrun wanted to explain that she had done nothing wrong, that she had merely been courteous to a guest and a neighbour, but she was reluctant to open her mouth. Why should she justify herself? If Abarhild hadn't censured her, then no one else had the right. But then why – if she had indeed done nothing wrong – this crawling sense of guilt? Her stomach was still growling audibly. She tried to nibble at the hunk of barley bread she was holding, but it was dry and a little stale and the crumbs stuck in her throat.

They had walked only a little way up the track behind the church when Fredegar stopped and turned to look down past the huddle of minster buildings to the sea, now visible beyond.

Elfrun braced herself.

But when he did speak at last his voice was quiet, and his eyes stayed on the sea. 'The world doesn't understand virginity.'

She stared at him, the bread forgotten.

'Perhaps integrity would be a better word.' He sighed, a long, juddering breath. 'Elfrun, dear child, you have such integrity. Such innocence. Like a candle-flame.' She could see his Adam's apple bob as he swallowed, his beaky profile dark against the evening sky. She had never known him struggle so for words, even though English was a foreign tongue to him and he patched his inadequacies with Frankish and Latin. 'Like a length of white linen. The note of a true bell.' He hugged himself, each hand clasping the opposite elbow. 'From time to time your grandmother speaks wistfully of sending you to some house of holy sisters, like Chelles.'

'But that's just her talk! Besides, I can't possibly go to Frankia.'

He shook his head. 'There are nearer houses. Hovingham – she says you have family connections—'

Elfrun forgot all about deference in her anger. 'She just can't stop meddling, can she? It's all about her, not me. She wants to retire, so I have to run the hall. She had to leave Chelles, so she makes these ridiculous plans for me to be a nun, because she couldn't. My father never wanted... He wanted...' But she had to stop then, because of the lump in her throat and the burning in her eyes. She pressed her lips together and stared at the restless far horizon, barely visible in the thronging dusk. She could not give in like this, not if she was lady of the hall, and lord in her father's absence.

But if he was really gone, forever, gone and not coming back, then who was she?

'Elfrun – your grandmother – don't dismiss her suggestions too quickly.' Fredegar sounded more uncertain than she had ever heard him. 'Child, I fear for you. The world...'

She waited for a long time, her heart slowing and her breath steadying. At last, trying to help, she said hesitantly, 'I know I haven't much experience of the world, but I do know folk do... stupid things. And say them... and believe them. I'm not so innocent...' She was breaking off little bits of bread, crumbling them between her fingertips, discarding them, trying to make sense of his words. Her feet were going numb.

'Stupid? Wicked, rather.'

'Is this about Thancrad, riding with him, just now?' She was feeling obscurely insulted. 'Because I didn't *want* to ride with him, Father, but I couldn't be unmannerly either, when he offered.'

'Unmannerly? *Be* unmannerly!' The priest was still staring out to sea. 'You must be less eager to please. Elfrun, you trust too readily.'

She shook her head at him. 'I am the lord of Donmouth. I can't possibly be rude to a guest. What would my father have said?'

Fredegar exhaled, another shuddering sigh, and she realized to her shock that he was near tears. 'These are the manners of the old world, Elfrun. But I am very much afraid that a different world is coming, and you will need to learn to stand up for yourself better. To fight.'

48

'**W**here's your father?'

Wynn hadn't even noticed the shadowing of the forge entrance, she had been so engrossed in her work. Jumping up, she pushed the chunk of cow shank and the little knife with which she had been whittling out her design into the dark corner with a casual sideways flick of her foot.

Her mother was squinting suspiciously into the gloom. 'Well? I want to talk to him.'

'He's not here.'

'I can see that!' Her mother had her arms crossed defensively and a little hard frown tugging at her neat, small-featured face. She took a few steps further into the forge. 'He's found no one to work with him then.'

It was a statement, not a question. Wynn saw no need to respond. That was public knowledge.

'What were you doing just now?' Her mother was peering into the corner.

'Nothing.' Wynn walked towards her mother, blocking her view. 'Father's gone way north, looking for ironstone. Up past Pickering marshes, he said. Days away.' She sighed and put her hands on her hips. 'He goes every year, Mam. You know that.'

'He's not taken you? He's left you here alone?'

Wynn wondered how anyone could be so thick-witted. 'Does it look as though he's taken me?'

'Don't you speak to me like that.'

She relented a little. 'He's left me enough to do while the

forge is cold.' She gestured at the oak slab. 'There's hammers need rehafting, tongs with loose rivets...'

'Wynn, will you not come home with me?'

Wynn stared at the floor.

'You're a girl grown, you shouldn't be here. You should be with me – or in the women's house...'

Wynn muttered something, deliberately pitching her voice below easy hearing.

'What?'

'The lady says I can work with my da.' Wynn had no idea whether this was true.

'Elfrun?' Her mother sounded startled. 'Aye, but what does she know? Another green girl! You're needed by me, I've a hundred jobs for you to do.'

Wynn could imagine only too well. A little pang of remorse needled at her, but it was small and swiftly blunted. She had half a dozen cousins who could hoe the beans and lug the babies around. Her father had no one else. She had fought too hard and risked too much to earn her place at the forge; she wasn't going to give it up now, never mind how her mother played on her guilt.

'Come on.' Her mother jerked her head. 'Let's go to the lady now, you and me. She'll understand; she must know this is no place for a girl alone.'

Wynn shrugged. 'Try it if you like. She's no fool, the lady, for all you call her green. Da can't run the forge on his own. And no one can do without smithcraft.' She put her hands back on her hips and stuck out her chin, hoping she looked bigger than she felt.

'Are you saying you're staying here till he finds another lad?'

Wynn nodded, sighing. She had lost patience with this conversation, and her fingers were itching to get back to her knife and bit of bone.

Her mother crossed the floor swiftly and seized her by the hair at the back of her neck.

'Ow!'

'Don't you dare roll your eyes at me like that, you stupid child.' Her mother's face was only inches away, twisted with fury. Wynn flinched, but her mother had her fast. 'What happens when he loses his temper with you, and shoves you in the fire, eh? You think I want to lose another of my children?'

Wynn ducked and ripped away, hissing with pain and leaving a hank of hair in her mother's fist. 'That's not what happened.' She glared from the far side of the cold fire-pit. 'Cudda was fuddled with drink. It was nothing to do with Da, and anyone who says otherwise is a liar.'

'So you're calling me a liar now?'

Wynn shrugged, feeling safer. She wasn't going to go back within reach, and she knew she could out-dodge her mother if it came to a chase. 'Cudda brought it on himself. And yes – you're a liar if you say otherwise, just as much as anyone else.'

Her mother raised a hand, and Wynn braced herself, but after a long moment her mother merely pressed her fingers against her forehead. 'Well, I tried,' she said quietly, her gaze lowered. 'Forgive me, but I tried.'

'Who are you talking to?'

Her mother looked at her levelly, light-blue eyes expressionless in her tired face. She seemed about to speak, but in the end she just turned and walked away.

Wynn waited a long moment. When she was quite sure she was alone she went to the pile of wood stacked in the corner and found the little knife and the hand-long length of bone. She was about to start work again, but looking afresh at her work she found it didn't please her after all. The proportions were wrong, the creature's head too small, its back-bent body too jerky and angular, the encircling tendrils lacking all force. She had been snatching furtive glances at the little silver creatures on Elfrun's cloak tags, but they were no bigger than her thumb, and she was rarely close enough for long enough to get a proper look. Just give her half a morning alone with those tags, to get under the skin of how they had been made, not just the finished thing, but all the stages of how they had come into being...

She refused even to think about the mirror.

Frustration and bad temper made her raise her hand, ready to throw the shank of bone back into the kindling pile, but then she paused. *He* had said something, the kind man with the lovely eyes. *You're a maker... If you truly love it, you can learn.* Elfrun had never thought to tell her his name, but Wynn had been very taken with him, the mirror man.

If *he* had thought she could learn, then she could learn.

Love, so that was what was needed. She didn't know very much about love, but maybe this was the time to start.

She huffed a sigh. It was bad enough trying to do this by eye, never mind from memory. There were rules about how you made these patterns: she knew that. But no one was ever going to tell her what they were. She squinted at her scratchings, brow furrowed with concentration. Another piece of bone was easy enough to come by; much harder to find beautiful things to look at. But if she were ever to get the knack of it, to make the patterns flow the way the best craftsmen could, then she had to have a teacher.

Or models to copy.

Wynn found her eyes flickering again to the long, wrapped bundle on the oak slab. Before he had left, her father had made her promise to leave it well alone. But she had had a glimpse when Athulf had brought it in, and though she hadn't been able to hear much of the urgent, low-voiced exchange, the firelight had shown her enough of the worked leather of the scabbard and the goldcraft of the hilt to make it clear that this was a finer thing than she would meet again in a hurry.

She had promised on her honour not to touch it.

Moving slowly, hardly daring to breathe, she got to her feet again and tiptoed round the forge floor to where Athulf's sword and scabbard lay swathed in a fold of woven wool, like a swaddled baby. She stood contemplating the bundle, her hands clasped behind her back. Then she stepped to the forge door and looked up the path to the hall, and down towards the river. No one in sight, other than a small child half-minding a gaggle of errant geese bigger than itself. Wynn drifted back inside, feigning innocence, purposelessness, just in case.

Once back inside, she arranged the faulty tongs together with the tools needed to mend them on the bench, again just in case. If someone did come in they would furnish her an excuse for being at the bench. And then she returned her attention to the sword.

Her first, and unexpected, sensation was one of disappointment. Scabbard and hilt alike were decorated with angular long-jawed creatures of a type she did not recognize. A long chain of them in the raised leather of the scabbard, and a pair facing each other on the pommel. They looked old, and ugly, and alien.

But as Wynn looked more closely the fine detail of the design, the control and the rhythm implicit in this hooky, overlapping band of creatures began to entrance her eye. They wove together so perfectly, the jaws of each clasping the leg of the one in front... This was the work of a master. It might be that no one would thank her for making something marked with these beasts today, but she could learn from it, for all that.

She wouldn't rush into it, though. Another long hard look at the pommel, drinking in the over and under, the angle of the jaws, the echoing relationship of oval eye and body-curve; and she squatted down with a stick to scrape out the pattern, as a first step, on the packed earth of the floor.

But it was no good, going back and forth. Her promise entirely forgotten, she picked up the sword in its scabbard and set it down on the ground so she could keep it before her eyes while she drew.

It was nearly impossible at first, so many little angles and zigzags, and as she copied each component was slightly more askew, so the pattern distorted further and further as she moved along. She looked back at the scratchings in the floor and felt the hot tears of anger. This was impossible. She was on the verge of snapping the stick and throwing it into the kindling-pile, when she had a thought.

Dirt wasn't like bone, or metal. Dirt was more like what she had heard of parchment. It could be rubbed out. You could build up layers of lines, rubbing out selectively...

She ground the floor smooth again with the ball of her foot, and began once more. But this time, rather than trying to reproduce the whole pattern at once, she drew a long, regular, swooping line. Then a second, dip intersecting rise at set intervals. And then a third. These would guide her. Now to draw parallel lines above and below each of her original three. Squatting, shuffling incrementally, using her finger, she erased, drew in new lines, turned other lines back on themselves, joined errant loops. Increasingly she began to notice intentional irregularities, places where the artist had aimed for the effect of symmetry where true symmetry was unattainable. How he had amused the eye with a spiral to distract from the impossibility of a hip joint...

The whole pattern, from hilt to chape, was making sense now, and she was working with greater confidence, no longer bothering to check every time that her wild scratchings on the floor corresponded to the design on the scabbard. Perhaps only she and the artist to whose vision she was responding would have recognized the pattern she was making, but she knew it was there, and she could feel that other maker's approval, as surely as though his hand were guiding hers.

'What the hell is going on here?'

She scrabbled backwards and away, but her first reaction was one of relief. The intruder was neither her father nor her mother. 'I was looking at the pattern.'

'You put my sword on the floor. The dirt floor.' Athulf had snatched it up and was cradling it protectively in his arms.

Wynn eyed him warily, and moved gently back so that the

fire-pit was between them, and she was closer than he was to the door. 'How'm I ever going to learn to mend it if I can't look at it?' She gestured. 'Or draw it.'

'You?' The contempt in his tone was withering. His eyes narrowed, and he peered at the floor between them. 'This?' Deliberately he dragged his heel sideways, scouring and obliterating her designs. 'Tell your father I'll bring the sword back later. And he's not to leave it unattended again.'

Wynn scowled at him as he barged past her. She knew she was at fault. He would have been well within his rights to strike her, but he had not. And still, she hated him.

49

They heard the music first, fitful and distant only, because although the high-summer day was bright the wind was coming in from the sea. Strange, high-pitched, trowie sounds that had everyone dropping their work and coming to the hall, to see the musicians coming, the girl in kale-green who played a bird-bone flute, and the man with an Irish drum against which he rattled a little stick, and the boy who danced on a ball that he turned with his feet – and the bear.

The bear!

Elfrun had never seen a live bear before. It was a long, baffling moment before she could work out the dark, hunched shape.

The bear-leader came shaking a leather rattle in his left hand and leading the bear with his right. It shambled along, its thick shaggy coat pale with the dust of the road. A mob of children came after it, shoving and pointing and egging each other to run up and tug at a clump of the fur. They were growing ever more daring, but the bear plodded on, giving no sign of having noticed their antics. It was bridled, with tags of coloured ribbon, green and red and yellow, fastened to the leather straps, and its nose was pierced with a rope which passed right through the soft flesh of its snout; it followed the bear-leader with impressive humility.

The musicians were playing a quick, catchy tune, the man with the drum shouting encouragement to the crowd, and especially to the children who were jigging from foot to foot.

The boy jumped down from his ball and kicked it sideways, then flipped over and began walking on his hands, his tunic falling about his ears and his bare buttocks flashing white in the cool, hazy sunshine.

But Elfrun couldn't look at anything but the bear.

The bear-leader had stopped quite close to where she was standing in the doorway of the women's house, drawn out like every other soul in Donmouth by the strange, wailing music. She was not at all sure it was fitting to watch the entertainers, or even to allow them to perform, but for the first time since the news had come of Radmer's drowning the bear drove all such anxieties from her mind, replacing them with a horrified fascination. Small, red-brown eyes glared out at her, almost lost in the fur which, now she was close, she could see was less thick than she had thought, even mangy, and rubbed bare in places. Its huge feet were tipped with massive claws, black paling to brown at the tips, each one as long and thick as her longest fingers, and she took a step back at the thought of the damage those could do. A powerful musky aroma came off the fur.

The swarthy, heavily bearded bear-leader caught her eye and grinned. 'You like him?' He winked at her. 'Think he's pretty, eh?' His voice was thick and deep, with a lilting accent.

'Is he' – she hesitated over her choice of words, not wanting to sound as though she doubted his power over the beast – 'is he friendly?'

'Acourse. Come here.' He beckoned, and she took an unwilling, fascinated, step nearer. 'Come on – I don't bite, either! Promise! I'll tell you a secret. He's like me' – he gaped and pointed – 'lost all his sharp teeth. Give him a little pat, little cuddle? And how about one for me?'

She recoiled. Already she was too close for comfort to either bear or man, with that yawning hole of a mouth. 'But what about the claws?'

'He won't hurt you with them. Maybe knock you down, rip your dress, give you a little scratch, a bruise.' He looked her up and down in cheerfully offensive detail and grinned again, eyes disappearing in his weathered face. 'Nothing your man won't do from time to time.'

Elfrun flushed and stepped backwards, but he went on smiling at her as though they had been sharing a joke.

She turned abruptly away from him, to find that the boy had started walking on a rope rigged up hastily between two sturdy tripods of birch-logs, some four or five feet above the earth. He was holding a willow wand for balance, but it was clear that he hardly needed it. The rope sagged a little, but he never lost his footing, moving faster and faster to the pipe-whistle and the drum-beat. When he reached the end he pivoted easily on one foot, threw the wand aside, and went back, this time reaching out to catch the weighted cloth balls that the girl was throwing to him – one, two, three – until he had five in the air at the same time. When he reached the end of the rope again and sprang down on to the earth the crowd emitted a collective sigh. There must have been sixty or seventy folk there now, all ages, and more arriving. Not all Donmouth, maybe, but all those who lived within a mile or so of the hall.

The girl in kale-green was passing through the crowd with her bowl, hoping for any little coin or pin that could be spared, tossing her long, loose brown hair that the sun made more copper and gilt-bronze, swirling her skirts, the radiant smile on her sun-freckled face never reaching her eyes.

The music changed. Wilder now, with high notes wavering and wailing and rapid pattering on the drum, and the bear-leader brought his charge into the centre of the circle the folk of Donmouth had made. He bowed to each side, north, south, east, west, and an extra, mocking bow for Elfrun that somehow made it clear he had known all along that she was the lady of this place. Then he clapped his hands, and the bear did the same, even down to the respectful dip of the head when it faced Elfrun. A ripple of laughter.

The show started slowly, with the man straddling his bear

and having it squirm between his legs; leading it around the ring as it went tumbling head over heels, rolling so close to the crowd that folk drew in their breath and stepped back before pressing eagerly forward again; raising a commanding hand and having the bear flatten itself until it looked like a flayed hide rather than a living animal. At long last he snapped his fingers, and the bear stood up on its hind legs.

A gasp.

Taller than the tallest man present, and grotesquely like a man, with massive shoulders and thighs. The fur was thinnest over its belly, but there were dark tufts thick at the groin. It stood flat on its feet and glared out from those little reddish eyes. The bear-leader clucked, a little low, almost loving sound, and he shook the rope, and the bear began to clap its heavy paws together and shuffle back and forth in time with the music, swaying its hips and nodding its head. The bear-leader gestured at the crowd. 'Come on, everyone, dance!'

Then the music changed again, darker, the drum thudding. The bear-leader gestured, and the bear sat heavily down on its haunches. The music stopped. The bear-leader walked up to the bear, coiling the rope in his hand as he went, and when he reached the animal he unfastened the bridle and slipped it over the animal's ears and snout. He backed away, raising his big hands with the bridle clutched in one, and turned to the crowd, once more facing this way and that. 'Now,' he said, 'who will fight my bear?'

Silence.

'Big men like you? This little soft bear I've had from a cub?' He turned his back on the bear, then jumped round. 'Boo!' The bear put its paws to its face and fell over backwards.

Some laughter.

'And I'd heard the men of Donmouth were hard men.' He looked around the crowd. 'I'll tell you. Someone stake a silver penny and I' – he made a pass in the air and abstracted something shiny from nowhere – 'I will let as many of you as you like fight my bear, and the man judged the winner will get a reward.'

Between grimy thumb and forefinger he was holding a tiny patterned disc of gold. 'Seen one of these before?'

The sight of gold was intoxicating. Elfrun could see eyes widening, fingers pointing, hear the hurried whispers.

'No one?' The gold glinted in the sun.

'I'll stake the penny!' Elfrun looked round to find her uncle at her shoulder. His eyes were shining and his face flushed. She hadn't even seen him in the crowd.

'Well done, my lord!' Ingeld lobbed the coin and the bear-leader put up his free hand to take it from the air. It and the gold disc vanished together.

The bear-leader looked around the crowd again. 'Here's what you do. My bear stands up.' He made that caressing little click again, and the bear shambled over to him, hunched and meek-looking. 'You wrestle him. No punching, no gouging. You push; he pushes. First one down is the loser.'

Still no one stepped forward. Elfrun was aware of jostling and whispers here and there in the crowd as the young men egged each other on, but no one was driving the matter too hard. They could see those claws and, unlike her, they didn't know about the absence of teeth. And even without teeth the force in those jaws must be immense... Who would have the power to challenge the bear? Dunstan would have once, but he had gone to join the king's retinue, much to Athulf's bitterness. Cuthred the smith perhaps, with his ropy strength? But she hadn't seen him or Wynn anywhere in the crowd.

The bear-leader whistled cheerfully. 'So, I keep your money and don't have to work for it?' He slapped his hip. 'Easiest penny I've ever made.' He looked around the crowd. 'Tell me – who are your neighbours? Who do the Donmouth men love to hate?'

'Illingham!' A voice from the back of the crowd, echoed here and there with approval.

'Illingham, eh?' The man's eyes narrowed. 'And what'll they say in Illingham, when I tell them not a man in Donmouth—'

'I'll fight your bear.'

Every eye swivelled. The voice had come from the far side of the arena, and at first Elfrun couldn't see who had spoken. Then the crowd parted, and Hirel the shepherd pushed his way to the front.

'I'll fight your bear,' he repeated. The men around him were whooping and slapping his broad shoulders but he was silent and his dark face was strained. He walked into the open space, but he was ignoring the bear and its warder, even though they were only a yard or so from him. Elfrun, puzzled, thought for a moment he was looking at her.

Ingeld was smiling.

The crowd fell silent.

The bear-leader squinted back and forth between the two men. His brows were knotted, and he evidently suspected Hirel's action in coming forth masked more than mere bluster. When Hirel turned at last to look at him, he nodded. 'A' right then and good luck to you both. You're not unlike a bear yourself, master, if you don't mind my saying so.' He scratched the bear behind its ears, and the creature sat up on its haunches. 'Go on, then, my lovelies. Go to it.'

Hirel approached warily, stepping right and left, eyeing up his opportunities. The bear swung its head to follow his movements, this way and that, for an eternity. Then Hirel sprang. He hurled himself forward, driving his right shoulder under the bear's chin, and shoved upwards, all the weight of his body behind it. His bare feet scrabbled for purchase in the dust. The bear lurched violently, and for a moment Elfrun thought that Hirel had won, so quickly that no fun was to be got from it, and the bear was going over on its back, but the animal rocked and danced from foot to foot, and resettled itself, as massive and implacable as it had ever been. Elfrun felt a cold breath on her shoulder, and looking round she realized that while she had been engrossed by the bear a mist-bank had been rolling in from the sea and closing round them. Already the trees the far side of the weaving shed were blurring and losing their colour. The east wind always brought the summer sea-fret; she didn't know why she was surprised.

Hirel still had his shoulder under the beast's jaw, and now he locked his arms around the great shaggy neck and hauled sideways. His face was buried in the fur but Elfrun could hear his grunts of effort. His feet skidded sideways and he fell, still holding the bear, and the animal came down on top of him. Hirel was back on his knees at once, shoving the colossal weight off him, but now the bear too seemed stirred and it rose on to its back legs and put its front paws around Hirel's waist. A gasp from the crowd at the sight of the extended claws. The bear was trying to get its jaws around Hirel's head, and Elfrun, sickened and excited, hoped the bear-leader had been telling the truth about its teeth. Hirel was flailing at the bear's mouth with his hands, but Elfrun could see the bear's grip getting tighter and tighter. She pressed her hand over her mouth, finding it hard to breathe herself.

Hirel ducked suddenly and twisted, down and out of the terrible grip.

'Enough?' The bear-leader was grinning. Hirel's tunic was torn and his face was dark red and beaded with sweat. He didn't answer, panting hard and scowling, and then he hurled himself at the animal once again. This time it was quick. The bear was up on its hind legs already, and it showed a fast, almost nimble, dancing step that was new. It grabbed Hirel with one arm and bore down on him, throwing him sideways as though he were made of straw, swiping across the shepherd's face with the claws of the other paw. Someone screamed. Hirel landed flat on his back, and the bear hurled itself on top of him, pounding him repeatedly with its whole body weight.

'I think the bear likes him!' The bear-leader was egging the crowd to laughter, but Elfrun didn't think it was funny. Hirel hadn't looked like a man who was doing this for his own entertainment or anyone else's. Blood streamed down his face. He was still trying to lever the bear up and away when the bear-leader whistled. At once the bear stopped fighting and slunk back to the side of its master.

Hirel twisted over and got up on to his hands and knees. He was breathing harder than ever, his face purple and contorted, and now Elfrun could see the torn back of his tunic was stained with fresh blood. He sat back on his heels and pushed the hair and blood out of his eyes with the back of his hand. 'Let me fight it again.'

The bear-leader shrugged. 'If you're game—'

'I'm game!' The blood was trickling thickly down from a cut above his eyebrow and he dashed it away again with his sleeve.

'No.' It was Ingeld who had spoken. He was smiling, but his voice lacked its usual warmth. 'You've done very well, shepherd. But you should know when to leave well enough alone.'

Hirel had clenched his fists. He staggered to his feet and lurched a few paces forward. Even through that gory half-mask Elfrun could see how bloodshot his eyes were, and smell his sweat mingled with the musky, smoky aroma of bear. 'You don't tell me what to do.' He looked around. 'Where's my wife?'

Saethryth pushed her way forward to the front of the crowd.

'How did I do?' Hirel sounded like a child. 'Did you see me, wife? Did I do well? Was it like when I won my keg?'

Saethryth had her arms folded across her breasts. 'Who's going to have to wash and mend that tunic?' To Elfrun's disbelief she sounded more bored than anything else.

'I told you: you did well, shepherd.' At Ingeld's words there was a stir of interest among the crowd, those further back pushing forward for a better view. 'Donmouth's honour is safe enough.' There was a taunting note to his voice which baffled Elfrun. Hirel had fought heroically, even if he had lost; he was hurt; and now Ingeld was trying to provoke him to anger? Hirel was their good servant: why on earth make matters worse?

But Elfrun could hear the amusement in his voice, and there was no doubt that Hirel could hear it too. 'You stay out of it,' the shepherd said in a low voice. He looked around suspiciously, and his eye fell on the bear-leader. 'You set me up. What's going on?' He wiped his sleeve against his bloody forehead again.

'Not I, master.'

'You, then.' Hirel swung round on Ingeld.

Somewhere behind Elfrun she heard a voice say, 'If he didn't know before he knows now.' But she couldn't look to see who had spoken, she didn't dare take her eyes off Hirel.

'Are you going to best me the way you have the bear?' Ingeld raised his eyebrows.

Hirel lunged, and Elfrun almost choked on her own indrawn breath.

But Luda was there, out of nowhere, and Heahred, and a couple of other men with them. Athulf, too, was at his father's side, grim-faced and fists clenched. They moved between Hirel and Ingeld, and Luda put his hand on Hirel's shoulder. Hirel flung it off, but Luda, his long face stern, said something inaudible. Hirel stared down at his father-in-law; then, casting one more furious glance at Ingeld, he turned and limped his way through the far side of the crowd, the blood still spreading dark and wet across the back of his tunic.

50

'Anyone else?' The bear had curled up into a furry ball, its face concealed behind its paws. The bear-leader prodded it with a toe, but it just pulled itself tighter. 'Any more of you want to take on my little honey-fed baby?'

'What about dogs?'

Elfrun stared at her uncle. He was snapping an imperious hand. 'Widia!' And back to the bear-leader. 'Your bear – will it fight my dogs?'

The bear-leader looked down at his animal, then over at Ingeld, his eyes narrowed. 'My bear's my livelihood, master.' His voice had taken on an ingratiating note. 'What if it's hurt? It's worth my meat and drink to me. What's it worth to you that can match with that price?' The crowd had fallen silent. There was no sign of Hirel.

Ingeld was smiling. He tapped his red leather purse where it hung by his hip. 'I don't know how much I've got in here.' He gave it a shake, tilting his head and raising an eyebrow. 'Want to take a chance?'

The bear-leader's face was flushed above his beard, his eyes bright. Ingeld gave the purse a shake, and Elfrun could hear the thin silver discs chinking faintly. The dainty leather bag was evidently well stocked. It occurred to Elfrun as she gazed around her that those pennies had been creamed from the hard labour of these people. Her people, slave and free. The strips and patches of land belonging to the abbot and those which appertained to the lord were so entangled that nearly everyone owed goods and work and coin to both minster and hall. Their back-breaking hours in the fields and the ditches, at the looms and the fish-traps and the hives, had made the profit which now sang that faint, seductive song from inside its fine kidskin.

And much they cared.

If their silver would buy their pride again, then it was well spent.

They had cheered Hirel on, they had laughed and been abashed by their own laughter when it looked as though the bear was trying to mount him. They had been silenced and shamed by his defeat. Now here was their abbot giving them another chance. Donmouth, down to the last man, woman, and child jigging eagerly from foot to foot, wanted this fight.

'Let me see the dogs first,' the bear-leader said.

Ingeld was nodding but, '*Coward*,' Athulf shouted, and the insult was echoed a few times from faces hidden in the crowd. Ingeld raised his hand for silence. The sun had been coming and going through the patches of drifting mist, and it was a good omen that it shone now, flashing on the fine silver wire on the cuff of his tunic and the massive gold of his abbatial ring. The folk quietened a little. Elfrun watched her uncle thoughtfully. He had folded his arms easily across his chest, and he was standing with his weight on one foot, looking around the crowd. That stray patch of sunlight was also picking out the silver in his brown hair where a lock fell over his forehead, and glinting on the fine stubble on his chin and upper lip. He had a little smile on his face that creased the skin around his eyes and deepened the lines that ran from his nose to the corners of his mouth. The fingers of one hand were tapping on his other arm, and she suddenly had the thought that he was looking for someone. He lifted his head suddenly, his eyes narrowed and the smile grew warmer. Elfrun looked across at Luda and Saethryth and Heahred, but she couldn't see whom he had been smiling at. She wondered suddenly why Saethryth hadn't gone to look after her wounded husband.

'Uncle?'

'Mm?' He turned and looked down at her, brown eyes under arched, insouciant brows, still smiling.

She had nothing to say; she wasn't even sure why she had spoken. 'I – Look, here's Widia and the dogs.'

Widia and the dog-boy, still nameless as when he had arrived. The hounds were leashed together, and as ever Elfrun was amazed that such a scrawny green-stick of a boy could hold those three powerful animals in check. He and the bear-leader would have had a lot to say to each other about their mastery of beasts, if only the boy could use his tongue.

Ingeld put an arm round Widia's neck and a hand on the boy's shoulder, bringing them and their charges forward into the makeshift arena. 'Here they are. What do you say?'

The bear-leader took his time, sucking his teeth, eyeing the dogs with their bearded, wedge-shaped heads and shaggy coats, storm-cloud-grey, and creamy-red, and ashy-black. 'Fine hounds.' He turned his head and spat in the dust. 'Had them long?'

Ingeld shrugged. 'A matter of weeks.' He brightened. 'But I've had them out against deer, and you're right. They are fine hounds.'

'And the silver is for my bear fighting? I get that anyway, whether I win or I lose?'

Ingeld nodded.

'Then, master, what's in it for you?'

Ingeld's lips curved in that smile which was never very far away. He gave a shrug. 'Pleasure. We've seen your bear's power, how it sent the strongest man in Donmouth home to lick his wounds. It would please me greatly if my hounds can beat the bear.'

'I see your bulging purse.' The bear-leader closed his eyes and cupped a hand behind his ear. 'I can hear the silver inside it calling to me.' He snorted a deep breath in through his nose. 'Aye, I can smell it, even. But the thing is' – he opened his eyes and suddenly all the jesting, all the whining, had vanished from his voice and face – 'the thing is, my bear can mince your hounds.

And now that I've seen what valuable creatures they are, and how you love them, I'm thinking that if I leave one or more of them wounded – dead, even – I don't value the chances of me and my people leaving Donmouth hale and well.' He made a little bow. 'With all respect, master.'

Ingeld shrugged, a little, careless movement. 'That's a risk you'll have to take.'

In all the excitement Elfrun had completely forgotten about the dancing-boy, and the man with the drum, and the pretty girl in her kale-green pinafore strung with amber beads who had passed the bowl around, begging for contributions. Now that she thought to look, she saw them standing in a little huddle behind her and to her right. And the bear-leader probably had the truth of it. He and his were there to amuse. If things turned sour, the travelling entertainers would be overwhelmed, and she didn't know whether she had the authority to quell an angry mob in the way Radmer undoubtedly would have.

But it came to her of a sudden that she could command them now.

No one but Hirel was angry, not yet. She could keep these strangers safe on her land, if she wanted to. A sudden tug on her sleeve and she looked down to find the dog-boy at her side. When he opened his mouth nothing but a shapeless moan emerged, but she knew exactly what he meant. He was pointing at the bear with his free hand, and shaking his head from side to side with a jerk. Elfrun looked at the dogs. They were excited; she guessed they were disturbed by the alien, smoky smell, and they were straining towards it. One of them, Braith with the red and cream mixed in the brindle of his fur, was whining softly.

'They're not my dogs,' she said to him in a low voice. 'I can't tell my uncle what to do.' She swallowed. 'I'm sorry. I can't stop the fight, but I can try and keep the people safe.' He stared at her, the sun bringing out the green lights in his eyes. Elfrun wondered if he had understood a single word.

She stepped forward, bracing her shoulders and lifting her

chin, to be met by a rustle of whispers then a hush. She faced the bear-leader squarely. He was standing by his bear, which was still curled into a ball, paws over its nose. She wondered distractedly whether it had gone to sleep. 'It is your decision,' she said, and she was surprised by how her voice carried. 'But if you choose to pit your bear against my uncle's hounds, I speak for the people of Donmouth when I promise that no matter the outcome all of you will be allowed to leave in peace.' She set her face hard, and stared right and left, not allowing her eye to meet anyone else's, defying contradiction. 'No one is to touch the bear, or his master, or the dancing-boy, or the girl with the flute. Any of them. They are all under my hand.' Not so much as a whisper now. Her jaws were aching, she had been gritting her teeth so hard. The mist was drifting back again, sucking the warmth from the day and turning the sun into a little disc of pewter. She could hear the hisses and mutters, but no one had defied her, and she had to hope that no one would. She let the silence hold for a long moment, then gave a little nod, and turned.

And there, next to the rope-walking boy and the girl in green, was Finn the pedlar, standing easily, his wicker pack down in the dust by his feet. Gazing straight into her eyes, he lifted an eyebrow, half-greeting, half-enquiry, and his face broke into a smile.

Carefully expressionless, Elfrun walked steadily back to her place at her uncle's side. The blood was roaring in her ears, and her mouth had gone suddenly dry. In the long half-year and more since she had last seen him she had forgotten the lines and planes of his face, his easy stance, the way his smile seemed to have been created expressly for her delight. Where on earth had he appeared from? Was he with the bear and the dancing-boy and the flute-girl? Chapmen did often take up with other wanderers of the road. Could she have been so fascinated by the bear that she had failed to notice Finn this last hour and more?

'A' right,' the bear-leader said. 'Someone drive a stake in for me.'

Ingeld was fondling each of the dogs in turn, scratching their heads and tugging gently on their ears. 'Gethyn, Bleddyn, good boys. Braith, come here.' He was slipping the leads from the collars. 'Don't do that,' he said to the bear-leader.

'Should I not stake the bear, master?'

'Where's the fun in that? Give the poor beast a chance.' The boy's hands were full, gripping the collars of two of the dogs. Ingeld beckoned. 'Elfrun, hold Gethyn for me?'

Her head still buzzing, she slipped her hand through the stiff leather band. She could feel the dog's warmth through the wiry coat, and his strength. Gethyn wasn't pulling to get free, but she could sense how strong he was. Were he to spot a hare or some other small creature, she would have to let go, or be dragged willy-nilly in his wake.

Gethyn twisted his head sideways and licked her wrist and she smiled. He grinned back at her, panting, the long pink tongue flopping between the terrible serrated teeth, and she wondered suddenly about the true state of the bear-leader's confidence. These hounds were no mean opponents.

Ingeld was unfastening the straps where the purse looped over his belt. He threw it up in the air and caught it again, one-handed. The purse itself was a fine thing, with its soft red leather and its silver fittings. Elfrun saw the naked longing on the bear-leader's face, and felt sick. Ingeld raised those arched eyebrows that gave his face such a guileless look.

'Here – catch!'

He lobbed it at the bear-leader, who made a wild grab, but it fell short and the man had to go down on his knees in the dirt. A roar of laughter.

Athulf was grinning, inviting her to share in his evident pleasure at the bear-leader's discomfiture, but Elfrun couldn't meet his eye.

'Sorry,' Ingeld said. 'I was off balance.' He was still smiling, and Elfrun found herself wondering against her will whether he could possibly have thrown short on purpose.

The bear-leader shrugged. He was occupied with stuffing the

purse down the neck of his tunic, but when he looked up he said, 'Oh, you'd marvel at what silver has made me do in my time, master. Back when I was young and pretty.' He paused, and looked at Ingeld sideways for a long moment, a knowing stare that made Elfrun hot and itchy. 'Then again, maybe you wouldn't, master. Maybe you wouldn't be surprised at all.' Without waiting for a reply he turned and extended his arms. 'All right, one and all. Let's make us some room.' He walked forward, and the crowd shuffled away. When he had made a full circuit, gesturing all the while as he went, a wide space of dry, rutted earth some fifty paces across was left empty. He made his little clucking noise and the bear rose to its feet and shambled over. The bear-leader jerked his head. 'Bring them on.'

The dog-boy released the collars and pushed the dogs forward. Elfrun just stared, until an angry hiss from her uncle brought her to her senses, and she pulled her reluctant fingers away from Gethyn's neck.

The dogs were a confident and coordinated pack. They hurtled forward and began circling the bear at a distance, yapping in strange, high-pitched tones. The bear shuffled round and round on the spot, trying and failing to keep track of all three at once. Two of them – with a lump in her throat Elfrun recognized Gethyn as one – stopped together and barked sharply, and as the bear lunged towards them the hound with red and cream lights to its coat darted in and nipped sharply at the bear's heels.

'Braith!' Ingeld was shouting and whooping. 'That's my true Braith!'

The bear spun in response to the repeated snapping, and now it was dark-coated Gethyn's turn to dart in and away. The dogs bounded back and forth, and the bear lolloped sideways, trying to escape and to attack at the same time. It snarled suddenly and lunged, and the people nearest in the crowd hurled themselves backwards, with gasps and screams of excitement.

The dogs regrouped, panting, and began their harrying again. The bear seemed much angrier, snapping and growling continuously at these little pests – and they did look small, against its bulk. Surely, one blow with a lethal paw...

Suddenly, as though of one united mind, all three dogs hurled themselves towards the bear, yipping hysterically. The bear tumbled sideways with the impact and they became a ferocious blur of dark and brindled fur, the bear rolling over and over as though repeating the tricks with which its master had started their show. One of the dogs – Bleddyn, Elfrun thought – had fastened its jaws around the bear's nose, and Braith was underneath, snapping wildly at the creature's throat. She had her hands to her face, fingers pressed to her cheekbones ready to shield her eyes, unable to bear it and yet powerless to tear her gaze away.

'Those are some fine hounds you have there,' a voice said in her ear.

She jumped and turned to find Finn the pedlar standing next to her. Somewhere, she registered that Finn's lilting accent was much the same as the bear-leader's. Perhaps they were kin or countrymen at least, travelling together. It would make sense. A lone pedlar was so vulnerable, but any thief would think twice about attacking a party which had that shaggy monster, even bridled and toothless, as escort. She tried to keep her mind on these practical questions, but Finn was so close, she could feel the hairs rising on her arms, the palms of her hands tingling, her breath tight; much the same effect the bear had had on her: and yet she was not afraid.

A whoop went up from the crowd. In the brief moment during which she had withdrawn her attention, the bear had collapsed. Bleddyn was still hanging on to its nose, and the great beast seemed maddened with pain. It swung its head, and Bleddyn was torn free and flung across the arena. He scrambled back to his feet, but it was clear that he was limping. The bear's muzzle was torn and bloody. Once more the dogs fell back.

'One round to you. Is one round enough?' The bear-leader was grimacing deep in his beard.

'Too quick.' Ingeld shook his head. 'Where's the fun in that? You've not earned your silver yet, my friend.'

'Best of three, then.'

Ingeld nodded tersely. Braith and Bleddyn had already started their nipping at the heels again, and grey Gethyn was watching for his moment.

Elfrun wrapped her arms around herself under her cloak, longing for the fight to end. A sudden scuffle, and the bear had Bleddyn in a headlock, gripping the dog's neck between its front paws and swinging the helpless animal backwards and forwards in a grotesquely human way. Then it rolled forward, still holding the dog, and Gethyn and Braith rushed in. The bear backed off a little, but it had its jaws clamped round Bleddyn's throat. Elfrun gasped, winded and nauseated as though someone had just slammed her in the belly. The bear-leader raised his staff, and the bear lowered his head, letting the dog drop to the ground. To Elfrun's disbelief, Bleddyn twisted himself round and scrambled back to his feet, earning whoops and cheers from the crowd. Widia and the dog-boy ran in and hauled the dogs back by their hind legs, out of reach.

'And one round to me.' The bear-leader was unsmiling. 'The third decides it.'

The dog-boy was feeling Bleddyn's neck and legs, his mouth pulled down at the corners. He had his back to the bear and was well within the reach of those giant paws, but he was oblivious to any threat. Elfrun looked beyond him to the crowd. The early brightness had utterly gone, swallowed up in heavy folds of mist. Damp prickled her face. She wondered what would happen if she stopped the fight. A glance at Athulf, his face ablaze with excitement, told her everything she needed to know. People would be angry, as drinking men were when you ordered the mead barrel stopped up. Perhaps if she asked – no, if she *ordered* – the dancing-boy to do some more of his rope-walking... Perhaps Finn could distract them with the exotic treasures from his pack. She sent her glance sideways, just to see if he had his basket by him, and found that he was looking at her. He raised his eye-brows again, a little smile curving his lips, and she turned her hot face away.

The dog-boy shrugged and turned his hands outwards. His face was glum, but Widia seemingly took his gesture to mean that everything was fine, because he released the hounds once more into the arena.

Again they circled.

When it happened, it was so fast that Elfrun could barely be sure, thinking back, that she had seen what she had seen.

The bear rose up on its back paws and gave a stifled snarl. The three dogs came running in together, teeth bared, aiming for the exposed belly. The bear tumbled forwards and swung head and paws together this way and that, and all three of the dogs were tossed high in the air. They landed, hard, with audible thumps.

Elfrun gasped, feeling suddenly sick. The bear-leader was running forward. Those terrible claws had raked Bleddyn across the belly, and there was blood, and now Elfrun could see the hound's pinkish-grey guts spilling out into the dust. The bear-leader was fumbling the bridle from where he had stuffed it in his belt, fastening the leash through the bear's snout and hauling his animal out of the way, and the dog-boy was crouching over Bleddyn. His face was calm but there were silent tears pouring down it. He lifted a hand, and Widia came over. Elfrun saw the dog-boy point, and draw a finger across his throat. She turned away to see Braith gazing at her, whimpering and struggling, back legs and tail dragging.

'Spine snapped.'

She turned. Finn's golden-brown face was a hard mask, with no trace of those smile lines which had so characterized it earlier. 'What a waste of fine hounds.'

Gethyn was crouching, whining softly. Elfrun hunkered down to join him, afraid of what she might find, but he was unhurt as far as she could tell, just terrified. She soothed him and fondled his ears, and he leaned his great bulk against her, shivering.

She was barely aware of Finn bending beside her. 'I'll be on my way, lady,' he said, his voice barely louder than breath. 'It seems I bring bad luck on your house. Last time a death, and today this. Now is no day for the peddling of trinkets.'

'Bad luck! No!' She blinked, still confused and sickened. 'You can't go. It's not your fault. My uncle—' She swallowed. 'Besides, the mirror – I owe you for the mirror...' How could she ever pay him? The mirror was so much more than just the *perfect thing* Wynn had called it. She felt as though it had woken her up, brought her out of childhood, taught her to perceive the world differently. Not just her own face as others might see it, but the wordless messages her body sent her...

She had so longed to see him again, and now he was leaving.

He put a finger to his lips, and shook his head. 'I'll not be going so far. Look for me, one of these days. But we need to get away.'

She glanced around at the crowd. Whether it had anything to do with her earlier orders she could not tell, but the mood was still one of shock, not yet of anger. But anger would come. He was right, though she hated to admit it.

'Yes. Go. Get your people away. Before mine turn so ugly that I can't hold them.'

Finn nodded, and he stepped back and away. Gethyn whined again, and thrust his nose into her hand, and she crouched down and put her arms around him. She badly needed to hold on to something, and the dog's warm, solid bulk was a sudden and immediate source of comfort. She held him firmly, and rested her cheek against his fur for a long moment, for once not caring what people might think. There was a rustle nearby, and after a moment she looked up to find Ingeld and Widia looming over them. Athulf was standing by, his face tense and white, and she wondered if he were going to be sick.

'What's wrong with this one?'

She shook her head at her uncle. 'I think he's fine.'

Ingeld stared down at her. 'There's no place in my kennels for a dog without good heart. I can't trust him in the hunt, not now.'

'He has plenty of heart!'

Widia was still holding high the bloodstained knife with which he had despatched Braith and Bleddyn, and Elfrun stared at him, appalled.

'It's kindest, lady,' he said.

Athulf nodded.

She stood up, and Gethyn, as if knowing the danger, cowered against her skirts, whining and scraping the soil with his paw.

'*Look* at him, Elfrun,' Ingeld said. 'Hopeless. He may have had his nerve once but he's lost it now.'

Elfrun rested her hand on the dog's back, feeling his skin shiver under the coarse curly fur. 'You can't.'

'I'm not wasting food on that animal,' her uncle said.

Widia was nodding in agreement. 'It wouldn't be right to take him on the hunt, not if you can't trust his courage. Not safe for him or the huntsman. You must see that, lady.'

They were so much bigger than she, and older, and she had been bred to deference. But then she looked beyond them to see the wan, drawn face of the dog-boy, standing over the corpses of his other two charges, and she felt a surge of power compounded equally of anger, nausea and grief. She held out her hand and beckoned the boy towards her. 'I will take charge of both,' she said. 'They are my business now.'

Widia was about to object further, but Ingeld raised his hands in a gesture of surrender. 'Put the knife away, Widia.' He beckoned her to one side and she went, her fingers still entwined in Gethyn's coat, still not quite trusting the huntsman. 'I'm sorry, little niece.'

She stared at him. *Sorry?* What was that supposed to mean? But before she could speak Athulf had pushed in between them, rounding on his father. 'What are you sorry for?' And Elfrun realized she had mistaken her cousin's feelings: he was white and pinched with fury, not nausea. 'They cheated, those scum. We should round them up—'

'Be quiet, Athulf.' Ingeld sounded exhausted. He turned back to Elfrun. 'I thought they would defeat the bear, the hounds, the three of them together.' He pushed at the crease between his brows with one well-kept finger. 'Everything they say about me is true, isn't it?'

Elfrun bit hard on her lip, but the words wouldn't stay back. 'Why on earth did you goad Hirel like that? He's my good servant and yours, and the whole place rests on his work, minster as well as hall. And as for the dogs – the waste, the dreadful, stupid waste...' She stared down at the fingers of both her hands twined in Gethyn's curly coat. The dog was still shivering. 'And you a priest. I should have stopped this.'

'Waste?' She was barely aware of Athulf staring at her, still livid with anger. 'They were ours to waste. The honour of Donmouth—'

'I told you to be quiet, Athulf.' Ingeld turned back to her. 'Elfrun, I'm sorry,' he said again. 'Take the dog, and the boy, with my blessing.'

She nodded, shocked at herself as well as him, not trusting herself to come out with acceptable words.

Widia was dragging the dead hounds to one side by their back legs. She knew he would feed their bodies to the living dogs in the kennels, and she was determined that Gethyn would not be part of that banquet, as eater or eaten. Widia wouldn't let him back among the hunting dogs, anyway. He would have to stay with her.

She looked for Finn, for the bear-leader and his ward, for the girl in green, but they were nowhere to be seen. The milling crowd had scuffed the bloodstains from the soil with their feet, and the band of travelling entertainers had vanished into the sea-mist as though they had never visited Donmouth at all.

51

Elfrun sat in her father's great chair, its bare wooden seat hard against her bones, fondling Gethyn's ears and trying to find her courage.

After the disaster of the bear-fight, she had moved out of the women's house and into the little bower annexe to the hall that had been her father's private quarters. It was lonely, sleeping by herself for the first time in her life, but it felt right, somehow. For the first time, she could look head-on at the fact that whatever the future might hold for her, she was the lord of Donmouth and she needed to behave like it. No more tolerating Ingeld's waywardness, or Athulf's aggression, or Luda's patronizing assurances. *Learn to fight*, Fredegar had said. Well, she would.

Strange that the rest of Gethyn's coat should be so wiry, but that there was such comforting silk in his ears. He whined slightly, and nudged at her hand, and she dug her fingers around the base of those lovely ears. Gethyn sighed with happiness, and slumped against her, as though he knew just how much she was in need of comfort.

Before the news had come of her father's drowning Elfrun had felt as though she were part of a makeshift plough-team, an uneasy but functioning alliance, yoked all together and heading in the same direction. Luda, and her grandmother, and her uncle, her companions at the looms, sheepwick and dairy and kale yard, everyone doing their bit to keep the complex, recalcitrant creature that was Donmouth moving onwards, to keep everyone alive, so they could work, and eat, and sleep, and work again.

Even Athulf, with his pilfered grain, and his whales, and that cow.

Like sun and moon and planets, all in their measured dance round an earth whose absence could be coped with, because it would only be short-term.

Now she had been forced into that central space, trying to fill up that vast absence, and she found herself alone.

It was the morning after Johnsmas, and every unmarried girl in the women's house and from the steads and wicks around had been up in the hills all night, with the young men, dancing and singing round the fires they lit for the Baptist's birthday. But she hadn't gone, not this year. They would have noticed. They would have been talking. She didn't care.

She couldn't stand the giggling and the gossiping and the coarse jokes that they made when they thought she couldn't hear – or pretended they thought she couldn't hear. And then they gave her those sidelong glances, and fell ostentatiously silent.

But still, she should have gone. Because she hadn't, they would think she held herself too lofty. There was no winning, whatever she did. Behind her back, the rumour mill would grind her name and her reputation into ever finer powder.

No matter how hard she worked, the king might take Donmouth back into his own hands, and use it to reward some loyal thane; no matter how many charters she might dig out of the chest to brandish at him. He had smiled at her after that dreadful spring meeting, plied her with reassurances, but he wouldn't go on smiling forever.

And what would happen to her when Osberht's expression changed? Would she be handed over, part and parcel with the estate?

She *had* to hold on to Donmouth. And she had to hold on to it with a sterner grip than she had used so far.

Gethyn was leaning against her with all his weight, pressing her thigh painfully hard against the edge of the chair, and Elfrun slapped him on his storm-cloud flank, harder than she had intended. He looked at her with reproachful eyes and she felt a pang of guilt. 'Sorry, boy.'

She pushed herself up from the chair. If she went to the weaving shed now, she would be there in time to give a similarly accusing look to the girls when they came in, bright-eyed and flushed, with their hems dew-soaked and skirts spattered with fallen petals. Some, always some, with the backs of their dresses green-stained.

She would do her best to channel some of Abarhild's snapping looks and acid words.

It worked.

The women and girls were tired, too, and the usual non-stop chatter was subdued and sporadic. Elfrun herself was sitting tight-lipped in front of her two-beam loom and beating the cloth down with more than usual vigour when a horn was heard sounding from the path that came down through the hills from the south-west.

'Go and see what that is.'

Within moments the excited girl came scurrying back into the weaving shed. 'It's a pedlar! Asking leave to open his pack! Please, lady...' She looked at Elfrun with enormous, hopeful eyes, and looking round the gloomy shed Elfrun could see that expectation echoed on every face there. She nodded, and before she could even open her mouth the girl had swung round, scooped up her skirts and raced back into the sunshine. Elfrun could hear her shouting all the way.

'May we, lady?'

'Yes – but don't just drop everything!' Almost too late, but shuttles and heddles were hastily stowed, and bobbins rolled at speed and tucked into their baskets. Moving much more slowly, Elfrun followed her women out and latched the door behind her. The last thing she needed was one of the goats getting into the weaving shed again. Gethyn had been waiting for her at the door, and now he bounced to his feet, tail an eager blur. She snapped her fingers, and he fell in behind her.

As she had expected, it was Finn.

He was standing in the open space outside the door of the hall, his hands resting on his pack, half-protective, half-teasing, and he was fielding questions and comments from the Donmouth girls with a merry smile. She could hear his laugh from where she stood.

Next to him stood a girl in a kale-green dress. Her hair was smooth and tightly braided, and it took Elfrun a long drawn-out moment to recognize her as the dancer whose rippling brown locks had shimmered so enticingly on the dreadful day nearly two weeks ago when the bear had fought the dogs. Elfrun felt her throat tighten. Oh God, what stupidity was this? She barely knew the man. Why should the foundations of the earth be shaken at the sight of him standing by the side of another girl?

But he had called her beautiful, and he had noticed that she had been crying; he had recognized that like him she had a burden to shoulder. She could feel her heart hammering: it had moved up into the space beneath her breastbone and was threatening to rise up further yet and choke her.

Did he know her father was dead? If he knew, surely he would say. Some word of sympathy, of understanding...

Not trusting her treacherous face, or voice, Elfrun kept her distance and watched the pair of them. The stranger girl was standing back a little, hands folded and gaze lowered, letting Finn have his moment of glory, very different from the way she had milked the crowd on her last visit, with her tossing hair, her gestures like withies in the wind, and her radiant smile. Finn was fending off those would-be customers who were trying to dart in and unlatch his pack, when he looked up and saw her. His face lit with his own heart-lifting smile, the one she remembered so well from her first sight of him, and she felt a sudden blaze of anger with him for his easy power over her and her women. These stupid girls, blushing and giggling. Bite it back, hard.

She might well be a fool, but no one else could be allowed to catch a glimpse of her folly. And it was *her* folly. It hurt beyond reckoning to think that any other woman might respond to him with the same delight as she did.

'See?' His voice was pitched loud for her to hear. 'I told you all I wouldn't open my fardel for anyone but the lady of Donmouth herself.' He beckoned with his free hand. 'Come here, lady. What can I lure you with?'

She walked across the yard straight towards him, head high, aware of the stares. 'What have you got for me, pedlar?' She looked right into his eyes, and he held her gaze until she felt the colour burn hard in her cheeks and her mouth go dry. She had meant to say, *Transact your business, and move on. Let my women get back to their looms.* But she was silenced. Her heart seemed to be beating in unfamiliar places: in her throat, in her belly, between her thighs.

'Nothing like good enough for you.' His fingers were working the buckles as he spoke. 'But pretty, pretty things, all the same, to tempt these Donmouth magpies.' He pushed the fall of his ash-blond hair out of his eyes and pulled the lid back, drawing out a length of coarse brown cloth at the same time. He handed this to the nearest of the giggling girls. 'Lay this out for me, will you, my darling?'

Little brooches of gilt copper, some set with enamel. A leather bag of beads, white and purple crystal, amber and jet, which he tipped rattling into a wooden bowl. Silk ribbons, some with gold and silver threaded in. Treasure piled upon little sparkling treasure until the brown cloth had almost disappeared under its tantalizing burden. The girl in green had moved closer. Elfrun thought at first that she too was drawn by the glitter though she must surely have seen it all before, and then she realized that the girl was watching for any hint of pilfering, leaving Finn at liberty to flirt and flatter and haggle. Elfrun bristled a little at the silent implication that her women might be light-fingered, and then she forced herself to relax. This was their livelihood. The girl's narrowed eyes meant no more than her own latching of the door of the weaving shed against that opportunist goat.

Finn was squatting, swirling his fingers in the beads, trailing the ribbons, smiling up through his lashes.

'What's going on? Why aren't you at your work?'

Luda had come limping up to the chattering group. His face darkened, and his eye fell on Elfrun. He beckoned, more abruptly than she liked. Had the steward not seen her when he had first addressed the group? He would never have spoken like that, surely, if he had known she was there.

'Those are two of the cheating vagabonds who came with that damned bear.'

'There was no cheating.' She squared her shoulders. 'That bear won both its fights, and fairly. Hirel is recovering cleanly.'

'I know that. But they should have asked me before they came back.' Elfrun stared at him. His face was turning purple, veins prominent on his forehead, in a way that the day's warmth couldn't explain, and glancing down she saw his fists were clenched. Had his son-in-law's defeat by the bear rankled so much?

'But they asked me, Luda.' She shook her head at him. 'Me.' She had to make this clear though she would have preferred a smaller audience. 'I'm the lord. If I say it's all right, what business is it of yours?' She was trying to keep her temper, trying not to say, *You're only the steward*. But it was in her voice, and her face, and she knew he could read her.

'The steward?' Finn was at her side, leaving the silent girl in green to watch over the goods. Athulf had appeared from nowhere, and Elfrun could see him both eyeing up the trinkets and listening avidly to the conversation. Finn said, 'They told us about you, on the road.'

Luda opened his mouth, but Elfrun held up her hand. 'What do you mean?'

'Look out for the steward of Donmouth, they said.' A teasing note had crept into Finn's voice, and Luda scowled even more furiously. 'He's got a name for it, they said. He'll make you pay a fee to open your pack, and a fee to close it again, and like as not set the dogs on you to close the bargain.'

'Is this true, Luda?'

'No less than I'm entitled to do.'

Elfrun folded her arms. It was bad enough when he patronized her and dismissed her questions in the privacy of the wool shed but here, with all her women looking on, was infinitely worse. 'The pedlar is welcome here,' she said through gritted teeth. She thought of her mirror, wrapped in its linen. Fit for a queen. 'He has already paid any fee required. To me. He and his are our guests.' She turned to Finn, angling her shoulder to shut Luda out but raising her voice. 'Will you do me the honour of coming into my hall and drinking some wine, when you have done here? Both of you.' It was an unheard-of courtesy. The most her father would ever have done for a chapman would be to send him round to the cook-house for bread and small beer. But it was worth it, if only to see the blind fury on Luda's face.

And worth it a thousand times to have the pleasure of Finn's company. She could feel how her longing for him was drawing her into duplicity, into lying to herself about her motives. And she didn't care.

And she suspected Finn knew exactly what she was doing. 'With pleasure, lady.'

Now she stepped back to include Luda in the conversation once again. 'See that cups and a jug of the Rhineland wine are set out in the hall.' After a long moment he turned without acknowledgement.

'And will he do it?'

'He is my servant,' she said, her jaw still painfully tight. 'He was my father's servant when they were boys.'

'Your father. We heard something – is it true?'

She couldn't speak.

Finn looked at her hard for a moment, then nodded silently and turned back to his customers. She was grateful for the opportunity to swallow down the sudden surge of misery that had threatened to overwhelm her. Speaking those words had summoned a vision of her father far more real than the busy court in front of her. For a blessed moment he had been standing before her, solid and foursquare, his hair more grey than blond but his eyes as bright as those of any young man in the yard. Why did folk always comment on how handsome Ingeld was, with his white smile and his high colour? There had never been anyone to touch her father.

She realized that the chattering group had slowly fallen quiet, and that a dozen faces were turned to hers. 'Lady? Please?' She gave herself a little shake. Her women, slave and free, all earned silver and bronze by their weaving, but she kept it for them.

'Of course. A moment.'

She turned and hurried into the hall. It had been a gloomy space since her father left, chilly today despite the spring sunshine, and she spent as little time there as she could. Though Dunstan had successfully steered most of the baggage home again the bundles were still tight-packed, stored in one of the barns. She could not bear to touch them, even to find out how sea-ravaged they might be. So the hall was dark still, the iron pegs forlorn without their bright, bullion-tricked hangings. Radmer's massive chair with its gilded finials likewise looked forsaken, bereft of its silk-trimmed cushion. The great table was dismantled, board propped against trestles. The one patch of colour in the whole gloomy barn of a place was her red cloak on its peg. Only now that she was to welcome Finn under her roof did she fully realize what a shabby apology for a house this had become. 'Get a fire lit,' she snapped at Luda, fumbling at her waist for the keys to the heddern and the little chest where the silver and bronze were kept.

The handful of coins exchanged, the women chivvied back to the weaving shed, she turned her attention again to Finn and his silent companion. 'It would do me great honour,' she repeated, feeling clumsy and stupid, 'if you would share that cup of wine with me.'

Finn nodded. 'I'll just pack all my clutter away.'

Luda, still glowering, had delegated the making of the fire to a small boy who came scurrying in with a bucket of glowing charcoal. The girl in green still hadn't said a word. Elfrun watched her settle on to a bench. They were much of an age. The stranger was no more than medium height, shorter than Elfrun herself, but so slender that she appeared tall. Her sleek brown hair was tucked into tidy plaits which were knotted into one at the base of her neck and fell from there down the length of her spine. Elfrun was intrigued by the girl's dress. She had a tunic of unbleached and fine-pleated linen, and over it she wore the kale-green pinafore. The back of the dress was pulled somehow up and over each shoulder, fastened to the front over each collarbone by a pair of big lumpy brooches. The dress had a band of sage-green woven decoration across the front, between the brooches, and below it that single string of polished amber. Her hands were folded in her lap and her ankles crossed. She had coiled bronze bracelets that went from her wrist halfway to each elbow, and an impressive belt-knife in an elaborate sheath nestled in her lap.

She still hadn't said a word, and was looking at the fire; Elfrun wondered if she were crippled with shyness when she didn't have her bowl and her smile to hide behind. Her clothes were so fine for all their strangeness, much better than Elfrun's own.

Was she Finn's woman? She had seen no sign of affection between them – indeed, she wasn't sure she had heard them exchange a word.

And, if she were Finn's woman, what difference could it possibly make to the lady of Donmouth?

Just as these thoughts were rattling thorough Elfrun's mind, Finn came in and set the wicker pack down by the door, Athulf at his heels. 'That's lighter by half.' He ruffled Gethyn's ears. 'Glad to see this fine beast still with us.'

'They can't have bought that much!' She glowed at his praise of Gethyn.

'And my wares aren't heavy.' He grinned and came towards the women. 'I was joking, Alvrun.' He looked around, his quick gaze seeming to rest on nothing and yet take everything in.

Blushing, she went over to the small table where the jugs were standing and poured wine into the waiting beakers. Only three had been set out, and she was determined not to let Athulf bully her into waiting on him as well. The wine was thick and almost black in the dim hall-light, and she tipped water in to thin it before bringing one to Finn. 'Does – will—?' She glanced at the mute girl.

'Auli?'

The girl said something rapid and incomprehensible, and inclined her head with dignity.

'Yes, she will. And she says that, to thank you for your hospitality, she would like to tell your fortune on this fine midsummer morning. She's famous at home for her fortunes. She and her mother both.'

Elfrun busied herself with jug and beaker, hoping they couldn't see how the hot blood was still coming into her face. The Donmouth women were obsessed with fortunes and omens, but she knew they kept it from her, as they had always kept so much from the lord's daughter. And she in turn had come to despise this kind of talk, as Abarhild was training her to do. Those girls were just stupid; all they were interested in was men and babies.

She looked sideways at her cousin, still lingering shamelessly inside the door. If she said yes to the fortune-telling, Athulf would doubtless tell everyone at the minster. Fredegar would despise her for it.

Abarhild would be angry. Very angry.

But this stranger girl, with her neat, oval face and her quiet authority, she was different from the gigglers in the weaving shed. She might know something different, something real. For a second she thought of vowing Athulf to silence, but that would be to give him too much power.

By the time Elfrun had mixed Auli's wine and brought it to her she felt composed again. 'How do – does she tell fortunes?'

'With running wax, or with lead, in water. Or reading the runes the fates have inscribed in your hand.' Elfrun felt her palms prickle and she balled her fists to hide any treacherous lines. Auli said something and laughed softly, and Finn went on, 'Or in the dregs of your wine cup, if you like.'

'How—?'

'Here.' Finn got up and came over. 'Pour the wine – no, don't add water. Swirl it. Let it settle. Now, drink the whole cup, slowly and steadily – don't drink the lees.'

When she had finished the cup she felt warm all the way through, as though her blood had been drained and replaced with the syrupy liquid. Finn was nodding. 'You need to think of a question. Something you really want to know the answer to. Have you got one?' He smiled at her. 'Think of one, but don't say what it is.'

Her thoughts scurried, frantic, like woodlice with their stone turned over. Half of her mind was telling her not to think of a question, not to get drawn into this dangerous game, just to observe. But the other half felt all the sick thrill that had run through her while watching the bear fighting Hirel, and the dogs. She didn't want shock, blood, danger, pain. But – and at one and the same time – she could feel the craving for the excitement that went with them.

And she could feel them looking at her, hooded-eyed Auli, and Athulf in the shadows, and Finn, whose eyes were limpid silver-grey, and kind, and sad.

Why was he so sad?

'Got a question?'

She shook her head, feeling stupid and exposed. What did she really want to know? There were so many things about which she longed to be certain.

Was Luda really cheating her in some way? Was Fredegar right, with his ominous warnings about the sea-wolves? Did Illingham still pose any genuine threat? Rattle, rattle, rattle went her thoughts, like the glass beads and gemstones that Finn had tipped into his bowl.

No.

The question, above all, to which she needed an answer was, *Is my father really dead?*

She had questioned Dunstan endlessly once the first shock had worn off, and the freezing numbness had ebbed a little. And the answer had always been the same. They had been beating up the coast of Iberia, with a powerful westerly and a lee shore, and the strain on the ship had had her bucking and twisting. There was no room for passengers on such a voyage, and Radmer and his men had been working as hard as they could, baling side by side with the crew, crammed in alongside the unstepped mast and the sodden heaps of sail. 'Nine men were lost,' Dunstan had said. 'It was a wave like I'd never seen, out of nowhere.' He shrugged. 'I loved him too. It was no one's fault.'

No land within a mile, and then jagged rock. No other ships. Just a remorseless mountain of cold water, breaking over the strakes, and sucking her father under.

'He was there.' Dunstan had swallowed and looked away. 'And then he was gone.'

She looked at Finn, and nodded that she was ready, her throat too tight to speak.

'Now, carry the cup in both hands to Auli.'

She did as she was told, the yellow-trailed glass cold and ridged against her palms. Athulf was watching, fascinated.

Auli twirled a finger in the air above the rim, and obediently Elfrun swirled the claggy lees round the cup, faster and faster, the must and fragments of grape skin straggling around the inner curve of the glass, until the other girl held up her hand abruptly and bent forward.

'What is she looking at?'

Finn shook his head and put a finger to his lips.

Auli was bent so far forward that Elfrun could see that the twist of plaits on the pale nape of her neck had been sewn into place with dark-red silk threads. She was muttering something under her breath. Finn was alert, still as a cat at a mouse hole.

Elfrun could feel beads of sweat prickling her scalp, forming on her upper lip. Were they trying to frighten her? She felt a sudden gust of anger. She had protected them, invited them into her father's hall. Why were they doing this?

Finn's voice startled her. 'Do you have your question? No! Don't say it aloud. Just hold it in your mind.'

Auli was jabbing a finger at the rim of the beaker furthest from her and gabbling something.

'What—?' Elfrun jerked the glass away.

Finn put a steadying hand on her arm. 'Wait. I'll tell you everything she says.' He was following the finger and the muttered words intently. His hand was still clasping her arm, just next to the wrist, where her skin was bare because she had pushed her sleeves up and out of the way when pouring the wine. His grip was gentle and firm, the skin of his palm warm and hard. She could feel the ball of his thumb pressing into the flesh below her wrist-bone. Her breath caught in her chest.

Auli finished with an emphatic statement of which Elfrun understood not a syllable. She was looking intently up into Elfrun's face, and Elfrun realized with a shock that the other girl's eyes were the same shadowed gold as her amber beads.

'This is you,' Finn said. He released her arm to point into the beaker, and the letting go was like a small bereavement. But any pang was overtaken by her almost equally shameful rush of desire to know what Auli had been saying. 'This part here, the wavy line. Frustration, delay.'

She nodded. That made sense. But they could have worked that out. They must have known that these had been the warp and weft of her life in the nine months since Radmer had sailed south.

'And this here, in the middle? The whale?'

'Whale?' Now that he was pointing she could see a blob with a curved back, but she would never have known it was a whale.

'That is your fate. A journey, and also a transformation.'

'For me? A sea voyage?' As ever, a shiver at the thought of the deep sea, and its creatures.

'Perhaps. Across water, for certain.' He was frowning, and said something to Auli; then, 'The answer depends on the question. And then this last bit, nearest you, this is the person who matters most in the world.'

Her breath caught again. 'And?'

'Alvrun, look at the pattern.' His voice was gentle.

She looked and saw nothing. She turned her face to him, shaking her head, frowning. 'I don't understand.'

'This person will be there for you. But it will be hard. Through deep water.' Auli said something, and he added, 'And blood. And fire.'

Deep water. She stood still. Gethyn lifted his head and whined softly.

'Is it my father?'

'Do you love him most in the world?'

'Your father?' Athulf was very close suddenly, crowding her, trying to peer in. 'Is that who it means? He's coming back?' Elfrun turned her shoulder, trying to block his view of the beaker. 'But he's dead!'

Auli said something further. Finn listened, nodding. 'Auli says she thinks not dead. Some other kind of change.' He took the beaker gently from her cupped hands. 'It could be good news.'

'My father is dead,' she said. A ringing in her ears; a tightness under her heart. 'You must have known that. Everyone knows it. Dunstan saw him drown.' She was amazed she could speak at all, her teeth were so tight-gritted. 'There is nothing there that you could not have learned from what I have told you already, or from the gossip you might have picked up around the place.' And now she could hear her words fraying round the edges, unravelling in the bitter wind. 'You are playing with me. You are cruel' – Luda's angry words of a few moments earlier came back to her – 'cheating vagabonds, and you abuse my hospitality.

You will please me by leaving.' Now she knew why canon law denounced divination. It was the Devil's own game.

'Alvrun—' Finn reached his free hand out towards her. 'Don't—'

She grabbed the beaker from him and hurled. It shattered against the doorjamb in a spray of splinters. Gethyn set up a frantic barking. 'Get out!'

52

'Did you see the bear? What did you think of it?'
It was a mild night. The hobbled horses were grazing not far off, and Athulf could hear them tearing up
mouthfuls of the sweet new grass.

'Which bear?' Addan sounded bored.

How many bears could there be? Athulf bit back his irrita-
tion. 'A few weeks back. It came through. Did you really not
see it?' Athulf's eyes brightened. The wolf pack hadn't run for
several weeks, and he had been afraid that the others would lord
it over him, but now he had something big to tell them. 'You
should have seen its claws! It beat our shepherd, and it killed
Ingeld's dogs.'

'A wild bear?' Addan sounded disbelieving. He reached out
and poked the fire with a branch. 'I've never heard of wild bear
in these hills.'

Athulf shook his head. 'No, a tame one. With a bridle, and
coloured ribbons.'

'Coloured ribbons!' Addan snorted. 'Listen to you. So a pet
bear killed your father's poor little dogs? What did you do in
return, skin it for its fur?'

Athulf flushed. 'We had to let them go. Elfrun wouldn't let
me sort them out.' He looked at Thancrad, who had been silent
for some time. 'Didn't it come to Illingham then?'

Thancrad shrugged. 'How would we know? We've been with
the king.'

'What – all three of you?' Athulf felt the slow burn of envy.

He did his best to keep his voice steady. 'There were danc-ers, too. Musicians. Acrobats. You should have been there.' He wanted the story to sound as good as possible. 'We've had lots of visitors. A pedlar came by later, just a few days ago, with a girl. She told Elfrun's fortune, and—'

'What did she say?' Thancrad's voice had woken up.

Athulf tried to remember. 'Some stupid stuff. About delays. And that whoever it is Elfrun loves most is coming to her through fire and water. Oh – and she's to go on a journey.'

Thancrad appeared to have lost interest. He got to his feet. They were in a sheltered little dip in the hills above Illingham, and the sparks from their fire swirled and eddied upwards in the slight breeze until they were lost against the midnight sky. The Milky Way was a silver stripe above their heads. Athulf, feeling slighted, watched Thancrad carefully. Thancrad was sometimes warm, almost affectionate, but at other times, like now, withdrawn, gruff, given to talking in riddles and ambiguities. His angular face was fire-lit from below, hard to read. After a long silence, Athulf said, 'So what were you doing? With the king, I mean?'

Thancrad shrugged, still looking off into the distance.

Addan said, 'Riding with the war-band, of course.' He laughed. 'What did you think?'

'Collecting taxes,' Thancrad added. He turned to the fire again and squatted, warming his hands. 'We weren't fighting. Don't worry. My father had business at court, and he took us all with him.'

'There isn't any fighting to be done,' Addan said. 'Not real fighting. What's the use?'

'My father's always saying that the king's too strong.' Thancrad sat back on his haunches. The firelight in his hair glinted red. 'And it sounds as though you agree with him?' He looked at Addan. 'I'd say he keeps us safe, rather.'

'Safe!' Addan stirred the fire. 'If there's no fighting, there's no winning. And no winning means no rewards. Look at the way Osberht treats us. We should be in his war-band.' He glanced at Athulf, then said, 'All of us. But he knows fine well that if he takes us on we'll be asking for prizes. Not just food and a roof.'

'I'd serve him,' Athulf said. 'I'd take him my sword, if he asked me.'

'So would I...' Addan broke his branch in half across his knee and threw both pieces into the fire, sending up a blaze of sparks. '... until something better came along.'

'Something better?'

Addan's teeth glinted in the firelight. 'Tilmon is promising better things. Hasn't he had a word with you yet? Switha said he was going to. Or that she would herself. She said you were important.'

Important? Him?

Athulf bit his lip. Switha had spoken to him more than once, and always with that affectionate, admiring tone to her voice. But never about her husband, and Athulf was still wary of Tilmon's solid bulk and gruff presence.

Thancrad was snapping pieces of tinder into smaller and smaller fragments. 'Something better? What's wrong with peace?' Athulf looked up and found Thancrad looking at him intently. 'I've been watching my father, all the while we were in the Danemarch, and ever since we came back this side of the sea. He never stops, him and my mother both. Him and Alred—' He stopped abruptly.

'I though Alred was up in the north. That's where he was bribed to be.'

'That's where the king thinks he is.' Thancrad sounded as though he was regretting having brought the name into their talk. 'But we've had him under our roof at Illingham. And my father's Hedeby men. And their friends, too.'

'Sea-wolves.' Addan bared his teeth. 'Not such bad souls, when you get to rub shoulders with them.'

Athulf found a cold knot of unease tying itself tight in the pit of his belly. 'Sea-wolves?'

'My father thinks we need to talk to these people. Make

common cause if necessary – use them to get what we all want. It's not what men at court want to hear. But like it or not, they're not going to go away – if we learned anything from seven years in the Danemarch we learned that. Things are changing over there, like here. More power in fewer hands.' Thancrad threw his handful of tiny fragments of twig into the guttering fire. 'Addan, go break up a few more branches.'

'Go yourself.'

They stared at each other. Thancrad seemed about to speak, and then his face closed down. 'Very well.' And he got to his feet. 'What difference does it make, anyway, who gets the wood?'

Behind his back, Athulf and Addan exchanged glances.

53

Something was amiss. Elfrun had known as soon as she lifted the cloak from its peg. An unfamiliar lightness, a loss of balance, a change in the swing of the fabric. A long strip of braid was stitched to the shoulder, weighted at each end with a solid silver tag which then pulled through a loop to keep the cloak hanging properly.

And now one was gone.

A glance around the floor told her that the tag was nowhere to hand. It was nearly the length of her thumb, and the silver was heavy enough that she would certainly have heard it if it had come loose and fallen inside, on the hard boards. Which meant she must have lost it outside. But when? She used the cloak day in and day out: she could not imagine the tag working loose without her noticing the gradual slackening of the stitches.

Fifteen whole pennies. And that was just the weight of the silver. Never mind the labour of the king's smith, and the value conferred by virtue of it being a royal gift, and doubly from it being her father's loan to her. She stood perfectly still, the thick red wool clutched in her cold hands. She felt as though she had broken some spell of protection.

The surviving tag was tucked up in its loop, and she pulled it free and contemplated it. The woven strap was gripped by the split end of the tag, and then held by two little rivets. She gave it a tug. Strong enough. She turned her attention to the other end of the strap, and her frown deepened. Something else was wrong.

The end wasn't frayed, as she had been expecting. It had been cut.

She could see quite clearly how the knife had struggled and slipped as each of the tough woollen fibres had resisted and given way at last. The overall effect was ragged but each separate fibre had been neatly sheared.

Fifteen pennies. To almost anyone in Donmouth it was a small fortune.

'I don't want this.'

She was fully aware that she ought to be moving already. Summoning Luda, ordering him to round up everyone in Donmouth, getting the men she trusted to strip bodies and rummage through bedstraw. That was what her father would have done. And in whose keeping would it be found, if they found it?

'It's no good.'

It was too small, too easy to hide, too easy to melt down. To hide somewhere about a desperate body, if the search got that close. They wouldn't find it. And then everyone would be talking, saying the lady knew fine well she had lost it through her own carelessness and was seeking to put the blame on some innocent head. How petty she would sound, shrill and vindictive, where Radmer would have channelled the wrath of God and king combined.

But was this reluctance merely cowardice by another name? Dodging her responsibilities? She was folding and pleating the woollen strip between her fingers, thicker and tighter, until she reached the place where it was stitched into its loop.

'I don't care who took it,' she whispered, 'and I don't care why.'

But if she didn't find it, she would have to wear that cloak in public, and sooner rather than later someone would notice. And then everyone would be wondering what had happened to the tag, and why she hadn't asked folk to look for it, and somewhere in the crowd there would be that one knowing, nauseating glance. Perhaps more than one. That was if it had been someone from Donmouth who had taken it.

Names offered themselves, but she batted them away. No profit in travelling that road, not as a first recourse. Later, perhaps.

For now she had to think.

Fight, Fredegar had told her. But there were other ways of fighting than going in bellowing and brandishing a sword.

She looked hard at the other tag. Its single spotted animal cavorted on a background of vines and tendrils. It was extraordinarily delicate work, and she knew that creating such a thing was far beyond Cuthred's capabilities. But could he *copy* one, with a model to work from? She could take fifteen pennies from the chest whose key she guarded, and Cuthred could melt them down. The prancing animal on the lost tag had not been an exact match for this one, although few folk ever came close enough to her to notice that kind of detail. Cuthred would know of the substitution, but no one else... And she could hold her head up, and pretend this abominable intrusion had never happened. And sleep in the cloak, if need be, from now on.

The fifteen silver pennies tight in her palm and the cloak bundled under her arm, Elfrun picked her way down to the forge.

But, 'Look at my hands, lady.' Cuthred spread them out and she stared at them, the scars and the burns, the thickened joints and the missing nail on one index finger.

'What am I looking at?' Elfrun fought back a gust of impatience.

'They shake.' His voice was flat.

It was true. Now she was aware of it, she could see the unwilling tremor that animated fingers, hands and wrists, the way a poplar's leaves would shiver even on the stillest day.

'I can do the heavy work well and good enough,' he said. 'But a dainty job like that?' He shrugged.

'But – I need you to do it.' Elfrun stared at the smith, wondering how to put into words her feeling that all the authority vested in her came from the shield and guard of her father's cloak.

'Don't you look at me like that, maid. I've not chosen this fate to spite you.'

'I never thought you had.' She shook out the folds of the cloak and pulled it around her shoulders. 'But you're letting me down, for all that. And after all this time you still haven't found some-one to work the forge with you.'

'I've tried.'

Elfrun knew that was true. And she knew exactly why the smith's quest was proving so hard. There wasn't a farm from here south to Dore and west to Elmet where they didn't know as cross-your-heart Gospel truth that the smith of Donmouth had killed his son by pushing him into the forge fire. She chewed her lip, remembering how she too had had her suspicions.

And now? Every time she remembered the smouldering depths and the charred edges of the craters in Cudda's flesh, she wondered again. The coals must have taken their time to have seared his flesh like that. She was willing to believe that the smith hadn't pushed his son into the fire-pit. But had he watched the boy stumble and left him there over-long, too angry to offer a hand? A son who ran wild, abandoned the forge to dream of a seat in the king's hall and a place among the young retainers of his wolf pack... enough there to have angered any father beyond reason. And everyone knew the smith's temper.

His wife better than any, and she was refusing to go back under his roof. Was that significant?

Elfrun sighed. If only she were Radmer, she would trawl the farm lads and the slave boys for some likely candidate and send him off to Cuthred with a cuff and a terse word. Her grand-mother, too, would do it without a second thought.

'He's got me.'

Elfrun turned, startled. She hadn't even realized that Wynn was there, so quiet and still the girl had been in the shadows beyond the fire-pit. Wynn came forward now, and without ask-ing leave she pulled the woollen strap free and looked hard at the surviving tag. 'I could do this, maybe.'

Elfrun started to protest but Cuthred held up a hand. 'How?'

'Sand mould.'

Cuthred frowned. 'Damp sand? Baked sand?'

Wynn was still studying the tag, turning it over and looking hard at the pattern and the rivets. 'Oiled sand, to get the detail. It'd be crude, but I could do the fine work after.'

Cuthred folded his arms. 'Are you telling me that thing you're holding was made in a mould?' It was as though they had forgotten Elfrun was there.

Wynn snorted. 'Acourse not. From a strip, folded and hammered and graved. But I couldn't make a new one that way, not if I wanted an eye-sweet match. I've not the skill, not yet.' She twisted the tag round and looked at the back. 'I'd have to take the rivets out... It might not work.'

'Sup it and see, lass.'

'Wait,' Elfrun said. The conversation was running away from her. 'You're telling me a child can do this?'

'You've only four years on me, lady.' Wynn's blue stare was bold. 'Even before Cudda—' she hesitated, '—there was nothing I couldn't do as well as him or better.'

'She's right, lady.' Cuthred ran a battered hand through his shaggy grey thatch of hair. 'You know I've been looking for a new lad, but it's not proving easy. Wynn's my right hand at the forge. She's strong and steady.'

'So what happened to the other tag, lady?'

Elfrun looked down at the determined little face. 'Why do you need to know?'

Wynn raised her eyebrows, folding her arms across her skinny chest. 'I don't want to go to all that effort and then have you tell me, *Oh, sorry, Wynn, I found it down the back of my linen chest*.' Her mimicry was pointed, and Elfrun winced.

'I don't keep the cloak in my linen chest.'

'Found it anywhere, then.' Wynn's hand darted out, and Elfrun pulled away, but not quickly enough. The other girl was

331

already tugging out the other end of the woven strap and eyeing it sceptically. 'Cut.'

'Yes.'

'Stolen.'

'Anyone could have taken it,' Cuthred said. 'Silver's easy enough to melt.'

Elfrun was startled by the defensive tone. Again, she wondered about the state of the smith's conscience. 'I know that.' Could he conceivably have taken it? Or Wynn? In a sudden rush of distrust she wondered whether they had planned exactly this, and they would take her coin and give her back her own stolen tag, claiming to have made it new.

But she would recognize it, if they gave her back her own. They had to know that. She felt as though a cloud of gnats were dancing around her face, buzzing in her ears, crawling in her eyes and mouth, making it hard for her to see the truth. It was all she could do to keep her hands from batting the imaginary creatures away. This was the road to madness.

Wynn was back, with a tiny pair of tongs. 'Let me get the rivets out, lady.'

'What?'

Wynn's voice was rich with exaggerated patience. 'I have to keep it, to copy it. It's high summer, lady. No one will notice if you leave the cloak at home for a few days.'

She submitted unwillingly to the girl's attentions, watching the neat, triangular face screw up in concentration, the tip of Wynn's tongue sticking out of the corner of her mouth. As the rivets parted and the surviving tag came free Elfrun felt another pang of loss.

54

'**W**here's Thancrad? I need to talk to him.' Athulf slipped down from Mara and knotted her reins over a low hawthorn branch.

'We've not seen him for weeks.' Addan's voice was sour.

'Days,' Dene amended. 'He's with the king. Him and his father both.'

'Again.'

Dene nodded. 'Nearly two weeks,' he added, his tone conciliatory.

Athulf had found them high in the woods on the steep slope between hall and minster. Addan's bitch had brought down a hare, and they had come under the shelter of the trees to light a fire and cook it.

'Hunting my hills,' he said. His tone was neutral but the words were offensive, as he had intended.

'Your hills,' Addan agreed. 'Your hare. Want to do something about it?' He was skinning the wretched creature with swift strokes of his belt-knife, and he paused, blade jutting upwards.

Athulf folded his arms and stared for a hard moment, before Addan turned his gaze aside. He smiled then and shrugged. 'It's all the same to me. I've plenty to go around, after all.'

Addan grinned. 'Don't mind us, then. Just scooping a few crumbs from the rich man's table.' With an abrupt gesture he flipped the hare, stripping the skin off whole and skewering the corpse with a sharpened stick before propping it over the fire.

'That'll take ages,' Dene complained. 'I'm hungry now.'

Addan wiped his knife front and back on the grass and thrust it into the sheath at his belt. 'Then hunger must be your master. That's the lot of younger sons and little cousins the world over. We do the dirty work, we can't afford pride or principles, and we're the last to be fed. Where have you been that you don't know that?'

Athulf tried to hide his pleasure in Dene's discomfiture. Dene eyed him sideways. 'Your hills. So, are you the heir to Donmouth minster? That's the plan, isn't it? Making a priest of you.' He grinned.

Athulf was surprised by the needling tone. It was usually Addan who led any riling. 'Plan? Not mine. My grandmother's, maybe.' He stretched out his legs and yawned, hiding his discomfiture. 'And I'm not sure about taking orders.'

Addan barked with laughter, but Dene looked more curious. 'Holy orders, you mean? And you're not prepared to do that?'

'Be a priest? Rather than be in the king's war-band?'

Dene shrugged. 'Donmouth minster's rich, they say. What are there, forty hides of land? Fifty?'

'Something like that. But what does it matter?'

'You wouldn't catch me turning an offer like that down because I thought I'd look silly in a tonsure. Being in orders never seems to stop your father from enjoying himself, from all I hear. Hunting, and women. Lots of women...'

'But not battle.'

Dene sat up. 'That matters to you?'

Athulf thought of the handful of times he had seen the king's war-band riding out, those young men glamorous beyond all measure in their shining corslets, the gilded saddlecloths, the horses with their oiled hooves and knotted tails. The youngest warriors were no older than he was himself. He said, 'With Radmer dead, maybe I'd rather have Donmouth hall than the minster.' Abarhild had been dropping hints. But he knew fine well the hall wasn't hers to give.

Addan spat into the fire. 'You can't join the war-band if the king won't have you. He'll have Thancrad long before you.' His tone was dismissive. He reached out to turn the hare round a little. 'Why is this taking so long?'

'I'm a better swordsman than Thancrad.'

'Thancrad's got a father.'

Athulf tensed. 'And I haven't?'

'A father who'll speak for him. Who'll take a proper interest. It's no good your being Switha's little pet if Tilmon doesn't know you exist.'

A father who'll take a proper interest... Athulf thought about Ingeld's offhand shrug and lazy smile. He bit his lip, hiding the slow burn of fury nestled in the pit of his stomach. 'The only thing he's interested in is his woman.'

'The shepherd's wife?' Addan grinned in his dark beard. 'Oh, we've heard about her. *All* about her.'

Dene reached out and poked the fire. 'They say the shepherd doesn't know, that he's too stupid to smell what's under his nose. Maybe you should tell him.' They were both laughing now.

Athulf was irked that they didn't seem to be taking him seriously. He rose from his squat and took a few paces away from the fire, into the nearest trees.

'Don't you go too far,' Addan said. 'We don't want to be using you for target practice again.' He patted his bow.

Athulf thought back to the swan-fletched arrow quivering in the birch-trunk, the first time he had met Thancrad and these two, and he laughed. 'You never sent that arrow. You're not good enough, not half.'

'And you think you're so sharp?'

Athulf wheeled. 'I'm better than you, anyway. I led that cattle-raid, didn't I? Any time you want—'

Addan's young bitch was on her feet, ears pricked. 'Stow it,' Addan said. 'Someone's coming.' He grabbed her by the scruff and clamped his other hand round her muzzle.

335

The three youths froze. It was too late to do anything about the fire, though, and the roasting hare appeared to gaze at them, accusing, ghastly and reproachful.

There was a rustle and a scrabble in the long grass, and a lop-eared hound appeared and rushed over to Athulf. He turned to the others, hiding his relief, fondling the dog's ears. 'It's all right. It's one of ours. The hall's, I mean. It must be Widia.'

The other two still looked wary. 'He won't mind? Us hunting Donmouth land?'

Athulf grabbed the dog's collar and stood as tall as he could. 'My land, you mean? Of course not. He wouldn't dare.' The dog was straining, longing to make the acquaintance of Addan's bitch, but Athulf hung on until Widia came in sight and whistled, and the dog, reluctantly obedient, went to his heel.

'There you are. Good lad.'

Athulf twitched and frowned before realizing that Widia was addressing the dog. He had been praying that the huntsman wouldn't treat him like a child, as he still did far too often. Not in front of the others.

'Fine hunting, lads. Better luck than mine.' He gave his twisted smile, and showed his empty hands. 'May I join you?' He interpreted Dene's scowl correctly. 'Oh, I'm not after your hare. Just your company.' His dog, released, went to nose in the pile of hare-guts, and was joined by Addan's bitch.

Athulf let out a long, slow breath.

'From Illingham?' At their nods Widia squatted awkwardly and made a show of warming his hands, though the evening was mild. 'Don't mind me. What were you talking about?'

Addan grinned. 'Athulf's father. The lord abbot of Donmouth, and the virtuous example he sets us all.' He reached out and turned the blackening hare. He made a face. 'It'll be dry.'

'I don't care,' Dene said.

Widia laughed. 'Quite right, lad. No need for butter and honey when you're out in the hills.'

Athulf came to a sudden decision. 'We were talking about

Saethryth.' He looked hard at Widia. 'We were saying someone should tell the shepherd outright my father's been tupping his favourite ewe. They say Hirel still doesn't know.'

'Aye, I've heard that.' Widia's face had gone taut, the scar tissue livid and stretched. 'But I wouldn't be so sure. It may be that Hirel doesn't want to force a confrontation. You were there when he fought the bear, you saw how that fell out.'

'The bear?'

Widia sighed. 'Are you stupid, lad? He can't challenge the lord abbot to a fight. The abbot is backing the bear, so he fights the bear instead. But the bear won. Put yourself in Hirel's place for a bit. Leave the man alone.'

Athulf felt mulish, and all the more so for being contradicted. 'But he ought to know what's going on. For his own good.'

'Stow it. He loves his wife, I know that.'

'What, that slut?'

Widia held up a warning hand. 'Never in my hearing, all right? And where does Hirel get his living? There's more at stake for him than honour. You shouldn't talk like that, not about him, or her, or your father.' Widia's dog picked up his master's mood and growled low in his throat.

'Why not? He's got plenty of time for her, but he's too busy to notice I exist.' Athulf reached out and snatched the spitted hare off the upright sticks. 'That's done.' Gripping it tight, he hacked off a back leg with his belt-knife and chucked the carcase to Addan. 'Yours, I believe.'

Addan was bristling. 'I killed it. I should have had the first share.'

'My hills, my hare. Want to come and get it?' Athulf waved the leg at Addan, then took a bite and chewed the charred meat, slowly and ostentatiously. Addan stared for a moment, then grunted something non-committal and began sawing at the pathetic little corpse with his own knife.

Widia looked from one to the other, a troubled expression

on his face. 'I'll be leaving you then.' He got slowly to his feet and whistling his dog he headed off down the slope.

As well as the hare, Athulf was still chewing over something Addan had said earlier. 'What did you mean, *Switha's little pet*?'

Addan grinned. 'Go and ask her, why don't you?'

55

'You come between me and the sun. You dazzle me.'

'Are you complaining?' Saethryth leaned forward so that her hair tickled his face, and Ingeld brushed it aside, laughing.

'No, not complaining. Never complaining.' He gripped her waist hard, delighting in the play of her strong muscles under the soft sheathing of skin, running his hands lightly over her ribcage and up to her breasts. 'Just thinking. Just looking.'

'Well, stop it! You have to go soon. Don't waste time.'

'Fredegar and Heahred can look after the minster for me.' He closed his eyes and lay back. 'Do that thing with your hair again.'

'Only if you tell me I'm pretty.'

'You are pretty.' He opened his eyes again and looked at her in mild incredulity. 'Do you doubt it?'

'And you've never loved anyone as you love me.'

'I have never loved anyone as I love you.'

'Not even your mother.'

He laughed. 'Not even my mother.'

'Not even Athulf's mother.' Saethryth lowered her head and drew her hair across his chest, a back-and-forth sweep of gossamer, and he sighed. 'Go on,' she said.

'I can't say that. I don't know if it's true.'

'You still think about her.' She shifted sideways on to the thick-piled stack of straw that made their bed.

The mood between them had sobered. Ingeld propped himself up on one elbow and tugged a strand of straw free. 'No, not really. It was so long ago, and we were so young, and she died. But she was my first girl, and I thought she was very lovely.' He pleated the straw over and over until the stem cracked and fell apart in many small fragments. 'Does it bother you so much?'

'Athulf isn't very lovely.'

'Athulf is a lumpen youth. Hard to believe I was no older than he is now when I got him. But nonetheless he has a look of her, and I find I tolerate him for it.'

Saethryth sat up with her arms around her knees. 'Move over. It tickles, with my arse on the straw.'

He shifted sideways, making space for her on their makeshift coverlet. 'She's dead. We're alive. Life is short.' He stroked her cheek with the back of his hand. 'Youth is shorter. *Life is on loan, love is on loan...*'

'Stop it.' She caught his hand and trapped it against her face, kissing the palm. 'Pass me the flask.'

'There's not much left.'

After she had sipped the sticky liquid she put the wooden bottle down on the floor, not bothering to replace the stopper. 'Why don't I feel guilty?'

He propped himself up on one elbow. 'What do you mean?'

'About this. About Hirel.' She made a circular gesture, encompassing the makeshift bed, their entwined legs. 'I never meant to be a bad wife. But I am, and I ought to feel guilty.' She shrugged. 'Why don't I?'

It was the most interesting thing he had ever heard her say, in nine months of her company. He knew fine well how the lord abbot of Donmouth ought to respond, that she was young and her conscience was unformed, that she needed instruction in the basic tenets of the commandments and the paternoster. *Ne nos inducas in tentationem.* Covet not thy neighbour's wife. But that all seemed too simple, and he would not insult her with it. Such matters were better left to those who believed in them, like Fredegar. Life's lease was too short, and the landlord ever-ready to foreclose...

'Why don't you answer me?'

'I don't know what to say.'

Saethryth wriggled, pushing the side of her face against Ingeld's shoulder as though she were a cat. 'What I really feel is relief. I've been pretending to be good all my life, but inside I know, really, I'm bad. I've always known. And now my inside and my outside match, and it's as though I've put down a heavy burden.' She lifted her face and looked him in the eye. 'Does that make any sense?'

He smiled and shook his head. 'I don't have an answer. You call yourself a bad wife. Well, I am a bad cleric and I always have been, but I come closer to being a good man with you than I have ever done in all my life.' There were tears prickling the edge of his vision, and he swallowed hard. She was looking at him intently, and he leaned forward and cupped her face, the palms of his hands moulding themselves to her cheekbones. 'You are so pretty,' he said, and again there was that obstruction in his throat and he had to swallow before he could speak again. 'How could anyone so pretty be bad?'

It was no kind of answer, and they both knew it.

She pulled away from him and dipped her face, her hair swinging forward. 'I am bad,' she said, 'and you love it.'

He reached for her and pulled her down on top of him into a bone-crushing embrace.

Afterwards, when the hot tide had ebbed, she said, 'Tell me again about running away.'

'Come close then.' He lay back and pulled her in tight-curled against his chest and flank. 'Let's go south. We'll take a boat through the waves of the Ocean, past Iberia and into the Middle Sea past the Pillars of Hercules.'

'Is it hot there? Hotter than here?'

'Always.' He thought of the maps in the pages of Isidore and Adomnán in Wulfhere's lovely library, the fruit and the music and the laughing girls in the old Roman poetry he loved so much. 'There will be figs, and olives, and spice trees. All the wine you could want.'

'What's it called, the land where we're going?'

'The Earthly Paradise.' He sighed, and she cuddled closer into him. 'There is no sin there, and everyone goes naked and unashamed, like children.'

'Like us.'

'Yes,' and he kissed the top of her head. 'Like us. The streams run with honey, like sunshine you can drink. And every daisy is made of pearls. There are wonderful creatures there. The phoenix, who makes her nest from aromatic twigs.'

'What's a phoenix?'

Ingeld began to tell her, but before very long her breathing slowed and deepened into a light snore. When he was sure she was asleep Ingeld pulled his tingling arm out from under her shoulders and lay down next to her.

He had no illusions. She was silly, and shallow, and capable of moments of spite that he found distressing. But at the same time there was an innocence there, a simple, childish greed for the good things of the flesh. She made no crippling moral judgements: she saw something, she wanted it and she reached for it. She wanted *him*. Eve, he thought, in Eden, must have been like this girl. He had never been so happy. He dropped a kiss on the lovely curve where her neck met her shoulder. Her skin smelt strong and musky, and he inhaled deeply.

Before long he too was asleep. In the long, slanting light the motes of dust and straw rose and fell in the warm air.

lfrun clicked her fingers and Gethyn fell in at her heels. Widia was coming away from the stables and she waved him over. 'Saddle Mara for me.'

His expression shifted subtly. 'Athulf is out on Mara.'

'Athulf? Again?' Elfrun glanced at Widia's carefully composed face. 'Oh, never mind.' She knew only too well that stopping Athulf – short of shutting him in a heavy-lidded chest and turning the key – was a near-impossible task.

'Where would you be riding to, lady?'

'Up to the sheepwick.' She wouldn't normally go herself, but she didn't quite trust Luda to give her a report she understood. 'I need a word with Hirel, about the shearing.'

Elfrun had thought Widia's expression guarded before, but it was nothing to the one he now assumed. She had never realized that his mouth and his dark eyebrows could make such perfectly stern, horizontal lines, broken only by the jagged-lightning line of his still-raw scar. But when he spoke his voice was mild. 'I'll saddle Hafoc for you, if you like?' He jerked his head. 'He's in the home field.'

Elfrun nodded. She watched Widia go into the stables and emerge with the fringed saddlecloth draped over one arm and a bridle in his hand. 'Lady,' he called, 'will you use your father's saddle?'

She was about to shake her head, but thought again. She had been wearing her father's cloak – though she was still waiting for the new silver tag – and sitting in his chair; and now she would be riding his horse: how would using his saddle be any different? Athulf may have been riding Mara without her leave, but at least he hadn't dared to take Hafoc again through the winter and the spring, not since the raid on Illingham's granaries.

Widia came back leading the dun gelding by the bridle and hitched him to a post while he went back in to get the great saddle. Silver-gilt studs sparkled in the late-afternoon sun. Widia stood holding Hafoc's bridle for her, but the horse jibbed, swinging his head, and Widia had to shake the bridle in his face and back him up a few paces before bringing him forward again. 'Restless,' he said. 'Not been ridden for too long, lady. I've taken him out when I can, but it's not enough. You should ride him regularly.'

She patted the snuffling whiskery nose and let Hafoc lip and nuzzle the palm of her hand. 'You're all right, aren't you, boy?' Widia made a step with his hands and boosted her up. She ran her finger over the studs, noticing where the gilt was rubbing off, where the underlying silver had the purple bloom of tarnish. 'I remember when I was a little girl, sitting up here perched on this saddle-bow in front of my father.'

'I don't like you riding out on your own, lady.'

'It's only to the sheepwick. And I've got Gethyn.' Still that grim face. 'Come with me then, if you're so fretted.' She didn't care what he did, as long as he made up his mind.

He paused. 'I have nets to mend, but...' He was forestalled by the sound of hooves. They both turned to see Thancrad of Illingham riding through the gate on Blis, sunshine glinting in the glossy russet of his hair.

He raised a hand in salute. 'I was looking for Athulf.'

Widia laughed shortly. 'Good luck. He's gone out on Mara. I thought he was meeting you – he said as much. Or at least that he was going to Illingham.'

Thancrad looked puzzled, then shrugged. 'I've not seen him on the way. We've only just got back from Driffield.' He turned to Elfrun. 'That's a fine horse you're riding.'

344

Elfrun reached forward to pat Hafoc's neck, hiding her smile. 'My father's.'

'Where are you taking him?'

She hesitated, feeling shyer than ever in the aftermath of her talk with Fredegar.

'She's going up to the sheepwick,' Widia said.

'On her own?'

'Yes,' she said, and at the same moment Widia said, 'I don't like it, either.' His eyes met Thancrad's, and there was a silent moment of masculine complicity which Elfrun found deeply irritating. Then Thancrad tugged Blis round.

'I'll ride with you.' He paused. 'If you like.'

She didn't like, but she didn't know how to refuse. Be rude, Fredegar had said. But how do you refuse simple courtesy?

It had rained earlier in the day, and now a light steamy mist was rising from the young barley. The sky had cleared, but there was more rain to come to judge by the dampness of the air and the shifting clouds to the west. Hafoc ducked his head and broke his stride. Lurching in the saddle, Elfrun gripped the edge of the pommel and pulled herself forward until she felt secure enough again to lean forward and pat his neck. He snorted and shook his head. She was very aware of Thancrad riding just to her side and behind her. Did he think she couldn't manage her father's horse? Warm damp air rose up from the long grass, thick and slightly sour with the scent of elder-blossom from the bushes that fringed the track. The sheepwick stood on the edge of the outland, three miles above the hall. They came up the little combe, following the dry course of the winterburn, and out of the stand of elder and alder, rowan and birch that grew on the little plateau which held the feed-barn and house and sheep-pens.

Elfrun jerked back harder on the reins than she had meant. A snowy mare was already there, dazzling in the sunlight, her back bare of anything but a blanket. She was tethered to a post of the fence that surrounded the lambing pens, empty now, with the flocks scattered across the rough grazing of the hills to which they were hefted. She had her head down, grazing among the sweet weeds that grew as high as her belly, but hearing other horses approaching she lifted her head and whickered an enquiry. The saddle was propped against another post.

'It's Storm. My uncle's horse,' Elfrun said. 'He must be here about the shearing too.' She frowned. 'Funny, that he would come himself.' Minster sheep and hall sheep ran side by side, with only the differently cut nicks in their ears to mark them out, but she would have expected Heahred or one of the minster servants to be running such an errand.

'Maybe someone's borrowed his mare?'

'Storm?' She tried to repress a snort. 'You clearly don't know my uncle. No-one would dare' – she thought of Fredegar coming to Cudda – 'not without it being a matter of life or death.' Elfrun looped the reins over the high, carved saddle-bow and grabbed it with her right hand before leaning forward and grasping a slithery handful of Hafoc's dark mane, swinging her right leg over the cantle and pushing herself away from his flank as she thumped down into the grass, winded but with her skirts in place and her dignity intact. 'Good boy!' Gethyn came trotting up, panting and pink tongue lolling, brown eyes eager. 'Not you! Well, you are too.'

She looked back at Thancrad looping Blis's reins over a post. 'Thancrad, could you hold Gethyn? There might be late lambs around, and I don't trust him.' Thancrad took Gethyn's collar with one hand and Hafoc's bridle with the other. He opened his mouth but she forestalled him. She had had more than enough of being fussed over. He was as bad as her grandmother. 'Wait for me here.'

Without staying for his answer, she went through the gate.

The place seemed deserted. Elfrun frowned. The overwintering shed stood to her left and Hirel's little house to her right, and ahead there were the hay store and the dairy. Hirel's old dog was tethered by the dairy. He lifted his greying muzzle and stared at her, but didn't bother to struggle to his legs. She went over to the house, noting the smoke trickling out here and there through the thatch, and the door ajar and sagging a little against the ground on its leather hinges.

'Hello?' The little house was dim after the enamel-bright sunshine of the midsummer late afternoon, but she could tell from the dull fall of her voice that the place was unoccupied despite the smouldering hearth. She came out again, past the stacked barrels and the cords of firewood and went over to the silent pens. Standing on tiptoe she peered over the top of the wattle panels, her gaze sweeping round the empty stalls. The door to the fodder store loomed, a gaping mouth waiting to swallow the imminent hay-harvest. Elfrun crossed herself hastily. If only this fine weather would hold.

She picked up her skirts to step over the high threshold. It was dark inside, punctuated by stabbing lines of bright light where there were holes in the thatch.

The entrance was flanked by mounds of last year's hay as high as her head, an old cartwheel looking for all the world like a giant spindle-whorl, random lengths of wood, little pots for tar and raddle. She took another couple of paces. This was silly. If folk were about they would have hailed her by now. Perhaps Hirel and Ingeld had gone on foot up to the high pastures, with the two lads who helped out.

But Saethryth should be here somewhere, surely.

Elfrun's lips tightened. Too many prickly memories of coming into the women's house to a babble of happy chatter that fell silent at the sight of her, and Saethryth's sidelong eyes, her sulky mouth and her muttering to her neighbour. But that was last year. Saethryth was a married woman now. She would be different.

The air in the barn was thick and sweet with the ghosts of last year's ingathering: hay and pea and vetch. Sparrows chirped incessantly in the rafters and from somewhere there came the buzzing of insects. A stir in the straw caught her eye, and a little sighing sound.

For a wild moment she thought it was a ewe, a marvellous ewe with a great cascade of long silky fleece, caught in a net of sunlight. And then she realized it was human hair.

Saethryth's hair, unbound.

It flowed over the girl's shoulders and down her back in a curly tangle that had all the pallid sheen of the best flax. A wooden flask, its stopper out, lay on the earthen floor beside her. Its contents had spilled and the sticky mess was alive with feasting wasps.

Saethryth shifted again and muttered some unintelligible words. She was deep asleep, lying with her near leg bent at the knee and her other leg over something colourful spread over the hay. Something with even more of a sheen to it than Saethryth's hair.

Silk.

A wasp buzzed in Elfrun's face and she batted it away.

Familiar silk.

Ingeld too was asleep, naked, his arm around Saethryth's waist and his face buried in her breasts. And they had spread out his chasuble, the best one, the yellow silk from Pavia, as a coverlet over the straw.

Elfrun blinked. The heat – it was hard to breathe.

Saethryth sighed and turned closer to Ingeld, wrapping her leg around his. Elfrun could see the pale swell of the other girl's buttock and her uncle's hand, sun-darkened as no priest's should be, cupped possessively around the smooth curve. Gold shone on his finger.

The air had so thickened and filled with dust, it was hard to drag it into her lungs. She took a careful step backwards, then another, and turned round. Her head jerked back. Thancrad was just a few paces away, a silhouette against the light, staring as she had stared. She walked straight past him, eyes fixed out on the rectangle of daylight. She could feel the pulse thudding hard in her neck, her wrists, her groin.

The yard was painfully bright and she shaded her eyes with her hand and stumbled over a long-dried rut. Where had this heat come from, this inability to draw breath?

Thancrad must not know that there had been anything in that sight to disturb her. She swallowed hard as she unlatched the gate. Gethyn came trotting up to her and she bent over the dog, making a fuss of his ears. Blis snorted and shifted from hoof to hoof, setting her harness-trinkets jingling.

'It's your uncle, isn't it? And the shepherd's wife.' Thancrad's words were bitten off at the end. 'What a risk to take.' Hot blood swamped her. She thought he was looking at her oddly. 'And you didn't know.' It was a statement, not a question.

'I knew... I knew there was someone.' She thought back four, no, five months, to that bitter day when she had inadvertently eavesdropped on her uncle and grandmother. She had almost forgotten that conversation in the shock of Fredegar telling her that he would be teaching her no more Latin. Thancrad turned his head sharply. He was looking away from her, up towards the hills.

'What?'

He lifted a hand. 'Listen.'

She frowned, concentrating. One of the horses snorted softly. And then she heard it too, hardly louder than the summer breeze in the birch leaves. Little bells, chiming and clanking in the far uphill distance, and behind the bells a soft steady bleating note almost too faint to hear.

Hirel was bringing the flock down for the shearing.

57

Thancrad vaulted the gate and pelted into the dark doorway of the barn. Elfrun could hear raised voices, muffled by the walls, and she felt sick again, imagining the panic, the vulgar, bare-legged scrabbling for breeches or overdress. It was humiliating to be associated with such a scene, even at this distance. She turned away to stare up the thickly wooded slope. The sound of those tinkling bells would carry some distance on a warm, still afternoon like this, but nonetheless Hirel might round the corner far too soon. She had to get up the hillside and forestall him.

Her only thought was concealing Ingeld's shame. She looked up at the great carved saddle on Hafoc's back and shook her head. Storm presented just as much of a challenge. Without a leg-up it would have to be Blis. Without Thancrad's permission? She glanced behind her, and swallowed. What choice did she have? 'Come on, girl. Stand still.' Thancrad was nowhere in sight. She kilted her skirt up and hurled herself over Blis's back, swinging her right leg over and tugging her skirt back down as far as possible with one hand while she reached for the reins with the other. 'Come on, darling. I've been up on you before. You know me, don't you?'

Blis walked obediently forward, and Elfrun found her balance, urging the pretty mare up the track with her voice more than anything else.

There was a furious barking ahead of her. Gethyn had gone questing up the hillside, sniffing this side and that, and now he was out of sight. From somewhere above her there came a high-pitched yelp.

Elfrun gave Blis a firm kick and the sleek little pony broke into a smooth trot that carried them several hundred yards further up the hillside's well-beaten track. Round a great clump of flowering elder and into a furious scuffle: two rough-coated sheepdogs and Gethyn in an all-out snapping whirl in the middle of the path. Hirel was wading through the terrified sheep, roaring away. The bleating from the sheep was tremendous. Hirel lashed out indiscriminately this way and that with his crook, and Gethyn went yelping back to his mistress. Hirel whistled sharply and his own two dogs slunk back to his heels. He shouted and pointed, and they went scurrying round the flock, nipping at the heels of the strays and the stragglers.

Elfrun had reined in. She and Hirel stared at each other. A horrified look was spreading over his face. He pulled the greasy felt cap from his head and made an awkward bow. 'Lady! Begging pardon, but you should have kept that dog back. Couldn't you hear the wethers coming down?'

Blis was restless, dancing and shuffling. She didn't like the slinking dogs or the mass of sheep still moving towards her, and Elfrun was having a hard time keeping her in the one place. 'I want to talk to you,' she called over her shoulder, trying to haul Blis's head round.

'I can't talk to anyone until I get these penned.' He had a handful of stones grubbed from the track and he threw these one after the other into the bushes ahead of the sheep, trying to startle them back into the flock. The two dogs snarled and slunk pressed low to the ground. 'Get your dog away, lady!'

Rounding up the startled and straying wethers would give them a little extra time. Breathing a blessing on Gethyn and his undisciplined ways, Elfrun let Blis have her head, and the little horse went almost skipping back down the path to the sheepwick.

Ingeld's grey Storm was gone. Elfrun's breath left her in a

gust. She slithered down from Blis, gave her a grateful pat and hitched her next to the patient Hafoc. 'Come, Gethyn.'

Saethryth was watching her from the barn door, her crumpled blue overdress back on, her hair a silver halo. 'You? Why are you here?'

'Your husband's coming.'

'Yes, I—' Saethryth's hands flew to her head. 'Help me with my hair?' And then, 'Were you here before, with that boy, the Illingham boy?'

'He very kindly offered me an escort.' Elfrun tugged out the bigger wisps of hay and straw, then divided the silky mass into three rough hanks and braided it quickly with the ribbon that Saethryth thrust into her hand.

'Thancrad of Illingham.' A teasing note entered her voice. 'You and him, up here for the same thing we were about?'

'Shut up!' The clanking of the sheep-bells was getting loud. 'You – should – be – ashamed – of – yourself,' she said between gritted teeth, emphasizing every word with a tug on the hanks she was plaiting. Saethryth waited until Elfrun was done, and then she spun round, her rose-petal face so contorted that Elfrun recoiled.

'You wait,' she spat, jamming her linen coif over her head and tying it in place with fumbling fingers. 'Just you wait till you have some man you loathe poking you between your legs and ordering you around. See how you like it. Then judge me, with your mouth pursed like a cat's arse.'

'My uncle—'

'I'm not talking about your uncle. I mean *him*' – she jabbed with her thumb – 'that great gormless oaf you married me to.'

'Me?'

'You gave us your blessing.'

'You can't blame me! You and Hirel were dancing happily enough at your wedding. I saw you.'

Elfrun watched the shutters come down over Saethryth's face. 'You don't know what you're talking about.' The approaching clank and bleat were very loud now. 'When he touches me it's like he's handling a ewe. A dead ewe. He's kinder with the live ones.'

'But that doesn't stop you – with him, Father abbot – my uncle. If it's so horrible why do you do it at all?'

The other girl's face was still closed and remote, but as Elfrun stared she saw a small smile begin to tug at her mouth's corners. 'Because Ingeld's different. So very different.' Saethryth turned her wide dark-blue eyes on Elfrun. Her husky voice was hardly above a whisper. 'You cannot imagine what it's like with him.'

Elfrun had a sudden blinding vision of Saethryth's white, sprawled legs, and Ingeld's caressing hand. Hot, sick fury took her. She hunched her shoulder and turned away.

Saethryth reached out a furious hand and pulled her back. 'If it had been anyone else but your precious uncle you'd have left me there asleep, wouldn't you? For my man to find us and do what he might with us?'

Elfrun stared in disbelief at the hand on her shoulder. 'Don't you dare touch me.'

Hirel unlatched the gate and the sea of wool, dirty white and grey, near black and warm brown, came pouring into the yard. Saethryth darted across to the entrance to the pen, shouting and waving her arms, and the flock went yammering past her, the slanting evening sun gilding their fleeces.

Hirel was resting on his crook, looking beyond weary. 'You'd not believe how far some of them had strayed, lady. I've been all night and all day on the hill.' He yawned hugely. 'And that's just the wethers. Saethryth, hurry up and pen them in.'

'I want to talk to you about the shearing.' Elfrun could hear her voice was too abrupt. The sweat was trickling down her ribs.

'The fleece? It'll be good this year. Strong. The grass—' Hirel's eyes flickered past her, and he frowned. She turned to see Thancrad coming out of the barn, a bundle under his arm. He had folded it carefully so that the silk didn't show but Elfrun recognized the chasuble's linen lining. She had sponged stains of oil and picked fragments of wax out of its lush folds too often not to know it, even inside out and folded as small as its stiff fabric would allow.

'What's he doing here?' The shepherd's voice was little more than a growl. One of his dogs cocked its ears.

Elfrun drew herself up. 'He is with me.' She didn't like the suspicious look on Hirel's face. Wordlessly, Thancrad went over to Hafoc and strapped the bundle up behind the gelding's saddle before turning back to help Saethryth drag the heavy hurdles across the entrance to the pen where the wethers were milling and bleating. Hirel's brows darkened further. He crossed the yard to take the other end himself, shouldering Thancrad out of the way. When the pen was secured, he turned back to Elfrun, ducking his head and avoiding her eye.

What was wrong with the man? She tried to remember the errand that had brought her up here in the first place.

'I want to talk to you about the shearing. We need to plan the feast, get the cooking-pits dug, choose which animals to slaughter. So let me know when you have in mind. I should have been up here before, I know – it's late already.'

Hirel nodded, but he still wouldn't meet her eye.

Something else struck her, something that had been in the back of her mind. 'I wanted to ask you about the lambskins, as well. I've been looking back through the tallies, and talking to Luda, and it's been getting worse year on year for the last several. But this year seems to have been the worst ever – at least as far back as I could see. Much the worst.' She looked up. 'Is there anything you can tell me about this? I'm not blaming you—'

Her words had literally wrong-footed him. She saw him pause and sway and stumble mid-stride. 'Lady?' The blood had drained from his face, leaving the raised line where the bear's claw had gouged him above the eyebrow dark and angry. He was shaking his head. 'No.'

'What do you mean, no?'

354

'Not me, lady. Not me. He said you'd never notice.' Hirel was gabbling, his hands blundering out in front of his body as though to fend her off. 'I just did what he told me.'

There was only one possible *he* in this conversation. 'Luda.'

'Last year' – Hirel looked at his wife – 'last year, there were too many deaths, all at once. That snow!'

'That's true enough, lady.' Saethryth straightened up from where she had been leaning against the hurdle, scowling and picking her teeth. 'I remember my father saying much that. They kept what they could but too many of them had got maggoty.'

'And two years ago?' Elfrun was feeling the almost pleasant heat that comes from righteous anger. 'And this year – the worst year? There was no lambing snow this year.'

'I kept some back. I've hidden them. He told me to.' Hirel looked pitiful. 'He said he would give me a silver penny.'

'You did what?' Saethryth sounded as startled and furious as Elfrun felt herself. Thancrad's face was quiet, watchful. Elfrun wished passionately for a moment that he wasn't there and then was grateful in equal measure that he was. This day would have been a nightmare on her own.

'It was for you,' Hirel said. He sounded like a baffled child. 'It was for you, wife, to buy you pretty things. But I lost it.'

Elfrun stared at her shepherd. 'And did it never occur to you that I would have rewarded you for your loyalty if you had come straight to me and told me of this?'

'Rewarded me?' Hirel sounded dazed.

Saethryth crowed with laughter. 'Now, you might, lady. *Now*. But last year? You were no more than a helpless little ean yourself, bleating for its dada.'

Elfrun wheeled on her. 'Did you know about this?'

'Not me.' She shrugged, and darted a furious look at her husband. 'No one tells me anything.'

'Enough,' Elfrun said. She was feeling sickened in equal measure by Hirel's stupidity and Saethryth's spite. 'Where are the lambskins now? Go and get them for me immediately.'

Hirel turned at once and shambled towards the barn. 'In the rafters, lady. Will you come?'

No power on earth was strong enough to make her go back in that barn.

'I'll go with him.' For all Thancrad's height he looked like a stripling next to the shepherd.

Saethryth was at her side. 'I hope they cleared everything out, him and Ingeld.' She smirked at Elfrun. 'It makes a fine bed, that silk. You don't sleep on silk, do you, Elfrun?'

Elfrun turned her back. The men were gone for a while. She leaned over the fence and made a fuss of Gethyn, who had been lying with his head on his paws, panting. 'Sorry, boy. Thirsty? Saethryth, fetch a bowl of water.'

'For the dog? I have to lug every drop of that water.'

Elfrun bit her lip. In high summer Saethryth would have to go a mile with her buckets. 'Sorry. I didn't think.'

Saethryth eyed her sideways. 'You never do, do you?'

The summer evening seemed to have gone on forever, but at last the sun was touching the rim of the hills in the north-west and the sky was flooding red behind great streaks and swathes of gilt-edged cloud. The air was thick and close. A curlew flew low over their heads, giving its shrill, unearthly cry as it glided into the long grass.

Thancrad and Hirel emerged at last, and Thancrad came straight over to where Elfrun was standing by the house door. 'There are two stacks of skins,' he said in a low voice. 'One hidden between two bales of straw in the rafters – about a third of the total, and looking to be the finest. Your shepherd says the steward was going to take them to York himself and sell them.'

'A *third*? The *finest*?'

Thancrad's brown eyes smouldered. 'Stupid, greedy fools. They've over-reached themselves. And if the steward was only giving the shepherd a single penny, then there'll be a fine stash of your silver buried somewhere around his own house.'

Elfrun opened her mouth and closed it again. She blinked a

few times, and glanced at Saethryth, who was staring at them. But too far away to hear what they were saying, surely.

'What is it?'

'Is this my fault? They would never have cheated my father.' She put one hand to her mouth, trying to keep the tears back.

Thancrad glanced over at Saethryth and Hirel, who were standing several feet apart. 'Are you sure of that?' He moved to stand between them and Elfrun. 'Not here. Don't let them see you weak.'

She nodded and squared her chin. 'I will send someone up for the skins,' she said loudly, and turned her back.

Thancrad followed her to the gate.

'You did well there.'

'You think so?'

He nodded. 'Here.' He offered a step with his hands and she swung herself into Hafoc's saddle, banging her knee on the cantle on the way. She pulled Hafoc round, her voice even louder and harder to hide her pain.

'Don't think you've heard the last of this, Hirel.'

But there was no sign of the shepherd. Elfrun looked furiously around the sheepfold, feeling authority slipping like sand though her fingers. 'Where is he?'

'You think he tells me?' Saethryth shrugged. 'He's gone lumbering off down the hill, lady.' The scorn in her voice made the courtesy sound like an insult. 'Maybe he's looking for another little lost lamb.'

58

It was dark under the trees, though the sky would be light for a long time yet. They rode carefully, ducking under the low branches, letting the horses find their own way through the ruts, following the dry bed of the stream.

After a few minutes, Thancrad broke the silence. 'What will you do?'

'About the lambskins? I will have to take it to the assembly. This isn't for settling at Donmouth.'

Thancrad looked across at her. She was pale and withdrawn, her shoulders hunched, her hands gripping the reins too tightly.

'But the assembly's weeks away. Months. Perhaps I should go to my uncle...' She put her hand to her breastbone.

'Come on.' He slipped down from Blis's back and took her bridle. 'You're going to fall out of that saddle in a minute.'

She patted the high pommel. 'You can't fall out of this saddle.'

'Have you eaten today?'

'Am I one of your hounds, for you to fret over?'

He smiled at that. 'You've had a hard day.'

'Yes, I have, haven't I?' She looked down at his hand on Hafoc's bridle. 'Do you think my uncle has gone back to the minster?'

'I would have thought so.'

'I need to talk to him about what we saw today. And the longer I put it off the harder it will be.' She gave a little, self-mocking laugh. 'Left to my own devices, I'll just turn up for compline as usual and sing along like a good girl as though nothing had happened.' Her throat was tight. 'Would you come with me? Now?'

Thancrad was quiet for a moment, then, 'Do you need to confront him?'

'Do I need...?'

'You could just let it go.'

She stared at him. This had not occurred to her. He was looking at the path ahead and all she could see was the thick russet hair of his crown. 'Are you saying I should pretend nothing *had* happened?' A drop of rain fell on her hand.

Thancrad clicked his tongue and tugged Blis away from a tall clump of summer grass. 'Elfrun, everyone knows about the abbot of Donmouth and the shepherd's wife. Everyone, it seems, but you and maybe the shepherd. It's a long while since they first started playing their bed games.'

Elfrun's face looked stiff. Her jaw muscles visibly tightened. 'But that's wrong.'

Thancrad sighed. There was a fallen tree beside the path. 'Look, you need to think, not go hurry-scurry in.' He gestured. 'Sit, and talk?'

At last she nodded.

He unfastened Blis's girth and put the saddle down, then spread her saddlecloth over the log. 'Your chair, lady?'

There was a wraith of a smile. She slithered down, and sat. Gethyn slumped at her feet.

There was a long silence, broken only by the brooding coo of ring-doves and the gentle patter of rain on the beech leaves above their heads. At last Elfrun looked up. 'I should talk to my grandmother, really. But Ingeld has been always her favourite. I don't even know if she would listen. Or care, for that matter.' But again she remembered that overheard conversation, and she knew Abarhild would indeed care, but also that she was powerless.

Thancrad squatted on his haunches in front of her. 'Even so, would you want to hurt her by making a scandal?'

'No.' Elfrun brushed her eyes with the back of her hand.

'Why has he never married?'

'I only know scraps from what I've heard. But putting them

together – she's always wanted him to be a bishop. Archbishop, even. My father for king's thane and her darling Ingeld a great prince of the Church.'

Thancrad snorted. 'Married bishops are not unknown.'

She looked up then, eyes dark peaty hollows in her pale face. 'But not in Frankia. Father Fredegar and my grandmother are always talking about how pure the Church is in Frankia, and how we are backward and degenerate... They think I don't understand their language but their Gallic words are enough like Latin... I've been learning some Latin.' She swallowed, her hands pleating the linen of her skirt. '*Il fuiet lo nom christiien*, Fredegar said. He has abandoned the name of Christian.'

'Your uncle, he means?'

'Yes. The way he behaves upsets Fredegar. And it makes my grandmother so angry she cries. I thought it was just hunting, and feasting, and playing dice.' A crease had appeared between her eyebrows. 'But this... And with Saethryth, of all people.'

Thancrad thought back to the vision of silver-gilt hair, soft curves and sensual abandon that they had encountered in the barn. The abbot had all his sympathy, and a small amount of his envy. He looked down at the clinging tangle of goosegrass and dead-nettle around his feet, not wanting Elfrun to see his face. He desperately wanted to talk to her, but he didn't know where to start.

She was still talking. 'I don't understand what men like so much about her.'

Thancrad sighed thickly. 'And that's probably for the best.' He stood up. 'So you'll hold your peace a little longer, then?' An unexpected gust of wind tugged at his hair, and the rain, which had been pattering lightly down, began to fall in earnest, darkening her fine linen scarf and sticking rats' tails of soaked hair to her temples.

'Come on.' He picked up the damp saddlecloth, pulled a face and laid it carefully over Blis's back. 'I don't want to have to explain to your grandmother how I came to let you catch your death.'

'Let's walk, though. I'm stiff.'

'If you like.' Now for the saddle. 'To the minster?'

She nodded, and they fell into step. The path, such as it was, was rapidly turning into a quagmire, and there were whippy trailing sprays of bramble waiting to snag the unwary. Neither of them had much time or energy to devote to conversation. They had left the line of the stream now and were cutting diagonally across the slope, heading south-east towards the minster inlands.

After a while her silence began to trouble him. The horses were between them and it was hard to see her face, but her steps were dragging.

'Are you sure you won't ride?'

'We're nearly there. There's only a mile or so, though the heifer field is heavy going.'

They came out of the trees and into the rough grazing, a wide dell that deepened steeply before rising again, where the minster heifers were kept. As they descended the slope Thancrad spotted them, clustered in the shelter of the bottom, stolid and shaggy, heads down and their backs to the wind and driving rain. Under its deceptive covering of lush green the meadow was pocked and pitted where the cattle had trampled the sodden earth, and Elfrun kept stumbling. Her skirts were soaked to the knee, briar-snagged and tricked out with goosegrass and burrs.

The cattle were restless as they approached the boggy bottom, stamping and lowering their heads. Thancrad frowned. 'They're not happy. Maybe it's Gethyn.' Elfrun grabbed the hound's collar with her free hand, and Thancrad nodded. 'I'll try and shift them. Am I right in thinking it's a long way round otherwise?' She nodded. 'Can you take Blis, too?' He passed her the reins to loop over her arm and took a pace or two, then turned to glance back at her, burdened with the two horses and the dog. Gethyn was no happier than the heifers, he was straining and whining, and Elfrun was having a hard time of it. He raised his arms and shouted, 'Get! Get!' The ground where the cattle had been was churned and filthy.

There was something there. Something wrong. He took a few more stumbling paces, waving his arms but his heart wasn't in it. As he drew closer the heifers' collective nerve suddenly broke, and they wheeled and rocked away.

There was a man lying there in the mud and the cow-sharn. Thancrad could tell he was dead, because the man's face was pressed deep into the slurry. But he would have guessed anyway, because the body was naked and the rain now falling was hard enough to send little splatters of mud across the drained white skin.

Thancrad stepped carefully closer, the mud sucking at his feet. A well-built, broad-shouldered man, pale-skinned and with a little fat on him. Shortish hair that looked dark, but with the rain and mud who knew? Thancrad took a deep breath. Hunkering down by the man's side, he put a tentative hand on the shoulder blade and felt an otherworldly chill. He tried giving the shoulder a little shake, wondering if by some miracle the soul was still present, but the body felt stiff, and heavy. It would be a struggle to turn it over. The face was buried up to the ears.

He had to be dead.

If he hadn't been dead when he went into the muck he would most certainly be dead now. Thancrad's stomach heaved at the thought of swallowing or inhaling that stuff. Sorry as he was that there was nothing to be done, it was still a relief to step back and wipe his hand down the front of his tunic. He had a premonition that the feeling of that cold, slick skin would haunt him for a while yet.

He nodded once or twice to himself, trying to order his thoughts.

Someone would have to stay with the body. The carrion birds would be down soon. He was surprised they weren't already here. Perhaps the heifers had kept them at bay.

Someone would have to go for help.

He turned and went back to Elfrun. Her eyes widened as he approached and he guessed his face looked wild. 'There's a dead man. Not dead long.' But very dead, for all that.

'Oh, my dear Lord. Who is it?'

'I don't know. I'll stay here and keep the birds off if you go to the minster for help? Take Blis, she's lighter on her feet.'

She hesitated.

'You rode her earlier, didn't you?' She bit her lip and he shook his head at her. 'No, of course I don't mind. Go on.'

Even before he had finished speaking she was thrusting Hafoc at him and hauling herself on to Blis. Her wet dress clung to her thighs, and she was gripping the pony's flanks with blue-white, goose-pimpled knees. 'Come, Gethyn.' She whacked backwards with her heels and Blis lurched off at a startled canter for the far corner of the field, Gethyn in lolloping pursuit. Thancrad picked up Hafoc's reins and walked back over to the corpse. The dun baulked and jibbed as they got closer, and Thancrad clucked soothingly, to calm himself as much as the horse.

He had hunted all his life; he helped slaughter the beasts for the table. He dealt with dead bodies as a matter of routine. Stag and boar and hare, bull calf and sucking pig, stiff and dull-eyed and smelling of blood. Thancrad hugged himself, tucking his hands into his armpits. Why was this so different?

It was hard to believe that that inert and pallid lump had lately been a warm man, breathing and eating and laughing.

Hafoc nickered gently, and Thancrad went back to him and started walking him up and down. 'I'm cold too, my friend. I'm cold too.'

It seemed a long time before help arrived.

They came on foot, heads down against the torrents of rain, that foreign priest and a couple of the minster servants. Thancrad was angry to see that they had allowed Elfrun to return with them, even though someone had had the sense to lend her a cloak.

'The ox-cart is on its way,' the priest said. He stared down at the body. 'The wheels will get bogged down. We will have to lift the body and carry it to firmer ground.'

'Do you know him?'

There was no answer.

'Father?'

'Help me,' the priest said.

Thancrad joined the other two men in the mud, and with their feet skidding away beneath them they heaved the stiff, heavy body over. It came out of the mud with a sucking noise and fell on its back with a thump.

Elfrun gave a little cry.

Even through the thick smears of filth and blood they could see that the face and chest were a dull purple, an inhuman colour that Thancrad found perversely reassuring. There had been nothing for him to do, no death on his conscience. The driving rain was washing the streaks of dirt away, and they could see the great gash that had hacked right through the windpipe.

It was clear to all who stood by that the dead man was, indeed, someone they knew.

Ingeld, abbot of Donmouth.

PART FOUR

The Chronicle, York Minster Scriptorium

There was nothing more that could be written. The ink dried to powder in the inkhorn, and between the corner of the vellum and the corner of the writing-slope a small spider spun its gossamer web.

59

It had been a beautiful day, the triumph of late summer, with barely a breath of wind to stir the clouds, so like handfuls of freshly carded fleece, that hung in the blue depths of the upper air. But Elfrun could not get warm. She forced herself to stay where she was, lips compressed, head held aloft. Under her father's cloak her arms were wrapped tightly around her ribs. At her feet Gethyn lay on the sand with his head resting on crossed paws. Every so often he gave a faint, crooning whimper, but he did not move.

The men came through the dunes and down the beach in a tight group, the long light of the evening sun behind them gilding their edges and leaving their faces dark, throwing their shadows far across the sand. Six of the seven moving with silent purpose, five of them with spears in their hands, their faces every bit as grim and set as Elfrun's.

There was a hiss, a sigh, from the crowd.

Abarhild wasn't there. Abarhild had spent the week since Ingeld's burial weeping, her veil discarded, tearing her hair and scratching her cheeks with her nails like a queen out of an ancient song. When she and Athulf had gone to her to bring her to the church, the old woman had clung crooning to Athulf, calling him Ingeld, her heart's darling and her last-born. And then later, at the graveside, she had turned to Elfrun and said, 'Where are my babies? I miss my babies. Why are my arms empty?' Her eyes had been bloodshot but dry and her voice scratchy and hollow.

The seventh man, a head taller than any of the rest, blundered and stumbled, jostled along, his cries muffled by the thick folds of the bag that was tied over his head. When he tripped he could not save himself, for his wrists were lashed tightly together behind his back. The others let him fall, then two of them jerked him roughly back to his feet. The slightest of them set him going again with a vicious jab from his spear-butt.

As they moved from the dry sand of the dunes to the firmer footing below the high-tide line the hooded man began howling, flailing his body from side to side, trying to lash out with his feet at anyone he could reach. It was a pathetic sight, almost a comic one, but no one was laughing. His guards merely stepped back a pace or two by some tacit common consent, waiting for the man to wear himself out with his antics and fall again. This time, when he tripped and measured his length, thumping heavily face down, his raddle-stained hands twitching and helpless, he landed only a couple of yards from Elfrun's feet. She kept her face like stone.

The hooded man was moaning now. The five men with their spears waited for a few moments, and then began their prodding, jerking and worrying him once more to his feet. Even the youngest of them was taking his cue from the others, acting in silence with a set, expressionless face. The sixth man, the one without a spear, had a troubled look on his sallow face.

Elfrun shifted her weight on to the other leg and turned to look out to sea. The four-oarer was waiting on the sand. The golden evening light caught the headland and picked out every breaking ripple. At the edge of vision white birds were rising and diving, over and over. Impossible to associate that serene prospect with anything as dark as the scene behind her on the beach. But Elfrun knew fine well that the diving birds would be feeding on frantic silver fish, that a storm could boil up out of nowhere to claim its share of lives, that the deep water hid monsters.

A thump. The six men had bundled the seventh headlong into the boat, his legs still flailing.

Six men. Luda the steward. Widia the huntsman. Cuthred the smith. Heahred the deacon. Fredegar the priest. And Athulf.

The seventh man was Hirel the shepherd.

Elfrun had insisted to Fredegar and the young deacon that they didn't have to be part of this, but Heahred had stared at her as though she had run mad. So she had nodded and let things run their course. Heahred had served at the minster since he was seven, and he had adored his father abbot all his life. Of course he needed to bring Ingeld's murderer to justice.

And Fredegar?

After Heahred had blundered out, still angry and confused, the priest had turned to her, his large, dark eyes remote. She had the sense that he was looking not at but through her.

'You're a foreigner. A mass-priest. You don't have to be part of it. You shouldn't—'

'This is my fault. I brought this about.'

For an insane moment she thought he was confessing to killing his abbot himself. 'You? I – How, Father? Hirel—'

He put up a restraining hand. 'Not Hirel. I am not to blame for anything Hirel has done.' He closed his eyes and turned away, and his words were low and rapid. 'But the abbot – *pro Deo amur*, Elfrun, I could have talked to him. Persuaded him to go to the bishop, to mend his ways. Become the great man his mother wanted him to be – the man he could so easily have been.' His eyes were fathomless. 'Instead I had nothing but contempt for his weakness. I turned my back. *Viso illo praeterivi...*'

'You saw him,' Elfrun whispered, 'and you walked by on the other side. But haven't I done the same?'

'You? You're a child. A girl child.' His voice was dismissive. 'But I? I might as well have done the deed myself.'

He had talked with Hirel, pressing him to confess and have his soul absolved in God's eyes, even though his body would still have to suffer the punishment the world dictated. Hirel had refused to say a single word in his own extenuation.

370

And here was Fredegar, weary and tight-lipped, in the execution party. Six men were needed, and he had said that he would help with the boat, and see that the others were no more brutal than they had to be.

Elfrun hugged herself tighter. Nothing felt real: it was as though the whole thing were happening in last night's dream, or an already distant memory. She watched Cuthred and Widia holding Hirel down in the boat. Athulf and Heahred binding those thrashing ankles. Fredegar and Luda pushing off, running the boat into the water and clambering soggily aboard.

Of all the men sending the murderer to justice, Athulf had insisted most loudly on taking part. She had stared at him, half-revolted by his feverish eagerness, half-baffled. 'Of course. You more than anyone.' She had not thought that he would grieve so violently.

The tide was turning, but still high. Four men now at the oars, pulling hard. They would have no difficulty passing the sandbank. There was a place of deep water off the headland. Everyone knew where it was. The men never fished there, even though it had not been used for this purpose in Elfrun's lifetime. She tried not to think of Hirel's weighted body sinking slowly down into the unspeakable monster-haunted darkness.

She had had no choice. She knew, however, that among the hundred or so folk who stood on the dunes there were several who did not blame the shepherd, who muttered that their rutting goat of an abbot had had his judgement coming, that harsh jokes at Ingeld's expense – and no doubt hers too – were common currency at some firesides.

But when minster and hall were united, and when even those who thought the shepherd's anger justified had no doubt about his guilt, there was only ever going to be one outcome. And when Elfrun relived the nightmarish sight of Ingeld's body being turned face upwards out of the mud, her guts curdled and her nails scarred her palms, and she was ready to join the executioners in the boat herself.

Hardly bigger than a leaf now, it looked, bobbing on the gentle swell beyond the sandbank. A bevy of oystercatchers flew busily peeping over her head to land at the far end of the strand. The full moon was just beginning to lift clear of the south-eastern horizon.

A rustle of sea-grasses, and Elfrun sensed someone too close behind her. She turned to find Saethryth at her side. The girl looked terrible, her eyes swollen and pink-rimmed, her skin almost grey, with violet shadows around her eyes.

'Go on,' Saethryth said quietly.

'What?'

'Ask me if I'm satisfied now? Everybody else has.'

'That wouldn't be appropriate.'

'Have you wept for him?' Saethryth spat out the words.

'My uncle? Yes.' Elfrun pulled the cloak tighter and turned away a little. She didn't want to listen. Saethryth was lucky that she too wasn't being taken out by Long Nab and tipped over the topmost strake with a stone bound to her belly. There were those who had pressed for it, Heahred the deacon among them, furi-ous, red-faced, stabbing the air with his finger as he argued that if she had kept to her wedding bargain then their beloved abbot would still be warm and breathing. And Luda had nodded, and looked from stony face to stony face, and growled his agreement. But Elfrun had simply refused to listen to the men.

The matter was bad enough as it was. There was no sign that Hirel had been at the slaughter-place. He had sworn by every saint in the calendar that he was guiltless, until Luda had ordered him gagged. But then, what would they expect the shepherd to say? His guilt was manifest, and only compounded by his denials.

Who else had such good cause to hate Ingeld?

She could hear Luda's voice even now. 'You have no choice, lady.' She had been disgusted by the steward's readiness in argu-ing for the death of his one-time accomplice, his daughter's husband, though she had said nothing to him about the theft of the lambskins – not yet.

Never mind his self-righteous eagerness to push for the drowning of his own daughter, who was now willy-nilly back under his roof.

Bile and acid rose from deep in her belly.

'Elfrun? Lady?'

Was Saethryth still there? Elfrun didn't want to hear whatever it was she had to say. Wasn't it enough for the other woman that she still had life and breath herself? 'What is it now?'

'Lady, my man never did it.'

And at that Elfrun did turn round. 'What are you saying?'

Saethryth was gazing out to sea, the setting sun gilding her uncovered hair. Elfrun saw her throat work as she swallowed. 'Oh, I grant you, Hirel would have been glad to see Ingeld in his grave. But never to cut his throat. They'd have fought, man to man, like he did the bear. And he would never strip him. He wouldn't stoop to take the gold that was on his finger. He's not that kind of greedy.'

Elfrun thought of the purloined lambskins and anger swelled within her. 'So you say. But maybe I know him better than you do. He is a liar, and a thief, and a cheat.'

'So *you* say, lady. But there's one other thing you know as well as I do, and that's that Hirel was wax in my da's hands. You know what my da is like.' There was a new, keening edge in Saethryth's voice. 'Hirel only hid those skins because he wanted a silver penny to buy me fairings, so I would love him.'

Elfrun felt her belly do a slow rise and plunge. She swallowed hard. 'They worked together to cheat me.'

'So you'll be sending my own da out to Long Nab next with a bag on his head?'

Elfrun turned on her. 'For all his sins, it wasn't Luda who killed my uncle! And don't pretend you care what happens to him. He wanted to do the same to you.'

Saethryth was silent for a long moment. At last she said, 'If Hirel killed Ingeld, then where did he put his clothes?'

'They could be anywhere.' Elfrun shrugged, trying to pretend that the question had never occurred to her. 'He could have buried them, burned them, thrown them in the sea, hidden them somewhere.'

'Had he time? Had he? Really?' Saethryth sounded as though she had been drinking a bitter brew. 'And another thing, lady. Ingeld's horse.'

Elfrun wanted to stop her ears. They had not found Storm. She had bolted, they had decided, floundered into the fen perhaps. There were places in there where a full troop of men and horses might sink and be lost in moments. But how far and how fast had Ingeld's grey mare had to run, that they had not found any sign of her?

'Why are you telling me this, now, when it's too late?' Elfrun gestured out to sea, where the little leaf-shaped boat was already far beyond the reach of a human voice. Hirel was guilty. Hirel had to be guilty.

'It wasn't him.'

'Who then?'

No answer.

'You can't just make claims like that. If not Hirel, who?' Elfrun's voice had a new edge of anger to it. Her own silent question of a few moments back returned to her. 'Who else hated my uncle enough to kill him?'

'I'd stake it was the priest. That foreigner.'

'That's ridiculous.' Elfrun turned away. She knew folk were watching her, and she herself should be watching the boat.

'Look how he put down Cudda, like a beast. He's a cold, hard man. And I know he spoke against us, me and Ingeld.' Saethryth's voice rose to a wail. 'And even if it wasn't the priest, it still wasn't Hirel. Couldn't you just have driven him away?' Saethryth sank to her knees and put her face in her hands.

Elfrun closed her eyes.

Unseen, unheard by either of them, a long dark shape slid overboard from the little bobbing leaf and splashed heavily into the sea.

60

'**N**ow about taking the four-oarer out to the sandbanks and hunting seals?' Athulf unhooked one of the big knives and hefted it admiringly. 'The dog-faced ones are pupping. Easy game.'

Widia shrugged. 'I don't fancy it.' The thought of going out in the boat made his stomach turn, although common sense told him that in the weeks since Hirel's drowning the crabs and little fishes would have picked him clean, and his bones would have sunk down into the dark. But it didn't take much these days to bring about that giddy lurch in his guts.

Athulf grinned. 'Get some white fur to make a hood for Saethryth?' He replaced the knife and half turned, watching Widia's face carefully.

'What do you mean?'

Athulf raised his eyebrows. 'Oh, is it meant to be a secret? The whole world knows, Widia. You're still besotted enough to hope to pick up dead men's leavings, when she's out and about again.'

'You disgust me.'

'I only know what they told me.'

'Who? Who told you?'

'You know what they say about widows.' Athulf shrugged, and smirked. 'Common knowledge – once they've had a man they're never happy without something between their thighs—'

Widia shoved him hard against the wall, grabbing the neck of his tunic with one hand. In the other he had a foot-long knife. 'Who?'

'Someone who thinks you can do better.' Athulf kept his voice light, but he was mesmerized by the killing edge on the blade. Perhaps he should have brought his sword to Widia after all. 'Maybe it was Elfrun.'

'Elfrun? I don't believe you.' They stared at each other across the gleaming surface of the knife. Athulf was unnerved by the speed with which Widia had moved, and by the contorted rage on the huntsman's damaged face.

'Put that knife away, you fool.' Athulf's mouth was dry. 'If it wasn't Elfrun it was some other silly gossiping girl. They're all the same. Why does it matter to you which one you take?'

'All the same?' Athulf watched Widia's knuckles whiten. 'My God, but you're like your dead da. People's lives are just one great joke to you, aren't they?'

'Put the knife down.' Athulf was breathing slowly, waiting for his moment. 'And don't ever say I'm like Ingeld.'

'I'll say—'

Athulf brought his knee up hard, at the same time punching Widia in the midriff, aiming for the scar tissue and the badly mended ribs, a blow with all his body weight behind it. The knife clattered as Widia bent double, choking and taken as completely unawares as Athulf had been a moment earlier. He straightened up slowly, clutching his ribs and his groin. The boy had put on weight and breadth of late, and Widia felt as though someone had driven a pile into his flank with a mallet.

'What a family you are,' Widia said, his voice ragged. 'Your da was a disgrace to the name of priest, your uncle broke his promises to me and abandoned his people, and you – you think you're a warrior and leader of men but you're no more than a spiteful child.' He bent down and picked up the knife, checking the blade for damage. 'The sooner the king finds a new lord for Donmouth, the better. And I don't mean you.'

Athulf shrugged. 'Luckily for me, nobody cares for your thoughts.' He moved towards the door, but on the threshold he paused and turned back. 'But don't think that means I'm going to forget a single word. I'm going to be master here, you know. Hall and minster. Then you'll see.'

The knife was undamaged, and Widia shoved it back into its sheath, his breathing still ragged. He wondered yet again why he stayed at Donmouth, when he was a free man. His mother's family were from north of York, and he knew his kin would welcome him. A place could always be found somewhere for a good huntsman. He wasn't going to stay to be at Athulf's beck and call, not for much longer. The mews felt close and airless, and he had a sudden longing to be out and alone. There was that young peregrine he was training, and he decided he would take her out with a lure. The summer evening was young yet and he could lose himself in the fierce joy of the bird.

'Widia?'

He paused, his back to the mews doorway, the falcon on his glove, his right hand reaching out for the lure.

'Can I come in?'

'Go away.'

'Widia? Please?'

He had known even without Athulf's insinuations that she would be back in the world soon. She couldn't hide in her father's house forever – and he knew fine well that she wouldn't, not her, even if she could. The pain and nausea racking him came from Athulf's assault, not from her presence.

'Go away,' he repeated.

'Just turn round and look me in the eye and say that.'

He obeyed, slowly. The bird on his wrist swayed and rebalanced herself. He could feel the grip of her talons, even through the thick leather.

'They should never have married me to Hirel. I should have married you.'

He stared at her in disbelief. 'Aye, maybe. And then it would have been my place in the bed Ingeld took.'

'You can't believe that.' She took a few quick paces towards him but he held up his free hand in warning, and she stopped.

'I would never have listened to Ingeld if I'd had you!' There was a shrill edge to her voice.

'Aye, but the boar put paid to that. Do you not think I've wished a thousand times I'd just stood out of the way and let it charge at the man it was meant for? That would have saved us a lot of trouble.' He was struggling to keep his own voice steady, not wanting to startle the sleek, hooded bird whose claws clutched his glove so trustingly.

'Elfrun would grant you land now, if you asked.' Saethryth was biting her full lower lip, her eyes beseeching.

'Aye, and maybe she would. She's a good lord, to me at least.' Widia felt a slow heat growing inside him. 'But you were glad enough to catch Hirel, and glad enough to betray him when something better beckoned to you. And look what came of that. He and Ingeld are not a month dead and here you are like a bitch in heat. Do you think me such a fool?'

A shuttered look came over Saethryth's face. 'Nothing came of it.'

He wasn't sure he'd heard. 'What?'

'Nothing *came* of it,' she said, still soft, but he knew he'd caught the words right this time. 'Hirel never killed Ingeld.' The flat certainty in her voice sent chills down between his shoulder blades.

'Who did, then?'

She shrugged. 'How should I know?' She looked at him sideways, dipping her head and glancing up through her pale lashes. 'I thought maybe it was you.'

He stared at her. There was a long moment of silence, but to Widia it felt as though the air was full of screaming voices. At last he shook his head.

'Never even tempted to kill him?' To his disbelief an intimate note had crept into her voice, and she took another couple of steps towards him.

Widia had a sudden, vivid memory of that jaunty back, Ingeld going whistling down the slope, and the ease with which he could have thrown his knife. How many folk were speculating, same as Saethryth? Everyone, was the answer. Every soul who had known he and she had been courting, before the boar... He had to stop this. Was she going round all Donmouth spreading her filthy lies? 'What does it matter what I wanted? I never raised hand or knife to the man, and I can prove it. I was in the mews when the word came to the hall.' He was thinking back, his thoughts suddenly frantic as a netted linnet. Had anyone been in the mews with him? Only the dog-boy, and he couldn't speak. But surely no one who knew him would believe for a moment he could have done this thing?

'Then maybe you didn't.' Saethryth shrugged, a lazy up and down of her shoulders. 'It was someone else, maybe someone else who wanted me. Or hated Ingeld, for another reason. But not Hirel.'

Widia shook his head. Everything pointed to the shepherd. He was not surprised that grief and shock had sent Saethryth off balance, but he found her presence unsettling, and he longed for her to go and leave him with his birds.

'I told Elfrun,' she said suddenly, a new hardness in her voice.

'And?'

'That's all.' Saethryth's face tightened. 'She didn't want to know, so I left it. I've not said anything. I wouldn't have spoken now, except for you saying it was my fault.' He opened his mouth, but she was still talking, in the same stiff, flat voice. 'And now I'm back under that roof, with Da and Mam, and so I thought I'd come to you. I always did like you, and maybe I could forget about your face. But now I see you've changed too. Everything's changed.'

61

S omehow the hay had been brought in in its time, and the barley and the oats harvested, and the sun had shone on Donmouth, and the celebrations in church and hall and harvest field had all happened in the right way and in due season. The sheep had even been shorn, by the lads who had been working with Hirel and as many extra hands as they could muster, and the raw wool baled; and the women's house had been busy dawn to dusk with the rustle and thud of the looms. Elfrun knew that behind her back the gossip and the laughter had risen to something like their old levels.

But not when she was there. Never when she was there.

Nor had Elfrun ever mustered the courage to bring up the matter of the lambskins with Luda. When she found time and nerve to tell Widia the bare outline of what had happened, and asked him to go up to the sheepwick and bring the skins down from the secret place in the rafters, he reported them already gone. 'What will you do?'

She had shaken her head. 'Be more watchful. What can I do?' She felt the familiar tightness in her temples. 'I've made the man drown his own son-in-law. Isn't that enough?' Somewhere around the place there was a bag of her silver, but Donmouth was big, and a little leather pouch was an easy thing to hide.

At the harvest meeting she had stood up in the assembly before king and archbishop, Donmouth and Illingham and all the hard-faced men, and for the first time found she didn't care what folk might say about her. She had reported her uncle's murder, and the drowning of Hirel, and she accepted the murmurs of shock, and approval, and the quiet words that came afterwards, when men who had known Ingeld from his boyhood stopped her to pay their respects. Never had the name of the abbot of Donmouth sounded so golden in men's mouths. She had had a brief meeting with the king in the splendour of his tent, the narrow-faced archbishop standing by. She had looked at their faces, knowing that her wellbeing lay in the palm of their hands, and murmured quiet words. For all the recent scandal Donmouth was still producing the renders and tithes king and Church demanded. They had let her go with their blessing, but she knew that with neither Radmer nor Ingeld to give her ballast her grasp on Donmouth's tiller was of the most fragile. They wouldn't take it from her yet – to do so now would look like a reprimand, and she had done nothing wrong.

But it was probably only a matter of time.

And she knew men looked at her curiously, sideways, a new calculation in their eyes.

She unhooked her cloak. Wynn had brought the new and the old tags, and riveted them back in place with sharp little taps of her hammer, squeezing them into place with tiny pliers. Elfrun had been bowled over by the skill of the girl's work. To be sure, the new one was cruder, its shape blurred, the etching and chasing nothing like so fine as its parent. But it looked much the same from a little distance; it weighed as much, it held the strap down and it flashed in the sun, and Elfrun had been effusively grateful to the gruff, defensive child. She had worn the cloak at the meeting and its red folds had been mail-shirt and shield to her.

And she would need it to keep her warm on her walk to the minster.

September was only midway through but the long days of summer were a half-forgotten memory. The ash trees were heavy with seeds and the thorn with haws, the leaves brown-edged and wind-burned, and the summer grasses, the dockans and nettles and hogweed were dying back in one great sagging mass of vegetation. The thin wind had swung round to the north-east and it nipped like a ferret, sending the dead leaves spinning before it and heralding winter, and she was gladder than ever that the harvest was safely in.

'We'll finish this tomorrow. It's too dark.' She wound her thread round the shuttle and rested it on a cross-beam, out of the reach of the kittens. Coming out of the weaving shed she could see that although the sun had already set there was still just enough light to make out the clouds of the upper air racing, like the leaves, before the wind.

There had been no time for her to walk even as far as the minster for the last two weeks, she had been so taken up with seeing that the dead bees were strained out of the honey and checking that the bales of wool were the right weight; and then the harvest meeting; and now that there was a little breathing space she found herself longing for the calm of the church and Fredegar's clear dark voice singing the antiphons. She would be too late for vespers, but sometimes she thought she loved the night hours best. That was such a simple world. She knew what the rules were. All she had to do was keep her face quiet and her hands folded and come in with the responses at the right time.

Abarhild had not mentioned sending her to a house of nuns in all the weeks since Ingeld's murder, but Elfrun was beginning to hanker for the haven her grandmother's plan had offered. Take a bag of silver from the chest in the heddern, saddle Hafoc, ask Widia to come with her for escort, and ride the three or four days north. Knock at the gate, ask for the abbess, mention Abarhild's name, and be received into silence and darkness, where she could give up being Elfrun of Donmouth...

Another foolish dream.

The equinoctial dark had come down quickly, and it was the last night before the new moon. But she wasn't going to let that stop her. She might not be able to walk away from Donmouth altogether, but she could still walk down to the minster to share in the night offices. Perhaps she would spend the night with

Abarhild, though there seemed to be nothing that comforted her grandmother these days.

And she would definitely take Gethyn.

At the thick stand of coppiced ash that marked halfway between hall and minster, she paused for a moment, one hand on the nearest smooth trunk, and tried to gather her chaotic thoughts, looking down through the clusters of bristling shoots and poles towards the tussocky grass and the salt marsh and the white-flecked sea beyond. The heavy branches of the untended standard trees were rustling and stirring with the wind; and it was a long moment before she realized that among all the slim dense verticals there was one that wasn't quite right, a tree not like the others. No, not a tree. A human figure, a dozen yards away or more and wearing much the same browns and greens as the trees, staring up at her through the dusk.

Her first thought was that it was some kind of trowie spirit, and she stepped rapidly backwards, out from under the shadow of the trees, sketching the sign of the cross like a breastplate before coming to the realization that the figure was vaguely familiar.

That girl, the one who had been with Finn, three months back. Elfrun groped for the name in vain. Something outlandish. She was too distracted by the hot, shameful memory of herself screaming like a stuck pig and throwing that valuable beaker to shatter against the doorpost.

Gethyn had come running back to her, and now he too was looking at the girl, ears pricked.

She hadn't moved. Elfrun went towards her again, back under the shade of the trees. The girl stood some way off the path, downslope, just where the trees began to thin out and mix with the long, fading grasses and brambles before running down to the salt-marsh edge. She was still looking intently up at Elfrun. There was something odd about her; it was hard to be sure in the failing light, but the darkness of her hair and her dress and the way the latter hung in thick clinging folds suggested she was soaked to the skin. Had she fallen in the stream? But that would never have got her so wet, not running summer-shallow as it still was. Elfrun frowned, and paused, and the girl beckoned imperiously. Ailu, was that the name?

'What do you want?' She could hear the peremptory edge and she tried to soften her voice. 'Why are you here? Are you all right?'

The way the girl was poised, her eyes wide and her shoulders tense, reminded Elfrun of those times when she had found herself face to face with a doe in the woods, that moment of stand-off while the animal assesses its danger, the knowledge that if she were to take one more step the wild creature would break free from the moment of enchantment and hurtle away into the depths of the trees.

But this was silly. Ailu – no, *Auli*, that was it – Auli was just another girl. Even if they didn't share a language.

She took another step, and Auli ducked her head and pelted away, hurtling down the hill despite having to haul her claggy, clinging skirts away from her legs with both hands.

'Stay, Gethyn. Wait! Auli!' Elfrun didn't know why she shouted – the other girl clearly had no intention of coming back – and all she herself really wanted was to say sorry for screaming at her and Finn and throwing them out of her yards, and she couldn't do that in words Auli could understand.

Elfrun looked for her but she was gone, down and out of the trees and vanished in the fast-fading light among the tall reed-beds of the salt marsh.

Auli had been trying to say something to her, with that peremptory gesture.

Why had she been beckoning if she was going to turn and run away? And what was she doing here, unannounced and alone?

62

Elfrun left the path, treading carefully among the mud and brambles as she worked her way down, trying to remember just where Auli had been standing. It was darker under the thickly pressing trees, and she thought angrily that here was another part of the life of Donmouth that had been neglected. With her father away there was little building going on, and less maintenance. Luda needed to send some of the men out here, from minster and hall both now the harvest was over, to thin the coppice and set the poles aside to season. The brambles needed cutting away, as well...

Gethyn gave a little whine.

'What is it, boy?'

The dog whined again, sniffing along the ground, and Elfrun looked down.

She had almost trodden on him.

The man lay on his right side, his back to her, his hands bunched in front of his face and his knees drawn up high. His hair was dark and plastered against his scalp, and he was shivering violently. As she bent over him, she realized his tunic and leggings were soaked as well.

And then she understood it was Finn, and her insides did a slow turning-over.

Auli had been wet, too. What had they been doing?

But just being wet wouldn't explain that curled, protective pose. Was he ill as well? Drunk? It was horribly reminiscent of crouching over Cudda's burned body, almost a year ago, and she remembered that the first time she had seen Finn she had thought him Cudda's walking spirit, coming up out of the depths of the sea. She reached out a tentative hand and touched his arm, braced for the scream.

It never came. Finn mumbled something and curled up even more tightly. It was sheltered here, but the wind still found its way in, those sharp little teeth. She gripped his left shoulder and gave him a shake, and when she took her hand away it was sticky, and she saw that her palm was darker than it should be. His tunic was soaked with blood as well as with water. Now that she knew, she could smell it.

Where was he bleeding from? Bramble scratches? No, something more serious, to soak his clothes. The dark-brown wool gave her no clues. She had to get that wet tunic off him, both so that she could get him warm and so that she could find the source of the damage.

If it was his blood.

'Finn?'

He sighed again, and a shudder went the length of his body. Greatly daring, she put her hand on his face, then slid it down to the base of his throat. His skin was cold and his pulse hard to find, and fast and faint when she did; and Elfrun understood to her horror that perhaps she didn't have long. She wasn't so worried about his underlinen, but that sodden, heavy tunic would just keep him chilled and exhausted. She had seen enough of this kind of thing when there were accidents with the fishing boats.

Where had that useless girl run off to? An extra pair of hands was badly wanted, and Auli had had a handsome belt-knife the last time Elfrun had seen her. She herself wore a small knife at her own belt, good for little more than unpicking seams and peeling apples, but it was all she had. Shrugging her cloak aside she got to work, snagging and sawing at each tough fibre, peering closely in the gathering darkness. The tunic was made from coarse, greasy wool in a tight weave, and she was going from the back of his neck downwards. She wanted to be gentle and her blade was none of the sharpest, but she was more afraid of taking too long than she was of cutting her finger. There was a nasty little jerk every time the fibres parted, and the knife slipped as often as it bit into the wool. At one point she put the knife down and tried to tear the heavy cloth, but it resisted her grip, and she had to go back to bunching the fabric in one hand and cutting it one plied thread at a time all the way down to the hem. It seemed to take forever but she got there in the end. Straightforward enough now to pull it forward over his left shoulder, and ease it down over his arm.

She found the wound at once, just above his left collarbone, a sharp slit rather than a ragged gash. There was some bruising, and she guessed there would be much more before long. It wasn't bleeding and it looked small, and Elfrun felt a moment of relief before realizing she couldn't be sure how far the blade had gone in. Someone had stabbed with force, aiming for heart or lung or windpipe and by an extraordinary moment of providence had missed all three. As far as she could see there was nothing left in the wound.

And then she realized this might not be his only hurt. Blind panic gusted through her.

'I'm going to get help.'

'*Ei...*'

She leaned forward, her face only inches from his. 'Did you say something?'

His eyes were closed. The gloaming was draining all the world of colour but she could see that compared to her own his skin was a worrying grey. 'Auli, *eigi hjálp.*'

'What? I'm not Auli. It's Elfrun. I'm going to get someone to help. My grandmother will—'

'*Alvrun?*'

He tried to sit up but had to stop and lean forward, visibly fighting nausea. When the shivering had lessened he said thickly, 'No. Don't get help. I don't need help. It's only my collarbone.'

'But you have to get warm – here...' And she bundled the

cloak from round her shoulders and on to his. 'Let's get that tunic right off you, it's chilling you.' It was easier now that he could shift his own weight a little, and when she suggested that the wet linen should come too he shrugged and let her peel it from his flinching skin. She stopped at the sound of his indrawn breath, but he gestured her to continue.

'Use the edge of the cloak to rub yourself dry, and—' She stopped.

'What?'

She was staring at him, back and shoulders and ribs.

'Alvrun? What is it?'

'Nothing.' She pulled the cloak over his back and tucked it quickly and gently around him, defying the wind to nip through those fine soft layers.

Scars. Her fingers had found them first but her eyes could confirm that tactile evidence. The whole of his back was criss-crossed with a fine network of old scars, raised white lines darting this way and that like strands of sunlit gossamer on an autumn morning, standing out even against the pale skin of his back. She shook her head, trying to banish the memory, and the other pictures it summoned of how that latticework might have been inflicted. There was more recent damage to address. What would Abarhild have done? 'Lie with your head downhill. You need to get the blood flowing back into your head and your heart.' She thought of all that rich red life seeping out of him. What was left had to be coaxed, encouraged, cherished.

He tried to sit up abruptly. 'Where's Auli?'

'She ran away. Shh.'

Elfrun was aware of a dozen pressing questions howling on the edges of her consciousness like wind round the eaves on a night of winter gales. Who had done this? Was it in a fight? Or had he been set upon? It was horribly reminiscent of Ingeld. And where had Auli gone running off to? If Finn was her man, how could the wretched girl ever have abandoned him in this state? But none of this mattered compared to the immediate challenge of luring the life-warmth back into him. The clang of the minster bell came to her faintly, its note fighting against the attempts of the wind to carry it away. She had forgotten all about compline.

'I'm cold.'

'I don't know what to do. You don't want me to go for help, but I can't leave you like this.'

'Hold me.'

'What?'

'Lie down with me. Hold me.'

'I—' *Can't*, she was going to say. But she could, she found. Hesitantly, she sat against him and pulled the cloak over both of them, before settling down behind him, her breasts pressed to his back and her arms holding the cloak tight against his chest. He was still shaking, and she held him closer.

'That's better.'

'Shh. You should let me go and get help. I don't even have my strike-a-light, or I'd get a fire going—'

'No fire,' he said. 'I don't want them—'

'Them? Who?'

She couldn't see his face but the violent shaking of his head was enough to frighten her.

'Shh,' she said again, helplessly. 'Stop it.'

Full dark was coming quickly. Inside her head there was a loud and assertive voice, telling her to get up and go, leave him with the cloak if necessary but get away. Someone had done this. Someone might come back. And even if there were no enemies, how could she possibly be here, lying down with a man in the dark?

He crossed his hands over hers and hugged them tight against his chest. 'I'm so tired. Cold.' He was still shaking uncontrollably.

'Finn, are you lying on the earth? Your skin on the earth, I mean?' She didn't need him to answer. 'You have to sit up. The cloak's big enough. I need to put it under you.'

'Don't leave me.' The fear in his voice broke her heart.

'I won't.' She managed to get him propped up on his right

389

elbow long enough to put a corner of the cloak between him and the cold ground before lying down again. 'Gethyn!' She whistled and pointed, and the dog lay down obediently on Finn's other side, pinning down the edge of the cloak. 'Good boy.' She reached across Finn to ruffle Gethyn's ears before pulling the rich fabric right over them both, from the crowns of their heads to their feet. Already it felt less strange than it had done only moments earlier to lie there holding this man; the darkness helped; and this time she squirmed until the full length of her body was against his and she could put her arms around him again, resting her right cheek against his bare shoulder. Perhaps the warmth of her breath would help, especially in the cave of the cloak. His leggings were still wet and she could feel the moisture seeping through the layers of her skirt, but there was nothing to be done about that now. Her hands were less hesitant, and she rubbed them gently up and down the smooth skin of his ribcage, trying to kindle some warmth without jarring him. His breathing was deeper and slower now and she began at last to feel that she was some use. Gethyn's warm, heavy presence, leaning against Finn from the other side and snoring faintly, was an infinite comfort.

Finn covered her left hand with his again, and brought it up to his mouth, pressing his lips hard against her palm. 'You have earned your mirror, Alvrun.'

He sounded so tired. 'Go to sleep,' she said.

63

When Elfrun woke, even before she opened her eyes or her soul had settled properly back into her body, she knew that Finn had gone. She lay motionless, sending out her awareness into the cold morning. He was not there.

But he had been there. Still she did not move, reminding herself of how his body had felt next to hers, and the pressure of his mouth against the palm of her left hand. The skin there still tingled. Perhaps if she went on lying there, not moving and not opening her eyes, she would find that it was still last night, that this was the dream and not the waking. But she could tell, even with her eyes closed and shrouded as she was, that it was dawn, and he had gone.

Gone. And he was wounded. The warm amber glow in which she had slept vanished like dew in the sun.

She pulled the cloak away from her face. It was a morning of mist, cold on her skin and so dull and thick that she couldn't tell if the sun had yet risen.

Finn was sitting three or four yards from her, his back against a tree trunk, gazing down the slope towards the sea. He had put his stained and still-damp linen undershirt back on, and the damaged wool tunic lay bundled against him. Everything looked grey and sad in that light, but it wasn't just the dismal morning that gave him that hollow-cheeked and weary aspect. He looked as though something inside him had broken. Gethyn lay next to him, with Finn's left arm resting around his neck.

Finn didn't turn as she approached, but he held up his free hand and took hers to pull her down next to him. 'Good morning.'

'You're cold.'

He shook his head. 'Last night I learned what cold is. I'm fine now.' He was still looking down towards the sea. 'Are you all right? Will anyone have missed you?' He let her hand fall.

'I'm fine too.' And at the hall they would be assuming she had been at the minster, but no one at the minster had been expecting her. She wondered suddenly how long she might vanish for, before anyone thought to ask where she was. 'Finn, what happened?'

He was silent for a long time, so long that Elfrun began to feel a slow burn of embarrassment at having asked such an apparently impudent question. She had no claim on him, after all. But at last he turned and looked down at her. 'An attack.'

'Was it Auli?' She meant to ask the question that had been in her mind ever since remembering Auli's efficient-looking blade. Had the girl stabbed him? But he evidently misunderstood.

'Auli was out in the marsh. I don't think they saw her. She hid in the reeds. The rest of us weren't so lucky.'

'Us? They? What *they*?' Elfrun sat up so sharply that Gethyn whined and pricked his ears. 'You're saying someone – more than one – attacked you, on my land? What do you mean, the rest of you?'

'Myr. Holmi. It was because of the bear.'

'The *bear*? Do you mean the bear turned on you?' She was frowning, shaking her head, trying and failing to match the stab wound in his left shoulder with what she had seen the bear's claws do to Hirel and the dogs.

He was silent again, but this time she could see it was only because he was struggling after words. He opened his mouth once or twice and closed it again before saying, 'Alvrun, there are things I can't tell you. But the others, I think they may be down there.' He jerked his chin towards marsh and sea.

'Waiting for you?'

'No, they won't be waiting for me.' His face contracted as

392

though he had tasted ale brewed with bitter herbs. 'If they were lucky, they'll have gone, thinking I'm dead. I need to go and look, though. Now that it's light enough.'

'I could go.' She started to get to her feet.

'No. This is not your business.'

'You're stabbed and left for dead on my land?' Her outrage made it hard for her to speak coherently. 'That makes it my business, Finn, whether it was your friends who attacked you, or your enemies, or even a band of sea-wolves.'

He was still for a moment. Then, 'Well, it wasn't sea-wolves, anyway.' He pulled himself up to standing. 'Come on, if you must.'

Down through the trees, across the rough grass and to the edge of the mist-wreathed marsh. A long brackish creek ran in here from the river. At low tide it was easy enough to cross over to Illingham. But as they drew closer to the eerie zone where land and water intermingled they could see that the tide was high now, lapping against the grasses and reeds that grew on the blotches of damp land. A heron launched itself into the air as they came close to the water's edge, flapping off on heavy, reproachful wings.

Elfrun stopped. 'They can't be here. They would have frightened the heron.'

Gethyn was stiff-legged and growling. 'He doesn't like me going too close to the water,' Elfrun said, but Finn shook his head.

'He's scented something.'

Elfrun looked down at the familiar grey muzzle. Gethyn was staring out at the marsh and the reed-beds. She put her hand on the dog's shoulder and realized he was trembling slightly with the effort of holding himself still.

'Shall I let him go?'

Finn nodded.

'Seek, boy, seek!'

Gethyn sprang away from her with a tense, rocking gait. He pranced along the water's edge, giving little high-pitched yips.

'Stay back,' Finn said.

She ignored him.

There was something dark, large, shaggy...

The bear's corpse lay half in and half out of the water. A broken spear-shaft jutted from its belly. The beast was still muzzled, the sodden tags of ribbon, red and green and yellow, floating on the water's surface.

'I told you to stay back.'

She had seen her uncle's body dragged out of the mud. She wasn't as nesh as he thought. 'How bad can this be?'

He had already turned away; she didn't think he had heard her.

Beyond the bear were two more bodies, human ones. Elfrun recognized the bear-master's heavy, dark-bearded face at once. It took another long moment to identify the boy who had danced along the rope, the blood was so thick, clotted across his face and matting his hair. It was immediately evident that they were beyond all human help.

Finn was hugging his ribs, staring down at them. The only sound was the little lap and wash of the water.

'Finn, who did this?'

There was a muscle jumping in his cheek. 'We were down here waiting for a boat to put in, to take us off. We had an agreement: we'd wait for each of the nights of the dark of the first moon after the harvest even-nights. They would aim to come at sunset, wind and tide allowing, and we would wait till they came.'

She could have interrupted then, demanded to know why they had been making free with Donmouth's waterways, but she pressed her lips together and waited.

'The first two nights, nothing. We lay low in the reeds. We thought no one had seen us. But I think now we were wrong, I think we were being watched, from up in the hills.'

She turned to peer along the misty slope in the direction he had indicated. There was nothing to see in this weather, but she knew that he could be right, that in the rough scrubby land of the hill-edge there was plenty of cover. 'Who?'

'I don't know who they were, Alvrun. They came down on us in silence; we hardly even heard their horses' hooves until they were right on top of us. We were looking out for the boat – we were off our guard, or we would have gone out into the swamp, where the horses couldn't follow. Three men on horseback, with spears. They went for Varri first, like it was a game. I think at first they only planned to attack Varri as a bit of fun, but it got too exciting for them.'

'Varri?'

'The bear. His name was Varri. Myr tried to fight them off. He had Varri from a tiny cub, you see. But they had spears, and swords too, and horses. We weren't armed like that. Why would we be?'

'Your shoulder...'

'Spear. I was the furthest out.' He gestured vaguely at the marsh. 'When it hit me it glanced off the collarbone, and the blow knocked me backwards into the water, among the reeds. They must have thought they had killed me too. Auli wasn't far from me. She came for me while they – they were busy.' He stopped and swallowed painfully. 'She pulled me up out of the water, and held me so I could breathe.'

'Three armed men on horseback.' Elfrun felt as though a cold hand had reached in under her ribcage to squeeze her heart. 'Finn, why? Who were they? What did they want?'

He shrugged lopsidedly. 'Thieves, I guess, though they weren't armed like common thieves. They robbed us, anyway. They took my pack, and Myr's purse.' He turned to look back at the corpses of his friends. 'As to who they were... It was getting dark, and they wore hoods. They were yelling, but I didn't hear any names.'

Elfrun too stared at the bodies lying in the reeds, but she wasn't seeing them. Thieves on horseback, armed like warriors. There were always rumours about bands of outlaws and lordless men haunting the hills and the wilder stretches of the king's road where it crossed moor and marshland, but she had never known them to come down into Donmouth lands before.

Except that she had.

'It must have been them. They're the ones who killed Ingeld.' Her lips felt numb, and she didn't recognize the fragmented, wavery sound that came through them as being her own voice.

Finn still had his back to her. 'Auli got me out of the water in the end, and we made it into the trees, but she had to wait till they'd gone. It took a while.'

'I ordered Hirel's death,' she whispered.

'You might have walked right into them.'

She pressed icy fingers against her temples. He was right. She could easily have blundered into that gang of robbers as she walked to the minster, her head full of her stupid childish plans to take the silver and run away. And Abarhild had been right too, about the road being dangerous. Abarhild was always right.

Finn had walked over to Myr's side and was crouching down, bending over the dead man's broad, dark-bearded face. He looked to be muttering something.

Hirel hadn't killed Ingeld.

But Hirel was dead and gone, and the big and little fishes had picked his bones.

That milk was spilled. There was nothing she could do to bring him back, nothing she could do to make amends to him, and if she were to stand up in front of the people of Donmouth and announce that he had been guiltless after all she would only undermine such authority as she still had. The shepherd's name, his reputation and his memory would have to be sacrificed in the greater interests of Donmouth. In approving his drowning she had only put her name to the consensus.

But what about these men, here and now, and their deaths? She thought back to that other misty day, back in June. The bear-fight, and everything that had come from it. She had stood up in public then, and asserted that these wandering folk were under her protection.

An attack on them was tantamount to an attack on her.

Three well-armed and mounted men were a serious threat. Now that she knew, she could see where their hooves had ploughed and churned the boggy soil.

She looked sideways at Finn. She had sent him and Auli packing weeks before Ingeld's body had been found. Had he learned of her uncle's death, wandering the green lanes? Had he even understood her panicked words of a few moments earlier? Was he likely to make the connection? She hugged herself, trying to stand up tall against the weight of guilt. She should call a meeting, confess her mistake, make amends – but how? There was not even Hirel's corpse to recompense with decent burial...

Sinking down through the cold dark water, with shapeless, predatory things moving just out of sight...

It was all her nightmares come home to roost.

She swallowed hard. If she did not draw men's attention to the parallels between her uncle's murder and these, then no one else would either.

No one but Saethryth.

She would think about Saethryth later.

'Finn,' she said sharply.

He rose and turned.

'Come with me to the hall.' She could hear she was too abrupt, and tried to soften her voice. He was not one of her men, after all. 'I need you to tell your story to the men of Donmouth. You have been robbed on my lands, and while you and yours were under my hand.'

He laughed.

She stared at him.

He was shaking his head. 'You drove me and Auli out, Alvrun. You set your dog on us. Do you think your men have such short memories? I would not underestimate your steward like that, if I were you.'

That hit home. 'I never set Gethyn on you! Don't say that! He just got excited.' Her face flushed hot yet again at the thought of that undignified scene in her father's hall. 'And I'm sorry

I behaved like that – I didn't want to hear what you were telling me. You didn't give me the chance to say I was sorry last night.'

Finn clicked his fingers and Gethyn went trotting up to him trustingly to have his ears fondled. 'No. No more I did.' His voice had softened.

'So will you come?'

He was still caressing the dog with his right hand. 'Where did Auli go?'

'Auli? She ran away.' Elfrun thought back. 'She was sopping wet – you both were; you can't have been out of the water long. She got my attention, and then she bolted. But she can't have gone far.'

'Unless the boat put back in for her. Did you see anything?'

It was Elfrun's turn to laugh. 'I was too busy saving your life. After she abandoned you. Whose boat is this, anyway? Illingham?'

'What? No – no – a merchant, that's all.' He was still staring at the waterlogged bodies, his voice quiet, distracted. 'Someone who takes an interest – helps – helped us...' He had straightened up and he was rubbing his left arm, and she felt a pang of conscience.

'How's your shoulder?'

'Sore. Been worse. It'll mend.'

Elfrun had a sudden vivid and painful vision – more than vision: all her senses conspiring to make the thought real to her – of Finn's body lying next to hers, his skin with its web of scars. She knew nothing about this man. She couldn't give herself to some wandering pedlar on a whim. And he had given no sign he was interested since their meetings on the beach last year; so why should she flatter herself that that had been anything more than his chapman's banter?

But he had called her beautiful! No one but her father had ever called her beautiful before. There was a pain inside her that she couldn't remember ever having felt, a keen, silent, acid wailing that brought water to her eyes and a lump to her throat and made it hard to breathe.

'Alvrun, you're crying. Don't cry.'

'I'm not crying,' she said furiously. 'Why do you always think I'm crying?'

He lifted a finger and brushed first one cheekbone, then the other. 'Look.'

She tightened her lips and shook her head. 'It's the wind.'

'Does it matter so very much to you that I come to the hall and you use me to assert your mastery over Donmouth?' He gave her the same smile that she had first seen on his face on the sand dunes less than half a mile from this spot, when he had come walking out of the sea in a silver dazzle of light, almost a year ago. The smile that stretched the skin over his high, smooth cheekbones and tilted his eyes and was so beautiful that she couldn't help returning it. 'My life is in the palm of your hand, lady. If you want me, I will come.'

64

Widia was already mounted, boar-spear in hand. 'Come on, Athulf.'

Elfrun watched them ride out: Widia and Athulf, and the handful of other men from Donmouth whom she could trust not to slice off one of their own mount's ears with an ineptly brandished hunting knife. Finn was also watching, his face hard. His eyes followed Athulf in particular, a little frown tugging at the patch of skin between his eyebrows.

'He's all right,' she said, wanting to reassure Finn that she was providing the best that Donmouth had to offer. 'He may look young but he knows how to use that sword.'

She had come roaring into the yard. All the way from the site of the slaughter she had been trying her hardest to bring her father's image forcibly before her, to remember the set of his shoulders and the tone of his voice, how he would bellow with all a bull's trumpeting force if he found one of his horses ungroomed or unfed after a day in the hunting grounds. What kind of voice would Radmer have used if he had found men murdered by outlaws on his own land?

And it had worked. Elfrun had simply shouted down any attempt by the men to interrupt, fighting the edge of shrillness that threatened to creep in, always aware of Finn standing quietly, grey-skinned and hugging his ribs in damp and muddy underlinen, the mute testimony to the truth of everything she was saying. She had ordered Widia and Athulf to lead the hunt, though Athulf had jibbed, complaining that he was tired, that his horse needed a rest, that he hadn't broken his fast.

'Come inside,' she said to Finn now, wanting to be away from those eager eyes. 'Sit down. Rest. You look exhausted.'

'Sit? Where?'

She pointed to her father's chair.

'I can't possibly.' He looked around for a bench.

'Don't be stupid. How's your shoulder?'

'Better all the time.' But still he didn't sit down, and she knew he was lying.

Elfrun interlaced her fingers and looked down at them, then up at Finn. 'What were you all doing on our land, without telling me – us?' It was the question that had been nagging at her all morning. 'Why didn't you come through by the hall?'

He paused before replying. 'You have no idea how terrifying you can be, do you?' He shook his head. 'I told you earlier – you sent us packing, me and Auli. I wasn't going to come this way again, not after we'd upset you like that.' His eyes met hers. 'But our meeting-place with the boat – that had been arranged back in April. We couldn't change that. So we came in over the hills and cut down by the stream...' His face closed down.

'This is my fault, then, for driving you away, in June.'

'That's not what I said, or what I thought.'

'That's as may be.' Her guilt hurt so much, it was as though the room had gone dark, as though she had swallowed knives.

'No.' He was stern. 'We didn't want you or yours to know about the boat. It would have been a secret meeting, even if we had come by the road. So we would still have been attacked. It is nothing to do with you, Alvrun. Nothing to do with your lordship of Donmouth.'

He was trying to stop her from being so hard on herself, but he could only do it by showing her how little she knew of him, how little she meant to him. She took refuge in anger. 'I don't like all these secrets.'

'I didn't choose them either.'

She stared at him for a long moment that drew out past all bearing.

'I'm cold,' he said at last. 'Cold and damp. Could I trouble you to find me a tunic, to replace the one you so recklessly hacked to pieces?'

She was about to retaliate in kind; and then she realized that the lift of his eyebrows should have told her he was teasing, that he was trying to draw the sting. To move their encounter on to higher, drier, less treacherous ground. She had a sudden image of him lying in the muddy marsh water, the red blood spilling out of him, getting colder and colder, knowing he was dying. Not knowing whether his friends were dead or merely wounded, only that either way he could not help them.

Finn.

She had come so close to losing him entirely.

'Sit down.' Blinded with sudden tears, she blundered her way to the heddern at the back of the hall, where she and Athulf had had their confrontation over the sword not six months since. She had lost that argument. She was determined not to lose anything else. It was dark in the little chamber and Elfrun thought belatedly that she should have ordered a candle brought. She would manage, though – she mustn't waste more time. Old tunics of her father's were stowed in the great chest, and Finn could have one of those. She had in mind that grey lambswool, summer-weight but warm and softer than most, and wide-woven – wide enough that a hurt man might shrug his way into it without the pain being beyond bearing. It had been one of her father's favourites, but he had left it behind in favour of more splendid garments.

But when she hauled back the lid of the chest and dug through the layers to the grey tunic, she found that the moth had got into the armpit. Her fingertips could poke right through the holes. Bunching it up and burying her face in it, Elfrun inhaled the scent of sheep-grease and the sprigs of costmary and mugwort that were supposed to keep the moths at bay. She had been no better at guarding her father's clothes than she had been at keeping any other part of his realm safe. *Lay not up to yourselves treasures on earth: where the rust and moth consume...*

All that labour, for this.

Breathe. *Breathe.* Finn was waiting. Would this one do, despite the holes? No doubt Luda would say that Finn, as a beggarly wanderer of the roads, was lucky to get it and should be grateful.

Her jaw tightened. She would not send him out in moth-eaten cast-offs for Luda to mock, not if she had a choice. She leaned forward into the chest again, her fingers leafing in the gloom through the neatly folded garments. She knew them so well, she didn't need a light. The dark brown was too heavy to sit comfortably on a man wounded in the shoulder. Not the blue – her father had never liked that blue one: she could see him running his finger around the inside of the collar, complaining that the wool was too scratchy, that it chafed him. Every single garment had memories threaded through warp and weft; and nothing was right.

Caution had been abandoned now: she was pulling out the clothes one after the other, only to reject each item in turn, drop it on the floor and reach after another. She could feel hysteria building like thunderclouds, memories thick as midges about her head.

Elfrun took a deep breath and sat back on her heels, resting her hands on her knees and trying to still her hammering heart.

Perhaps she should send down to the minster and see what Ingeld had left in his chest, although Abarhild had refused to let anyone touch her darling son's possessions, even Athulf, to whom they surely belonged by right. There were some fine things there – finer than anything Radmer had left behind him. Despite her grandmother's intransigence they would need sorting, and sooner rather than later to judge by the state she had let her father's clothes get into. Less than a year of neglect... She swallowed painfully, thinking back to Athulf's righteous fury about the rusty sword, its cracked, flaking harness and tarnished silver buckles. He had been right, but she had been too angry to see it.

And she would have to see these clothes put back into the chest, in some kind of order. Finn needed a tunic now, not in half a day. Perhaps the grey would do after all. If she took it into the light and had a better look at it...

'Alvrun?'

'What?' He was right behind her.

'You took so long. I wondered if you – if everything was all right.'

'Sorry. I – I was thinking about moths.' She thrust the tunic at him blindly.

He grasped her wrist instead, and the grey tunic slithered to the floor. 'Alvrun... have I thanked you? Thanked you properly? I would have died. What can I do for you?'

The moment trembled between them. Elfrun felt something huge swelling under her ribs, like some great creature of the deep sea, rising and breaching the water and coming darkly shining into the air at last.

She went with a rush into his arms, burying her face in his right shoulder, feeling the renewed warmth of his skin through the damp linen. So different from the corpse-chill of last night. His hand cupped the back of her head, stroking her hair.

Him and his secrets. There were so many questions to which she should demand answers. She had no idea what Auli was to him. How had he come by that spider's web of scars? Why these secret assignations with strange merchants on her land? But none of those buzzing, wasp-like issues mattered, not just at that moment. Someone had taken out her blood and replaced it with sun-warmed mead. She turned her face up to his and kissed him, hard and clumsy, right on the mouth, her arms around his waist.

He was startled: he rocked slightly and found his balance again before kissing her in his turn. She could feel her knees caving in, the earth tugging her downwards, and she found herself pulling hard until they were both kneeling on the floor, among her father's rejected finery, still kissing, fierce enough to bruise lips against teeth. He was cupping her face with his good hand, stroking his thumb over her cheekbones. '*Alvrun...*'

She tried to tug him closer, to make him lie down beside her as she had lain by him in the ash coppice, but he jerked away with a wince. 'Sorry – my shoulder.'

Her heart was beating so hard she could hardly breathe; it was like some frantic wild bird struggling in the huntsman's lime. She felt that if she spoke she would break the spell, that she would lose this ferocious determination, so she just nodded and shifted round and tried to pull him down against her on the other side. He groaned and buried his face in her neck, and suddenly she was terrified she had really hurt him.

'What is it?'

'Alvrun... Alvrun...'

'What?' She was properly frightened now.

'Not here.' The breath was catching in his throat. 'I – My shoulder hurts. The bones grated. But it's not that. Your charming steward might come in.' He was sitting up, his breath steadying. His eyes were shadowed in the filtered light. Somewhere up in the rafters a mouse or a rat squeaked and scrabbled. 'He might come in any moment. And then what about your name, and your reputation, Alvrun? And what price my life? You didn't save me last night to see me die at the rope's end.'

She batted away the buzzing, unwelcome cloud of words, hanging on to the first two. 'Not here? Then where?'

He sighed. 'What is it you want?'

'You.' She was amazed by her own boldness.

'As a means to what end?'

'What?' She shook her head at him, not wanting to talk, wanting to recapture that honey-warm energy of a moment since.

'There's something going on with you. You're frightened of something. What's frightened you so badly that you want to use me to bring your world crashing down around you?'

'That's not true, any of it.' She was appalled by his words.

'I'm not using you. I dream about you.' She closed her mouth, because it had been about to say, *I love you*.

'Then what is true? A dream?' He shook his head. 'You have the right of it, Alvrun. I am no more than a dream. A thief in the night. A creature of shadow. You don't want me.'

That torrent of blood and desire was ebbing now: she could feel it slowly withdrawing like the turn of the tide and the slow retreat across the sand; and a deep mournful longing taking its place. There was anger in there too, but she didn't know why, or with whom she should be angry, and she bit it back.

'You're right in one thing.' She breathed out sharply, a short huffing sound. 'Luda could come in, or anybody really.' She pulled away from him, rearranging her rucked skirts. Too late, her modesty was reasserting itself, and she could feel hot shame staining her cheeks. 'Here.' The grey wool. 'It's the softest, although the moth have—'

Finn caught her wrist. 'Would you come away with me?'

65

Of course she had turned him down.

But first there had been a long stunned moment, like the floating time of shock after a bad fall; a moment in which a whole other life had unfolded itself before her, one in which she was free of Donmouth; in which guilt and grief and terrible responsibility were no more than the rags of last night's dream; in which she and Finn wandered the green lanes in some endless summer.

It was so real, she could see the cow parsley and the meadowsweet and the loosestrife, all in bloom at once and as high as her head, the air fragrant and buzzing with the laden bees, and Finn's face warm and golden and turned towards her own.

Then, 'No!' She had shaken her head at Finn, furious with him for even summoning up that tantalizing illusion. 'How can I?'

It was like her stupid dream of taking her father's silver and fleeing to some haven with Widia as escort, but a thousand times worse because it was Finn and it was real and he was looking at her with those silver-grey eyes and the little lift of the eyebrows that somehow put all the humour and the charm back into his weary face.

She scrambled to her feet, thrusting the grey wool into his arms and backing towards the door. 'Don't look at me like that.'

He followed her out into the lighter space of the high-raftered, echoing hall. 'I mean it. Come with me.' There was a tight look to his jaw now, and she wondered whether he was angry with her. She felt her own temper rising in pre-emptive retaliation.

'I can't. Don't be ridiculous. Put that tunic on. Be careful with the left sleeve – the moth—'

'Never mind the moth!' He stepped forward quickly and took her by the hand. 'I really mean it, Alvrun. You should come with me.' His gaze flickered towards the door and back to her face. 'You have no idea.'

'Donmouth—'

'Donmouth can shift for itself. There's not a soul here who cares for you as they should. Look at you! I thought you were too thin when I met you a year ago—'

'You said I was beautiful!' She hadn't meant to speak, but this betrayal tore the words out of her.

'You are beautiful.' He was shaking his head. 'And strong, and brave. And kind, too, for that matter. Kinder than you have any call to be. But your face...' He lifted his other hand and stroked a finger down from her eyebrow to the corner of her jaw, holding her gaze with his until she felt as though she were drowning. 'You're all bones and hollows and corners, Alvrun. Donmouth isn't hungry, not this year. You aren't looking after yourself, and no one is looking after you.' He gripped her wrist tighter. 'But this isn't what I meant to be saying. Alvrun' – and his voice was sombre suddenly – 'I've heard things...'

'About me? What things?' The floorboards seemed to shift beneath her.

'No, no. Not about you. About... things. On – on the roads.' He paused, hunting for words. 'You do, you know, travelling. At markets. Folk – I think folk forget I'm there.' His eyes were shadowed, remote, as though he were looking into the depths of his memory. 'Bad times are coming.'

'To Donmouth?' The ground was still lurching.

'To all Northumbria. But from what I've seen and heard – yes, perhaps particularly to Donmouth.'

The gravity of his tone terrified her. She tried to fight the fear with anger. 'Then how can I possibly go? My folk need me, Finn. How can I go with you? Are you asking me to be your woman?' A flash of memory: Ingeld's brown hand resting with such affectionate possession on the soft pale curve of Saethryth's hip; and she battled a sudden hot rush of tears. 'What makes you think I'm so easy?'

'Easy? *You?*' Finn closed his eyes. 'I should never have asked you. Never. And if bad times do come it's at least in part my fault. Better for both of us maybe if you had left me where I lay, last night.'

She was speechless for a long moment. His words made no sense. Then, 'But you would have died.'

'Yes, most like.' He shrugged his good shoulder. 'Men do die, you know. They die all the time.'

The flat fatalism of his tone drove her to fury. 'Do you think I don't know that?'

'I don't know what you know, Alvrun. And I don't know what you want. I wish you would come with me. But never mind.' He turned a little away from her and started to pull the grey tunic on over his head, flinching as he worked his left arm gingerly into the sleeve. He lacked some of Radmer's breadth, and she could see that the seams sat awkwardly across his shoulders and upper arms, but at least the moth damage was invisible. 'I'll stay here tonight, if I may.' His voice was stiff. 'I need to rest, with your leave. Then I'll be off at first light tomorrow.'

'Where will you go?'

He shrugged, and winced again. 'York, probably. After that, who knows?'

'But you're hurt.'

'I've been hurt before. I'll live.' He turned towards the main door of the hall, the one that gave out into the yard.

'Finn!' She was knocked by a sudden gust of panic, a longing to hold on to him, to regain some of the ground they seemed to have lost. 'You must be starving. Come with me to the bakehouse. It must be about time to give out the bread to the slaves.'

Finn stopped, one hand on the doorjamb, his back to her. 'Indeed. My life is yours to command.'

'What?' She pushed her hair out of her face.

'So feed me with your other thralls. I've known worse masters.'

Elfrun felt a terrible draining despair, as though someone had turned a spigot and let all the life and mirth run out of her veins. Only a few minutes ago they had been so close, and now he had cased himself in ice and bitterness, and she had no idea why.

'Go then.' Without wanting to she was mimicking his own bitten-back tone. 'Speak to Luda. Tell him I said he is to give you whatever you need. Then go and sleep.'

'Alvrun...' He pivoted.

'Just go.'

He stared at her for a long moment, then turned and did as she had ordered, and his very compliance only made her feel worse. After he had gone she gazed at the empty doorway, numbed, a lump in her throat. Then she went into the weaving shed and sat herself down at her loom and forced herself to concentrate on thread count and colour and not bashing the cloth too hard with her batten. She stayed there in the half-light for the whole day, speaking only when she had to.

Widia came back late, with all his companions but Athulf. The mist had retreated at last, to leave a warm golden evening as its legacy. One of her women stood awkwardly in the door of the weaving shed and beckoned her out to the yard.

'We found nothing. Oh – hoofprints, and dung, and a smoth-ered fire. And this.' Widia jerked his head, and one of the others urged his mount forward, swinging a crushed and battered wicker basket from his back. It was Finn's pack. She didn't need to look inside to see that it had been emptied of its treasures.

'But no clue as to where they went?'

'Athulf's still out there. Still looking. He said he would be late, and not to worry.'

'On his own?' She couldn't hide the shrill edge of alarm.

Widia shrugged. 'He can look after himself.'

'Against three armed men?' And there could be more than three.

'Lady' – and Widia's voice betrayed that he was weary to the bone – 'you've tried quarrelling with him before now. How far did it get you?'

She nodded, suddenly beyond all arguing. He was right. Somewhere in the last year or so the little cousin whom she had thought she knew had vanished. Athulf was a man now. He had his sword. He could look to himself.

'Thank you, Widia.'

His face softened. 'You're more than welcome, lady.' He paused, then said, 'I'd like a word with you, when you've time? Something important. But not now – I need food and fire, and you're too weary for me to burden you further.'

'Of course. Whenever it suits you.' Too saddened to be curious, she bent to lift the pack, and carried it through to the stable. The horses were still out in their summer-field and the place was quiet; at first she thought it was empty, but then she saw that Gethyn and the dog-boy were there, and as she approached the dog-boy put a finger to his lips, eyes wide and nodding his head.

Finn was lying in the straw, fast asleep. When she had first gone into the weaving shed that morning she had ordered one of the women to make a bed for him in the stable, and to dress his shoulder; she could only guess now how massively the bruising had spread, as it was hidden by the soft grey wool. He looked as calm and comfortable as he was ever likely to. Bones and hollows and corners, he had called her, but he was little more substantial than a shadow himself. She hunkered down and looked hard at his face. A gross intrusion, to take advantage of his oblivion, but she couldn't help herself. The air in the stable was warm and sweet with new hay.

'Is this your man then?' Saethryth had come in silently. Gethyn padded up to her, tail wagging.

Elfrun rose hot-faced and stepped back swiftly, a denial on her lips, but it died unspoken. *My man.* She tried out the words, shaping them with her lips but giving them no sound.

'I was wrong then,' Saethryth said. 'You do understand.' She moved round to stand at Elfrun's side. 'My da says he's some beggarly pedlar who should be whipped out of Donmouth. He says to tell you he's sent men down to the marsh to deal with the carrion. Burn them. His words.'

Elfrun nodded, carefully ignoring Saethryth's first sentences. Yes. The bodies. It had to be done.

'Who hurt him? Who killed them?'

It was the question Elfrun had been dreading. 'We don't know. Outlaws.'

'So they're all saying. You know what I'm thinking, don't you, lady?'

'Thinking?' The two young women stared at each other, until Elfrun had to lower her gaze.

'I told you before. You should never have drowned Hirel.'

Elfrun swallowed. 'Ingeld's throat was cut. He was stripped. Not speared and left to drown. It's not the same.'

'But like enough. Robbed and killed.' Saethryth paused, looking down at Finn. 'What are you going to do? He's pretty, isn't he? But he looks a cold fish. Not much life in him. That Thancrad, he's the better bet.'

Elfrun fought her fury. 'Of course there isn't much life in him, not just now. But that isn't – isn't normal. He's wounded, that's all.' She squatted down beside him again, blocking Saethryth's view of him as though Finn needed protecting from the other woman's limpid cornflower gaze.

'Wounded?' Saethryth laughed, the old gurgling laugh that had set Elfrun's teeth on edge for so many years. 'That's his excuse, is it?'

'Anyway, he's leaving tomorrow.'

'And you'll just stand back and let him go.' Saethryth shook her head. 'You'd better get him to take you to that house of nuns your gammer's always talking about. Best place for someone like you.'

'What do you mean by that?' Elfrun half rose, but Saethryth just shrugged and vanished into the yard.

Just stand back and let him go...

Elfrun sat down at Finn's feet. Someone had put an old blanket over him, and his breathing was easy and regular. Her own cloak was hanging in the hall, matted and filthy, in need of careful brushing and sponging after the night's trials. She crossed her legs and folded her hands in her lap, looking down at her interwoven fingers, brown and grubby against the faded blue of her patched dress with its ragged and muddy hem. Her nails were a disgrace. Abarhild would have something to say – would have had, she emended. Her grandmother was so vague, these days, so lost in her memories. A reprimand would have been a welcome sign that she was engaging with the world again.

Elfrun came to a sudden decision.

She would go to the king and the archbishop, and ask them to take Donmouth hall and minster under their protection. She could do no more. She had been trying for a whole year, and all had been disaster. Rust and moth, theft and corruption and adultery, and now outlaws running free on her hills.

And what of her own fate? Elfrun lifted her head and gazed unseeing at the far wall of the stable, the bridles and halters hanging from their pegs.

A house of nuns, if the great powers agreed with Abarhild.

Marriage. Most women her age were two or three years married, one baby at the breast and another in the ground. It was more than likely that the king would give Donmouth into the hand of some proven and deserving retainer, a hard-eyed, heavy-bearded man of thirty or forty with a wife or two behind him already, her body as the seal of the bargain. Someone like cousin Edmund. *And is the maiden willing?* Of course, she could always say no, but she could imagine how coldly that would be received.

And if she did refuse, then what?

She could see the king shrugging, pointing to the open door, clear as though she already stood before him.

She could go and find service on some other estate. Her weaving skills would make her welcome in the homes of any

413

one of a number of distant cousins. Useful, worthy women could always find a roof, until they were too old to work. And a kind household would even find the old woman a sunny corner and a rusk to mumble.

But she had grown used over the last year to having choices and making decisions. Of having men listen to her. Even if they listened and promised and lied. Even if her choices and decisions were the wrong ones. She would have to forget about all that, as a poor relation.

So then what?

The road was open to her, as Finn had seemed to know.

Elfrun felt a deep bone-weariness that was only partly to do with her long night in the open and the horror of what had happened to Finn and his companions. It was herself, her guilty conscience, and her foolish vanity and fear of what might come: these were the burdens which were crushing her. Where was her much-vaunted faith when it was needed? She looked down at Finn. His lips were slightly parted, and one lock of his hair, ashy-fair and fine, had fallen over his forehead.

As she watched, his eyes opened.

As if in a dream that turned to nightmare, she saw his face light from within, and his right hand reach out to her, and then full wakefulness and memory bring the shutters down; and he turned away, lifting his shoulder against her.

'Finn?'

'Lady.' He still had his back turned.

'What are you and Auli to each other?'

She had no right to demand. She wasn't even sure why that question, of all the burning questions, had come from her lips. But she knew that Auli had abandoned Finn into her care; and although that granted her no claim to an answer she felt it at least gave her permission to ask.

He didn't respond for a long moment, and then he turned back, with a rustling of straw, and half sat up carefully, propping himself on his good arm, the blanket falling to one side.

'Auli.'

'Yes.' She had to bite her lower lip, to stop herself from supplying his response. Sister. Cousin. Chance-met companion on the road. Anything but the answer she dreaded.

But the words, when they came, were not any of the ones she had foreseen.

'Alvrun, Auli is my owner.'

She stared, literally making no sense of the separate syllables, unable to combine them into meaningful words. 'What do you mean?'

He sighed. 'I am her thrall. I work for her. She owns me, she and her father.'

'Her father? The bear-leader?'

'Who, Myr?' Finn laughed scratchily. 'No, no. Myr and Holmi and me, we're all their thralls.'

'So who is her father? Where is he?'

'I don't know. It was his boat that was putting in for us, but whether he was in it...' Finn shrugged and made a face. 'A lot can happen in a summer.'

'So when you asked me to come with you...' A slave with his eye on freedom. No wonder he had been buttering her up. Right from that long-ago encounter in the sand dunes he must have known her for what she was. A green girl with access to her father's silver, pathetically ready to lie down with the first man who called her beautiful.

Vanity. Vanity. She hadn't known it was possible to feel so utterly humiliated.

'I think I had better go.'

'Alvrun!'

She turned and walked out of the stable, into the autumn dusk.

66

The yard appeared deserted, but for the loops and skeins of hearth-smoke hanging in the still September air, and the smell of cooking. Everyone would be at their evening meal, and for this favour Elfrun was profoundly grateful. The last thing she wanted just then, hot-cheeked as she was and fighting tears, was to confront Saethryth and another half-dozen gossip-avid women, who might so easily have overheard anything she and Finn had had to say to each other. She would go back to the weaving shed – no, first she would go and beg half a loaf and some cheese. She hadn't eaten since – and she realized then that she hadn't eaten that whole day, nor the previous evening, and she was suddenly, bestially, hungry.

But she had taken no more than half a dozen paces from the stable-door when there was a thunder of hooves, loud and unfamiliar in the narrow, enclosed space of the yard.

Elfrun spun around, drawing in her breath to shout a warning and a reproof, but she wasn't given the chance. There was a rider either side of her, their hoods pulled low, and a third coming straight at her who had looped his reins and was leaning sideways from his saddle, holding a grey cloak outstretched between his hands. Before she had time even to wonder what he was about, her head and upper body had been trapped in the coarse, scratchy fabric, and it was being bundled about her. Outraged, she put up her hands to shove the stifling cloth away, but now she was being grabbed under the armpits and hauled on to the back of one of the other horses, flung to lie face down over the saddle-bow, which dug more painfully into her midriff with every long stride. She shouted and tried to heave herself sideways, but the horse was wheeling now and the lurching trot flowing into a canter and then the crazy thud of a gallop, and she was suddenly more frightened of falling off than of staying on, no matter what was happening and who these riders might be.

But she knew exactly who they were.

Who had killed Ingeld? Who had speared the bear, and Finn's friends, and Finn himself? Three men on horseback. Outlaws.

They would take her up into the hills.

Elfrun tried desperately to think, though the panic burning through her veins like fever fuddled her brain, and the saddle-bow was bruising her and winding her in equal measure, the rough wool pressed hard and stifling against eyes and nose and mouth.

They would have to slow down. They couldn't ride like this once they were out of the cultivated ground and on to the waste, not unless they wanted to break a horse's leg among the rough and the gorse. That would be her chance. When they slowed… No, let them ride a little way into the hills. She knew that landscape, every copse, every hollow. She could run and lie low.

The day was fading. They would have to slow down soon. The darkness would be her friend.

She just had to wait.

But the hectic pace wasn't slowing, and she could hear the other horses galloping alongside, and then she realized she was slipping slowly forward with every great stride, her head a little further towards the ground, that there nothing she could do to stop it, and that if she fell she could be trampled. Every rise and fall of the horse's head, every jolt of its withers, and she was another inch towards the ground. She twisted wildly, moaning with terror, knowing it was useless, knowing that she was letting fear win; and then she felt the cloth around the waist of her dress clamped in a strong hand slowly hauling her back to the centre. She was sick and dizzy with relief, and then furious with herself at her gratitude.

And then the pace did slow, and to her bafflement she heard the sound of splashing from the horses' hooves below her. She had had it so clear in her head that they would ride out of the Donmouth yards and head uphill that she was genuinely mystified for a long moment, before cold realization could break through. They were taking her across the river.

Dark of the moon. Low tide.

They were taking her to Illingham.

Outlaws in the pay of Illingham. There were too many implications here for her giddy brain to grasp.

She could hear the water around the horse's legs as it pushed its way through, the sound getting louder in her ears as the water deepened, and then she realized that either her dress or that grey cloak they had bagged her with was trailing in the water and wicking it up, because her legs were wet now, and she was getting cold. Colder still when they reached the other side and the horses lurched and swayed back up on to the opposite bank.

The horsemen had been riding mostly in silence, apart from the odd gasp or grunted word of encouragement to their mounts, but now the one who was holding her shouted something, and there was an answering call from ahead, and a whinny. Another horse trotting up.

There were words she couldn't hear, and then a deep voice saying, 'Did she fight?' And a laugh from the man who was gripping her waist, echoed by the others, but nothing more. And then trotting, horrible trotting that bashed her ribcage repeatedly against the saddle's pommel until she felt bruised to the bone and giddy with nausea. And then the soft thud of hooves on grass slowing and giving way to the clatter of a metalled surface: they were coming into a paved or a cobbled yard with a jingling of tack and soothing words and slowing again, and stopping. And then someone was hauling her down and setting her on her feet, turning her round and pulling the wool away from her face.

'You got the right one then.'

He wasn't talking to her. She blinked, light-headed.

Tilmon.

She had guessed as much already. But why?

If she spoke she risked being sick, and she was afraid of what she might say if she were to open her mouth, so she turned away and looked at the others, still mounted. A slight fair lad with a sulky face. Another young man, solider and with a dark beard that made him look older than she suspected he really was.

And Athulf, on Mara.

Elfrun closed her eyes, wrapping her arms around her ribs. There was nothing to say which could restore an ounce of her dignity. She had been wearing the same dress for two days and a night; she was dirty and wet. What price Elfrun of Donmouth now?

Athulf was watching her avidly, but when she swung round and stared him full in the face he dropped his gaze and wouldn't meet her eye.

Now they had her, they didn't seem to know what to do with her.

'Where's my son?' Tilmon was moving away, towards their hall, a longer, more looming building than she was used to.

But it was his wife who came, Switha, that dark-eyed, kind-faced woman with a beaming smile and the manner of a hen fussing over errant chicks. Elfrun felt relief swamp her with all the shock of a freak wave.

'Look at the state of you, child! Do I have to pick you up every time some Illingham oaf dumps you in it? Come with me,' she said pointedly, 'into the women's house,' shooting hard dark glances at the young men. Athulf was scowling, but he didn't open his mouth. Suddenly Thancrad was there, with that set, immobile look to him. 'Leave this to me,' his mother said, and he stared for a moment, then nodded and shrugged and turned away.

She was already shepherding Elfrun, who was trying hard to fight the sense of being overwhelmed. 'But what—'

'Never mind all that now.' Thancrad's mother was opening the door, ushering her into the cosy dark interior. 'Here, Ada, get some warm water,' she snapped to another woman, who ducked her head and scuttled out. Switha was pulling Elfrun closer to the hearth. 'Where's my comb? Let's get your wet things off.'

Elfrun hugged herself tighter than ever. She was beginning to shake, now that the shock of the ride was over, and she staggered suddenly as her knees threatened to give way beneath her.

'Come on, girl.' There was a new edge to her voice. 'You're soaked.'

And it made sense. Elfrun didn't want to be cold and damp and dirty either. Unfastening her girdle with its burden of keys, she hauled her dress off over her head and passed it to the older woman.

'And your shift.'

'My shift?' Elfrun stared at Switha. She was painfully aware now of other eyes, other voices, in the dark corners away from the hearth. 'But I'll have nothing to put on.'

'We'll find you something.' Thancrad's mother was the voice of sweet reason. 'You're soaked and filthy. I knew your mother, dear child. What would she say to me if I failed to care for you properly? Or Abarhild? I don't want her telling me off for not looking after you, do I? Just *look* at yourself!'

Obedient to the tone of command, Elfrun looked down the length of her body to where her pale ankles and mud-spattered feet emerged from the sorry hem of her linen. Tattered, and stained, and wet enough to cling. Switha was right. 'Yes. I'm sorry. If you can find me...' But when she heard the note of apology in her tone she was furious with herself. She had not asked to be here, after all.

'Come on, then. Hand it over.'

Hot-faced and shivering, Elfrun pulled off the linen shift,

more aware than ever of those eyes on her exposed skin. The room was too warm and close, and she could feel trickles of nervous sweat running down her ribs. She had her girdle and keys and pouch bundled awkwardly in her hand.

Trying to shield her nakedness with her hands, she looked around for the promised garment, but instead to her disbelief she saw Thancrad's mother pick up her discarded dress and shift and drop them on the fire.

'I – You – What – what are you *doing*?' She darted forward, but the linen was already darkening, charring, red-gold edges appearing to the holes, the old blue dress half smothering the flames, the room filling with the stink of burning wool.

'Don't be silly. You won't need that patched old thing.' There was a purr of complacency in the older woman's voice that made Elfrun uncomfortable. 'Come on, dear one. Let's get you clean.'

The diminutive slave woman at whom Switha had snapped when they first came in was now reaching into the hearth with a pair of tongs to pull out a hot stone; she dropped it, with a hiss and a bubble, into the bucket of water she had just fetched. Dipping a rag into the water, she stepped forward and reached to pull Elfrun's arm away from her body.

It was an effort not to scream and fling her off. 'I don't need washing,' Elfrun said through clenched teeth. She wrapped her arms around herself again.

'Don't be so silly,' Thancrad's mother repeated. She didn't sound so patient now. 'Mud from top to toe. Anyway, what have you got to be so shy about? More like a boy than a girl.' She stepped forward and grabbed Elfrun's wrists, forcing her arms aside and scanning her up and down. 'Look! I can count every rib. We'll have to do something about that.'

Elfrun was far beyond humiliation now. She twisted violently out of the other woman's grip. 'Let me go! I want to leave, now.'

She had expected a fight, but: 'Go on then.' Switha stepped back and crossed her arms. 'There's the door. It's not locked.' She jerked her chin. 'Off you go.'

'I can't go naked!' Elfrun could hear the beginning of ragged, childish tears, and again she was furious with herself. 'Give me something to wear.'

'Then let us help you get cleaned up and we'll find you something to wear.' Soothing, unctuous tones. 'You must be hungry, too.'

Elfrun closed her eyes. Again it sounded so reasonable, even attractive now that the jolting nausea had ebbed. Hadn't she been on her way to find herself food when the horsemen came riding in? She had told Finn to get some bread, but she had eaten nothing herself that day.

Finn.

Tears pricked her closed eyelids. How stupid her pride felt now. That sudden blaze of self-righteousness had been fuelled by anger too, and the shame that had come in the backwash of desire.

Pride, anger, lust. Such familiar words.

Three of the seven capital sins.

Abarhild had been lecturing her about sin all her life, but now for the first time she began to realize what the word might mean. This wasn't really about disobedience, wilfulness, the way Abarhild made out – though that might yet prove to be part of it. Sin was a bramble thicket made of her own selfishness, tearing at her, blocking her view, stopping others from coming close. Hurting them too.

She knew she had hurt Finn: she had seen his face.

Worse: she had meant to hurt him.

And the fight went out of her.

She stood passive as a post, her arms outstretched and her eyes closed, to let a couple of the Illingham slave women wipe her face, her arms and legs with warm water; unplait her dishevelled hair and go through it as gently as they could with fine-toothed combs. Being tended; giving up her will to theirs: it was deeply soothing. She was almost asleep on her feet, swaying slightly and longing for oblivion, only the occasional sharp tug on her scalp keeping her awake, not responding even when she heard them muttering about the bruises rising on her ribs; and she was almost sorry when she heard Thancrad's mother say, 'Lift your arms above your head,' and she felt the fresh, crisp linen slither against her skin and fall to her feet. It was too long, and too large for her, the hem pooling around her feet, but it was such a relief to be covered again, and she hugged the extra folds of fine white fabric around her as though it afforded as much protection as a mail-shirt.

'Here.' And turning she found at her elbow a wooden platter with warm wheaten bread, and new butter, and honey. The smell of the bread was almost more than she could bear. She tried not to stuff herself ravenously, to take small mouthfuls and chew properly as Abarhild would have told her, but it wasn't easy, with the bread soft and crumbly on her tongue, the thick layer of faintly salty butter, the unbearable sweetness of the honey. She had to stop, however, when she realized to her shame that the other women were standing around her, just watching her cram her face while trying to keep the honey out of her hair.

'Is no one else eating?'

Thancrad's mother was smiling. 'We're looking after you just now. Here.'

A horn beaker of mead, sticky and syrupy, with that under-taste of bitterness she always found present, that sense of something lurking in the depths. She sipped and tried to hand it back, but the smiling, tiny slave woman pressed it into her hand, and she had to be polite, to drain it to the cloying, emetic dregs, and then have her hands and face wiped again. Her hair was pulled back, and combed again until it crackled. Thancrad's mother was standing back a little and eyeing her critically, and again Elfrun noticed the unsettling way she had of darting out the tip of her tongue to touch the bristle at the corner of her mouth. Perhaps the woman didn't know she was doing it.

Old Ada was tending the fire, dragging Elfrun's charred clothes from it and dumping them in a corner, feeding the flames with curls of birch-bark from a wicker basketful that stood hard by.

'Here.' A dress was being unfolded, a warm length of wool the colour of ripe wheat, and Switha looked approving. 'That'll look fine well with your hair.' She was nodding. 'Darker than Thancrad's, but not by much. You two could be brother and sister instead.'

Instead of what? But the dress was being pulled over her head, and her question went unspoken. It was beautiful, a fine diamond twill, softer than anything she had ever owned, soft as the moth-eaten grey she had given Finn and even lighter. There were bands of dark-red braid around the cuffs. She retied her girdle, and began to feel more like herself again.

'Lovely. Stand up straight.' Thancrad's mother was moving towards her, unfolding a length of white linen, fine as cheesecloth but a tighter weave, with white-on-white embroidery around the edge. 'Here, let me.' And she lifted up the veil to drape it over the crown of Elfrun's head. 'Funny to see a bride who already has her own keys.'

And Elfrun screamed.

She couldn't help herself. She stumbled backwards, batting at the cloud of white fabric, suddenly aware of the spider's web into which she had blundered. Accepting those ells of gauze would be tantamount to saying yes to Thancrad's family. If she took it then no accusation she might make, of abduction, of rape, would be believed. How had she not noticed, not understood? How stupid they must have thought her!

But no. They hadn't thought her stupid: they had believed her acquiescent, meek, even pleased. Happy. Grateful for the honour they were doing her.

All this flashed through her mind while she was stepping backwards, breathing hard, her arms up in front of her to fend off the danger.

'Of course you're nervous.' Thancrad's mother was smiling, but it didn't reach her eyes. 'You should have seen me on my

wedding night. I was a lot younger than you, my dear.' Flick
went her tongue on the stiff dark bristle. She looked at the slave
women. 'Do you remember, Ada?'

'Frightened senseless, lady, like a vole in the cat's jaws,' the
little woman said, bobbing and ducking her head obligingly.

They really weren't helping.

'I'm sorry,' Elfrun gabbled, hating herself almost as much
she hated them. 'I didn't understand – you didn't tell me... No
one told me...' The dress felt heavy, the extra folds of linen were
hampering her legs. She was almost in the corner now, backed
and stumbling against a loom, the door as far away as it could
possibly be, the three of them closing in on her, holding up the
linen veil as huntsmen might a net.

But then Thancrad's mother stopped, and she gestured to the
other two to do the same. 'You poor thing. You're exhausted,
and no surprise. We've asked too much of you. Settle down in
here.' She was folding the veil in precise squares, corner to corner, while she was talking. 'Ada, put a good log on the hearth,
and make a bed. Put some ash in a bucket for her needs. Then
come and find me in the hall.' She turned back to Elfrun, all
smiles. 'There's no hurry, after all, now that you're here.'

'I just want to go home,' Elfrun said, squirming at the polite-
ness, the apology in her voice. 'They'll be worrying.' But would
they? She couldn't imagine how they would be responding to the
raid. Somewhere in the remoter wilderness of her weary mind,
there was a lurking fear that no one would have noticed, that
Donmouth would be trundling on, that her presence or absence
would make no difference at all. But surely that was fatigue and
fear talking. Abarhild would be half-mad with anxiety, surely.
Fredegar, too. Widia – she could rely on him to track the horsemen here and retrieve her.

And Finn...

Would Finn care that she had vanished? Why would it matter
to him what she did, or what was done to her?

Again her midriff contracted and twisted and a wellspring

of misery threatened to overflow. She fought it back with anger. Did she need them to help her, any of them? If she could just get away, get down to the river, she would be fine. She would be out of this ridiculous situation.

And she hung on to that comforting word. *Ridiculous.* Not frightening, not nightmare. Nothing had changed. She wasn't hurt. She hadn't consented to marriage. Nothing had been done that could not be undone.

She watched Ada shuffle out, leaving her alone among the Illingham looms. Forcing herself to wait for as long as she could bear to after the door had closed behind the old slave woman, Elfrun counted a long hundred, then crossed swiftly and lifted the latch. The door didn't budge, wrestle with it as she might.

Barred from outside.

She counted again, trying to think, to get her pulse to slow, the panicky blood to ebb from her cheeks. Solid boards, pegged and lapped. Hard-packed earth floor. This wasn't some wattle hut through whose wall she could simply tear a hole.

But she could sleep. She was clean and warm, and she had eaten well, and there was an ash bucket. There was a straw pallet and a blanket. Yes, she could sleep. And make them let her go home in the morning.

PART FIVE

THE CHRONICLE, YORK MINSTER SCRIPTORIUM

'Don't touch!' The novice snatched his hand back as though he had been burned. 'Those things are to be left as they are.'

'But they're dusty, *magister*!'

'Aye, they are. And your novice-master will beat you unless you do the job properly. I know, I know.' The boy was nodding emphatically. 'But I will beat you too, harder and longer, if you meddle. Do you hear me?' The librarian had tears in his eyes. 'Anything else in here, yes. Do your worst. But not this desk.'

67

Widia had seen the hawks and hounds properly tended, and was at last on his way to the kitchen for bread and broth, and a nip of ale if there was any going. Get himself fed and braced, and then it was time to have a conversation he'd long been planning. That done to his satisfaction, and he would go for a much-needed word with Elfrun. He was already close enough to smell the warm, savoury odours from the cook-fire, his mouth watering and belly growling, when he felt a frantic tug on his tunic hem. Turning in surprise, he found the dog-boy, his face twisted with evident distress.

'What's the matter?' Was the boy hurt? Did he even understand the question? Widia was more than half-minded to send the boy away with a cuff round the ear.

But more tugging followed, and anguished gesturing, and in the end Widia was convinced against his better judgement to follow him back into the twilit courtyard. The child was pointing at the dog, that wretched dog which had failed in its fight with the bear. Widia's lips tightened. Elfrun was soft, even if it was her good companion. He still thought it should have been destroyed with the others.

Elfrun's shadow.

Why was it here? And what was it doing?

Gethyn was crouched, his tail down between his legs, his head lifted, and he was making odd noises, half-whine, half-bark. An uncanny sound that made the hair prickle on the back of Widia's neck. The dog was staring fixedly into the distance, but when Widia turned to follow his gaze he could see nothing but the track that wound in and out of the buildings and enclosures on its way down through the fields and ultimately to the river. Gethyn took a couple of paces forward, followed by another couple back. That whine again.

'What's wrong with him?' Widia crouched down and held out a hand. He might not have much respect for a dog with no fight in him, but it went against the grain to see an animal so distressed and not lift a hand in response.

Gethyn ignored him.

'Is he hurt?'

The dog-boy shook his head. So, he did understand something.

'Where's Elfrun?'

The boy shrugged expressively, lifting his hands up and out, then pointed down the track.

'But why hasn't he gone with her?'

'She went on horseback.'

Widia swung round to see the grey-faced stranger, that wounded man Elfrun had brought back with her to the yards that morning. He had come out of the shadowy entrance to the stables, his left arm held across his chest, with his right hand cupping the elbow.

'But surely she would still take Gethyn? I've told her enough times, God damn it, always take the dog.'

'I don't think going anywhere was in her mind.' The stranger shook his head. 'I didn't see. But I was in there, and I heard the pounding of hooves. Not a sound you'd expect to hear in the yard. It was only a few moments ago. I couldn't get to my feet in time.' He gestured at himself in evident frustration.

'You mean this has only just happened?' Widia shook his head, frowning. 'Which horses? Ours?' He pushed past the stranger and walked briskly along the stalls, peering into the gloom at the shadowy animals. 'Mara's not here. Was she riding Mara? The little chestnut?' Widia was frowning. Athulf had been out on Mara all day. The lad would have had to come back and stable the little mare, and then Elfrun have her out again; and he didn't think all that could have happened without him noticing. And Elfrun wouldn't take out a tired horse.

But, 'She didn't take a horse out.' The stranger was frowning, evidently trying to make sense of the sounds he had heard. Widia was tempted to shake him. 'She walked out of here on her own feet. She was angry with me.' He closed his eyes. 'And then almost at once I heard the horses.'

'*Horses?* More than one?'

'Yes, two or three. I'd swear to it.' He sighed thickly. 'But it took me a moment to get to my feet. By the time I was at the door they were gone. There was nothing to see.'

Widia had already moved away from him. He crouched down, looking at the hard earth, and shook his head. 'There have been too many horses in and out of here today.' He started walking away, in the direction in which Gethyn was staring, still making that unearthly sound.

'I'll come with you.'

'What use are you?' The stranger flinched at that. Widia went on walking. 'You're hurt. He's voiceless.' He gestured at the boy. 'That damn dog isn't worth the feeding, as I've told Elfrun half a dozen times.' Bafflement and hunger were making him snappish. 'And you don't belong here. This – whatever it is – is nothing to do with you.'

'The damn dog saved my life last night,' the stranger said quietly. 'Him and his lady together.'

Widia stopped at that. 'I see. Yes. Very well. That – that gives you an interest.' He turned back. 'Did no one else see what happened? One dumb boy and one useless dog?'

But the boy was there again, pointing insistently down the track. He took Widia by the elbow and began trying to push him onwards. The stranger had turned back to Gethyn, and was fondling his ears with his good hand. When he straightened up the dog was calmer, and he came trotting after them. 'Let's go.'

It was getting dark, and darker as they went under the trees and down the slope, but Widia crouched from time to time, checking the tracks, once they were well away from the churned and trodden ground around the sheds and the common pathways.

'Three horses,' he said at last, straightening up. 'Going flat out by the time they got down here.' He was beginning to take the story more seriously. 'We know there are outlaws in the hills, but here in the yards? And heading for the river?' He shook his head. Attacking wandering bears and entertainers was one thing; attacking a woman in her own yards was another matter altogether.

The stranger was staring at the path where it went down to the water. 'They've taken her to Illingham. I should have known.'

Widia swivelled. 'What do you mean, you – whatever your name is.'

'Finn,' the stranger said bitterly. 'I've heard enough. I knew they had their eye on Donmouth.' He stared into the darkness across the river. 'I should have tried harder to keep her safe.' He had his hand on the back of Gethyn's head. The dog was still whining softly.

'That's not exactly your job.' Widia was baffled, trying to make sense of all this. If they were taking her to Illingham they were likely to be Illingham men. Not outlaws, who might grab a girl at random for their use. Not slave-dealers. If Illingham men had taken Elfrun it was because she was the lady of Donmouth. It would not be in their interests, surely, to treat her badly. 'Best not meddle. For all we know she went willingly.'

'We don't know that,' Finn said.

We? Widia turned on him with a curse. 'Would you let me think?' He exhaled heavily. 'We can't barge into Illingham making wild accusations, after nightfall, unarmed, just the two of us.'

'The steward?' Widia watched Finn's face hardening.

Widia thought about it for a moment, then shook his head.

He had no love for the steward. 'No, the lady Abarhild would be the person to turn to. I'll send to the minster.' He eyed Finn sideways. 'But it can wait. If she's at Illingham they'll treat her well enough.' His belly growled, and he gave his twisted grin. 'I haven't eaten all day, and I've things I have to do. Time enough in the morning.'

68

This was her chance. Her aunt would be brewing, and her mother had taken the little ones over so they could be up and doing before dawn. Only a few hundred yards away, but they would be busy gossiping around the warm hearth. She neither knew nor cared where exactly her father was. Somewhere up at the hall, making other people's lives a misery for a change. Some risks had to be run.

Saethryth looked round the dim room. If she were her father, where would she have hidden it? A lot of silver could pack into a very small space. The worst would be if he had buried it. She couldn't dig up the whole floor. And it might not even be inside. The earth of the floor was hard-packed, filthy and rush-strewn. Well, there was a job for her. Clear those to the midden, and bring in fresh from the stack, and while she was at it look at every inch of the surface, to see if it had been disturbed.

It took her long enough, but she was sure in the end that her father had dug no hole inside the house. That only left the whole of the outside world.

But the sunset was still warm in the western sky, and the waxing moon would soon be rising. She picked up a digging stick and went out to hoe the little kitchen-garden, looking, looking all the while in the thickening light, poking among the dying beans. He would have had to mark the place somehow, surely. The hens and the ducks followed her, pecking at the slugs and creepy-crawlies her stick unearthed. As the light faded she worked harder, peering under the withered leaves. The pile of hoed weeds had grown impressive, and the poultry were looking sleek and cheerful, but there was no sign anywhere that the soil had been disturbed out of the usual way.

Saethryth gritted her teeth.

It could be anywhere.

Her back ached and her hands were blistering. Why, when she worked so hard at the churn and the cheese-press, should a digging stick still raise these weals?

'Do you still think about him?'

She lifted her head.

Widia, with a dog as always at his heels, was standing at the fence, looking down at her. She stood up. They were very much of a height.

'Let me put the fowl away for the night,' she said.

'I'll help.' He clicked his tongue at the dog to lie down and came inside the enclosure. Shooing chickens and cockerel into their house, the ducks into their pen, was so much easier with two, and she was grateful. Once the little wooden door had clunked into place, she turned to him.

'You asked me something.'

He nodded. 'But it doesn't matter.'

'Yes. It does.'

'Very well.' And he repeated, 'Do you still think of him?'

She closed her eyes briefly. 'All the time.'

'Ingeld.'

'All the time.' She looked at him defiantly, waiting for judgement, but his twisted face was sombre. She said, 'He once told me I came between him and the sun. That's how it feels now, something between me and the sun. But he meant I was brighter than the sun, and for me, now, it's all gone cold and dark.' Her teeth were clenched hard against the burning rush of tears, but still they came, forcing their way upwards and choking her. 'I was alive with him. And now I wish I was dead.'

Widia thought of the difficulty he was having in getting the youngest of the peregrines to take the lure, and how she panicked and shrieked at first whenever he took the hood off. Calmer in the dark, with his voice soothing her and his hands stroking her neck feathers. He ought to hate this woman. Despise her. But he had a suspicion that all she had ever needed was proper handling.

'Can I come inside?'

'I've nothing to offer you.'

'It doesn't matter.'

She nodded, and after a moment she brushed the dirt from her hands and led the way; but just inside the door she turned, startling him.

'I think about Hirel as well, you know.' The old aggression was back in her voice. 'I'm not making a mistake like that again.'

'Why did you marry him?'

She shrugged. 'Da wanted me to. I – I thought I might be having a baby.' Her eyes flickered to his. 'I wasn't. And I thought you were dying. Or crippled.'

'I was mending by the time you married Hirel.'

She swallowed. 'They said the boar had damaged you. I didn't want a gelding for a husband.'

'It never got me there.'

'Well, you should have come and told me!'

'I sent for you. I sent Elfrun to get you. And you wouldn't come. I might have been feverish, but I remember that fine well. If you had come, then...' But looking at her furious, scarlet face he couldn't complete the thought, never mind the sentence. 'Anyway' – and he took a breath deep enough to tug at the scar tissue that took a gather in the skin across his ribs – 'I've come to say goodbye.'

'What?'

'I'm leaving soon. I've been planning this for weeks. Months. There's nothing for me here.'

'Where will you go?'

'Back to my kin. North. It's not so far. Three days. Other side of Pickering marshes.' But he could see that the name meant nothing to her.

'Have you told them? Elfrun? The old bitch?' But she bit her lip when he frowned.

'I'm heading to the minster now.' He frowned. 'I wanted to tell Elfrun, but she's gone to Illingham. There's something odd about it. She didn't take Gethyn.'

Saethryth was not remotely interested in whether Elfrun took her dog for a walk or not, and her face said as much. 'Are you leaving straight away?'

'In the next day or two. Why?'

'I'm coming with you.'

'What makes you think you're welcome?'

Her face had gone quiet, thoughtful, though her colour was still high. She said, 'If you wanted to hide a bag of silver, where would you put it?'

'Round my neck.'

She shook her head. 'Not that. Maybe bury it, but I haven't found it.'

He made a wry face and shrugged. 'Thatch, then? Rafters? How big a bag?'

'I don't know.' Then, 'Help me.'

His eyes narrowed, he gave her a long look. She stared back, defiant, and after a moment he nodded. As with the chickens, it was a quick job with two of them. The rafters were low, and it was a matter of moments to run their questing hands along every surface, into the corner of every beam and purlin. She was just about to move on to the underside of the thick-packed eaves when she heard him grunt. 'There was a hollow. Inside.' He was clawing with his fingers at the further edge of reach, hauling down a little bag. 'By... there's some wealth in here. Thirty – forty coins, maybe.' His fingers tugged at the fastening thong, and he groped inside, tipped the little discs into his palm. 'And all good silver. Where's this from?'

'It's what my father's stolen from Donmouth.' She held her breath. This was the gamble. Would he purse his lips and march to Elfrun, either from honesty, or from a desire to see her father brought low? She thought to herself that if it were the latter she would understand, although she might not be able to forgive.

Or would he simply stuff it in his own pouch and walk out?

She said, 'It's my way out of here. I'm sick of him lamming me every time I turn round.' Which way would he jump? She watched the way his fingers tightened around the leather purse, and she took a deep, silent breath, slow in and slow out.

'You, and the silver, to come north with me? Is that the deal on the table?'

'There's more.'

'What?'

'Kiss me.'

He scowled at her.

'Come on. I need to know what it's like.'

'You've kissed me before.'

'Things are different now.' Her cheeks were blazing but she held his gaze. 'You're scarred. And I've more knowledge of kissing.' There, she had said it. He could just turn round and go, and take the silver with him, and there wouldn't be a blind thing she could do to stop him.

But instead his eyes met hers, and ducked away, and came back, and he took a step towards her. 'If I kiss you,' and his voice was thick, 'there'll be no more abbots.'

She nodded, and he pulled her hard against him.

69

lfrun drifted up out of sleep and dark, muddled dreams.
There was someone there, hands, body pressing close
against her. It was dark and the air was thick, and so
perhaps she was under her father's cloak, but she was warm
and comfortable, so she couldn't still be on that bitter hillside
where Finn was lying bleeding, and the body whose warmth and
weight were pressing against hers *smelt* wrong.

She was fully awake in a moment, sitting bolt upright,
shucking off the warm folds of cloth and shoving herself away
backwards with hands and heels. The room was dark except for
the glow round the edges of the banked fire, but it was enough
to show her Thancrad, kneeling by the place where she had been
lying, his eyes hidden in the shadow thrown by his cheekbones.

'What are you doing?' he asked.

'What am *I* doing?' She pulled her knees close up against her
chest and looked wildly around the dim space.

He patted the blanket. 'Come back here and lie down.'

She shook her head at him, speechless, her face stiff, brows
tugged into a frown.

'Don't be silly,' he said. 'This is what's needed. We need to.'

She stared, light slowly breaking in on her confusion, and
panic coming in hard on its heels. 'But I'm already promised.'
It was the first thing she could think of to say.

'What?' There was shock and anger in his voice, and he was
on his feet suddenly, moving towards her.

'A nun,' she gabbled. 'My grandmother says I'm to be a nun.'

And he laughed.

It wasn't unkind laughter, or loud; she could tell he really thought it was funny, but he was trying to keep his amusement under control. Perhaps he didn't want to hurt her feelings. When his face was straight again he said, 'Oh, yes. Athulf told me all about that. Your grandmother, and her conviction that the Church is the safest haven for both of you.'

'Athulf?'

'Athulf tells me all about you.' His face hardened again for a moment, and she wondered what unwelcome thought had crossed his mind.

'So can I go now?' She scrambled to her feet and started making her wary way past him and the hearth, towards the door, keeping a careful distance. *If you threaten me with wild beasts, know that at the Name of Christ they grow tame...* St Agatha's words to Quintianus were rattling though her mind: *... if you use fire, from heaven angels will drop healing dew on me...* But the words seemed so sensational, fitting perhaps for a saint confronting all the pagan powers of Rome, but many worlds away from this dim room, this reasonable young man.

As soon as she had her hand on the latch she knew that the door was as immobile in its frame as ever.

They had been locked in together.

And at that the whirlpool of panic she had navigated around successfully so far came swirling up from the depths on a flood tide.

This had all been planned. That kindly, heavy-faced woman, with her honeyed bread and her soft words... Elfrun could feel her heart galloping, threatening to choke her.

'I'm sorry,' she said. 'This is all a misunderstanding. I won't be angry if you let me go. I won't tell anyone. I won't tell the king, or...' She was fighting to keep the pleading note out of her voice, to keep her hands at her sides.

'I understand,' he said. 'Don't worry.' His voice was kind and friendly, as it had been when she had ridden behind him on Blis, and she felt the tide of fear turn and flow away from her. He got to his feet and began walking towards her, smiling down in the dim light of the banked hearth. 'My mother said it wouldn't be easy for you. That you'd be afraid, that you might change your mind.'

'Change my mind? About what?'

'She said that girls are often afraid, the first time, but I shouldn't take too much notice.' And without warning he shoved her shoulders hard, and she sat down on the floor, winded and shocked. Before she could recover, he was down there next to her, and she twisted round on to her hands and knees, trying to crawl away, but Thancrad pushed her flat on to the pile of bedding, and then the weight of his body was pinning her down from above and behind. It was all happening so fast, and she couldn't get air into her lungs, but air or no air she began to scream.

'Stop it,' he said.

But she couldn't stop screaming until she ran out of air, and had to stop in order to drag more into her burning lungs. Only then did she realize that the crushing pressure had eased. For some reason he had rolled away, and she was free. She could breathe.

She clawed her way up on to her feet and spun around, ready for the next attack, but he was sitting with his back to her, his arms encircling his knees and head bowed. She could hear his ragged breathing, but he didn't move. Her heart was thudding within her ribcage, and her eyes flickered to the door. What next? Would he call in his friends to hold her down?

Still he didn't move, and slowly her panic lessened. She would be on her guard, next time. No knife, but she could go for his eyes.

'Come here,' he said at last. 'Sit down. Let's talk.' He turned, and she could see the pale oval of his face. He jerked his head, and she took a step backwards. 'Come *on*.' He got to his feet, and started walking towards her. She forced herself to hold her ground. What good would it do her to be backed into a corner? 'We need to talk.'

Elfrun swallowed the hysterical laughter that threatened. Her throat was so tight with holding it back that she couldn't have spoken even if she had wanted to. But his hand was on her shoulder, and he gave her a little shake.

'Don't be upset. Don't worry. Things will get better. We'll try again, later.'

Get better? Try again? She had to stop this, now. She shifted away from his hand, then turned to face him, swallowing hard and wiping her damp palms down her skirts. 'What do you think I am?' She didn't recognize her own voice, so flat, so hard. 'One of your slave girls, who has no choice?'

'What?' He was shaking his head. 'Don't be stupid. You accepted the veil. You're my wife.'

It took a moment for the words to get through to her. When they did it was as an icy drench. 'Is that what your mother told you?' She drew herself up and squared her shoulders. There could be no possibility for doubt in this message. 'I am not and never will be your wife.'

'Of course you are.' He was like his mother earlier: so reasonable, so assured.

'How can you say that? You kidnap me. You – you try to violate me. No one has asked me. I told your mother, *no*. My father is dead. My uncle is dead. No one has the power, no one—'

He was frowning. 'Have you forgotten?'

'What?' She wanted to fly at him, flay him, claw that reasonable look from his face with her nails. 'I haven't forgotten anything. You – it's you who've forgotten. I'm lord of Donmouth. Nobody can treat me like this.'

'But you sent me your token, and your consent.' He sounded blind, baffled.

'My what?'

He was fishing for a leather thong around his neck, pulling out a little, tight-fastened pocket, fumbling with the neck, tipping something out into his palm. 'Look. I've been carrying it for weeks. Months.'

She didn't want to see, but he was coming close again, pushing whatever it was he held in front of her face. 'You can't pretend it's not yours. Come on, Elfrun. Love. I've seen it on you.' There was a puppyish quality to him now, insistent, like Gethyn when he knew he had done wrong and was trying to wheedle his way back into her affections.

She folded her arms and turned her shoulder, not caring – more than not caring – dreading what he might have to show her. A bout of nausea hit her. 'Leave me alone.'

It did her no good. Thancrad pulled her back with one hand, thrusting the other, fingers cupped protectively, under her gaze.

A little silver tag, decorated with a cheerful, prancing animal, black on silver. He tilted it to catch the glow from the fire. There was still a scrap of red wool trapped in the riveted end. Even in this dark room, it was as familiar as her own heartbeat, as her father's face. The room reeled around her.

'Where did you get this?' But she knew the answer before he ever opened his mouth.

'Athulf brought it, with your messages. All summer, you've been sending me word.'

'Not me.'

'You're teasing me. Stop, please, Elfrun. This isn't funny.'

'Thancrad' – she could hear the high note of rising panic and choked it back – 'I never sent you any word. If Athulf said I did he was lying. That tag was stolen from me.

'I don't believe you.' His mouth had gone square, corners tugging downwards, and for a dreadful moment she thought he was going to cry. 'Those words, kind words...'

She half stamped her foot in frustration. 'Call him in. Ask him, see if he'll lie to my face.'

She watched his own face tighten. He closed his fist around the silver tag. 'Well, no harm done. You're here now.'

'I never accepted the veil. I never said yes.' She could hear her voice shaking and she couldn't have said herself whether it was with fright or fury. She knew it happened, that a girl was taken and married by force, whether she and her family liked it or not. But she had never thought it might happen to her.

Whose account of this dreadful night would be believed, when the world learned of it? She could see the avid faces, the gleaming eyes, the wagging tongues, at spring and harvest meetings. How they would relish this.

'Don't be afraid.' He tried another smile. 'I shouldn't be surprised, I suppose—'

'I'm not *afraid*, you oaf.' She glared at him, her fists clenched in front of her. 'I'm angry. Are you so stupid you can't tell the difference? Athulf stole that tag. He lied to me, and he is lying to you. What sort of loyalty is that? And you're *surprised* that I want nothing to do—'

'What is wrong with you?' For the first time there was an edge of anger in his voice too. 'Do you think this was my idea? Flatter yourself that you're my first choice?'

She stared at the floor, shocked at his sudden turn from coaxing to hostility.

'You should be counting your blessings,' he said bitterly. 'There are other girls in the world, you know.'

'Then why me?'

'You call me stupid, and then you ask that question?' His hurt was evident but she felt no urge to console him.

They glared at each other for a long moment before Elfrun realized. 'Donmouth.'

He nodded.

She turned away from him, hugging her arms around her body. This wasn't about her at all. It hadn't even been desire for her body that had fuelled his assault just now. It was the land she embodied, the reed-beds and the water meadows, the fields of barley and oats, and the sheep on the hills. And not only what, but where. Donmouth, the gateway to Northumbria. Hold Donmouth, and you have the kingdom in the palm of your hand.

Hot tears burned her eyes but she had no intention of giving in to them.

'Elfrun?'

She ignored him. She was thinking too hard.

'You should have this back,' he said. 'If it wasn't a token from you, I don't want it.' He took her hand and she felt him pushing the little silver tag into her palm, curling her fingers about it. But as soon he released her she let it drop into the rushes.

'Are you going to keep me here?'

'This wasn't my idea,' he said. 'Don't blame me.' He was looking beyond her. 'I didn't want it like this.'

'Do you really think I care whose idea it was?'

Thancrad stared at her, then pushed past her and headed for the door. He shouted a name and battered the wood with his fists, and there were muffled answering voices from outside. Elfrun heard the bar being taken down with a clatter and a thump. She had thought it was still this same endless night. But the long early-morning sun came in horizontal through the doorway, outlining Thancrad in gold, and beyond him the yard was full of people.

And among all the strange faces, sharp and clear, was Auli.

70

Finn's eyes snapped open.

He had waited for a long time, and finally, somewhere in the midnight, still waiting, he had tumbled against all desire and good sense into sleep.

Widia had been as good as his word, finding Finn a strip of cloth to tie around his neck and support his left arm, and the pain from his damaged shoulder had faded into a dull throbbing ache and a lingering nausea that he knew would pass. Eventually.

Waiting for Widia to return, his thoughts had been more taken up with the lingering sense of bruising on his mouth, the memory of Elfrun's clumsy, reckless kisses that had come out of nowhere in the half-dark of the heddern, her passion that had touched him and terrified him in almost equal measure. Why had he ever thought, even for a moment, that it was a good idea to ask her to come away with him?

What could he ever offer her? Not just the absolute poverty of his pouch, but the poverty of his way of life, the poverty of his heart. Whenever Finn thought of what a priest might call his soul he had an image of one of those leggy beetles that run so fast, so lightly, on still water that their tiny feet only dent the surface, skittering this way and that. To stop would be to sink. So fast, so light, evading blows and attention equally. Passing across men's awareness for a moment, and then gone, like the swallows, and forgotten.

But Elfrun had looked at him. Him, not the trinkets and tat

he peddled. She had turned that thoughtful, dark-brown gaze on him, eyes like pools of peaty water, and he felt that she had seen right down through the shallows and into the places deep down, where the monsters lurked. She had looked, and she had not flinched. He had a sudden tactile memory of her fingers, light as moths, on the old scars on his back.

How on earth, after all that, had he slept? And it seemed he had slept for hours.

Fully awake now, he was squatting with his back against a tree trunk, watching Donmouth coming back to life as the sky paled. It was a morning of mist and echoes, the call and response of the cocks on the dunghills, wild geese honking as they descended to the estuary. A child trotted past swinging an empty basket. He could hear the rise and fall of voices from the women's house. Those girls would have no interest in him now that he had lost his pack. Gethyn sat at his side, and the dog-boy, his twin for silence and patience, just beyond.

There was still no sign of Widia.

Finn closed his eyes. What kind of welcome would he be given at Illingham? He knew he had an obligation to go there, and to go now, and this had nothing to do with whoever had taken Elfrun. He had lied to her, saying that he would head for York. If Auli were anywhere up and down the Humber coast she would be there, and so would the rest of the crew. And he would be coming back to them with their most valuable assets squandered. Never mind the variously cheap and costly treasures from his pack – it was coming back having lost Myr and Varri that would anger Tuuri.

Holmi less so. Boys who danced on ropes were easily picked up in any market. But a good bear was hard to find, as was a man to lead him.

Varri had been an excellent bear.

Nothing to do with who had taken Elfrun – and everything. He might not know the ins and outs of the rivalries between Illingham and Donmouth, but he knew who Tuuri's paymasters were, and he could guess at which target they were aiming their first shots.

Finn stared into the darkness behind his eyelids. He should have told Elfrun everything, warned her properly, not let her touchy pride – and his – stand in the way. What business did he have hanging on to the rags and shreds of his pride, anyway? He thought of Elfrun's upright stance, her strongly marked eyebrows and the dusting of freckles across her nose. The earnest little frown that tugged constantly between her brows, and how from the first time he had exchanged words with her, almost a year ago, he had felt the urge to touch a fingertip to those furrows and make them vanish.

He should have told her of the threats that hung around Donmouth, as present to his eyes as the skeins of mist and hearth-smoke that even now were looping and curling around the low, reed-thatched roofs. But he had not told her. Stupidly, he had thought her burdened enough. And he had let her walk away from him, straight out of the stable and into immeasurable danger.

Widia thought she was safe at Illingham?

Then Widia was a fool.

The sun was rising, reddening the blood in his closed eyelids. Elfrun had been gone all night, and him just sitting here.

'It was you. You brought that mirror.'

His eyes snapped open. The mist was tinged with gold.

The speaker was a skinny creature who looked as though childhood were reluctant to relinquish her. She wore a dress that she had clearly outgrown, all bony wrists and bare calves. It was a moment before he recognized her. Her mention of the mirror was the clue. The child from the drear November beach with her skirt full of cockle shells. Her eyes were huge, her face shining.

'Yes,' he said mildly.

She nodded, as though satisfied with his brief answer, and hunkered down beside him. 'I was looking for the lady.' There was a pause. 'I even went into the hall. Her red cloak's hanging up there, so she must be around somewhere. She always has it

449

close by her, now. Always, always. But no one has seen her.' She looked him up and down. 'You're hurt.' An observation, that was all.

He nodded. Then, 'Go and get her cloak.'

Her light-blue eyes widened.

'Go on,' he said.

She looked at him hard for a moment, then slowly rose to her feet. 'God help me if that sour-faced misery guts Luda catches me.'

She was a long time.

When she came back she was bright-eyed and tight-lipped. 'I've given it a brush,' she said. 'I've never seen it in such a state. And I told Luda the lady was asking for it.'

Finn reached out to touch the soft red folds, but Wynn pulled away. 'The lady trusts me with her things,' she said pointedly, and he nodded, accepting her suspicion as his rightful portion. 'Are we taking it to her?'

Finn made up his mind. 'Yes,' he said. 'Now.' He had to break this inaction or go mad. He pushed upwards, using the trunk of the ash for support.

'Where is she?'

'At Illingham.'

Wynn nodded thoughtfully. 'She'll want her cloak.' She fell into step beside him, with Gethyn and the dog-boy at their heels.

The tide was coming in and the river was high. They stripped off to wade across, the water chest-deep on the dog-boy, their clothes and Elfrun's cloak bundled on their heads. Gethyn was unhappy but took to the water in the end when he saw what they were all doing.

Hardly were they dressed again – Finn taking the longest, clumsy with his bruised and swollen shoulder – when his ears pricked. 'I can hear horses,' he said. 'The far side of the river. Into the bushes.'

Just one horse, with a young man in the saddle, heading for the ford. He would pass very close to them as he emerged, but it was too late now to move. Finn watched, hardly breathing. He recognized Athulf at once, but, just as he had the previous morning, he kept his suspicions to himself. The men who had attacked him and Holmi and Myr had had their hoods pulled down. One stubby chestnut with a stiff blond mane looked much like another. But he had been fairly sure, watching Athulf ride out of the Donmouth yard yesterday, looking at the set of his shoulders, the defensive jut of his chin, the way he held the reins; and watching him now as he encouraged his horse down to the river's edge Finn was ever more convinced that those initial misgivings had been right.

Elfrun's young cousin, the lad with the hunched shoulders and the permanent sulk, was one of the killers.

One of the men who had come thundering out of that little valley cut by the stream and made straight for Varri, circling and jabbing with spears, howling and whooping now, and then when Myr had pushed in front of his beloved animal, shouting for help, for mercy, his empty hands spread wide, they had attacked him too. Finn and Holmi had been out on a little swampy island, and Auli further out still, keeping watch for the boat, but Holmi had loved Myr and Varri and he had gone floundering back, for all Finn could do to stop him. And then that spear like the wrath of an angry god out of nowhere, with such force, sending him flying backwards...

He still couldn't quite believe that he had not been transfixed by the spear, that his blood had not all seeped out into the brackish, muddy water of the estuary, that his body was not even now rolling, cold and limp, with the tide.

And so he should have been. But Auli had come back.

It was something he never would have expected from her, to hold him just out of the water, and half float, half drag him somehow on to the land, to stagger with her shoulder under his armpit into the shelter of the brambles.

And Elfrun had found him there.

Elfrun, who had given the cloak off her back and the warmth

of her own wonderful, fragile, sturdy body to stop his life ebbing away into the damp ground.

Was it remotely conceivable that the arrogant young man who was now urging his mount up the bank only a few feet from them carried out deeds like this with her blessing? And her other men – what about them? Who were the other two members of that murderous band? Finn had looked hard at Widia and the other men in the Donmouth search party yesterday morning, but no one except Athulf had brought him that sickening lurch of recognition.

Finn watched Athulf and his little mare vanish among the trees, her wet hide gilded and dappled by the long transverse rays of autumn sun. Long experience had taught him that no deed was so bad that someone wouldn't do it; and that, no matter how dark his imaginings, the truth was usually darker still. But he nonetheless could not, would not, believe that Athulf had been acting with Elfrun's benediction, or even her blind eye.

'One way or another, I am going to get you, young cock of the walk,' he said below his breath. 'Let's see how you crow then.'

71

The hall was thronged with strangers, even though most of the crews were still down with their boats. Only the masters and a couple of men from each boat were here, but with Tuuri's own men that still meant a dozen fighters who answered to someone else, and in Tilmon's considered opinion that was quite enough. Over their heads he could see Tuuri and his crew of eastern Balts, talking in quick voices, their foreign babble which Tilmon found infuriating. Bad enough when men spoke in Danish or Frankish, which were enough like proper human speech that he could get the gist. This incessant sibilant nonsense, however, which sounded like nothing so much as the twittering of birds in the rushes: this felt like a personal insult.

But a wise man doesn't say these things, not when the incomprehensible chatter is being uttered by folk who can call on sixty well-armed men within a few hundred yards. He looked around the hall, taking in the known and the unknown faces. He was not relying on the men of Illingham. The king had granted him the land but Tilmon knew he was still on probation, that Osberht had been testing him this year, tapping him all over like a bell-maker with a newly cast bell, listening for the false note. He had been holding his breath, all the while. But now it was time.

He stood tall and took a couple of steps forward.

So did Tuuri.

Tilmon stared at the other man, his face hard. He needed Tuuri, the information he brought and the links he embodied.

The ships' crews took their orders from him only because Tuuri vouched for him. But Tuuri was not master here, in the hall.

Silence had fallen when he had first stood up, but now he could hear low murmurs, whispers running round the walls like the wind in the cracks between the boards.

Alred was in the north, beyond the Tyne in his own family's Bernician heartlands, raising his own men. They had talked, months ago now, about starting the war against Osberht by burning Donmouth, hall and minster alike, but when he had told Switha she had come up with her own ideas. 'Save your men. The girl's the key to Donmouth. Quiet little thing. Thancrad likes her, for some reason.' She had smiled. 'Leave this to me. It'll be easy.'

And so it was proving. He looked down at his wife with affection. She understood girls.

Girls. Useful creatures.

Another girl, the disconcerting one, Tuuri's daughter with the pale gold eyes. She was at her father's elbow, and she was looking angry, her head high and her lips thin.

After that susurrus of whispering the hall was quiet again. North and south door stood ajar, and Tuuri's men were between him and both. It occurred to Tilmon for the first time that, just possibly, this was a mistake. But his men outnumbered the strangers.

And besides, he had promised them silver. And more than silver, if the dice rolled right.

A horse whinnied outside, and another one answered.

Tilmon beckoned to Tuuri. 'Come here.' Bring him over, put an arm over the man's shoulders, show the world they stood side by side. But Tuuri just stood and stared at him. Much more of this, and men's hands would be creeping to their hilts.

The south door darkened, and heads turned.

Tilmon raised a hand in greeting. That Donmouth lad. Athulf. Ingeld's son.

And Auli shrieked. Not a sound of fear, more like the scream of a tern about to attack some foolish trespasser on its nesting

454

field. The cry of one of the old war goddesses, whom men still offered to in the north. She had drawn herself up, and she was pointing at the boy in the door. Every eye followed her accusing finger. The boy stood in a beam of low light, a cloud of dust motes. Tilmon couldn't make out the look on his face.

Two of Tuuri's men moved forward and grabbed the boy by his elbows, dragging him forward.

'What is this?' Tilmon felt wrong-footed. This was his hall. No one else gave orders here. Switha's grip on his arm tightened, and he understood the silent message. *Steady, steady.* Other men might think that sudden clutch a sign of fear, but he knew his wife far too well for that.

'Auli says there are two more. They killed three of my men, and my bear. They tried to kill her.' Tuuri's voice was harsh, his face red and blotchy.

Tilmon swivelled. Thancrad was only a few feet away, his face frozen in that habitual arrogant mask that infuriated his father so much. 'What do you know about this?'

'Nothing.'

Tilmon swung a massive back-hander that sent the boy reeling into the man next to him. They staggered for a moment before both went crashing down on the floorboards. When Thancrad picked himself up again his nose was bleeding.

'Don't lie to me.' Tilmon gestured angrily towards the boy in the doorway. 'He's your man. You've been shoulder to shoulder for months. What have you been doing?'

Thancrad was wiping the blood away with the back of his hand, staring at his father as though he was a stranger. He turned and levelled much the same look at Athulf. 'He's not my man, though he may be yours.' His voice was thick, but there was no mistaking the anger. Tilmon raised his hand again, but Thancrad didn't flinch. He had the back of his hand pressed to his nose, and his lower face was a red-smeared mask. 'Where are Addan and Dene? Go on, ask him that. What have they been doing behind my back?'

There was a long silence. Then Athulf said, 'Addan and Dene are where they belong. Shovelling sharn outside. In the stables.'

'Get them,' Tilmon said rapidly. He didn't want Tuuri to beat him to it. He gestured furiously at his son. Thancrad pushed his way out, past the men who were still holding Athulf.

'You then.' Tilmon stared at the boy. The same question. 'What have you been doing?'

The boy stuck his chin out. 'It was my right.'

Tuuri growled something, and the boy turned to stare at him with that same fearless gaze. He looked so young, especially flanked by two war-battered Balts, but he held himself with an effortless arrogance. 'Your men insulted Donmouth.'

'My men,' Tuuri said slowly. 'Finn, a wandering pedlar. Holmi, a little boy who danced. And Myr, who cared for nothing but his bear. Even if they were disrespectful – which I doubt – is Donmouth's honour so brittle that it cannot survive a little challenge from such as these?' He clicked his tongue. 'Take his sword.'

Athulf turned his head and spat eloquently into the straw, ignoring the man fiddling with the buckles at his waist and shoulder. He stared straight into Tuuri's eyes. 'First, they mock our shepherd. Then they deceive my father into pitting his valuable dogs against the bear, in a fight your friends know the bear will win. And thirdly the pedlar and that girl' – he glared at Auli – 'frighten and insult my cousin.'

'And for this they have to die?'

Athulf jerked his chin at Auli. 'We weren't going to kill *her*.'

Tuuri put a hand on his daughter's shoulder. 'I'm glad to hear it.' His voice was quiet; Tilmon thought dangerously so.

'We were expecting a fight. They had a bear! We didn't know they weren't armed.' Athulf spat again, and there was a rumble and a murmur from the men ranged along the wall. Tilmon didn't know how much they understood, but he could tell they were getting restless. Athulf said angrily, 'We only meant to attack the bear, and frighten the men. I don't know what happened.' His voice tailed away, and for the first time, Tilmon thought, he looked uncertain.

And one thing was puzzling him. 'Why wasn't Thancrad with you?'

To his astonishment Athulf looked up then, his face breaking into a smile. 'I know he's your son, but Thancrad – Thancrad's soft.' His voice was intimate, confident, one equal addressing another. 'I'd been watching them – the bear and the men – for a couple of days. I knew it was time, and that Addan and Dene would be with me. But we didn't want Thancrad. We all knew he would duck out. Or worse.'

'Worse?' Tuuri asked, his voice a growl.

'Try to warn them.' Athulf shrugged as eloquently as he could with his arms still gripped and forced backwards by Tuuri's men. 'He's not to be trusted in a tight corner. You should know that.'

'Stow it.' But Tilmon was impressed, both with the boy's courage and his tolerance of pain. He had been watching this lad for a while, and he liked everything he saw. He and Switha might not care to admit it, but Athulf was right. Somehow, at Thancrad's core, there was a fastidiousness, a distance, detachment, that made Tilmon profoundly uncomfortable. *Soft*. It was as good a word as any. Too soft for a hard world.

Where had Thancrad got to, anyway?

72

The door had thumped shut in Elfrun's face. She stared at it helplessly for a few moments. Had she been seen?

All those people out there in the yard, surely someone there would help her?

She should hammer on the door, kick and scream until someone came, but she found she still had a horror of an audience, goggling at the spectacle she presented, emerging smudged and blinking into the daylight in Thancrad's wake, sporting her straw-strewn wedding finery. Everyone would think that they were man and wife in truth...

No, she could not do that. There would be no retreat from that kind of public exposure. The folk outside would bear witness to what they had seen. What they thought they had seen. And then she would be trapped.

She put her hand to her breastbone, trying to breathe more slowly. This was stupid. Think like that, and she would indeed stay locked in this room for the rest of her life. She had not chosen to be here. And nothing had happened. Thancrad hadn't hurt her. Not in any way that really mattered.

Thancrad had heard her scream, and understood that she meant it, and let her go. She should hate him too much to be grateful, but she was grateful nonetheless.

But he thought they were married. And in his place – lied to by Athulf, lied to by his mother – she might well have thought the same.

Oh God.

Athulf.

She sank down with her back to the wall, and the glint of silver in the rushes caught her eye. She had thrown the little cloak-tag away in revulsion in the night, but now she scrabbled for it, her heart thumping painfully. Her fist closed around it, the edges digging into the soft flesh of fingers and palm.

Why had Radmer ever gone away?

Athulf was the traitor. She should have known that, all the way through. There she had been, agonizing over Luda and the petty pilfering of lamb-leather, and all the while Athulf had been plotting her destruction.

How he must hate her.

She uncurled her fist and looked at the blithe little prancing animal, black on silver. It had its head thrown back, and it seemed to be laughing at her. Or rather, inviting her to laugh with it. Such energy. The king's gift to her father, and it had come back to her.

Elfrun closed her fist again, feeling how the silver was warming under her touch, and scrambled to her feet, tucking the tag into the little pouch at her waist. Something had been nagging on the edge of her awareness for the last few moments. There had been no second thump when the door had fallen shut behind Thancrad. Had he neglected to bar it?

As soon as she realized that the heavy oak was yielding to her hand her movements became more tentative. She eased it away from her until a minute crack appeared, and peered out.

She had expected to see the yard crowded, but it was sunlit and empty, at least of human life, though there were bags and rolls and bales in abundance. Had she really caught that fugitive glimpse of Auli? The girl was so distinctive, with her neat, oval head, her stitched and coiled braids, her amber eyes, but what on earth could she have been doing at Illingham? Elfrun peered this way and that, trying to orient herself in this strange yard. The direction of the sun told her something, but she had to remember that she was over the other side of the river now, and familiar clues would lead her astray; and she was muddle-headed with weariness.

That way, it must be.

Another cautious glance through the crack, and she eased the door a little wider.

Still no one, though she could hear the mutter and rumble of voices from the hall. Its door was closed, though.

Elfrun stepped out into daylight, the hampering folds of the alien wool and linen bunched in her hands, placing her bare feet carefully on the unknown soil. Her senses felt strained, scalp tugging, shoulder blades high and twitching, nostrils flared. Another swift look around. There was no point in dragging this out. If they saw her, they saw her. She walked fast and straight across the yard, aiming for the gap between the buildings which by her reckoning should lead out towards gate and river.

The buildings were laid out differently from home: Illingham's long block of horse-stalls stood right on the far side of the yard, away from the hall, and blocking the view of the gate. She had almost made it when she heard new voices, clearer and closer. Two of them: young, male, question and response; and then a third, further away, calling their names.

Not shouts, just a brief, hard-edged exchange from around a corner, but enough to make her throw herself through the open door of the stable and hurtle, clutching her skirts, to the far end of the row of half a dozen stalls, waiting for the doorway to darken.

She crouched herself down against the wall, as much out of the sightline as she could manage, and waited, hardly daring to breathe, eyes darting left and right, looking for better places to conceal herself. There was a mound of hay, with a pitchfork left in it. Hiding place and weapon in one? Her dress was much the same colour as the hay.

Or among the horses?

She shifted her weight and rebalanced, a tiny, silent motion, so that she could look into the closest stall, the end one.

A grey mare stood with her head down, tugging wisps of hay

from a manger. Elfrun couldn't see her face clearly, and she had
never tended her day in and day out as Athulf had since Ingeld's
return from York, but she knew the ripple of that tail, the whorl
of the hair on her flank, the fall of the mane.

'Storm,' she said, disbelieving.

The mare's ears pricked.

Elfrun clicked her tongue, and the mare lifted her head and
looked round.

'Hey, girl.' Still making soothing noises, she eased herself in
alongside. Her hands were damp and her heart was hammering,
but she moved and breathed as gently as she could. There was no
question but that this was Storm.

She looked well tended enough, even fat, if not quite the
gleaming creature on whose care Athulf had prided himself.

Elfrun glanced around, but there was no sign of Storm's tack.
'Oh, Storm.' And for the first time she missed Ingeld with a vis-
ceral intensity that astonished her.

Slowly, with her arm around the mare's neck and leaning
against her warm, infinitely comforting bulk, Elfrun began
to think.

In all the time since her uncle had died, they had found no
trace of Storm. Floundered into the marsh, Widia had specu-
lated. Or panicked at the smell of blood and bolted so far that
she had never found her way home.

Or stolen, he had postulated bitterly only a few hours since,
by the same outlaws who had robbed Finn and killed his friends,
two nights ago now.

Stolen.

And ended up here.

The same outlaws...

Elfrun was cold suddenly. She stared at her right hand where
it was stroking Storm under her mane and behind her ears, and
it looked like the hand of a stranger. That couldn't be right.

Illingham wanted Donmouth. Illingham had always wanted
Donmouth.

Kidnapping her, forcing her into marriage was one thing. This was another. Was their hostility directed against the minster as well as the hall?

And why not? The estates might be held and managed separately, but their lands were intermingled, their flocks ran together, and the lord of Donmouth hall and the abbot of Donmouth minster had been brothers or cousins for as long as anyone could remember. You could not take the hall and leave the minster as it was.

And how easy it would be to let the minster drift, with no priest, no services, until the archbishop was ready to relinquish any claim and it simply became part of the hall estate? Why, under Ingeld they had floated halfway down that stream already.

She had a sickeningly vivid image of Ingeld's body thumping over to lie face up in the mud and sharn. The same outlaws... Myr and Holmi and the bear, dumped in the tide-washed marshes, with the coloured ribbons, green and red and yellow, moving in the water. Finn, wounded. She was blinking fast, a nervous muscular twitch over which she found she had no control. Her hands clenched, and Storm nickered and shifted her weight; and she had to force herself to breathe slowly, to relax her hands.

To think.

Could all this be the wildness of her over-tired imagination?

Perhaps Storm had indeed bolted, and found her way to Illingham, and for some explicable reason – perhaps nothing more than an unscrupulous stable-master all too ready to appropriate a handsome mare – no one had ever thought to enquire about her origins.

It was plausible. If you didn't know Storm, her intelligence and loyalty. Elfrun had no doubt that if she were to challenge Illingham she would hear some story much like the one she was dreaming up now.

But she wouldn't, and didn't, believe it.

Illingham had killed Ingeld. She wasn't too concerned just then with why, or whose hand had held the blade.

Her guts lurched and contracted. This was no place for her. And no place for Storm. With any luck they could leave together. Breathing carefully, she gave Storm a reassuring pat and untied the tether to lead her carefully round and out into the yard. She was only wearing a head-collar, so Elfrun brought the rope as well. She fairly sparkled in the early-morning sunlight.

'Where are you going?'

She spun on her heel, and gasped. Blood streaked his face and his hands, and she thought for a moment it was some trowie fetch, come to take her soul. She was scarcely less frightened when in the next stuttering heartbeat she realized it was Thancrad, standing against the rising sun, in that same pose he had assumed at the spring-meeting, arms folded, weight on one long leg, mouth hard and straight. It seemed so long ago.

'Where do you think I'm going? Home. On my uncle's mare.' She glared back at him, defying him to interrupt, before turning back to Storm.

Hell and damnation. There was no easy hauling herself up on to the mare's back, not in these hampering yards of wedding linen and wheat-hued wool. She could feel his eyes on the back of her neck.

'Your uncle's mare?'

Why was he repeating her words in that fatuous way? 'Don't pretend you don't know what I'm talking about.'

'But I don't.' He was staring at Storm, at her, then swivelling to look back at the hall. The door was ajar now. 'Truly, your uncle's mare? Ingeld's?'

And now she wanted to smack him. 'Of course Ingeld's.' Her voice was a low scream. 'What is she doing here?'

'I didn't know,' he said. 'Elfrun, you have to believe me.' His words were oddly articulated, as though he'd just had a numbing blow to the face. And then she realized that that was exactly what must have happened, that someone had hit him hard, only

463

moments ago. The thought gave her considerable pleasure. He threw another glance behind him, at the open door of the hall, and now she knew why. He was afraid.

'The son of your father's house, and you didn't know about this? For all I know you were part of it.'

'I was with you the whole time!' He couldn't hide his hurt.

Oh, God in Heaven, it was true. She had entirely forgotten. Yes. It wasn't only that they had found Ingeld's body together. They had spent so much of that awful day together. Whoever had raised his hand to Ingeld, whoever had dragged her uncle's head back and slashed that killing cut across his windpipe, it had not been Thancrad. Thancrad had not so much as stood by and held the killer's horse.

Maybe he was telling the whole truth, about not knowing. And maybe not. Perhaps he had done a lightning-swift calculation and concluded she would be more compliant if she thought him stupid rather than guilty. A fine mare like that appearing in his father's stables out of nowhere. Better not to ask questions.

'A gift.' His voice low. 'My father said she was a gift.'

'You saw her that day at the sheepwick. Didn't you recognize her?'

He stared. 'You think I was paying attention to the horse? All I could think about was you.'

Elfrun flushed, half-angry and half-confused by the intensity in his voice. She refused to let herself be distracted. 'And Athulf? What story did your father tell *him*?'

He stared at her. The skin around his eyes contracted. 'Athulf has been in and out of these stables a hundred times. He's seen this mare. He never said anything.' And again, 'Are you *sure* she's Ingeld's?'

'Don't be stupid.'

Thancrad shook his head and winced, pressing his fingers to the bridge of his nose.

But their eyes met, and Elfrun somehow knew that he was thinking of the little silver tag. Her face grew hot. 'We know

Athulf is a liar,' she said in a low voice. 'He has betrayed both you and me. But that he would have even the faintest clue as to who killed his father, and do *nothing*?' She shook her head.

She could accept, against all her desire, that Thancrad was telling the truth about his innocence in the killing of Ingeld, his ignorance. But what about killing the bear-leader, and the dancing-boy, and Varri the bear?

And Finn. That Finn was still alive was a miracle.

Her lips tightening, she turned back to Storm.

He was at her side. 'Here. You need to go. Fast.' Making a step for her with his hands. She stared, and swallowed.

'What about Finn, then? Who attacked Finn? Was that you?' She wanted him to admit it; she needed more reasons to hate him.

'Who?'

'Finn and the others. The bear.'

'What bear? What are you talking about?' The blood was crusting dark around his nostrils, and his face was pale and frowning. 'Athulf said something once about a bear. It killed some dogs, he said? That's not important now. You need to go, Elfrun.'

She placed the ball of her foot in his interlocked fingers, gripping the rope with one hand and her skirts with the other, and he tossed her up on to the mare's back. Elfrun urged Storm forward with her knees and pointed her head towards the gate.

Finn stood there, framed.

73

'Get them! Stop them!'

The shout came from behind, from inside the hall.

Storm jibbed, and Elfrun was flung forward, hanging on to the mare's mane. She jabbed her bare heels into Storm's flanks. 'Come on, girl! Come on!'

Thancrad was running alongside her, shouting something. 'Go to the river. Get to the river!' She was through the gate, barely registering that the figure standing there was indeed Finn, his weary face suddenly alert, his eyes seeking hers, his arms full of bundled cloth. And he was accompanied for some unfathomable reason by Wynn and the dumb dog-boy. But she was through the gate and past them before she could respond. A movement at her heel caught her eye, and she realized that Gethyn was running alongside her, keeping pace even as Storm's brisk, jolting trot moved into an easier, rolling canter.

She had put a couple of hundred yards between her and the gate now. They were just coming into the trees and, against all her better judgement, Elfrun half twisted to assess the pursuit. She had thought she would see Tilmon, Switha, Athulf, some of their men, *somebody* coming after, but the track that led out from the gate was empty.

Elfrun felt a ridiculous sense of anti-climax, after the exhilaration of scrambling on to Storm's back, of Thancrad's exhortations. Why was no one coming after her?

Had that shout even been for her?

And what in heaven's name was Finn doing here, with her dog and the Donmouth children?

Storm slowed again, sensing that her rider's interest was elsewhere. Gethyn trotted beside them, head turned up to her, mouth open and tongue lolling. She was torn in half. Thancrad was right. She should get home. But Finn was here.

And if she had one desire in the world that transcended all thought of her own safety, it was her wish to put things straight with Finn. Whatever happened, she had to tell him she was sorry. Coming to a sudden, unreasoned decision, she slithered down from Storm's back, knotted her halter over a branch, and turned back.

'Finn.' She was out of breath, too agitated to be embarrassed at the recollection of the last words she had spoken to him. 'What's happening?' Gethyn panted at her side, red tongue lolling.

'I came to save you,' he said. 'To bring you this.' He offered her the bundle of red cloth, and she took it, barely even registering what it was. 'But you didn't need me.' He looked beyond her, to Storm, and back again. 'What are you doing? Are you all right?' His eyes sought hers.

She knew what he meant, and she wanted to reassure him. 'All right? Yes. Yes, I am.' And she was, she realized, with that wary grey gaze of his finding hers, looking into her eyes, her very soul, with such concern and affection. She struggled to find the words to tell him that she was sorry, and that she would come with him, but all that she could manage was to repeat, 'What's happening?'

Suddenly Thancrad was at her side again out of nowhere. 'Why are you still here?' He looked at Finn. 'I've seen you before. You're one of Tuuri's men.'

Finn nodded.

'He thinks you're dead. Killed.'

Finn smiled, but his eyes had gone cold. 'And I would be, if it weren't for the lady of Donmouth.'

The shouting was coming from the hall, getting louder.

Thancrad swung round, then said urgently to Finn, 'They're arguing – about the killings. The bear. They're debating what to do with Athulf and the others. They tried to run for it but Tuuri's men grabbed them at the door. You need to go in there and show them you're alive.'

Finn nodded and turned, but they were forestalled. Men were spilling out from the hall, pulling their belt-knives, shoving and swinging their fists. It was impossible to tell who was fighting whom.

Elfrun stared, appalled, and suddenly realized that Athulf was pounding towards them, three or four men hard on his heels. There were other scuffling tangles forming. Tilmon, a head taller than anyone else. And Switha, her hand on his arm.

And it wasn't just men chasing Athulf. Auli too was in the little knot of furious pursuers.

'Out of my way.' Athulf was gasping, running hard.

Elfrun stepped aside, but she saw Finn and Thancrad exchange a glance, and they moved closer together, blocking the way.

'Move!'

But they didn't, and he didn't stop, he came barrelling towards them, and his momentum was too great for them to do more than slow him down. He sent them spinning, and he was through the gate, and making headlong for tethered Storm.

He had to slow, to stop, before he reached the mare, in order not to frighten her; and suddenly a small figure – two small figures – darted out of the clump of hazel and thorn. The smith's girl and the dumb dog-boy. The boy was going confidently up to Storm and untying her halter. Why were they helping Athulf?

They weren't. Wynn may not have fully understood what was going on, but her astute gaze had taken in enough of the situation at a glance, and she flung herself at Athulf like a furious cat, claws out and going for his eyes. The dog-boy was jogging Storm down the slope, towards the river, towards Donmouth.

Elfrun had her free hand pressed to her mouth. Even with

468

the ropy strength the forge had nurtured Wynn could never be a match for Athulf.

But she didn't need to be. She only needed to slow him down. The others were catching him up now, circling him. He had flung Wynn sideways, his face bleeding and excoriated from her nails.

Elfrun swallowed hard and walked forward. Wynn was getting to her feet, her face expressionless. Athulf darted a look of pure hatred at the girl. No one was touching him, but he was surrounded.

Elfrun took a deep breath. Athulf was her man. This was her call, to judge him or to hand him over. And before anything else, she had to ask him about Storm. She opened her mouth to speak, but even as she did so Auli raised a hand, catching Elfrun's eye. Finn was at her side. Finn, Auli's slave. Auli's amber eyes met Elfrun's, limpid yet inscrutable. Her head was tilted slightly to one side, and she raised her eyebrows.

Elfrun became aware of the crowd forming behind them, the pressure of eyes on the back of her neck, the crawling of the collective gaze on her shoulder blades. Fear prickled, without her quite knowing why, and she leaned over to Wynn, her voice low and urgent. 'Take Gethyn. Follow the dog-boy. Go back to Donmouth.'

Wynn nodded, her gaze intent. 'He may not come with me, lady.'

'Do your best.' Elfrun turned to Auli, and took a deep breath. If the stranger girl had something to say about the assault on her property, her men and her bear, then she should say it.

Auli murmured something to Finn. He nodded, and she stepped forward. Suddenly her big knife was in her hand. Athulf's eyes were wide, his gaze flickering, the whites fully visible. There was nowhere to run.

'Wait!' Elfrun hardly recognized her own voice. She hadn't seen this coming.

Auli said something further to Finn, her eyes never leaving

Athulf. A big weather-beaten man with a broken-toothed grin was moving closer to Athulf now, and her cousin was shuffling, side-stepping, trying to watch for danger in all directions at once.

Her cousin. Little Athulf with the fringe that always got in his eyes, the sticky chin, the perennial anxiety about being left out, the cry of *Wait for me.*

And Finn said, 'Wait? Why?'

Elfrun knew he was only translating Auli's query, but his flat voice twisted her heart. Was this the same person who had noticed when she had been crying, who had called her beautiful, about whom she had been dreaming those hot, inchoate dreams in the fireside half-world between waking and sleeping? Dreams that seemed so real...

She gave herself a little shake. '*Why?*' Scrabbling to justify her indecision. 'Because it wasn't just Athulf. What about those two?' She gestured. The young men who rode out with Athulf and Thancrad. The dark-bearded one and the slighter, fairer one. She could never remember which one was which.

And another voice said, 'Kill them both.'

Both? Not *all three*? Elfrun turned to find Switha staring at her, her gaze hard-edged. She was next to Tilmon, but for all his bulk and force her husband seemed insignificant next to her, with her dark, gleaming eyes and crackling energy. Tilmon was frowning. He seemed to be having the same difficulty under-standing her meaning as Elfrun was herself.

Switha looked up at him. 'You want Donmouth, without having to burn it first? Now's your chance.' She gave a little side-ways jerk of her head, towards Elfrun. There was something she wasn't putting into words, something Elfrun still wasn't getting. There was an unspoken conversation going on: she could see it, tangible as a spider weaving its deadly gossamer, a web made of sidelong glances, lifted eyebrows, the quirk of men's mouths. She could see it, but she didn't know what it meant.

Finn got it, though. He grasped Auli's arm and muttered something, and she tensed, swinging half round with her knife still held out. Her eyes met Elfrun's again. She pulled away from Finn and reached out a hand. Hesitating, Elfrun clasped it with her own. Another little tug at the weave of the web. The ruddy, weather-beaten man with the broken grin was next to her. Elfrun looked nervously up at him.

Finn said, 'Elfrun, this is Tuuri. Auli's father.'

'What does he want?' She didn't want to take her eyes off Switha. Every nerve in her body was screaming, and she still didn't know why. Auli's hand was warm and dry and hard, squeezing hers – a spurt of comfort – and then relinquishing it.

'He speaks English.' A gruff voice, and she looked up, startled, at Tuuri. He was smiling at her, and she realized there had been movement, closing in, an inner circle forming about her and Athulf. Tilmon and Switha on the outside. No weapons had been drawn, yet, other than Auli's knife. Tuuri said, 'My daughter tells me you protected her and my men, and the bear. And then she left Finn with you, knowing you would help.'

Elfrun flushed. 'That was just chance.'

'Chance, yes, but also choice. You could have left him to die, but you warmed him and tended him, and you tried to find the killers. I am in your debt, by any reckoning.' His face was kind, his voice respectful. 'And at the bear-fight, from what Auli tells me, that was not chance.'

It seemed so long ago. She cast her mind back, trying to remember what she had done A day of mist and shifting damp, and horror. Ingeld, so solid and vital and handsome, with the sun glinting on his ring of office.

She had found Storm, but her uncle's ring and his clothes were still lost.

Who had killed him?

'I think maybe you need my help now,' Tuuri said.

74

They were closing in. Elfrun could see the steady movement out of the corners of both eyes. Athulf was staring at her, his face white but calm, his eyes narrowed. Just as she had at the bear-fight, she had mistaken his anger for terror.

'What happened? In the heifer field?' She knew that this was no time to be asking questions, but she had to find out. 'Athulf, how did Ingeld die?'

And Athulf smiled. 'His blood's not on my hands, cousin. Was that worrying you? *I am not my father's keeper.*'

But surely he was quoting – misquoting – scripture out of season? For all his flippancy Cain *had* killed his brother Abel. And Abel's blood cried out from the ground for revenge. 'So what did happen then?' Elfrun took a step towards him and stopped, repelled by the half-smile which was still hovering. He did have that look of his father Abarhild commended so often. But lacking Ingeld's easy charm, the effortless way in which her uncle had made everyone to whom he spoke feel that time with him was time in sunshine. Athulf's smile had an awful coldness about it, and she wondered why she had never quite realized that before.

Athulf jerked his head sideways and she glanced at Dene and Addan.

'It wasn't me!' Dene's voice was strained, as though on the verge of breaking. 'I never hurt him, I just held his bridle. Like when we got you, yesterday, all I did was ride with them… I never killed anybody. I did throw a spear at the bear, but I missed. I swear it.' And he was paler even than Athulf, greenish-yellow about the corners of his mouth. A dark stain was spreading across the front of his breeks. Elfrun was revolted.

The circle around them had fallen still. Tuuri's face was intent, flickering from Addan and Dene to Tilmon, and back again. Without shifting his gaze he reached out a hand and pulled his daughter closer to him.

'So you – Dene? – you held Storm's bridle. And Athulf never touched him – what *did* you do then, Athulf?'

'I talked to him.' There was a note of savage satisfaction in her cousin's voice. 'I told him what I thought of him. He didn't like it.' His eyes flickered sideways. 'And while I was doing that Addan came up from behind.' Athulf jerked his chin backwards and drew his finger across his throat in one easy gesture.

'It wasn't my idea.' Addan's tone was defiant.

'I didn't think for a moment it was.' Elfrun was fighting faintness, but the contempt in her tone was loud and clear enough. 'I'm sure Athulf can take all the credit for that.' Her mind was fluttering like a moth in a candle-flame. She had drowned Hirel for killing Ingeld. *Athulf* had drowned Hirel. Athulf had begged to be one of the execution party. She felt as though she too were sinking ineluctably down into deep, dark, cold water.

A hand cupping her elbow, steadying her.

Finn. She breathed more easily, hoping he could see her gratitude.

'Sadly,' Athulf was shrugging, 'it wasn't my idea, though I wish it had been. Any more than taking the cloak tag was my idea.' His eyes flickered from Elfrun, with the cloak bundled awkwardly under her arm, to Tuuri, from Tilmon to Switha. 'Oh, getting revenge on the bear, *that* was my idea. We only killed the men because they tried to protect the bear. But the inspiration for all the rest came from the lady of Illingham.' And he offered Switha a little bow.

Elfrun spun on her heel and stared at Switha, standing with her beringed hand resting on Tilmon's arm. Switha's sweet face, her dark eyes, the tendrils of silver-black escaping from the veil edge, even that little bristle in the corner of her mouth: Elfrun could see her every detail with extraordinary clarity. She was smiling. And she said, quite lightly, to her husband, 'I told you we should kill them both.' And then, to Athulf, 'What a little fool you are. So easy to play. Did you really I think I was going to help you to Donmouth?'

Athulf stared at her, mouth twitching, his face deathly pale.

A shift in the pattern, a movement of men. Elfrun had a sudden sense that she had been here before, on an April morning a year and a half ago, watching the men outside the king's tent, the alliances breaking and re-forming like clouds in the summer sky. Tilmon's men; Tuuri's men: so little to distinguish them. The angle of a cap, the way in which leggings were bound, the nature of a pattern on a braid...

But Tuuri's men were putting themselves between her and Tilmon's men, and Finn and Auli were either side of her, and Finn was saying, '*Run*.'

So she ran.

Other than Finn and Auli she had no idea who was with her, and who in pursuit. Behind there was shouting, grunting, a cry of pain and then the clash of metal. She had a terrible desire to look back, but she had done that once already, and to do it again would be to tempt fate beyond endurance. They hurtled under the trees, heavy-berried rowan and elder. Nor did Elfrun have any idea where they were going, or any time to wonder. Her hands were too full with the cloak easily to manage the extra hampering yards of her Illingham finery, and while it did briefly cross her mind that she could escape on Storm there was no sign of either the mare or the dog-boy. Had he guided her home to Donmouth, with Wynn and Gethyn? He was a miracle with animals, that child.

Her heart was too big, it would surely burst, or swell and splinter her ribs, and her breath was burning. More shouts from behind, and a howl, cut short. Blade meeting blade.

Out from under the trees, into the light and air where the mid-morning sun dappled the ripples with gilding too bright to bear. They were running straight down to the water, the river broadening out to estuary and open sea. The tide was high, little waves lapping at the top of the strand. A flock of outraged oystercatchers took wing with their shrill peeping.

And straight into the water, to where a sleek, pointed ship rode at anchor. Not an Illingham fishing boat, they were smaller and blunter, and they were all pulled up on the foreshore out of the reach of the tide. Elfrun and Auli were floundering in their skirts, the heavy suck and drag of the water on fabric slowing them down.

They were alone.

And at that Elfrun did look back.

Three figures on the beach, a mere fifteen or twenty paces away. Tall, russet-haired Thancrad, and slighter, fairer Finn, and Athulf. The first two had Athulf wrong-footed, he had his back to the water, and they were moving forward, and he was stumbling back, into the lapping shallows.

None of them was armed, but the look on the two faces she could see was deadly. A splash next to her, and she saw Auli, her knife drawn – still? – again? – wading back to the shore. Gulls bobbed on the water.

Auli was moving quietly, keeping right behind Athulf. Stalking him, Elfrun realized. She was only a couple of yards behind him, and she raised her knife. And Elfrun gasped.

Was it that gasp that alerted Athulf? He swung round, fast as a stooping peregrine, and lunged for the knife. He had Auli's wrist, and he was forcing it back, and the knife slipped from her grasp and splashed into the water. He dived, and scrambled up again, soaked to his skin, the knife in his hand held low, blade upwards, ready to thrust up into a man's heart, or lungs.

Elfrun could see glances exchanged between the other three. Then, again faster than she could quite understand, Finn hurled himself at Athulf's waist, tackling him around the ribcage, below the field in which the knife could be brought into play, hoping to bring him down. But, while Athulf staggered, he kept

475

his footing. It only took a moment for him to reverse the knife and bring it down, jabbing hard at Finn's grey-clad back and wresting the blade free for another blow.

And in that moment Auli came up behind him, put her knee in the small of his back, grabbed the sides of his head, jerked backwards, and broke his neck.

Elfrun heard the crack.

There were figures stumbling out now from under the trees.

Auli let Athulf's body fall into the knee-deep tide, and stooped to retrieve her knife, driving it hard into the sheath. Finn had fallen too, and she and Thancrad lifted him, their arms under his shoulders. Elfrun followed them to the boat, which rocked in waist-deep water. Further out three more keels rode at anchor.

Auli hauled herself over the topmost strake and turned to help Thancrad lift Finn over the side. He was streaming seawater and blood, and Elfrun heard the thump and saw the boat rock with the force of his landing.

'Elfrun?' Thancrad took the cloak from her. She wondered why on earth she had clung on to it, when a wiser woman would surely have dropped it when she ran. Thancrad pushed it over the side of the boat, and now he was making a foothold for her with his hands as he had done earlier to get her up on to Storm.

She shook her head. If Auli could slither over the side of the boat like a seal then surely she could do the same. The edge of the strake hit every rising bruise on her ribs, and for a moment she thought she would simply crash back into the sea, but in the end she managed it.

Auli was crouched over Finn. The boat creaked and lurched again as Thancrad pulled himself aboard. Finn lay on his side in the bilges. It was slowly turning red, little thick coils of blood snaking through the sun-tinted water.

Auli was shaking her head.

Elfrun opened her mouth but no sound came out. She reached

forward and together she and Auli began to turn Finn carefully on to his back. The fine grey wool was stained with red, and his skin was turning grey as they watched. His eyes were open, but they were dull. When they moved him his arm flopped to one side, as though there were no bones, no sinews, no tendons.

Thancrad had withdrawn into the bows, his face closed.

Auli leaned down and kissed Finn on the forehead, and then drew his eyelids down with the first and second fingers of her right hand. She said something under her breath, but Elfrun did not hear.

All her senses seemed to have left her. She could only see grey, hear nothing but the rush of the blood in her ears, taste and smell nothing but ashes, her body numb and cold.

Not even tears.

Not even breath.

There was a hand on her shoulder, and then she felt herself being drawn into a warm embrace. It was Auli, and Elfrun let herself lean, let the other girl support her. She could feel Auli's breath warm on her neck, and her hands on her shoulder blades, and for a long moment they clung together, kneeling in the bloody water. They were interlaced in perfect balance, each holding the other, stopping the other from falling. It was bitter, and sweet. Elfrun had never in her life been so close to a girl her own age as she was to this foreigner, with whom she could not exchange a single word.

The boat heaved and lurched again. It was Tuuri. He took in the scene at a glance, and said something in an alien tongue which was self-evidently blasphemous, turning and punching the side of the boat as he swore, bloodying his knuckles.

Auli let Elfrun go gently, and turned to her father. She was pointing to the shore, and to the boat, miming the fight as well as presumably describing it. Elfrun looked back to where the tide was washing the long, dark shape of Athulf's body to and fro. Would anybody care to bury him?

Tuuri was looking at Thancrad, face tight, but Auli said

something else, and he relaxed. Other men were splashing out to the boats. Smoke was trickling up from beyond the trees.

'Tilmon?' Elfrun asked. 'Switha?' She too glanced at Thancrad.

Tuuri gave his infectious, broken-toothed grin. 'They made a big mistake. Let themselves be outnumbered. A second, bigger one. Barred themselves in their hall.' It took a long moment for his meaning to sink in, but when it did she turned and looked again at Thancrad, properly this time. He too was watching the smoke, like a fledgling bespelled by a snake. Darker now, and thicker, beginning to billow up above the trees and eddy sideways away from them in the wind. The crackling of flame was faintly audible.

'*Blis!* The horses!' Thancrad had blenched under his tan, his mouth a square black hole of terror. He scrabbled for the side of the boat, but Tuuri put out a hand. '*Nej*, lad. We've not fired the stables.'

Elfrun thought of the hundred clear yards between hall and stable-block. The breeze was off the sea. They should be safe enough. But just one rogue spark might do it.

Thancrad had stopped, his mouth working. 'Even so,' and he was clearly battling for self-possession, 'the smell of the smoke... I can't just leave her there. Her and the others.'

His parents, trapped in the burning hall, drawn swords to drive them back at every door; and all he could think of was the horses? But Elfrun thought she understood. Switha and Tilmon had brought this down on themselves, warp and weft of their fate woven on a loom they had built and strung with their own hands. The horses, though, were guiltless.

And Tuuri seemed to understand as well. He barked an order, and one of his men set off back up the beach, as fast as he could stumble over weed and dune. 'He will lead the horses down here, and hobble them. Will that do?'

Thancrad nodded, a little muscle twitching in his jaw.

Auli grasped her father's sleeve and said something in that high clear voice like a bird chirping. Tuuri nodded. 'Alvrun?'

She jumped. Everything still seemed so thin and dim and far away.

'My daughter wishes you to know that, had he lived, she would have given Finn to you as your own.'

Her own? Elfrun blinked and shook her head like a dog with a flea in its ear. The words made no sense. How could such a quicksilver soul as Finn be owned, or bought, or given?

How could the lady of Donmouth love a slave, or a freed-man?

Better, maybe, that he was beyond all that. Gone like the summer geese or the winter swallows, to some place she knew nothing of. She half opened her mouth, to ask about the faded lattice of scars on his back, and then closed it again. None of that mattered now, with his body cooling at her feet in the bilge water which slopped to and fro with the rocking of the boat. His blood had sunk and settled, a lower, darker layer.

Finn's death was impossible, and yet it was the only solid thing in her shifting, restless world, caught between smoke and water. There was no profit in fighting it.

She looked back at the rising smoke of Illingham, and then across the glittering water to Donmouth. She had never seen her home from the seaward side before. Where to go now, and what to do?

She was lord of Donmouth. And Thancrad, she supposed, was now the lord of Illingham. Until the king chose otherwise.

That was what they had to do.

'The king.' She had spoken aloud. 'Osberht. We must tell him.'

Thancrad turned his eyes away from the smoke. 'York. The king is in York, with the archbishop.'

Tuuri nodded, half turning to wave at his men on the shore. 'We can take you, up the Humber and the Ouse.' He grinned, and laughed a laugh with no mirth in it. 'But you will forgive me if we do not come with you, into Osberht's hall.'

Elfrun nodded. 'That would be a great kindness.' She turned and looked at Auli, who was sitting back on her heels gazing down at Finn's body. Even soaked and bloodstained, the stranger girl had a swanlike composure to her, her neat head so graceful on her long neck. Those amber eyes, with their trowie light. And Elfrun gave a laugh, a little, bitter thing which caught in her belly and her throat. 'You got something wrong, Auli. Blood, yes, and fire. But shallow water.'

75

Cobnuts, this time. Another of the simple, finely plaited little rush baskets, and a couple of dozen nuts tucked inside. Fredegar stood in the church doorway looking down at the gift in his hands and shaking his head. An ordinary enough object: the hedgerows were ripe, even overladen, but the basket was cunningly woven and the nuts laid carefully within, giving value to the everyday.

When he looked up the girl-child stood in front of him. The smith's child, the one who had stayed on with him at the forge when the wife had taken the little ones back to her father's house. He had tried to speak to them, but there was a wall of silence there. He had wanted to explain to the woman why he had done what he had done, that it had been done with the smith's blessing, that the boy would almost certainly have died in the end, after slow agony.

All empty words, to justify the unjustifiable. He had killed Cudda merely to soothe his own distress, because he could not bear to see the pain.

And now this girl. She had a bruise on one cheek, he noticed. He held out the basket of nuts.

'From you,' he said. It was not a question.

She nodded.

'Everything was from you – flowers, hare, strawberries.'

'The little cross.' It was barely a whisper.

He tugged it out from the collar of his robe and showed it to her, and something relaxed in her taut, pointed little face. He nodded, thinking. 'Why?'

Her eyes flickered to the church door.

'Come on then.' There was a long bench along the back, for those such as Abarhild who could not stand for the length of the mass. Fredegar sat down in the dimness, and indicated that the child should do the same, but instead she stood in front of him, plaiting her fingers together, twisting one ankle round the other in unselfconscious agony. It made him uncomfortable to watch. What was tormenting this child? It came to him that he couldn't remember her name, and he said as much.

'Wynn,' she whispered.

Joy. It seemed ridiculously inapposite for this whey-faced little creature.

He took the cross from around his neck for the first time in months and looked at it properly again. The bone was warm from his skin. 'This must have taken many hours.'

She nodded.

'You are a craftsman.'

The first flicker of something lively in her eyes.

'Why have you been bringing me gifts?'

He could see her swallowing, running a dry tongue over her lips, trying to find words, to meet his eye. At last she took in a sharp breath, and fixed him with her blue stare. Then, very fast, 'To say thank you.'

That took him aback. 'To *thank* me? For what?'

'You made it all right.'

'I made it...' He was feeling stupid. He looked at the little cross. She had made it, not him.

'*Cudda*,' she said, and burst into tears.

Feeling helpless, Fredegar put out his hands and she grabbed them with astonishing force and clutched them to her face. 'Child.'

Her grief was astonishing, like a wind from nowhere that tears through the woods, blasting branches and toppling oaks. Her whole body shook with the force of her sobs, and she pressed his knuckles ever harder into her eye-sockets as though trying to gouge out her own eyes rather than to stem the flow of tears.

And she was silent, or as nearly silent as someone crying her heart out can be. Gasps, and snuffles, but never a sob.

Fredegar let her grip his hands, and waited for the storm to blow itself out. And he thought. *Cudda*. And she wanted to thank him for making it all right.

Was it possible that this child would understand? That the forgiveness he sought could be found at her hands?

The spasms were fewer, further apart, less frantic. But still he said nothing, just let her clutch his hands to her eyes and weep.

At last she gulped one last time, and stood back a little, still holding his hands. She was staring down at them, the sallow skin, her tears still wet on the prominent knuckles. Fredegar too stared at his hands as though he had never seen them before.

Her left hand gripped his right in a sudden convulsion. 'This hand?'

'This hand what?'

'You killed Cudda with this hand, and my father's knife.'

He nodded slowly.

She slipped her hands from his and held them out to him. 'I pushed him with both.' Her face and voice were flat.

Her words sank into his brain as though into deep and murky water, swaying and settling into the silt.

After a moment he said, 'On purpose?' But he knew, he didn't need her nod.

'You were angry?'

A little shrug. 'He was drunk again. He was laughing at me, again.'

'But you never meant to hurt him?' He was offering her a reprieve, a way out of the net, and he could see she understood. But she lifted her pointed little face and stuck out her chin, the tendons of her neck taut.

'It's not that easy. I meant to hurt him. I don't know if I meant to kill him, but I wanted him to die.'

'But' – and he had to be clear about this – 'you did not mean for him to fall in the fire and be burned?'

She shook her head, a little frightened gesture, eyes huge, and he was reminded how very young she was.

'Oh, child.' He remembered her name. 'Wynn. Living with other people is the hardest thing God asks of us.'

'I thought he would just stumble. I was going to run. I thought he'd lam me. But he tripped on the stone, and he fell, and he didn't get up. He fell in the fire!' Her voice went up, and he heard the scream building and he grabbed her hands again and clung on until she was breathing once more. 'And I didn't try to get him out. I thought he was faking it. And then I could smell burning. Him. Burning. Smelling like a roast.' She shuddered. 'I couldn't look. I just ran.'

Fredegar could feel his own heart pounding. The shock of finding the boy so damaged was very present to him. He had not been thinking, he realized now, that day in the forge. He had moved in an eerie calm, administering the last rites, and despatching the boy, and then haranguing Ingeld to admit the body into the minster turf, as though burial so close to the altar of the sacred mysteries would somehow compensate for a life unshriven. As though ending Cudda's pain and digging a hole in holy ground through which the boy's soul might just find its way to paradise would somehow make amends for all the pain at Noyon, for the slaughter that he alone had somehow survived. He uncurled his fingers and she slipped her hands from his.

'You made it go away,' she whispered.

He shook his head. 'It will never go away. Look at me, Wynn.' Obedient, she lifted her gaze. 'You have to confront what you have done, just as I do. What we have done, and what we have failed to do. And we have to be sorry, so sorry that it breaks our hearts again every day for the rest of our lives.'

Her face was frowning, intent. She nodded.

'But,' and he lifted a hand, though she had not so much as opened her mouth, and as he spoke he realized that he had never allowed himself to think these thoughts before, 'but we must not take up guilt that does not belong to us. God hates that as much as he hates the proper guilts we don't admit. You were angry with your brother. You pushed him. Terrible things came of it, but your intention was so much less than your deed.' Could she possibly understand?

He wondered if he should tell her about Noyon, about how he had rung the bell that – without him knowing – had been the signal for the attack, when all the pilgrims and all the tenants, all the brethren but him alone, had already been on their way to the church for the great mass.

Ring the bell, and unleash the Devil.

'No.' He hadn't realized he had spoken the word aloud until her pale face swam back into view, frowning at him.

He half smiled and shook his head. He was helping her to set down her burden. Could she do the same for him? Perhaps he would go to York and make his confession to some minster priest; and perhaps not. Had Ratramnus sent him here as his penance? They would make Heahred first priest, and then abbot of Donmouth. He knew that now. But if his place were here he would have to try and do better, put down the burden of guilt and take up the one of love, with more force than he done hitherto.

And where better to start than with this child, to whom he was irrevocably tied in blood?

'Wynn,' he said thoughtfully. 'Your father, would he let you make things for the church?' A cross for the altar. Candlesticks. They needed so much. She was young, but she would learn.

She shrugged, expressionless, but he wasn't fooled.

76

'Shall we start again?'

Thancrad held out his hand.

Elfrun stared at it, as though this collection of fingers, thumb, palm, knuckles, were some alien object. The waves rustled endlessly, like the rushing of the blood in her ears, and the herring gulls shrieked overhead. Her own hands were hidden, clutching the folds of the red cloak around her. She had kept Wynn's tag on the cloak-strap, with the original still tucked in the pouch at her belt. The cloak was stained now, the red fading, the hem tattering; and she suspected Radmer would have disdained wearing it in its present state. But it wasn't her father's cloak any more. It was hers.

All Hallows' Eve, a whole year since she had waited here for Finn in the rain, scrabbling after cockles. This year the day was fine, with thin sunlight, mist-filtered, a cold grey-gold that reminded her of tarnished parcel-gilt.

'They have played me for a fool,' he said. 'I was lied to from beginning to end by my father – and my mother, my friends, and Athulf most of all. I thought you loved me, and I thought everything I was doing was with your blessing. For us and for the best. I was wrong, and I am sorry.'

Elfrun listened carefully to each word, weighing and measuring, tugging it and testing its strength. Everything held. And more, she could hear in his voice how hard it was for him to say these things, and yet he was saying them.

'I hurt you.'

She nodded.

'You are still hurt.'

Another nod, and at last his hand dropped to his side.

She swung away from him to look out over the river and the estuary. Early mist hung low across the water. No foreign merchants' boats, no red-and-white sails. Misery welled up in her throat like a solid ball, blocking all air and light. Finn had gone, taking his secrets with him. She would never know what had caused that spider's web of scars across his skin, or where the much deeper damage had come from, that kept him so light and merry on the surface, and so quiet and remote down deep. *A cold fish*, Saethryth had said. She was sure that was not true, that she had prompted some real warmth from him. She would never forget his gift of the mirror, his naming her as beautiful, that sudden impulse that had spurred him to ask her to come away with him. Down all the green lanes of summer, with the cow parsley as high as their heads, and a single fork-tailed kite soaring and mewing far above, and the warm dust of the roads...

Behind her, Thancrad said, 'I have no right to ask, but I wish you would say something. There are hard times coming, for us and for all Northumbria, and we would be stronger, together.' He exhaled sharply. 'We may yet be very grateful to have Tuuri and Auli as our friends.'

Elfrun shook her head, not denying the truth of his words, merely indicating that she could not answer him, not quite yet.

But no more could she follow Finn's elusive shape down that winding road. And how safe would those green lanes have been, or the sea-roads, with war looming? She still could not bear to turn round and look at Thancrad, so she went on staring out to the mist-hung sea. Higher, the sky was clearer, and the geese were arriving from the north, arrow after arrow of them, little black shapes writing words on the sky in a language she could not read, crying their alien music. They began to appear at the turn of the leaf, they left in daffodil season, year in and year out, like the in-breath and out-breath of the world. And she had no idea where they went, or what they had seen.

'I found this for you.'

She turned to face him at last. His hand was extended again, and this time cradled in his palm was a white shape, long and curved and folded, the length of her thumb. She could make no sense of it at first, it looked like the drawn-out bud of a creamy flower, or some monstrous tooth. But when she reached out from inside the cloak and took the thing from his palm its meaning discovered itself. The innermost spiralling core of a big dog whelk, shaped and smoothed by the sea. She looked at it from the side, and from above, noticing where tiny, long-ago worms had bored through the shell, how the outer whorl of the spiral folded in to embrace the core as a parent might a child. Peering into the folds, she could make out a scatter of tiny barnacles, deep-embedded. How long had this shell been tumbling in the sea, to be so broken and polished and transformed? The relentless, impersonal perfection of that spiral tugged at her memory: the maker of her mirror must have spent hours looking at shapes like these. She wondered what Wynn might make of it.

He was looking embarrassed now. 'It's a worthless thing. I just picked it up on the foreshore. But I thought you would like it.'

She gripped it tight, and it moulded itself to the shape of her palm. 'I do.' She looked up into his face. His brown eyes held concern, and she wanted to reassure him. 'It's beautiful.'

She hardly knew him, this reserved, proud young man, despite the strange intimacy that had been forced upon them. But then, she had hardly taken the trouble to look. The sea-fret was clearing; those rags and skeins of vapour that had seemed so solid were disappearing in the morning sun. Still holding his gaze, Elfrun fiddled with the ties of her pouch and tucked the worn heart of the shell safely away, and made up her mind.

When her pouch was fastened again she held out her left hand to Thancrad. She didn't know what her face looked like, but she could guess from the look of relief and – yes – delight, on his; and she marvelled at the transformation worked by the play of tiny muscles across his strong, bony features. Her hand was cold, but he gripped it firmly, and slowly she felt a little kernel of warmth begin to grow in the secret hollow where their palms met.

Coda: The Chronicle, York Minster Scriptorium

'What shall I do with this, my lord?'

Archbishop Wulfhere pulled the quire of vellum towards him. He unfolded it and smoothed it out, but only the area which would become the front page of the still-uncut quire had been written on. His eyes widened briefly, then narrowed as they scanned the close-packed lines of text.

In this year died King Cinaed ap Alpin of the Picts; and also Athelwulf Ecgberhting of the West Saxons. Domnall ap Alpin and Athelbald Athelwulfing succeeded to the kingdoms. Also in this year the pagans burned the minster at Tours. In this year a girl gave me a flower on the kalends of March. Her face and bosom were freckled, and her eyes were blue. She made me think of a songthrush egg. In this year there was no famine, no murrain of cattle. The pagans were elsewhere. In this year Ingeld was made priest against his better judgement and appointed to the abbacy of Donmouth.

In this year, also, Amlaibh and Imhair made an alliance with Cerball against Mael Sechnaill, and Meath suffered greatly because of it. Athelbald of Wessex married his father's young widow, and the bishops of the West Saxons were much troubled thereby. In this year, King Osberht of the Northumbrians brought Tilmon back into his favour, and granted him Illingham. In this year also, the same king sent Radmer of Donmouth to Rome. Men wondered at both these things. In this year the swallows came back to their wonted places on the ides of April. The cuckoo called in the woods. The sun shone.

In this year, a woman's breasts were like mounded cream tipped with strawberries, and they moved me more than pen can express. In this year, I have trespassed on other men's woods and fields, and hunted their private runs. In this year, I have lost my soul, and found it.

'Ingeld?'

The librarian nodded, but Wulfhere had not needed to ask. He had wanted, rather, to turn his friend's name over in his mouth one last time. But he would have known Ingeld's distinctive hand anywhere, with its square *a* and its long, jaunty descenders.

And even more than the hand, the voice.

'Perhaps I should give it to his mother. I hear she is in need of comfort.'

The librarian cackled. 'Give it to his girl, rather. But which one? Songthrush or strawberries?'

A smile twitched Wulfhere's cautious face. 'More fitting, to be sure. But even if I knew who they were, I doubt either of them can read.' He folded the quire over on itself again, once, twice, three times, and handed it to the librarian. 'Put it with the archive. Maybe one day someone will find it interesting.'

HISTORICAL NOTE

Donmouth is a real place, yet no one knows where it was. Inevitably, therefore, the maps in this book are almost as fictional as the narrative. In 757/8, a century before this story begins, the Pope wrote to the King of Northumbria, demanding that the king return to their rightful abbot three monasteries which he had confiscated. Two of these are the well-known North Yorkshire sites of Stonegrave and Coxwold; the third is *Donaemuthe*. No site of this name is known, and yet the name itself tells us that it must be where a river known as the Don flows into the sea. Of the various candidates, I have chosen the Humber estuary, and the borderland of moor and marsh between the kingdoms of Northumbria and Mercia. However, you will not find my landscape on any map, and the modern, drained and reclaimed landscape of the region is very different from how it lay twelve centuries ago. Much has also been lost to coastal erosion. The shifting landscape and the ambiguous evidentiary status of Donmouth are like folds in the space–time continuum, allowing me to slip my river, estuary, hill and salt marsh seamlessly into the real geography of the Humber hinterland.

Further gaps and ambiguities govern other aspects of my story. In 866 York fell to the viking 'Great Army'. The way in which that army's leaders exploited the politics of Northumbria's Church and State to establish themselves in the landscape between the Humber and the Tees suggests that they were very well informed; yet there is little in the historical record to tell us how they gained that information. The kings and archbishops of ninth-century Northumbria are hardly more than names: we cannot be clear about their family relationships, their alliances, or how they died. One of the few facts that we do know is that Northumbria was embroiled in civil war when the vikings invaded. Please note that this is the first paragraph in this book in which the word *viking* appears, and that it is lower case on purpose. The word means *pirate*, and it is a job description, not an ethnicity. Nor is it a word which we find in contemporary English sources, applied to the bands of first raiders, then invaders, who are recorded from 793 onwards. The ideas exploited in this story – that there were Baltic and Scandinavian traders and wandering entertainers travelling the coasts of Eastern England who were in the pay of viking warlords, and that those warlords were themselves ready to take up the role of mercenaries on the different sides of the Northumbrian factions – are plausible hypotheses, but the evidence does not survive. I am indebted here to the work of Shane McLeod; and very grateful to Clare Downham for discussions about the nature of the viking trade diaspora, and the way in which such mercantile networks are based fundamentally on trust and shared interests. Her argument that the vikings and the churchmen formed mutually beneficial alliances from very early on in their encounters is powerful and persuasive. There is no viking attack on Northumbria recorded in the 850s: of course this need not mean that there *were* no attacks, but for the purposes of my story I have chosen to read the record in this way. The evidence provided by coins suggests that there was disruption in Northumbrian politics in the mid-ninth century, but this could equally well have been caused by the civil strife attested in the chronicles.

One fascinating type of coin evidence illustrates both the complexity and the ambiguity of the data. In the eighth and ninth centuries the various English kingdoms had established a consensus on currency, the widely accepted and standardized silver penny, weighing 1/240 of a pound, often beautifully designed, and minted under licence from the kings and occasionally the archbishops. A single silver penny represented a sizable amount of wealth, and cannot have been used for the smaller, everyday transactions. Northumbria, uniquely, moved away from the silver-penny model in the ninth century, and introduced a small debased silver/bronze coin known as the *styca*, with comparatively crude imagery, and worth much less than the silver penny. A previous generation of historians and numismatists interpreted this as indicating the isolated and backward nature of Northumbria; but these coins are now being seen by some revisionist scholars as evidence of a sophisticated economy, focused on external trade.

These coins are perhaps the best contemporary source for the politics as well as the economics of mid-ninth-century Northumbria, which are painfully obscure. We have a list of names of kings, found both on coins and in annals, but almost no recorded events, and the dates of those kings are very hard to pin down. The evidence of the coins does not match easily with that from the annals (which are themselves contradictory). Although I have placed Osberht on the throne in this story, as he is generally thought to have succeeded in around 850, other scholars have wanted to put the start of his reign a decade or more later. Almost the only thing we know about Osberht is that his civil war with the non-royal claimant Ælle (whose name I have expanded to Alred) was entrenched enough to continue even after the viking assault on York on 1 November 866. Nor do we know much about Archbishop Wulfhere, other than his dates (to which the same caveat applies).

Historians and archaeologists of Anglo-Saxon England may recognize aspects of the two excavated sites which underpin my vision of Donmouth: Brandon in Suffolk and Flixborough in north Lincolnshire, just south of the Humber. Both of these are complex sites, unrecorded in the written record, with many buildings and rich finds, including convincing evidence of literacy and Christian practice. They have been published to a very high standard. The debate rages as to whether they should be read as monasteries, as secular aristocratic residences, or some sort of hybrid. They also contribute to a wider academic debate about the extent to which the complex, wealthy and largely sheep-based economy of the High Middle Ages can be traced back into the Anglo-Saxon period. I have used elements of this, combined with those little bronze *stycas*, to paint a portrait of a rural centre combining ecclesiastical and secular elite foci with links to local, national and international markets, and royal and episcopal elites, specializing in high-quality wool and treated skins.

Despite these and other excavations, the built environment of the middle Anglo-Saxon elite remains frustratingly elusive. Here I am profoundly indebted to John Blair for stimulating conversations, and in particular for his allowing me access to his then-unpublished research. The conclusion may be drawn that regional power at this period was not yet entrenched in particular dynasties; that prosperous households were all on much of a level; that any one of these might do well in one generation, but the next might not be so favoured – especially as partible inheritance is likely to have been practised, making it hard to retain wealth in a small number of hands across the generations. Posts in the royal household were awarded on merit rather than only on family connections. A good analogy is probably with the society depicted in the Icelandic sagas of prosperous peasants, some of whom, by wit, canniness, charm, brute force and/or a willingness to take risks, did much better than their neighbours. The absence of archaeological evidence for notably grander residences in the eighth and ninth centuries means that the houses inhabited by people like Radmer and Tilmon may have been sumptuously decorated, but the glamour and luxury with which they surrounded themselves was portable, more like the trappings of a stage-set than the kind of long-term investment in statement buildings which becomes visible from the tenth century onwards. It is worth remembering that these people would have spent a significant part of their lives in tents, at royal and local assemblies and church synods as well as on military campaign, and that temporary dwellings and portable display would have been an integral part of the way they presented themselves to the world.

Perhaps the hardest kind of story to write set in this period is a love story. The vast majority of Anglo-Saxon writing, in Latin or Old English, is mediated through the Church, and one looks almost in vain for the kind of love lyric common from Classical Antiquity, or the later Middle Ages. Explorations of sexual passion are rare, and often presented negatively. When we do read about a woman torn between loyalty to two different men, they are likely to be her brother and her son, fighting on different sides of a family feud. Loving women in Anglo-Saxon literature are typically shown alone, anxious, bereft and either grieving or anticipating grief, not romantically happy or erotically fulfilled. I have tried to rectify this, within the bounds of social and cultural plausibility.

I owe a great debt to Alex Woolf for exploring with me questions of age at marriage in early medieval Britain. The evidence is neither comprehensive nor consistent, and when we have details they are usually concerned with the very highest levels of society. However, we would be justified in imagining a world in which most girls would be married by fifteen or sixteen, often to men significantly older than themselves. It goes without saying that pregnancy and birth were often death sentences for mother, child, or both. Nonetheless, a girl probably had the right to refuse a suitor; she retained some economic independence in marriage; as a married woman she had considerable status within the household; and she could choose to end a marriage if she wanted to. Marriage was a social contract; it was not to become a religious ceremony for centuries.

I am sure that this story is riddled with anachronisms, although I have tried to keep them at bay. However, the gaps in our knowledge are huge, and range from the minutiae of everyday life to some very large questions of how society was structured and culture was practised. We know little about how the Anglo-Saxons stabled their horses, for example, and yet I have to put my horses somewhere: the needs of horses have not changed much over 1,200 years; and the word 'horse-stall' is found in Old English. Another example: I have given my travelling entertainers a drum, based on the Irish *bodhrán*, but this is simply wishful thinking. We have no evidence that drums were in use in this part of the world in the middle of the ninth century – but then again it's hard to imagine that they were unknown. Dress is another problem. While the differences in dress between mid-ninth-century Scandinavian, eastern Baltic and Anglo-Saxon women would have been readily apparent to the casual observer, it is much less clear whether men's dress would also have served as an ethnic identifier at a distance. Estate management is another problematic issue. Carolingian estate stewards kept written records (or some of them did), but we do not know much about how an Anglo-Saxon estate was administered. Similarly, we have very little idea of whether there were itinerant pedlars at this period. There were certainly merchants who sold exotic goods, but who they were, how they got their stock, how they sold it, and in what currency (barter, bullion or coin) it was paid for, are all grey areas. In the end, and inevitably, I have made a lot of this story up (it is a novel, after all), and if anyone better informed than me reads this book, please contact me through my website, *vmwhitworth.co.uk*, as I'd love to know more.

I have invented the Keg game, but it is based on a number of local sports, ancestral to games like rugby. The one I know best is the Orkney Ba', fought out between Uppies and Doonies every Christmas and New Year through the narrow streets of Kirkwall. The Haxey Hood Game is another example, played every January in north Lincolnshire, very close geographically to my imaginary landscape.

One conscious anachronism, for using which I make no apology, is the adjective 'trowie'. This is an Orkney dialect word, referring to the supernatural people, the trows, a name derived ultimately from Old Norse *troll*. The Anglo-Saxons would probably have referred to these humanoid, mound-dwelling, musical, often malevolent and always uncanny creatures as 'elves'. But 'elf' is a word which has been commandeered by modern writers of fantasy and has gone in very different directions, whether twee or Tolkienesque, from how it would have been understood in the ninth century. A later medieval word is 'fairy', which is just as misleading. 'Troll' is equally inappropriate. 'Trowie' is still in use in Orcadian – an unwell or recalcitrant sheep, for example, is referred to as a 'trowie yow', although modern farmers no longer use the phrase literally to mean that she is from an otherworldly flock, or has been overlooked by some ill-wishing power. Other Orcadian and/or Scots words have slipped into my narrative, as well, such as 'smirr' for a drift of rain, and 'sharn' for excrement. I make no apology for this either: Northumbrian Old English is ancestral to Scots, a much closer relationship than the better-recorded Old English of the southern kingdoms.

The modern convention of dating the New Year from 1 January was known in Anglo-Saxon England, but not universally practised by any means, and there is little consistency. *The Anglo-Saxon Chronicle*, for example, uses a variety of dates to start the year, including Christmas Day, the Feast of the Annunciation on 25 March (which Ingeld uses in his own chronicle), and 1 September. Much more important was the cycle of saints' days, solar and lunar milestones such as the solstices and equinoxes, and agricultural celebrations, the dates of which would vary from year to year depending on the weather.

According to strict definitions, there were no horses in Anglo-Saxon England, only ponies. The nature of Anglo-Saxon horsemanship has been much debated. In the mid-ninth century the metal stirrup had not yet been introduced, although the word *stirrup* comes from *steer-rope*, suggesting that there were antecedents in materials which have not survived. Tenth- and eleventh-century evidence such as the poem 'The Battle of

Maldon' and the Bayeux Tapestry suggest that the English did not fight on horseback, at least not in the south-east. In contrast, the eighth- and ninth-century carved stones of Pictland (modern eastern Scotland) bristle with mounted warriors, and the care given to the depiction of the horses' gaits suggests that the breeding and training of horses was a subject of great interest, investment and skill. The English poem *Beowulf* also gives us a picture of flamboyant aristocrats who care deeply about their horses, racing them and composing poetry while riding. This is the culture I have evoked here.

Languages: Abarhild and Fredegar's native language is Gallic, a descendant of Latin which was to become French. They also speak Frankish, a Germanic language related to Old English (and Old Norse). For the purposes of the story Frankish and English are mutually comprehensible with a bit of effort, as is Old Norse (compare modern Swedish and Norwegian). Finn and his shipmates use Old Norse as their *lingua franca*, but Auli and Tuuri are Finnish-speakers from the eastern Baltic, and they also use that language (the one that Tilmon finds so objectionable).

Ingeld's reading: the great library of York has vanished almost without trace. We know it existed, and to some extent it can be reconstructed from the works of Alcuin, its most influential graduate. The *de luxe* manuscript of Pliny's *Natural History* now in Leiden has been ascribed to the York scriptorium by Mary Garrison, and Alcuin's poem on York suggests that the natural world and classical poetry figured largely in the curriculum of the minster school. There is no evidence that Ovid's love poetry was popular among the ninth-century Northumbrian clerics, but a contemporary Welsh manuscript of Book One of the *Ars Amatoria* ('How to Pick up Girls') came into the hands of a tenth-century monk, Dunstan, who later became Archbishop of Canterbury. The scholarly consensus is that Dunstan read and annotated the *Ars Amatoria* out of interest in Ovid's grammar, vocabulary and style, rather than its erotic content. But life is seldom so simple.

Many kind and wise people have helped in the writing of this book. I have mentioned some of them above, and I must also thank my wonderful agent, Laura Longrigg and publisher, Rosie de Courcy. Carolyne Larrington, Christina Lee, Alex Sanmark, Ragnhild Ljosland, Donna Heddle, Paul Macdonald, Kristin Lindfield-Ott, and Kiersty Tams-Grey, Jim MacPherson, Susan Oosthuizen, Donncha MacGabhann are some of the friends who have significantly boosted morale and/or made helpful contributions; and Julia and her staff at Julia's Café in Stromness, Orkney, have provided a lovely warm corner in which to scribble away. Special thanks must go to the Dark Lord of manuscript criticism, Martin Rundkvist, for helping me through several sticky patches.

GLOSSARY

- Airt – quarter from which the wind comes (Scots).
- Aula – a Latin word with a range of meanings such as court, and hall. Here referring to the abbot's private quarters.
- Ave – the greeting of the angel to Mary, *Ave Maria*, before telling her that she had conceived a son. The riddle-loving medieval imagination delighted in this being a reversal of *Eva*: i.e. through Eve's weakness we fell; by Mary's strength we are redeemed.
- Bernicia – northern Northumbria, usually thought to be from the River Tees to the Firth of Forth, including the modern Scottish Borders, the Lothians, Dumfries and Galloway, etc.
- Bower – from Old English *bur*, a private chamber. In later usage it is a specifically feminine space but in Anglo-Saxon England it is largely gender-neutral.
- Creepie-stool – a small, portable stool (Scots).
- Danemarch/the Danish marches – Denmark, but more specifically the border between modern Denmark and Germany.
- Deira – southern Northumbria, usually defined as the River Humber north to the Tees in the east. For both Bernicia and Deira the western territories and their borders are less clear than the eastern ones.
- Dore – now a village on the edge of Sheffield, the name Dore (same word as 'door') refers to the confluence of three waterways which formed the borderzone between Northumbria and Mercia.

- Ean – a newborn lamb.
- Elmet – a British kingdom in the Leeds area that hung on until the seventh century, and still survives as a regional identifier for villages such as Sherburn-in-Elmet and Barwick-in-Elmet.
- Even-night – equinox.
- Frankia – roughly modern France, the Netherlands, Germany, Austria, Switzerland and northern Italy.
- Haysel – hay harvest festival
- Heddern – a small inner chamber used for storage. We do not know if they were really lockable.
- Hedeby – a great 8th to 11th century trading centre on the east coast of the Germano-Danish border.
- Hyperborean – at the back of the North Wind.
- Ides – the fifteenth of the month.
- Kalends – the first of the month.
- Mont Jouve pass – we would call it the great St Bernard pass, through the Alps.
- *Prefecti* – senior royal officials and administrators.
- *Quale rosae fulgent inter sua lilia mixtae* – 'So roses shine when lilies round them blow' (Ovid).
- Sharn – excrement (Scots).
- Smirr – a drift of light rain (Scots).
- Trowie – an Orcadian world for the otherworldly people who inhabit mounds (see discussion in the Historical Note).
- *Trux aper insequitur totosque sub inguine dentes* – 'The wild boar thrust its tusks entire into his groin' (Ovid).
- Yole – a small fishing boat, pointed fore and aft, with one or two masts.